T5-AFH-398

WITHDRAWN

THE STARDUST KID

Pat Richoux

FOUNDED 1838

GPPS

MADISON COUNTY LIBRARY
DANIELSVILLE, GA.

THE
STARDUST
KID

G. P. Putnam's Sons
New York

ATHENS REGIONAL LIBRARY
ATHENS, GEORGIA

Copyright © 1973 by Pat Richoux

All rights reserved. This book, or parts thereof, must not be reproduced in any form without permission. Published simultaneously in Canada by Longman Cananda Limited, Toronto.

SBN: 399-11156-5

Library of Congress Catalog
Card Number: 73-78622

PRINTED IN THE UNITED STATES OF AMERICA

THE STARDUST KID

175759

I

FOR a high school auditorium it passed the minimum standards. In case of fire no assembled student bodies would perish at William Jennings Bryan High, protected as they were by one green asbestos curtain, three aisles, five sets of outward-opening doors with panic bars and nine hundred unpadded tip-up seats on a sloping concrete floor. The only combustible decorations were splashed along one side wall in flaming crayon on butcher paper:

V for VICTORY!
Buy War Bonds and Stamp Out Hitler!
Slap a Jap with a Hunk of Scrap!

The audience rows were empty now, but the stage was open for business. Beside the ragged semicircles of folding chairs and music stands a baby grand piano huddled slantwise in the right wing, half on, half off the proscenium. Stage directions on the floor marked the passing of last week's senior play, "The Case of the Laughing Dwarf." Given fair warning and a willing setup crew, the stage could accommodate pep rallies or bond rallies, jitney show or Christmas pageant. Amateur talent, backed by amateur musicians, played to an amateur audience.

But the kid on the stage was blowing "Stardust" and he blew it like a professional. Literally. Note for note à la Bill Rhodes.

7

Any swing fan at Bryan High could recognize that classic trumpet solo, smooth unrationed golden syrup on a half a million black wax hotcakes, still the top-selling record of 1942. Rhodes currently commanded ten thousand dollars a week at the New York Paramount for blowing that tune and a few others. His fans lined up in freezing November dawn with brown bag lunches and jitterbugged in the aisles through five shows daily, six on Sunday.

The kid on the stage knew the record cold, every last lip smear and eyebrow twitch reproduced with jukebox fidelity. Just once in the second chorus when he dropped one note from a complicated cluster he stopped, said, "Oh, hell," backed up and took the bar again. He hit the high notes lightly with a shrug of padded shoulders, ignoring the echoes of the big empty house before him and the small buzz of comment behind.

Junior Band stood wide-eyed and slack-jawed, an unguarded freshman flock ready to panic. Who let this hotshot into our rehearsal? Does Mr. Kessler know about him? The scaredest kid in the crowd was Roger Peterson, first chair trumpet. First chair until now. "It's a mistake," he said hopefully to a huddle of nervous young brassmen. "Maybe he misread his schedule and thinks it's fourth hour. Somebody should tell him."

A splendid idea, agreed the band. Go on, Roger, tell him. When the boy finished playing, Roger walked over, forcing himself not to tiptoe.

"Hi there." His voice squeaked a little; he cleared his throat and tried for a more mature register. "Do you, uh, know where you are? This isn't ROTC Band."

The kid's face twisted into a forced grin, his voice into a parody. "*That's* what I keep *telling* them down at the *office*. Too late, sonny, the man says to me. ROTC is all full up. You should have been here in September, he says."

"Full up? They never take freshmen, but— Are you sure Mr. Trimble said that?"

"Whosoever he was, he sure as hell said it. When I tried to explain where I was in September, he says T.S. for you but don't cry on my shoulder. I've got no time to hear alibis from bomber-plant punks. Consider yourself lucky we let cheap trash like you into this school at all, he says, and go blow your nose in Junior Band. Well, if that's what the man wants, that's what he'll get." He raised the trumpet carelessly and flicked the spit valve. A slobbering Bronx cheer spattered the floor and Roger jumped

8

back. "Consider it blown, friend. There's variations on that theme too, but not with ladies present."

Roger looked doubtfully at his wet shoe, at the fascinated faces behind him and back to the new attraction. "Say, how long have you played?"

The kid smoothed back his reddish hair. "Son," he drawled in a new voice, "y'all see these dents? Toothmarks. I cut my teeth on this here horn. When I was but a mere babe, I could—"

"No, honest, how long? Five, six years?"

"Three."

"You must have had a good teacher."

"Teacher? The best, man. Bill Rhodes himself."

"*Bill Rhodes!*" The band gave a genuine scurry of excitement. "You're kidding," Roger said without confidence. "For a hundred bucks a lesson?"

"No, for free. He don't need the money. Here, you see this mute? It's his own special design, like he uses on the record of 'Melancholy Baby.'" A soft tear-jerking phrase slid from the muted horn, coaxing them to believe the incredible. The band listened eagerly, unaware that two dollars and ninety-eight cents could buy anyone a genuine Rhodes Special at the nearest music store.

"Gee, you're lucky! What else did you learn?"

"Everything. You know how he hits about thirty-three high C's in a row where most guys turn blue? There's a trick to it. Listen." He unfolded like a six-foot rule, sucked a deep breath and took his Bill Rhodes stance again, eyes shut, horn aimed at the balcony.

Paul Kessler walked in on the thirteenth high C, the stage door clanging sharply behind him. Caught in his act, the kid with the trumpet let his last note dribble down two octaves in the whinny of an impatient young stallion challenging the leader of the herd. In sudden silence the man and the boy faced each other across the width of the stage for a moment of looking over, of sizing up. Junior Band, sensing drama, held its collective breath.

Then Kessler smiled. "Well, that's a relief. I thought it was an air-raid drill."

Laughter shattered the tension as the kids scrambled for their places in a late but loyal recollection of routine. Only the trumpeter stood firm, center front stage, as though he waited to play an encore.

Okay, Kessler thought, so let him wait.

9

He crossed the stage slowly, making the forced deliberation look casual. He didn't use a cane anymore, but his knee still tricked him often, locking one moment and giving way the next. The slash down the left side of his face had healed in a clean white line from temple to jaw, not disfiguring. Not a movie-gangster scar, not even an honorable Purple Heart war wound. Combined with the blond hair and solid build, it almost suggested a sporting souvenir of Heidelberg '33, dangerously unpatriotic in wartime Nebraska. He could live with it, even joke about it now. My dueling scar and football knee, he told the kids, but most of them knew better. Less than a year had passed since the accident and word got around, old-timers informing new freshmen in sympathetic undertones ("Last winter . . . a drunk driver . . . forced into the ditch . . . pinned under . . . and his wife . . . an hour before the ambulance . . . "). Junior Band knew the story. This cocky young stranger would hear it soon enough. But for today, for now at least, Paul refused to limp.

Just as he reached the director's stand, Roger Peterson burst out self-importantly with the big news. "Mr. Kessler, this guy says he took from Bill Rhodes!"

"How about that?" Paul said in a level tone. He sat on the high rehearsal stool and tossed his roll book to the nearest clarinet. She caught it neatly and began the routine checkoff.

"*Bill Rhodes*," Roger repeated, underlining the message. When Paul didn't spring to unroll the red carpet, Roger nudged at his neighbor in second chair. "Move down, Bob."

"Move down where? What for?"

"I have to sit where you are now."

Bob looked bewildered. "You told me this was my place. You always sit on the end. You said—"

"Not any more I don't," Roger said through his teeth. "Move *down*, stupid."

Bob's move triggered a confused chain reaction along the whole trumpet line while Paul waited, trying not to laugh. Trust Roger to rearrange everything the hard way. Early in the fall Paul had explained traditional concert seating to the kids, just theoretically, just to let them know how it ought to work. When eager beaver Roger proclaimed himself first-trumpet-first-desk-first-chair, Paul thought it might stir up some healthy competition. So far it hadn't. In Junior Band trumpets came overpriced at a dime a dozen. Some of them needed both hands to find their proper pitches, let alone their proper chairs. For two months Roger had sat proud and undisputed king of the molehill. But today he read the handwriting on the wall and vacated his throne without a fight.

No need for Paul to check the invader's credentials. He gestured at the place Roger had all but dusted off with his handkerchief. "Take a seat, friend. Care to give us your name for the records?"

"Records?" the kid said in a startled tone. "You mean you cut— *Oh*. Riley."

"O'Reilly?"

"Riley, Mike Riley. That's R-I-L-E-Y, *Riley*." Much more than a simple clarification of spelling, it rang like a barroom challenge.

Paul wasn't about to oblige any hotheaded Irishman, in school or out. "Okay, people, let's warm up. And somebody close that curtain, there's a heck of a draft blowing down my neck." He made a gesture of turning up his coat collar. "Why so cold in here today?"

"Fuel oil rationing, they announced it," Roger said, first as usual with bad news, and all the clarinets chorused, "Dontcha know there's a war on?"

He tuned them rapidly. Cold stage, cold horns, late start and a belligerent new first trumpet—this should be one really rotten rehearsal. "All right, Number Six in the blue book, let's go."

Mike Riley gave the page one glance and proceeded to make retching sounds.

"What's the matter, can't you play it?"

"This crap, are you kidding? In kindergarten I played it." He raised one eyebrow independent of its mate, looked at the music again and said, "Jeeeez," on a long scornful breath. Paul could hardly fault his taste. "Onward to Success March" was strictly warm-up stuff, "See Dick, See Jane, Look, look, look," set to four/four time, every phrase trite and every chord predictable, easy even for Junior Band. But today the cold-fingered clarinets stumbled again on their long climbing run. One sax overlooked the first ending to the second strain and marched single-handedly Onward to Chaos.

Mike stuck his right index finger into his ear and wiggled it in the familiar musicians' gesture: *Am I hearing things, or how sour can you get?*

"Hold it!" Paul rapped the stand. "Two dots before a double

11

bar—what does it mean, anybody? Repeat the strain, that's right. Take it again from Letter B, first time through and repeat." That was the story in third hour, Mickey Mouse music and basic instruction forever bracketed by two dots and a double bar. Play it once and play it again; tell them today and remind them tomorrow. *Watch the key signature, count the rhythm. You're playing flat, Johnny, push the mouthpiece in.* Grin and bear it for an hour a day from September to June. Then the hopefuls will advance to ROTC Band and Concert Orchestra, the hopeless will switch to art and woodshop. But next fall a new green freshman crop springs from the top of the same old page, *DC* but never *al fine*. And once in a while, once or twice in a lifetime of teaching, a real talent can turn up to make it all bearable. . . .

At the trio Paul saw Riley facing new irresistible temptation. He began doubling the melody a Rhodes-octave higher. When Paul shook his head, Mike quit altogether and laid his horn in his lap while the others plodded home without him.

"Play what's written, junior," Paul said. "No ad libs."

Mike gave him a devilish blue-eyed smile.

The rest of the hour was murder. Riley played with one eyebrow up and one down, his cheeks puffed out, translating the "Stadium March" into "Der Biergarten Polka." He schmaltzed up a waltz with Lombardo vibrato. He stuffed his right hand into his pocket and played stiff-fingered with his left, a jerky mechanical toy. During the rests he sat on his shoulder blades, stretched his long legs out past the music stand, yawned broadly, picked his nose and burped. After every trick he looked around for applause. Unfortunately he found it in the giggling clarinet section, where Frances and Pam and Joanie thought each new stunt was the snappiest thing since bubble gum.

It was inexcusable behavior, disastrous to the rehearsal. Paul knew he ought to squelch it on the spot. But if he ignored it, it might stop sooner. Let Little Boy Blue blow his horn and get whatever was itching him out of his system today. Tomorrow he could either settle down or else drop Junior Band if he found it so tedious.

By way of compensating the other kids for their destroyed rehearsal—not that *they* minded a free comedy hour—Paul let them wind up with "Elmer's Tune." They butchered it, as always, but he could forgive the sour notes because they were having so much fun, such hopeful swingers on a creaking gate. Even Mike Riley didn't turn up his sharp hawk nose at this one. He caught the spirit and played along sincerely. When the bell interrupted the second chorus, he joined the disappointed groan. "Oh, heck, can't we finish? That's neat, man! You got any more good arrangements like that?"

"Sorry, that's all," Paul said in answer to both questions. The great Bill Rhodes' protégé might like to demonstrate his flashy style on "Trumpet Blues" or "Two o'Clock Jump," which he could turn blue waiting to find in Junior Band's library. But if he enjoyed a simple novelty like "Elmer," his tastes were pretty normal for his age. And when he forgot to clown and act smarty, he seemed normal enough too—a tall, thin, good-looking boy, perhaps fifteen, with a proudly well-shined trumpet. "Nice horn you've got there. What is it?"

"Holton." Mike fingered the valves absently. "It's supposed to be worth a hundred new, with the mutes and everything. But we only gave fifty for it, Jerry jewed the guy down—" He stopped abruptly. "Rhodes uses a Bach trumpet. They're the best, man."

Rhodes uses anything they'll pay him to endorse, Paul thought, but he didn't say it aloud. "Where's your next class?" he asked as Mike continued to slouch, caught like the baker and the meandering gander under the spell of "Elmer's Tune."

Mike sighed and fished out a schedule card. "English. If I find Room 208."

"Upstairs, just south of the library. You've got exactly two minutes to get there or you'll be late."

"Keep your pants on, dad. I'm off in a thundering cloud of dust and hi-yo Silver away." Mike tucked his trumpet into its plush-lined bed and stood up lazily. "Speaking of pants, your fly's unzipped."

Paul very nearly fell for it. With an effort he managed not to reassure himself until Mike had sauntered off the stage. A joke, of course. As a joke it had whiskers, but he had never expected to hear it from a brand-new student on his first day in school. Wow, what brass. The only thing unzipped around here is your lip, sonny. Far too wise for Junior Band, too wise by half for his own good, Mike Riley was asking for trouble. He'd find it, too, before the day ended. Some less patient teacher with a thinner sense of humor would nail his ears to the wall.

And that was only Tuesday.

On Wednesday Mike arrived in sunglasses and wore them straight through rehearsal. "Doctor's orders," he said proudly to all who asked, as of course all did. "I went skiing and got myself snow-blinded." Snow blindness didn't seem to impair his ability to read Dick-and-Jane music. He sat up straight and played everything loudly and correctly and, Paul was sure, a deliberate quarter-tone sharp to make the others sound flatter than ever. But apart from the giggling clarinet obbligato, the rehearsal didn't suffer much damage. No rule in the book against sunglasses. Paul let them pass unchallenged.

On Thursday Mike reported with a broad grin on his face and his right arm in a homemade sling.

"Skiing again?"

"Yup. I slalomed when I should have christied. Sprained my wrist in two places."

"You can always play left-handed."

"Oh, no, sir, not on this difficult music, sir, I haven't the manual dextrosity. I might ruin your whole rehearsal, sir."

"Then sit out front and study." Paul's standard answer for all unprepared or incapacitated musicians—"Can't play today? Study, then"—saved a lot of argument and discouraged the chronic alibiers.

Mike looked startled. He smiled with less assurance and pretended to double-check his wrist. "Oh, well, I guess maybe I—"

Oh, no you don't, Paul thought. Not this time. He gestured firmly at the audience section. "Go on, take your books."

Mike opened his mouth, closed it again, then shrugged and went down the steps to slouch in a front-row seat while a calm, normal, mediocre rehearsal proceeded without first chair trumpet. Paul wondered what he was thinking. *Okay, mac, now listen how your tinhorn band sounds without the Great Riley?* It sounded lousy without him, even worse than it had before he came. The other trumpets were already learning to lean on his lead. But Mike didn't seem to be sneering. He sat with an open book, massaging his twice-sprained wrist and staring glumly into space, as thoroughly bored as Paul intended him to be. A wasted hour, but it might do him some good.

Friday morning dawned darkly cloudy after a sleepless night. Paul's head ached, his knee ached. He cut himself shaving—a

14

fresh nick across the slowly fading permanent scar—and scowled at the mirror. One more smart trick today, just one, and the great Riley would get his golden Holton shoved straight up his . . . nose.

Mike arrived without slings, crutches or hand grenades, his only visible weapon a surrealistic necktie of red and blue sunbursts. He sat in his chair and played his part like two men, his tone so beautiful against the sour section that Paul almost forgave him for the whole week. Maybe it was over. Maybe benching him yesterday had taught him at last who was boss.

But then Roger Peterson began to have trouble. All week he had sulked in second chair beside Mike, sharing the music and stand with a jealousy so acutely acid it tarnished the brass of his horn. Roger played adequate trumpet. He could fight his way up to a top line F and find his note at least three tries out of four. But Mike could outreach him by a full octave and he *never* missed an attack. Each time Roger flubbed a note this morning, Mike cocked a quietly patronizing eyebrow. The harder Roger tried, the more notes he flubbed. By the end of the second march Mike's right eyebrow had vanished into his hairline. Roger laid down his horn and wiped his mouth, red-faced, so outclassed he was sniffling.

"Want a handkerchief?" Mike asked. "If you can't blow a horn, you should try blowing your nose."

Goaded beyond all reason, Roger shut his eyes and swung wildly. By sheer bad luck he happened to connect. Mike exploded out of his chair, swearing blue murder.

"All right, Riley, that's it!" Paul snapped. "Go to the office."

"Me? *Me?* What about him? He hit me right in the lip, the goddamn little—"

"*Out*," Paul said fast but not quite fast enough to drown it. "Right now, *out*. Report to Mr. Trimble and tell him I'll come later."

"Trimble!" Mike gave a shiver of disgust as though he had said "Hitler!" His face looked pale now, as much awed as angry. "Listen, I don't want to talk to *that* guy again. How about if we just—"

Paul jerked a thumb toward the door.

"Listen, Mr. Kessler, I—" Mike teetered on the verge of an apology, but Paul didn't let him reach it. He gestured toward the door again and waited while Mike packed up. The locks of the

15

trumpet case snapped like two gunshots on the silent stage. And who were the targets? Paul wondered. Roger, Trimble, himself? Or maybe Mike committing suicide? One thing sure—a session with the vice-principal would lead to someone's bloodshed.

As soon as the stage door slammed behind Mike, Roger slid over into first chair. He played the next march in shaky triumph, slightly flat and missing some high notes. Paul felt shaky too. It was dirty one-sided discipline to nail Mike and let Roger home free. He ought to send them both out. The fight was probably inevitable. Roger couldn't help being miserably second-rate and eaten up with jealousy. Mike couldn't help being able to play rings around him one-handed, but he could have refrained from rubbing Roger's nose in his lost glory. It was mostly Mike's fault. He kept asking for trouble; now he'd finally got it. Paul hated to send any kid to the office, hated ever to imply that he couldn't handle his own problems. Sure, Junior Band was sloppy. He refused to crack the big whip over a bunch of beginners who needed patience and encouragement more than demerits. But he couldn't let one misplaced hotshot explode the whole rehearsal with fistfights and foul language.

At eleven o'clock Paul went to the office; ROTC Band could begin without him. In a stuffy cubbyhole beyond the typewriters Vice-Principal Herbert Trimble was plowing through paper work. He looked up accusingly as Paul came in. "And what's *your* problem today?"

Do I get a choice? Paul wondered. He nodded toward Mike, slouched in the corner, his lip puffed sulkily where Roger had hit it, his faithful trumpet case tucked between his feet.

"Oh, yes, that one. Causing trouble already, is he?" Trimble picked up an enrollment card and studied it casually. "Yes indeed, I remember. The young man had considerable difficulty filling his card out the other day. He didn't seem to know anything about himself. Well, I'm not surprised. Another bomber-plant baby, they're all alike. We're lucky if they can spell their own names, let alone know their father's. I don't know who drew up those new enrollment boundaries, but I swear we're getting more than half, and the worst half at that. Most of them belong at Morton, obviously. You can tell by their names and the looks of their faces. DeFranco, Wozniak, *Washington!* Would you believe that just this morning we inherited one Everett Amos Washington from Verbena, Alabama, may the good Lord help

16

us? Now you can't tell me *he* lives north of the highway. Even that shantytown of trailer houses out on West Thirty wouldn't let— And the white ones are just as bad. Riffraff, war-plant riffraff! It's a shame, it really is, a shame and a crime to let them take the whole town over." He shook his head sadly. "I always knew that bomber plant was a bad mistake, but what can we do?"

Not a damn thing, Paul thought with wry amusement. Not a goddamn thing but quit bitching about it. No wonder Herb found such a high percentage of troublemakers among his transfer students. He certainly went out eagerly with a lantern to meet them halfway.

"Troublemakers and foreign scum pouring into Connor City every day, like this Irish John Dillinger here from Chicago. Now that's what I call a nice tough place to spring from—Gangstertown. How about it, Riley? Is that where you went to school, with the pigs in the stockyards?"

"Stockyards!" Mike looked bewildered by the attack. "I never lived anywhere near— What's wrong with Chicago? I don't get it—"

Trimble cut him short. "Never mind. We'll teach you some better manners here. Report to study hall for third hour from now on."

Mike's face went white again. "You're kicking me out of Band? Permanently?"

"That's right." Trimble drew a sharp line on Mike's enrollment card. "Mr. Kessler doesn't tolerate troublemakers either. And with an extra hour of study—*if* you don't waste it—you might even catch up in your more important classes."

Mike swallowed hard. "I—I'm not much behind— I could study more at home. I—" He looked at Trimble's face again and then, helplessly, toward Paul. Paul felt as much at sea as Mike looked. What in hell caused this furor? Mike only needed a lecture, a little calming down. Trimble didn't even know the offense and didn't seem to care. Instead, he dispensed Instant Justice with one stroke of his pen.

"Put him in ROTC Band," Paul said.

"*What?*"

"I said put him in—"

"Yes, I heard you." Trimble's pen tapped an impatient cadence. "But you're making a mistake."

"If I am, it's not the first one," Paul said pointedly. Now that

17

he thought about it, something smelled very fishy there. Mike was a sophomore, an excellent trumpeter, obviously cadet caliber. How could he ever get stuck in Junior Band? Didn't he know any better? Did anyone give him a choice? "Dumping him in with the freshmen wasn't so bright. You could have asked me first."

"Asked you?" Trimble jabbed his pen at the file drawers. "Sixteen hundred students in a building built for twelve hundred! Ninety-five new since September, scuttling in here like cockroaches out of the woodwork! I should consult with you personally about the musical talents of each and every one of them? Really, Paul, I haven't the time. And this one—*this* one didn't even bring transfer papers or a report card! I've only got his word for it that he belongs in tenth grade at all. He gave me trouble. He's giving you trouble. Now you want to risk him in your best band? What makes you think he'll behave any better there?"

"Ask him," Paul said.

Trimble made a sour face. "Well, Michael?"

"Sure," Mike said. "I'll take ROTC."

"*If* you get it." Trimble studied Mike's card again, hoping to find insurmountable drawbacks. "English in fourth hour; that's bad."

"You can switch it," Paul said.

"It causes trouble, shifting them around. Unbalances the class loads."

"With ninety-five new kids enrolled since September, one more change will upset the apple cart? Oh, come on, Herb, fix it up."

"It's irregular," Trimble grumbled, but he reached for the master schedule and began checking. Paul suppressed a grin as the radio commercial's words flashed across his mind. *Are you troubled by irregularity?* Old Herb certainly was, and he looked it. He wanted everything to move through proper channels and by the clock, smooth and easy. Mike Riley was an awkward lump in the daily duty, hard to get rid of. "All right. As of Monday you've got him fourth hour. I hope you won't be sorry."

"Thanks," Paul said. "You're a real prince." *And next time try Ex-Lax.*

When he left the office, Mike came out right behind him, trumpet case in hand, a musician ready to travel. He grinned and

18

wiped a dramatic hand across his brow. "Sheeesh! What does that guy eat for breakfast, Kellogg's Hate Flakes?"

Paul shrugged. "I wouldn't worry about it if I were you. Anyway, it looks like you're in the Army now. That suit you okay?"

"Yeah, it's fine."

"You're sure? No complaints? Everybody happy?" Considering the narrow squeak he'd just survived, the least Mike could do was to say thank you.

"Sure, yes, it's great. Uh, well, thanks." Mike's grin widened. "I mean gee whiz, thank youse, Fadder Flanagan, thanks a million! Down at the stockyards we'd say youse was a real square guy." Mike threw up a defensive arm, pretending to dodge a blow, then laughed nervously and ducked away toward the stairs.

You'd better run, you little wise guy, Paul thought, before I really split that lip for you.

Snow was falling again, big lazy flakes drifting to the ledges outside Paul's history classroom windows. After a brief mid-January thaw the temperature had snapped to below zero overnight. Slush refrozen in a glaze of ice made streets treacherous and unsalted sidewalks worse. He had nearly broken his neck this morning between the parking lot and the school south door. His knee betrayed him often enough without the complication of ice underfoot. He hoped the Ford would start when he got out there. It balked in cold weather too, just like the knee. Secondhand, both of them. Faulty makeshift equipment that must somehow last for the duration.

It had been, all things considered, an incredibly lousy day. Getting up in the dark to wrestle with tire chains . . . that sprawl in the snowbank and a solicitous senior boy rushing to help him up and brush him off as if he were a wheelchair case . . . sour notes from cold brass horns . . . macaroni and cheese in the cafeteria dished up by a coughing cook . . . a history class who couldn't distinguish Richard the Third from Eric the Red. And then to top it all, not half an hour ago Herb Trimble had delivered his personal sock ending to the Wednesday Blues. Mike Riley, Herb said, was in trouble again right up to his neck. Someone must read him the final warning, the shape-up-or-ship-out lecture before they booted him out of school.

"But I can't do it." Nervously Herb shuffled a stack of enrollment cards as if to deal a fast hand of gin rummy across his cluttered desk. "I have to see Madigan downtown at three thirty. Those district idiots must think Bryan has rubber walls, the way they keep dumping students on us. I don't give a hang about their new boundary line, it's just not fair. Let them jam three kids to a locker at Morton if they like. Morton wouldn't know the difference. So you'll have to talk to Riley. Here's his file, and good luck—you'll need it."

"Why me? I'm no counselor."

"Well, somebody has to. Frankly, Paul, *I* can't take him on again; I wouldn't be responsible for the consequences. You know I'm a very patient man, but that little brat makes me want to commit murder!"

"Oh, Mike isn't so bad."

"Bad! He's broken a dozen Student Council rules in six weeks. They caught him smoking twice on the front sidewalk and once in the rest room. Every one of his teachers is screaming—"

"I'm not. He's fine in ROTC Band, no problem at all."

Trimble sniffed. "So he likes music. That's why you were elected to give the warning. Maybe you can reach him, but personally I doubt it. Believe me, the only thing that impresses the bomber-plant brats is force, plain simple physical punishment. When a dumb polack kid wises off at home, his father—if he's got a father—knocks him across the room. A clout on the head, the kid understands." Trimble rapped his deck of cards hard on the desk to square them up. "But all we can do here is expel them, boot them down to Morton with the rest of the garbage where they belong. And that's exactly where our Michael will find himself, sooner than he thinks. The kid is incorrigible. I knew it instinctively the minute I laid eyes on him. Smart young mick full of excuses and blarney, full of the devil—red hair and a cleft chin, you can't miss it. I tried to be patient, but I knew all along he was a lost cause. Well, you'll be wasting your breath, but you can talk to him. Let him know his kind isn't welcome here."

Trimble laid aside his stacked deck and went off to talk to Superintendent Madigan once again about Bryan's trash-filled halls. Paul sighed and carried the Riley file back to his empty history classroom to watch the snow fall and wait for Mike.

The dismissal bell triggered a rush in the hall, voices, laughter, lockers clanging, then a lull and the ninth-hour bell. Paul sighed again and wished for a cigarette. The kids sneaked their smokes in the rest rooms; he had to set a good example. They went home free at three o'clock while he stayed to struggle with another man's problems. And why should he? Lectures and discipline weren't his job. But Mike was a good trumpeter and a nice kid, in a weird sort of way. Even if he did sometimes act like a little shit, he shouldn't be flushed down the drain to Morton High branded with Trimble's biased judgment—"Incorrigible brat, beat his head in!"

At three fifteen Mike strolled in, whistling. He dumped his books and trumpet case and jacket on one front desk and sat down on top of another. "Ehhhh, what's up, doc?"

"Where were you since three o'clock?"

"Oh, man, you won't believe it. First they told me to see Trimble after school. Then the secretary said no, he left already, but I should see you instead, so I started up here. You know old Miss Jennerly who teaches English? Well, I just accidentally brushed against her passing by in the hall. I mean like my elbow just barely happened to touch against her sleeve, but she took it very personal like she thought I made a pass at her. She grabbed me and backed me into a corner and clicked her teeth at me for ten minutes. Then she offered to straighten me out further in her room, but I said no thanks, I already had a date with you. You better watch out for her, man, she's got big problems. *I* think she's sexually frustrated. What's your opinion?"

Caught off-balance, Paul said the first thing that crossed his mind. "Did you ever find out what Ivory soap tastes like?"

It hit the mark. Mike made a face before covering up with a guilty grin. They both knew the story was nonsense, a showoff stunt, a kid scribbling dirty words on the bathroom wall to impress the world with his sophistication. In Paul's world—and apparently in Mike's also—kids who talked dirty got their mouths scrubbed out. But Mike was due for worse punishment than a mere dose of Ivory. If this was the way he'd been behaving for Trimble and the others, maybe he deserved it.

Paul flipped the pages of the Riley file and wondered how to begin the lecture. "Shape up or ship out"? A neat phrase, but it wasn't true. If Herb Trimble had decided to ship Mike out, he couldn't shape up now. Any excuse would do to sink him. Whether he dropped a gum wrapper in the hall or raped the librarian, whatever he did next would be the Last Straw. So why lecture, why not just skip it? Turn him loose, pick up your hat and go home. Grade those miserable history papers. Then put on a stack of records and mix a drink and try to forget what kind of rotten day this has been, what kind of day you'll have tomorrow, and the day after, and all the other days ahead.

Mike jiggled on the desk, swinging his feet in a syncopated rhythm, waiting uneasily to hear what would come. He cleared his throat a couple of times. "Uh—Mr. Kessler—"

"Yes?"

"I—uh—you know that dumb stuff I said to you outside the office that time? I mean after Roj hit me in the lip and Trimble wanted to make me drop band and you wouldn't let him?"

"I remember," Paul said. Fadder Flanagan. He wasn't mad now, but he remembered.

Mike's jiggling speed increased. "Well, I'm sorry. I didn't mean it, honest, not like it sounded. I was just trying to thank you for what you did, only it—well, it sort of got away from me. I guess I was mad from all that talk of Trimble's about the Chicago stockyards. But I'm sorry I said it to *you*. I mean it was real nice of you to let me into ROTC. It's neat."

Shocking stories one minute, a shy apology the next. Paul couldn't keep up with the reversing moods. He had seen the clean, obedient cadet every morning for six weeks now, uniform neat, brass shined, not a smart remark in a carload. But according to the evidence of the Riley file, everyone else had been seeing a different student, smoking and sassing and spreading hate and discontent all over Bryan High. Today, within five minutes, he'd met them both. But how could you punish one Mike without wounding the other? No wonder Trimble was climbing the walls.

"You like Band, do you?"

"Sure, it's my only good class. Everything else stinks. I can't stand that bunch of jerky teachers."

Paul had to smile. "They seem to feel the same way about you. Why? How come you give them so much trouble, but none in the band?"

"Well, *you're* not asking for any."

22

"And they all are? I doubt that."

Mike looked confused. "Oh, heck, I don't know. Maybe not. But in Band—well, a guy knows where he is, there, because of the demerits and promotions and regulations and things."

"The school has regulations too."

"Oh, sure, millions of them. Walk *up* the end stairs and *down* the middle stairs and don't take cuts in the lunch line. Bunch of dumb rules you never even heard of until you happen to accidentally break one. Then they act like you just murdered your mother. If you do something wrong in Band, you get clobbered, sure, but it's by the officers and strictly by the book, not personal. They don't pick on you for no reason because they don't like your looks or something. And if you work hard, you can make officer too. It's fair, see what I mean? A guy has a chance."

"Well, maybe if you tried working harder and following the rules in your other classes things might go smoother for you. I know English and geometry aren't as much fun as Band, but you could give them a chance too."

Mike made a face. "Now you sound like old Trimble preaching his phony sermons. 'Young man, these are the valuable formative years of your life. If you pass up this opportunity to receive a priceless education at the taxpayers' expense, you will jeopardize your en-tire future, et cetera, et ceteras, unquote.' Shit! What does he care about my future? He thinks I was born in Hell's Kitchen and earmarked straight for the reformatory. But I'm not scared of that creep. He's all gas and no guts, a real politician like that clown they named the school after, old three-time-loser Willie."

Paul shifted his weight in the chair, easing his leg into a less cramped position, and tried to ignore the twinge of pain. Aspirin and a drink and a stack of records. They don't cure everything, but they help. Nothing cures everything, not even time. "Well, you'd better be scared of him, because he can alter your future so fast it'll make your head spin."

"How?"

"Expel you, buddy, and he's not fooling. You may as well start cleaning out your locker and get ready to head downtown to Morton."

"Morton!" Mike nearly fell off his desktop. "Me go to Moron Tech, are you kidding? Listen, I've heard about that dump. All the hoods go there. It's a concentration camp with a crew of

Gestapo to knock the guys down and the girls up. They all carry knives and brass knuckles." Under the bravado Mike's face looked pale green. "You know what happened there the other day? This big guy pulled a knife on the principal—what's his name, Richter?—and old Richter hauled off and knocked his three front teeth out, just like that, pow! And last month there was a little freshman girl who got cornered by six colored guys after school, and they laid her right in front of her own locker, *all six guys,* and now she's pregnant. Man, doesn't that make you sick? I wouldn't go there if you paid me!"

The first time Paul heard those two famous Moron-Tech stories—six years ago in his first season of teaching at Bryan—he had felt sick. Now he was merely sick of hearing the old chestnuts retold each year as shocking new gospel. Sometimes it was a gang of four Italians who raped the freshman, sometimes a .38 automatic that the tough kid pulled on Richter, but it always happened "just last month" and the punchline never varied—"*I wouldn't go there if you paid me!*"

"I'm afraid you will, though. It's the only other school in town. Give my regards to Joe Danielson; he's their bandleader."

Mike's face turned greener. "But I *can't!* Oh, man, this is horrible. If I get expelled, my mom will lose her mind. I mean things are messed up enough right now without— Can Trimble really do that, throw me out for no reason at all?"

Paul tapped the file folder. "Here are his reasons, three pages of them. Do you want to hear them all again? 'Insolent answers, inattention in class, smoking in the rest room—' "

"Never mind, I know. Sure, I did all that stuff, I busted his rules. But *he* started it. He hated my guts before I did *anything.* They sent me in to see him the first morning because I didn't have transfer papers from my other school, see, and the minute I walked in he started calling me dirty names. You know, you heard him yourself—bomber-plant trash and Chicago shitbird and the pigs in the stockyards. When I asked about ROTC Band, he said no, it was all full—but it really wasn't—and he shoved me in with the beginners just for spite. I mean *why?* What'd I do to deserve that? What's he so down on me for, anyway?"

Paul shook his head. "I don't know, Mike, that's the truth. But it's not just you. He's itchy about all the new kids lately. They're overcrowding the school and causing him big problems; it makes him pretty nervous. You probably said something that teed him off—"

"No, honest, nothing. I only left some blanks empty on my enrollment card."

"Why?"

"Well— Oh, never mind, skip it. But he started raving about foreigners off the cattle boat who couldn't read and write basic English. Me? I'm off the boat? Michael Boyd Riley, does that sound like a German Jewish refugee? Then he starts in with 'bomber-plant trash' and that made me mad. I mean, my mom works there, she's a secretary, but nobody in the world can call her trash! He talked like she was Rosie-the-Riveter in tight slacks and a lunch pail—and she's *not*. And even if she was, what business is it of his? That man is weird! But he kept saying I was a troublemaker, so finally I figured, okay, so I'm a troublemaker. If he wants trouble, he'll get trouble. Only not to get *expelled*. I didn't mean to do that. Listen, how can I get out of this mess? Bryan isn't such a marvelous place, but I sure as heck don't want to go to Morton. I'll quit making trouble, honest. Can you tell him? He hates me so bad he wouldn't listen even if I crawled in and licked his shoes."

Paul hesitated. "Well, I can try. He thinks you're an incorrigible lost cause. If you pulled a switch and reformed overnight, he'd probably drop dead from the shock."

"Hey, great! Let him drop. I'll play 'Taps' at his funeral."

"They'll play 'Taps' at yours if you keep on wising off. That's exactly the attitude that put you into the soup. If you zip the lip and behave yourself, maybe you can survive. I don't promise, but you can try. What have you got to lose?"

"Blood," Mike said soberly. "Oh, jeez, I don't know. Some days it just doesn't pay to get up in the morning."

How right you are, Paul thought. He took a pencil and doodled a coda of eighth notes across the bottom of the Riley file. QED, mission accomplished, message received and duly acknowledged. Mike Riley has had the shit scared out of him. Now we can both go home and rest up to face tomorrow. "That's all; you can go now." As soon as Mike went, he could leave at his own pace, solo without accompaniment. It was hell to move like a creaking old man at the age of thirty-two, and even more painful with smart kids watching. That idiot this morning, half his size, rushing over

25

like a damned boy scout on good deed duty—"Are you okay, Mr. Kessler? This sidewalk sure is slick, isn't it?"

Mike slid off the desk, but he didn't pick up his jacket. He walked to the window—quick, easy, long-legged strides—and stood looking out. Tall, almost Paul's own height, and light on his feet as a dancer. No, that was too effeminate. A prizefighter? He was too thin for a fighter, no meat on his bones, no muscle to back up his anxious arrogance. Battling Kid Riley couldn't survive ten rounds at Moron Tech. Richter's tough crew would batter that sharp hawk nose and muss up the handsome auburn hair, too well combed, too greased, too long on the sides and back. His skin would bruise and show the marks. Not the fair freckled complexion of brighter redheads but almost unhealthily pale, pasty, as though he'd been raised in a cellar or under a rock. The dark-lashed blue Irish eyes didn't smile like anybody's morn in spring. Herb Trimble had landed some wicked jabs in the preliminary match and now Kid Riley didn't feel so good.

Mike stared out his window. "Still snowing."

"Umm-hmm."

"Nebraska weather is for the birds, man, I mean the penguins. Would you believe . . . in California . . . there's oranges growing on trees right now?"

"So I have heard." Paul turned the eighth notes into sixteenths and added a key signature of six sharps. Wouldn't this Kid Riley ever leave?

Mike breathed on the glass and wrote something, then smeared it out. Suddenly he turned around. "Hey, you know that thing we played yesterday? The 'Suffocated Lady'?"

"Sophisticated." Paul grinned at the aptly twisted title. He had tried a concert arrangement of the Ellington jazz classic, but the ROTC brass beat the living breath out of the poor old gal. They couldn't find that subtle balance point between straight march rhythm and literal rickyticky syncopation, a blend that couldn't be written but had to be felt. Suffocated, indeed. "What about her?"

"Remember where the first trumpets messed up so bad and you took Fred's horn and played it for them?"

"Umm?" He blackened in the last note of his doodled composition while he waited for the punch line. But naturally Bill Rhodes could do it better. He didn't play like Bill Rhodes, never had and never claimed to. An adequate lead trumpet he was,

26

fantastic he was not. He rarely touched an instrument during school rehearsals. He was paid to direct, so he directed. Let the kids blow their own horns.

"That was neat, man! Where'd you learn to play like that?"

Surprise, surprise. A compliment instead of a slam. A real compliment coming from the boy who measured all musicians against the Colossus of Rhodes. "It wasn't that hard. They just didn't have the idea."

"No, I mean where did you learn to play swing? Are you professional?"

Professional, the way Mike pronounced the word, rang with a rather holy sound that made Paul cautious. "Well, I have a union card."

"Who with?"

"Nobody now. I served some time with Jack Herron around here, that's all."

"On the road?"

"Not since the summers in college, and that was ten years back, 1932, '33." Ancient history, Paul thought, Depression days when anybody did anything to make a buck. Way back when I had two good legs and a fifty-dollar horn and I hadn't yet met anyone to keep me home nights. A *long* time ago.

"Did you ever hear of Jerry Riley?"

"I don't think so. Should I have?"

"Well, you might have. He's played piano all over hell and back for about twenty years, with Dorsey and all different bands. He's— He's my dad."

"Oh, really?" The kid never learned, did he? Not even out of Trimble's personal frying pan, yet here he was spinning yarns again.

"He can play anything, swing, barrelhouse, old-time jazz. He was in a pickup group once with Bix and Tesch when they cut 'Shadyside' and 'Jamming the Blues.' That's a real collector's item, you can't buy it anyplace now."

Now that much I'll believe, Paul thought. You *can't* buy it because it's recorded on the Fantasy label. What a dandy story, better than the Bill Rhodes episode and harder to disprove. "Where is this versatile pianist nowadays?"

"He was with a USO Camp Shows unit last year. You know anything about them?"

"Sure, they entertain the troops overseas."

"Some of them do. We just played shows at different camps and hospitals around California, Camp Ord, Camp Pendleton."

Oh, did we now indeed? The blarney grew greener every minute. Not just Riley, but Riley & Son. "You were there too?"

Mike hesitated before he answered. "Yeah. Yeah, I was there. He bought this new car in Chicago last June, see, a big Buick convertible, and—"

"Red," Paul said involuntarily.

"Yeah, how'd you know? Red as a fire engine. And fast? Man, she'd do ninety like nothing at all. Jerry let her out on the desert just to see. But he never let me drive over sixty."

"That was conservative of him."

Mike reseated himself on his desk top, getting comfortable for a long story. "Yeah, a real sweet car. And would you believe when we got to Reno, he turned around and sold it? He didn't lose it, I mean, he sold it. Isn't that crazy? A practically brand-new Buick with whitewalls, would you part with it right now? But that's Jerry—easy come, easy go. So we hopped a train to L.A., where he caught a patriotic urge to entertain the boys in uniform. The USO travels by train and bus, real crude style, though, no comforts whatsoever. You ever tried to sleep rattling around mountain hairpin curves in a bus? It's creepy. You look out the window and there's nothing, I mean like vacuum right straight down. Some people got carsick, but I didn't and Russ didn't either. Nothing ever bothered Russ. He could eat pizza for breakfast. I did too, for that matter. If my mom knew some of the junk I ate, she'd—well, that's another story. Mothers get very antsy over nothing."

"Occupational disease of mothers," Paul said. Interesting, the way Mike's story kept veering off into miscellaneous details, unconfirmable but equally undeniable. You could find mountain scenery nearer than California. Most families took vacation trips. And who was Russ, who ate pizza for breakfast? "Tell me about the show. How big was the band?"

"Well, they carried four permanent men. Five, I mean. The rest was soldiers from the different camp bands where we played. The permanent group was piano, drums, first trumpet and first sax. And me, I played second trumpet."

"Oh?" Enough was enough.

"Yeah, uh, that's right." Mike ran his tongue over his lips and

28

looked nervous, as well he should. Nobody, *nobody* could buy that, not even the starry-eyed freshmen girls who swallowed the my-friend-Bill-Rhodes line.

"Second trumpet," Paul repeated. "That's quite a responsible job for a boy your age. I'll bet your dad was proud of you." Mike said nothing. His foot beat a rapid tattoo against the metal desk frame. "Paid a good salary?"

"Hundred a week."

"Not bad. For a young guy like you, no wife, nobody to worry about but yourself, that should have been great. I can't imagine why you gave it up and came back to school?"

If Mike could answer *that* one, Paul thought, he'd concede the match and send him home with the Liar's Cup. But Kid Riley looked pale now, awfully tired of sparring and dodging loaded questions. His answers came slower, the thoughtful pauses longer. Paul's last question stopped him cold. He swallowed hard, slipped off the desk and turned away, staring into the gray afternoon beyond the window. No help for him out there. No USO bandstand, no sunny orange groves or Hollywood stars. Just cold gray Nebraska winter on a high school campus, flat empty ground, bare trees, bare truth. Nothing exciting at all.

"I had to quit," he said finally. "Jerry got mad and sent me home."

He waited, but Paul refused to cue him again. Any second trumpet worth his salt should be able to ad-lib one more chorus.

"Me and Russ were— Did I mention Russ? Russ Kelbert, he was our drummer. Real nice guy, great on the drums, beautiful, really the greatest. Only nineteen, but he's been with three or four good bands, even with Rhodes before he joined the Navy. He wanted to join a service band, see, serve Uncle and see the world at the same time. But the Navy discharged him before he ever left San Diego. So then he joined us in September, figuring he'd get overseas one way or another. And he still didn't, because our unit never left the States. He just couldn't win."

Paul felt confused. Some details sounded so genuine and others so phony. Mike seemed to be weaving real acquaintances into his fantasy, generously sprinkled with show biz stardust. Jerry cut a record with Bix; Russ worked for Rhodes. But the anxious kid trying to reach the action, thwarted by medical problems and bad luck—there was nothing incredible about that, nothing at all.

29

Russ Kelbert was real, and Paul could feel for him. "He might make it yet. There's plenty of war left."

"Not for him." Mike kept on staring out at the snow, seeing something that Paul couldn't see. "You don't see no action where he is now. Four walls and bars on the window, that's your view. I just about landed there myself, and I wish— But they wouldn't. I'm too *young*. It was my fault he got busted, but they turned me loose and wouldn't even tell me where they sent him—Alcatraz, maybe, I don't know. I'm just an innocent *kid*, see, I didn't *know* any better. Like hell I didn't. I knew it's illegal, but what the hell, who does it hurt? Nobody, as long as they mind their own business and leave you alone. But no—people have to come busting in and clobbering other people around and calling the cops, being the big heavy father like he was suddenly so concerned about my morals. *My* morals! That's a laugh. My morals didn't inconvenience old Jerry getting gassed and screwing chorus girls every night. That's all right, see, that's a healthy, normal pastime. But messing around with your only true friend, the only guy in the world who—who cares about you—that's a crime. Feeling good is a crime. You ever tried it?"

Paul caught his breath at the abrupt question. Lying? Nobody in his right mind would lie his way into this kind of trouble. Out, yes, but not in. "Tried what?"

Suddenly Mike saw the edge of the cliff and the rocks below. "Never mind. If you don't know, I'm not telling. But they tossed Russ into the jug and sent me to Siberia, and that's the end of the story, man, the bitter, bitter end."

And what a story, Paul thought dazedly. A real cliff-hanger fantasy with the last chapter missing—censored, torn out or more likely never written. Mike must have spent a long dull summer inventing it, but he couldn't dream up a climax wild enough to satisfy his gory imagination. It was almost a shame to hand him a rejection slip. But of course he couldn't be allowed to publish such crazy trash around the school. The naïve and sheltered Bryan kids would believe any story if it sounded sufficiently shocking, like those hairy old Moron-Tech tales still going strong in their umpteenth year of circulation. The dirtier it was, the more eagerly they bought it. Mike's True Confessions would top the best-seller list next week and bring Herb Trimble down on him with screams of outrage. "Kill this little monster before he corrupts the whole school!"

30

"I can see why you screamed when Trimble stuck you into Junior Band. What an insult for a man of your professional experience."

"I'll say. Me and Russ were going to start our own combo, but— You know, if they kick me out of Bryan, I could get a job in a dance band. They're crying for sidemen now. Russ worked wit. Rhodes once. I bet I could myself."

That's what you think, Paul said to himself, and reached for his briefcase. He pulled out a folder of manuscript sheets. Scoring arrangements for Jack Herron's band was an easy way to pick up a few extra dollars, a very good way to fill empty time. It wasn't finished, but perfect for his purpose at the moment. "Okay, get your horn."

"What for?"

"Go on, get it out."

With a puzzled look Mike opened the case. "What's coming off?"

"An audition. I'm Rhodes, and you want a job." He flicked the sheet of second trumpet music across the desk. "Play it for me."

Mike took it, grinning broadly at the chance to act his role. Then the grin started to fade. "What is this? There's no name on it."

"There's notes on it. Play them."

"Uh—you sure it won't disturb old Trimble?"

"He's downtown. Come on, shove in a mute and quit stalling. I make ten grand a week and my time is valuable."

"Okay, okay." A slight frown creased Mike's forehead as he fingered the valves and blew a couple of low warm-ups. "My horn's pretty cold."

Paul leaned back in his chair and looked impatient. "Whenever you're ready, Mr. Riley."

"I'm ready, Mr. Rhodes," Mike said. He attacked the introduction bravely, floundered through the top line with mistakes and faked passing tones, lost his place and jumped a line. He stubbed his toe on a syncopated figure and fainted dead away at the first delayed triplet.

"Who copied this foul stuff? I can't read half the notes."

"You can't read, period."

"I never saw it before, I never even heard it. How do you expect a guy to—"

"Thank you, Mr. Riley. Don't call us, we'll call you."

31

"Aw, listen, will you? I can play it if you give me a little time—"

"Are you kidding? You not only never saw this music before, you never saw *any* orchestration before. Get lost, Riley. You couldn't hold down second chair with Smiling Joe Corntassel and his Kernels of Melody!"

"I could too!" Mike shouted like a cornered four-year-old on the verge of tears—trapped, outweighed, outnumbered, but still yelling in sheer desperation. "I could."

"Not if you can't read. You didn't even come close. I don't see how you've been getting by in ROTC."

Mike swallowed. "Faking, that's how. I've got a very fast ear. You just play through this thing one time and I bet you ten bucks I can fake it. You want to bet?"

"It wouldn't matter if you could. The union won't take illiterates. Do you think Bill Rhodes would say, 'Okay, men, everybody stand by while I play Riley's part through once so he can hear how it goes?' Come on, Mike, let's face it. You're no professional. You never held a swing-band job and you never will hold one by faking fancy stories."

"They weren't stories," Mike said hopelessly. "It was true." He couldn't even convince himself. His face had been red; now it was going pale again, greenish-white and miserable. He sat silently, staring at the floor, punching his first valve down over and over.

Once upon a time, Paul thought suddenly, there were two little boys and a big red birthday-party balloon and a tired man reading a newspaper. They batted the balloon around recklessly, up in the air, giggling each time it drifted down between the reader and his evening news. At first he batted it back. Then he said, "Cut it out now, that's enough." But they kept on punching it in there, living dangerously, giggling harder. So he lit a cigarette and waited until it came down again. Zap!—no more balloon. The giggles turned to tears and he felt like a first-class rubber heel. Sure, they'd asked for it. Sure, he warned them. But try saying "Tough luck" to tearstained nephews. They don't understand about being careful or about the low tolerance threshold of a tired uncle with a racked-up knee. All they know is they want their balloon back, and if you're half the man they think you are, you'll give it back, like a lost-and-found teddy bear or the magic reappearing penny. But when you zap a balloon, it's gone forever. You *can't* give it back, even when they cry.

32

Now Mike was all sad and bent out of shape, clutching the remnant of his beautiful show biz balloon. Sure, he'd asked for it. He blew his story far too big and batted it around far too enthusiastically until it popped right in his face. He was old enough to know better. But it would have popped anyway sooner or later. No one needed to reach out with a stealthy cigarette and hasten its demise.

"This is a hell of a mess," Mike said in a low voice. "I know I can't get a job yet. But I can't stand it like this either, not alone, not three more years. If I could just do something—"

"Why don't you learn to read swing music?"

"Read it? I don't even know where to get it, except those piano pieces in the dime store. All my Rhodes solos I just learned off the records, listening. I need stuff like this—" He touched the manuscript sheet that had betrayed him. "You copied this, didn't you? Can you buy them already printed?"

"Stock orchestrations at Hoffman and Franks, eighty cents per set."

"That's too much. All I need is the trumpet parts."

"Well, I might have some lying around at home. Old stuff, though, not the latest."

"Could you loan it to me? Seconds, thirds, that's what's rough. Melody you can fake."

"Not if you haven't heard it," Paul said.

Mike grinned, already beginning to recover his brass. "Another thing—you know those hot solos like Rhodes makes up? How can he tell which notes will sound good?"

"Good ad-libbing takes talent. But you need to begin with the basic rules of chord theory."

"Could you show me sometime?"

"Well, I don't know, I'm pretty busy." It was true enough, he was busy. The days were accounted for, one way or another; they had to be. "Preparation for history classes takes a lot of time, and I have fifteen private students, that's—"

"Students? You give private music lessons?" Mike grabbed at the words, and Paul realized his mistake too late. "Could I take from you? Not classical, just about ad-lib chords and reading those stock things. You'll do it, won't you? Please?"

Paul stared out at the falling snow. Oh, Lord, now what do you say? Make one friendly gesture and you're caught, involved,

33

committed to more. You've done too much already. Give him a handful of old stocks and tell him to blow. All he needs is a little solid groundwork to support the flash and dazzle. He can pick it up by himself if he wants it bad enough. And he does. He wants it so bad he can taste it.

When a kid feels that bad, there's only one thing to do. Wipe his tears and blow his nose and buy him another balloon. Or something better, sturdier, a strong rubber ball that will bounce instead of pop under the pressure. Paul sighed. "Talk it over with your folks and let me know. The price is a dollar for a half-hour lesson, two bucks for an hour."

"Cheap at twice the price," Mike said. "You have just enrolled yourself a new two-buck student, man."

Sundays were the roughest. No school to teach, no private lessons, no rehearsals, no sponges to absorb the time. He had nothing to get up for this morning, and a decent excuse to stay in the sack if he cared to. But he couldn't sleep either, not with that unholy racket going on upstairs, three little nephews thundering around and around the kitchen.

Last night he had filled a chair with Herron at the Charles Hotel for the first time in several months. When the band quit at midnight, Jack twisted his arm to stay on for a couple of beers. "I tell you, Paul, the war really plays hell with keeping a band together. Talk about turnover! Eleven different trumpets since Pearl Harbor and God knows how many saxes, I lost count. They get drafted, they work swing shift, they leave town right and left. Listen, why don't you come back with us regular? I need a reliable man."

"I'm too old," Paul said into his beer glass.

"You're what? Shut up talking about old; I've got five years on you."

"Yes, but my left knee is going on eighty-three next August."

Jack sobered a little. "That bad? I thought it seemed better. You don't limp so much now."

"It's fluky, I can't trust it. Goes fine for a while and then *pow*, flat on my face. And while we're on that subject, Mr. Herron, those new jack-in-the-box brass section tricks don't help. Four

bars up and four bars down, doowah-doowah with the hats. Who⁻
do you think you are anyway, Glenn Miller?"

"Oh, you know, the kids like it. Makes them think they're
getting extra for their money, genuwine big-name band straight
from the Hollywood Palladium."

"Well, you've big-named yourself straight out of my league. I
couldn't stand your frantic pace anymore, all that travel and
one-night stands."

"Travel, shit. How far can we travel on rationed gas with half
the sax section riveting bombers at six A.M.? All the way to
Lincoln, maybe. I'm not hurting for local dates. Roseland would
book us every weekend for the duration if I'd sign their exclusive
contract, which I won't, get myself committed forever so I
couldn't take any better offers. I'll play at Roseland next
weekend, God willing, maybe the week after that if I've still got a
band. Six months from now, who knows? I could be building
bombers myself by then."

"But you won't be."

"No, I won't be. That's too much like work. I'll keep it going.
But I sure would be happier with you in the section every night,
like old times. Those were pretty good times, you know it?
Remember the summer we toured two weeks around Iowa and
Minnesota, those lake resorts? 'Sunrise Serenade,' must have
played it a million times. And you sent those damn picture
postcards home every day, wish you were here, wish you were
here, like a broken record—"

"Forget it," Paul said so sharply that Jack sloshed beer on the
counter. "I won't be back."

"Well, sorry, I didn't mean to— Oh, Rosie says, when are you
coming to dinner again? She's been worrying about you. How
come we never see Paul, she says, has he lost our address? Come
on over tomorrow. She'll make her lasagna special just for you."

Paul hesitated. "Tell her thanks, but some other time, okay?"

"Sure, any time, you're always welcome. And any time you
should feel ready to take the chair, it's open."

He finished his beer and refused another, refused lasagna again
with all honest respect to Rosie's cooking and drove home with
tire chains clanking, home to the dark, empty basement apartment.

And now it was Sunday morning with the Battle of Stalingrad

echoing right overhead. He rolled on his side and wadded the pillow against his ear. Whoever wrote that line about the patter of little feet was never a parent or a resident uncle. More than feet got into the Jansky Brothers act. Huey argued and Looie wailed and Dewey jangled his tricycle bell. Helen's sweet maternal patience sounded dangerously thin for 9 A.M. as she tried to hush them up. She was earning her halo the hard way: ration points and mad-dog cyclists in the kitchen, novice trumpet students in the basement, a husband riveting overtime at the bomber plant and a widowed brother who dragged along on the rim of the family circle under his black cloud of private misery.

Paul knew he was Helen's final straw. He never should have moved in. He knew it a year ago when he was in no position to defend himself, flat on his back and dopey with pain. John and Helen insisted he had to live somewhere. *No, I don't,* he told them, *I don't have to live at all now.* But that was a futile statement born of despair; he lacked the strength to argue it or the guts to prove it. When a young man loses his wife, he doesn't die of loneliness; he only wishes he could. While he lay helpless in the cast and bandages and paralysis of grief, Helen went ahead and made his decisions for him. She arranged for Beth's funeral. She sold the Pine Street house with his apathetic agreement—yes, yes, go ahead, anything, it doesn't matter—sold it furnished to eager war workers and turned a profit. She moved his personal stuff—books, clothes, records, trumpet—and did with the rest whatever is mercifully done in such cases; Paul never asked and didn't want to know.

The Janskys let him pay OPA rates for a knotty-pine bachelor suite while they spoiled him rotten with home-baked streusel, tenderly starched shirts and all the family life and companionship he could bear. Insurance replaced the wrecked Dodge with a sober secondhand Ford, mournfully black and asthmatic on hills. By Easter he was back at school, picking up his work again, stumbling on through life with a permanent limp and scars that wouldn't heal.

He didn't want them to heal.

He kicked back the blankets—carefully, with the right leg—and rolled out of bed. Too many people worried themselves about his health and welfare. How he spent his lonely nights or what song he dreamed of was nobody's damn business. Why must the whole world try to cheer up a bereaved man? They wanted him cheered up and fixed up, rehabilitated and remarried before the grass grew decently green on Beth's grave. Willy-nilly, never mind who, just shove another woman into his bed, mate him up quick with some other odd sock. Why couldn't they leave him alone?

Unshaved, dressed in weekend clothes, he climbed the stairs not quite late enough to miss the family breakfast. John Jansky worked a six-day week, but Helen insisted on family Sundays, double overtime be darned. Children needed to see their father, she said, and nobody challenged her decisions about *Kinder, Kirche, und Küche*. A big blond-braided Rhinemaiden in a scuffed corduroy housecoat, she rose from her coffee to fry Paul's eggs.

"I can do that," he said halfheartedly.

"So can I," she said, and had them dished up before he could locate the spatula. The kids were racketing around in pajamas, scuffling over the comics. Dewey, the middle one, the one whose given name, Duane, had inspired Paul to the trio of duckling-nephew nicknames, tugged at his sleeve with a jammy hand. "My plane is busted, the wheels came off. Can you fix it?"

"Your father is the bomber expert."

"That's no bomber," Huey said with six-year-old scorn. "It's a P-38 fighter plane, my gosh, everybody knows that. Anybody who doesn't know the difference between a fighter and a bomber—"

"Shouldn't be an air-raid warden," Paul said. "And I'm not, so go read your funny papers, Flying Jack, and hand me the news section, please."

"Are you coming to church with us today?" Helen offered the question as routinely as she offered Paul's second cup of coffee, knowing just as accurately what the answer would be. Yes to coffee, no to church.

"No, not today."

Helen accepted that, but the kids didn't. "Why do you always say not today? Are you going someday?"

"Maybe. I don't know."

"Why can't you go today?"

"Because my wheels came off," Paul said absently into the newspaper.

Dewey giggled. "You don't have wheels. Your feet didn't come off."

"Smart, aren't you? Okay, it wasn't wheels. My internal rubber

37

band busted so the motor doesn't wind up anymore, and they're not making rubber bands for the duration."

"What's a duration?"

"It's a store, stupid," Huey said. Paul looked up then; he couldn't help it. "Everybody knows that. A big apartment store downtown where we used to buy radios and bikes and tires. Only there's a war on, see. The Army and Navy took all the rubber and steel to make guns. There's none left to make radios and bikes for the duration to sell. So now it's empty and they closed it."

But of course, Paul thought. Beautiful. That's what you learn in first-grade Curneyvence. Last week the Russians captured Hitler at Staltongrab. This week we closed the duration. Everybody knows that, stupid. You've seen the sign on the door, haven't you?

"Huey, you want to hop downstairs and bring the cigarettes off my desk?"

"If you call me Huey, you have to say it in duck talk."

Paul mentally measured the number of steps down, the number up and the strength of his need for an after-breakfast smoke. With a sigh he translated his request into sizzles and quacks. Huey quacked back, "Okay, Unca Donald," and flapped away with Dewey-duck hot on his tail feathers. Paul had time to read nearly three full pages of bad news before they returned, chanting, "Lucky Strike Green . . . has gone . . . TO WAR!"

"Thanks. What took so long, couldn't you find them?"

"No, we made your bed while we were there."

Paul said, "Thanks a lot," with restrained enthusiasm. Life here came studded with unexpected gestures of goodwill—a smudgy shoeshine, a broken cookie, a sticky good-night kiss from Looie, the two-year-old. He could accept them or move out to do his grieving alone. But he couldn't cling to grief forever like Looie's ragged baby blanket, a thumb-sucker's security. Other men lost their wives in tragedies equally sudden and senseless and undeserved, but they survived it. Good Lord, man, the world is overrun with tragedy now, new horrors every day. Pick up the Sunday paper and read all about it. Wives lose husbands, parents lose children, half the civilized world is slaughtering the other half. Why don't you go to church and pray for the souls of the million Jews that your German cousins murdered? That's a loss big enough for a man to cry over.

But the road back to faith still loomed too steep for his crippled leg and broken spiritual mainspring. Too many memories roosted like crows inside that sanctuary, five crowded years, from the wedding he had proudly attended to the funeral he had mercifully missed. Even the good memories—choir practice, church suppers—would hurt too much. Too many old friends in that congregation, Beth's friends and his, too many sympathetic faces and welcoming handshakes and meaningless words intended to comfort. While the Janskys went to church, he stayed at home and read the news—*Life* for the pictures, *Time* for sardonic cleverness, the Omaha *World-Herald* for unchallenged Midwestern insularity. He kept an eye on the roast, as directed, and when the faithful flock returned, they ate Sunday noon dinner together. While his nephews flaked out for afternoon naps, Paul went downstairs to his studio, downstairs to boredom.

He wished he too could nap to pass the time. Doze the day away, hibernate for the winter like a lonely bear. On Pine Street afternoons like this they had lit a fire and loaded a stack of records, unobtrusive background music, and sat close together on the couch planning. . . . No! *Don't.* That's no good, no damn good at all, the worst thing you can possibly do. That's deliberately picking off the scab to make it bleed again.

Today's mood demanded discipline, not stardust memories or baby-blanket nostalgia. He found a book to study, a Middle Ages survey full of meaty concepts to be chewed carefully before digestion. If Bryan High insisted on making him teach history, the least he could do was teach it right. He was deep into it when the phone rang, jarring him halfway through five centuries with its abrupt demand. Impatient, preoccupied, he reached for the receiver.

" . . . speaking Mr. Kessler . . . demand an explanation . . . what kind of arrangement . . . with one of your *students* . . . think I don't know what's going on—"

"What?" The words were undeniably English, but they made no sense, a rapid stream of anger, a message lost between bursts of emotional static. Some woman was madder than hell about something, but what? One of his students? One of his arrangements?

"—stand for this underhanded sneaky—"

"Listen, you're not—"

39

"—behind my back! A child of that age can be pretty easily influenced, but I am amazed that a grown man and a schoolteacher of all people should be party to anything so contemptible, underhanded and *low!*"

Whatever it was, it was trouble. When she paused to reload for the next attack he grabbed the chance to speak. "There's some kind of mistake; I don't—"

"*Your* mistake, Mr. Kessler! I don't know how long you've been carrying this on, but if the school—"

"Listen," Paul said dazedly. "Listen, will you, just one minute? Will you please tell me two things? Who are you and what are you talking about? I didn't catch your name and I honestly don't know." But he knew what it sounded like. If she thought that, she was out of her mind. Him, with a high school kid? Frances, Joanie, the giggling Junior Band bobbysoxers riding home occasionally in his car? Those *children?* Good God, no!

"My name is Katheryn Ashton," she snapped.

Ridiculous, nightmarish. Ashton? No girl in any of his classes was named Ashton. "I'm sorry, I still don't know who—"

"My son's name is Michael Riley. I believe you know *him?*"

Oh, boy, do I, Paul thought, and suddenly he felt his skin crawl. If that little liar had begun a new fantasy, a sequel adventure involving *him!* Rumors were easy to start and hard to stop. Schoolteachers, especially unmarried schoolteachers, sat like ducks for a morals charge, guilty until proved innocent and left in a doubtful shadow even then. One juicy lie, no matter how ridiculous, could send his reputation down the drain forever. And Mike had just the dirty little mind to invent that lie. *Messing around with your only true friend—feeling good, man—you ever tried it?* Two Saturday-morning private lessons in the studio, and now Mike's mother was on the line screaming bloody murder about low contemptible goings-on. The longer he hesitated, the guiltier he must seem. He cleared his throat. "What—does he say I did?"

"He didn't need to say it. I've got proof right here. I found the stuff you gave him!"

Stuff I gave him, Paul thought desperately. Stuff *I* gave— What, for God's sake, does she think I gave him? Gin? Dirty postcards? Nazi propaganda?

"What stuff?"

" 'Moonlight Cocktail' and 'King Porter Stomp'!"

The relief was too sharp; he exploded in uncontrollable laughter. Sheet music! This whole fantastic stormy scene over two sheets of trumpet music! Now he knew where Mike got his marvelous imagination. She made it sound as subversive as Studs Lonigan and Karl Marx, but as a nasty rumor it wouldn't even raise an eyebrow. Have you heard the latest? Paul Kessler of Bryan High corrupts his innocent little students with, forgive the expression, lowdown dirty j-a-z-z music. And he corrupted, of all people, young Mike Riley, whose innocence had teetered two months on the verge of school expulsion. If Mike's mother was only now beginning to worry about him, she was quite a few years too late.

"I'm guilty as charged," Paul said finally when he found control of his voice again. He hadn't laughed so hard in a long time; it felt pretty good. Wait till Herron heard this yarn. Jack loved to kid him about being a straitlaced schoolmaster. Moonlight cocktails, anyone? Who stomped on old King Porter? Who put the sin in syncopation?

"Along with Arden's Studies to play for my benefit while—"

"Arban? No, he doesn't use—"

"He certainly does, I paid for it. A big brown paper-covered book, and the same boring exercises over and over every night last week until I nearly lost my mind. That was your little scheme, wasn't it? Classics to cover up the smell of the garbage?"

"Hey, now hold it. Swing music isn't garbage, it's a legitimate style."

"Well, there's nothing legitimate about your two-faced teaching technique! I call it amazingly shabby behavior from a man that the *school* board considers morally fit to teach *children*."

Back to morals again. He almost slammed down the receiver, but not quite. Ridiculous or not, this woman was mad enough to call up Madigan and start making hysterical waves. "Listen, I don't think I've committed any crime, but before you get carried away, I'd like a chance to defend myself. Shall we meet and arbitrate this thing?" She could sizzle for hours, but the threat of a face-to-face encounter should cool her down. Anyone could be rude over the telephone. Insults in person took more nerve.

"No!" she said quickly, and he relaxed. Then she spoke again, less confidently. "Well, yes, maybe we should. When?"

Oh, hell. "Tomorrow at school? I'm free between—"

41

"No, I work until five. Could you— are you too busy today?"

He didn't want to meet her now or ever. In a few days she might cool down and forget about it. On the other hand, she might build up a head of steam that would blow the roof right off. "All right. Where and when?"

The first practical problem of melodrama met him at Sutherland's Café door, riding on a blast of steam heat and fried chicken grease. He didn't know who he was looking for. Luckily the place offered him little margin for error—few customers in midafternoon and only two unescorted women in sight. One of them looked rather old to be Mike's mother. The other was younger but hardly tough enough to have delivered that blistering tirade.

He took a breath and approached the younger one. She looked up expectantly. Oh, God, he'd forgotten her name and it wasn't Riley. Something with an A. "Mrs.—uh—Ashland?"

"Ashton, yes."

Well, close enough. "I'm Paul Kessler."

"Yes, I know. Please—sit down?"

Getting into the left side of the booth was awkward, his knee cramped suddenly straight and refusing to bend. She didn't seem to notice but waited in polite silence while he fumbled his way out of his hat and overcoat. "Been here long?"

"No."

Silence. He reached for his cigarettes. "Smoke?"

"Thank you." She didn't wait to accept his light.

"Want some coffee? If we're going to use their booth, I guess we should order."

"All right."

He flagged the waitress. "Anything else—a piece of pie or something?"

"Just coffee."

"Knowing restaurant pie, you're probably right."

"No, it's really not bad. We eat here sometimes."

Silence again. For a person who talked so volubly on the telephone, she was remarkably quiet now. Quiet, polite, almost shy, not at all what he had pictured. He had half expected Mike's reddish hair; she certainly had a red-haired temper. But she was plain brunette, brown-eyed, hardly resembling Mike at all except for being thin, sharp-boned, possibly tall—and, come to think of it, as confusingly double-natured as her son, sometimes quiet, sometimes explosive. Her voice was controlled now, but she didn't want to meet Paul's eyes, and her hands betrayed nervousness. She fiddled with her cup and spoon, spilled a drop of coffee and scrubbed it away with a paper napkin. Her nail polish was as bright as her lipstick, but her nails were trimmed short. He wondered idly if she played the piano. Or the typewriter? Yes, of course; Mike said she was a secretary. "Bomber-plant trash?" Hardly. In her dark tailored suit and white blouse she looked more teacherish than Paul himself did today; he had only thrown a sport coat over his old sweater and slacks.

Well, Mrs. Ashton was pleasant enough company now, but he didn't want to waste the whole afternoon with her. "About those lessons—"

"Yes," she said quickly. "We have to settle that."

"As far as I'm concerned, it's settled. If you don't want Mike to study with me, then he won't. No more lessons. We'll forget the whole thing. There's no need for hard feelings."

She shook her head impatiently. "You don't understand. The damage is already done. Oh, I know you think I'm some kind of old-fashioned nut who doesn't believe in swing music. Mike told you that, didn't he? So you thought that covering up with a layer of classical do-re-mi was a good joke, a harmless way to keep us both happy. But it's not harmless. Swing lessons for Mike are like—like feeding ice cream and cake and Coca-Cola to a child who is already suffering from a bad infection. They'll only make him sicker." Her tone picked up throbbing vibrato with each new line.

"Listen, I'm sorry, but you're wrong. Mike never mentioned your tastes. I didn't know he was laying down the classical camouflage and I still don't know why he did, but if you want the money back—"

"No, no, of course not." She gave him a small rueful smile. "This is terrible. You must think I'm crazy, yelling at you on the phone that way. But I didn't know what sort of person you were; I pictured—"

"What?" he asked curiously. "If you doubted my qualifications as a trumpet teacher, you could have checked at Bryan. I've been there six years."

43

"Yes, I did. Your references there were fine. That's why I never gave it another thought until I found that music in Mike's room today. He admitted it was yours. He said you worked with a dance band in town, Jack somebody, and that did it, I just— I just—"

"Yes, you sure did." He rubbed his ear reflectively, remembering the force of the blast. "Well, never mind that. It's too bad about the lessons, because Mike is an awfully good student, he picks things up fast. That's his big trouble, of course. He learns so fast by ear that he hates to sight-read. But he's got to, if he ever means to play for a living. He—"

She almost dropped her coffee cup. "Play for a living! But he can't!"

"Sure he can. With his talent he'll have no trouble finding a job when he leaves school. Being a sideman is nice clean white-collar work, good money. The hours are pretty wild, but you can travel, see the country. It's not a bad life if—"

"Don't you tell me about musicians!" she exploded, her eyes suddenly blazing dark in a pale face. "I can tell *you* a thing or two about the hours, *and* the travel, *and* the nice clean life they lead— *and* where the money goes. I was *married* to a goddamned piano player for six years! They're crumbs, all of them, filthy no-good rotten crumbs!"

Paul looked at her for one stunned moment. Then he said, "Excuse me, Mrs. Ashton," and reached for his hat. Obviously there was nothing else to be said, and nothing to do but walk away. He didn't know which startled him more, her wrathful explosion of hatred for musicians, or the realization that Jerry Riley, the piano man, actually did exist. He was not a figment of Mike's wild romancing, he was real. And the red convertible and the rest of the teen-aged moonshine, also true? But it couldn't be.

"Don't go," Katheryn Ashton said quietly. Her hands trembled, but her voice was controlled again. "Please. I—I'm the one to apologize. After I dragged you away from your home on a Sunday afternoon to discuss my son's problems, I could at least be civil. But it goes much deeper than a question of trumpet lessons, you see, and some of it is very personal. I don't quite know how to—"

"Never mind. If it's about Jerry Riley and the USO, I already heard it."

"You knew about Jerry, and still went ahead with—" She

looked startled and, for a moment, hurt. "Oh, well, of course Mike would make it sound marvelous. You can't trust his version."

"I didn't, it was too fantastic. Frankly, I thought he was spinning the whole yarn. Did he really travel with them?"

She took a sip of coffee, almost a gulp, as though searching for Dutch courage. "Yes. Yes, he did."

"But not as second trumpet with the band. I mean, he couldn't have—"

Her sigh was almost a sob. "He might have. I really don't know what he did, except to live like the King of Swing and learn a hundred bad habits. What I do know is that I worked hard to give my son a decent upbringing in spite of his father, and I did a good job of it. Mike finished ninth grade last June a fine decent normal boy. When I had to leave him for a little while, I left him with respectable people in a perfectly safe place where nothing could have hurt him if he had just stayed there. But no. Jerry Riley swaggered onto the scene with a sudden hot impulse to play Long-lost Father. No sooner were Donald and I safe aboard ship than he kidnapped Mike just like the handsome stranger with a bag of candy. 'Hop into my big red car, sonny, let's go adventuring. Mama's on her way to South America, and what she doesn't know won't hurt her.' And Mike said, 'Gee whiz, sure, let's go!' and away they zoomed into the sunset."

South America? Now who was romancing him? The cosmopolitan Rileys were far out of his class. Even in his college summers he'd never traveled east of St. Louis or west of Denver.

"When Mike wrote no letters, it worried me, of course; we'd never been separated before. But Donald said oh, you know kids, having such fun at the lake that he forgets to write. If anything were wrong, the Johnsons would contact us. Mistake number two. They didn't even peep. When I came home in September, they casually said, 'Oh, but Mike's father took him last June, didn't you know?' Can you feature that? Those decent respectable business people let my child go and didn't say boo, didn't even bother to mention it. Oh, they were *sorry*, of course. And how do you track down a shiftless, footloose swing musician with three months' head start? How would you do it?"

Paul considered. "The union, I guess. Local 802 or whatever. If he was working they'd have some record."

"Oh. Yes, I'd forgotten that. But I couldn't think straight, I was

45

too upset. My boy was gone, lost, dropped right out of sight, not a clue where to begin looking for him. Can you imagine how I felt? Of course you couldn't."

Oh, lady, don't say that. Paul felt the knife twist in him. I wouldn't know how it feels to lose someone I loved. I wouldn't have any idea. At least you could look for him. "But Mike's home now."

"Oh, yes, he's home," she said bitterly. "When Jerry finished thoroughly ruining Mike's life, he got bored with the game and just stuck him on a train for Chicago. It broke my heart when I saw him. Three inches taller but thin as a rail, grease on his hair, shadows under his eyes, his face all broken out from the awful junk he'd been eating. He was in a terrible state, you can't imagine. Swaggering like King Show Biz one minute and nearly crying the next. Pacing around the apartment with the radio full blast, drumming his fingers on the furniture. Lighting up cigarettes and blowing smoke in my face and saying 'jeez' every other breath to prove what a big tough man he was. Fifteen, barely fifteen years old! It was just pitiful, pitiful what they did to him. An innocent young boy perverted by a bunch of rotten crumbs, gypsying around the country, no school, no supervision, just bright lights and loud music and dirty jokes and chorus girls! The poor kid was too dazzled by the glamor to see the rottenness underneath. I couldn't calm him down or even talk to him; he just wouldn't listen to me at all."

"What about your husband, couldn't he help?"

"My hus— *Jerry?* How could he—"

"No, I mean Mr. Ashton."

She looked confused, then embarrassed. "Oh. You thought— Well, of course you did, it was a natural mistake. No, I'm not remarried. Ashton was my maiden name. I took it back years ago, after the divorce. In Chicago Mike was always Michael Ashton. But he registered here as Mike Riley, and I couldn't stop him. It is his legal name, I guess."

Paul nodded, still confused. What happened to Donald, whoever he was? Sunk with the ship off South America? Oh, well, forget it. None of this soapy tale was his business, though they all seemed determined to drag him headfirst into it. But if there was no Mr. Ashton, no stepfather to lay down the law and keep Mike in line, then Mrs. Ashton had her work cut out and no mistake. If

46

ever a kid needed a firm hand on the seat of his breeches, Mike Riley was the boy. No wonder his mother was riding the edge of a nervous breakdown, blowing her top at strangers one minute and begging for sympathy the next.

"He didn't want to go back to school. He talked nonsense about joining another band in Chicago. I said nobody would hire a boy, but he insisted he had experience now. *Experience!*" She shuddered. "I can imagine what sort of experience— But Chicago is so big, so many dance halls and bars and theaters, so many temptations to keep him stirred up and restless. Or if Jerry took another impulse to cause more trouble, he knew where to find us. So I thought the best answer was to move clear away to somewhere smaller, someplace quiet and decent and a million miles removed from *anything* that smelled like show business."

Paul smiled. "Welcome to Connor City. How did you happen to find us?"

"Just luck. My Chicago firm supplied parts to the bomber plant. A man from my office came here last year to supervise the installation of some new machines. I thought it sounded nice, so—here we are. Moving was an awful hassle, of course, and Mike nearly blew apart at the idea. But now he's safe in a decent school, and I *hope* things will settle down soon."

"Yes, well, good luck." Paul reached for the check. What a stupid waste of a Sunday afternoon. Two cups of bad coffee and a bucketful of soapsuds tragedy. But he'd swallowed it all, every last bitter drop. She ought to be satisfied now to let him go in peace. "It's been nice talking to you, Mrs. Ashton," he lied politely. "Like you say, it'll work out. Mike's a smart kid. If he doesn't get kicked out of school, he should come through fine."

"Kicked out of school!" Her shocked voice rose half an octave. "Why? Is he in trouble at school *too?*"

Oh, Lord, why couldn't he keep his mouth shut? "Well, yes. Didn't anyone notify you?"

"Not a word. No, I take that back. Some man did phone me once at the plant and muttered something about a conference, but I couldn't get away. We're absolutely buried in paper work out there, you never saw such a mess. What did Mike do wrong?"

"Oh, brother, you name it. Smoking and cussing and talking back, late to class, breaking rules. Our Mr. Trimble was ready to pull the plug on him."

47

She pressed a hand to her forehead. "I just don't know what to do with that child. He's under a spell and I can't break it; he simply won't listen to me. Mama is a square; what does she know about show business? I do know, believe me, I know more than he thinks, but what can I do if he won't listen? He needs a man to pound some sense into his head. Could your Mr. Trimble?"

"Not a chance. Herb can't even communicate with his own generation."

"Then maybe *you* could—"

"No, thanks. The only lectures I deliver are on world history and everybody goes to sleep, including me."

"You teach history, as well as music? I didn't know that." She looked even more hopeful. "I don't mean you should lecture to Mike, of course. He wouldn't stand for that. But if you could just be his friend and show some interest? I think he admires you, and there's nobody else for him to admire, except Jerry and those other crumbs I want him to forget. Couldn't you, somehow?"

"How? Teacher's pet? There's no room for that in ROTC Band."

"No, no, of course not. But those private lessons. . . . I've been thinking. . . . Maybe you should go on, what do you think?"

Paul stared at her. "Go on teaching him to sight-read and ad-lib? After what you said about feeding candy to a sick child? You've got to be kidding!"

"Some other kind of lessons, then. The regular sort, you know, classical."

"No chance. Mike may have bought an Arban to fool you, but he wouldn't be caught dead studying it seriously. No, his lessons are over, finished, kaput. I didn't want to start them, but I'm awfully willing to stop."

"I was afraid you'd say that. After the way I acted, I don't blame you. I didn't understand then, and maybe you don't understand now."

"Sure I understand. You want me to wipe Mike's nose and mold his character and set him a good Christian example every Saturday morning for two bucks an hour, with some sight-reading and ad libs thrown in to cover up the smell of the garbage as you so cleverly put it. Well, I'm sorry, but I can't do that."

"Why not? You've done it for two weeks already, haven't you?"

The justice of the remark caught him short. Put that way, of course he had. But not intentionally, not with any sense of personal responsibility. She had no right to ask that. "Remember I play in dance bands myself on occasion. Are you sure I'd be a good influence?"

"If Bryan High respects you, that's good enough. You needn't preach or be phony. Teach him ad libs or whatever you think will amuse him now, but not for a career. Just for an interest, for a hobby in the world he has to live in."

"Your world, you mean. The square world."

"It's your world too, isn't it? The only world there is, really. Show business isn't a world, it's a—a dope addict's delusion, all distorted and crazy. Mike can't live there any more than you or I or any other sane person. Jerry isn't sane. No sane man could do the things he's done, believe me. But with Mike it's just a passing craze. He'll recover if we help him." There were tears in her eyes and her voice was trembling again. Her fingers twisted the remains of a mangled paper napkin. "I can't do it alone. Please don't make me beg you now to do something you were perfectly willing to do an hour ago."

Paul drew thoughtfully on his cigarette, the last of a crumpled pack. This whole business was crazy. He came to vindicate himself for daring to corrupt a child with swing music. Now his accuser begged him to continue the selfsame course. He was right, he was wrong, he was right again. He had won, apparently. But won what? The right to play substitute uncle to a mixed-up kid, to wipe his nose and see him through his troubled adolescence. Some victory. Now he had them both on his neck, both mother and son begging him to solve their fantastic family problems. Solve their problems? He couldn't even solve his own.

"You're sure you want me to give him more swing lessons?"

"We have to start somewhere. Can you think of any other answer?"

Yes, there's another answer. Get out. Grab your hat and get out fast before it's too late. Tell this woman to go to hell and take her wise guy son with her.

Paul sighed. "We can give it a try, but I don't guarantee anything. It may be a mistake." May be a mistake? You know it's a mistake. Anything you do that involves Mike Riley or his relatives is bound to be a mistake.

II

WHEN Jerry Riley turned up—unannounced and un-welcomed—at the Ashtons' Chicago apartment in June, his son didn't know him from Adam.

A salesman was Mike's first thought when he opened the door, but four o'clock on a Sunday afternoon was a funny hour for a salesman. He didn't ask for the lady of the house. He asked for Mrs. Ashton, specifically but doubtfully, as if he might be at the wrong place. Mike said, "Just a minute," and went to the kitchen where she was cleaning the cupboards. "Hey, Mom, a man wants to see you."

"What does he want?"

"Maybe he's an OPA agent snooping for hoarded sugar."

"He's welcome to whatever he finds." She made a face and jumped down off the chair. "We shouldn't have agreed to sublet, it's worse than moving altogether—" Then she saw the man at the door. She stopped cold and her face went white, literally, frozen under the sweat she'd raised scubbing cupboards. They stood there looking at each other in a silence stiff enough to slice but quivering a little like Jello. And still Mike didn't catch on. She said, "Well, what do *you* want?" in a much ruder voice than she ever used on salesmen.

"I want to come in, Kathy," the man said, straight and businesslike. "I want to shake hands with my son here. Hello, Mike. Long time no see."

51

ATHENS REGIONAL LIBRARY
ATHENS, GEORGIA

175759

And then Mike finally tumbled, and there he was, shaking hands with Jerry Riley for possibly the first time in his life. Quite possibly the first time because a little kid under five wouldn't do that, would he, to his father? Hug him or kiss him or something but not shake hands awkwardly, like strangers meeting on the street.

Mike felt pretty stupid not to have recognized him right off. But on the other hand, how? Mom kept no pictures on the mantel and didn't talk about her ex-husband any more than she could help. It was a weird feeling to stand face to face with him now, almost eye to eye, not two inches difference in their heights. He would have expected Jerry to be taller, more than five ten. Red hair was no surprise. Way out of the past Mike could vaguely remember a big redheaded man rassling him around for fun, tickling him, swinging him upside down in the air until he was scared and dizzy—"Attaboy, Mikey, take a walk on the ceiling!" And it figured, of course. The red in his own hair must come from somewhere, just like the slot in his chin. And suddenly Mike realized he had never thought about his father much. He hadn't presumed him dead; he hadn't presumed him anything. It was easier that way, and safer.

But here he was, thought of or not, and getting a very chilly welcome. Mike could feel the early June temperature dropping straight down to December. Jerry—well, yes, Jerry. What else should he call him? First-naming an adult was rude but "Mr. Riley" would be silly and "Dad" just stuck in his throat somehow; he couldn't get it out after all those years. He could say "sir," but he wouldn't.—Jerry sort of grinned as if he had been expecting such a reception. "Am I interrupting anything important?"

Mom shrugged without explaining. But it wasn't fair to let him think this mess was the normal state of things. "We were cleaning the kitchen, that's all," Mike said.

"Cozy way to spend a Sunday afternoon. She's got you working too, has she?"

"Yeah, well, somebody has to. There's a lot to do before—"

"Michael, would you—open that other window." Mom cut right across his explanation. "All the way. It seems stuffy in here."

Jerry grinned again. "Funny, I'd have called it cold myself." He settled more deeply into the armchair. "Real nice place you have. Looks like a pretty classy neighborhood, grass lawns and all. Must cost a bundle for rent. How you managing it? Did you kiss and make up with the old folks at home?"

"No," she said shortly. Old folks, Mike thought. What old folks? "We're getting along just fine, Michael and I. Alone."

"No kidding, this is real nice. Very—ah—genteel. I was afraid I'd find you stitching shirts in an attic and little Michael peddling papers on a windy corner."

"It's not your fault we aren't."

"Oh, hey now, let's keep it honest. Who refused alimony? I could have sent you money any time, easy. The bands I worked with lately paid more dough than I knew what to do with."

"What kind of bands?" Mike asked.

"All the kinds that use a piano. Swing, sweet, big, little, hot, corny and pistachio. You name it, kid, I've been there."

"Bill Rhodes?"

"No, I never happened to work for him. But a potful of others—Tommy Dorsey, Bradley, Stabile. . . ." Jerry ran through a dozen more names, some that Mike knew, others he didn't. The man had really been around. And he looked the part too, just like the swing bandmen in movies and magazine pictures—slick, longish haircut, padded shoulders, no cuffs on the pants, ventilated shoes and a splashy tie. Really sharp. Obviously he spent money on himself, and why not, if he had it? Mike thought, with a small pang of frustration, of all the chocolate malts and comic books he had wished for guiltily over the years, of all the hamburger dinners and mingy Christmases he had accepted as simple facts of life. They had never starved in any attics. Even in the toughest Depression years when Mom filed records for the Cook County relief office and hung on by her fingernails not to be drawing relief herself, they'd always gotten by somehow. But if Jerry *offered* to help and she *refused*—well, it made things a little different, didn't it?

Mike felt puzzled. To hear Mom talk about Jerry Riley, you'd swear he was one hundred percent rotten, the lowest scum of the earth. Clear back when Mike was a dumb little six-year-old kid new to Chicago, he had told people—almost bragged to them—that his father was a bad guy in jail. They immediately assumed the worst, and Mom nearly died of embarrassment before she straightened everybody out, including Mike. Getting

53

divorced was just getting unmarried, when a man and woman decided to live happily apart instead of unhappily together. Mike understood that. They were lots happier in Chicago than they had been in New York, even if she did have to work to earn their living. So then he knew his father was not a jailbird. But he still always pictured a real Brooklyn bum, a dese-and-dose character who lay around drunk as a skunk all day and pounded gin-mill pianos all night.

But here was Jerry himself in the flesh, obviously not a bum and obviously not drunk. Mike could spot a drunk on the street or a crowded bus; he knew the smell, the blurry look, the seedy old overcoat. Jerry was nothing like that. A man with expensive sporty clothes and a gold wristwatch and tie clip and even a heavy red-stoned ring on his finger—well, he wasn't hocking his belongings to finance his drinking habits, that's for sure. So Mom was wrong somehow. Mike didn't know how she could be wrong about something so important. She'd lived with the man for five or six years; she of all people should know. She certainly had no reason to lie about him. The only answer must be that Jerry was different now. He must have reformed during the last ten years, reformed and changed his ways. Maybe the shock of the divorce had sobered him up. You needn't be ashamed of a man who did that. You could be proud. "Whose band are you in now?"

"None at the moment. Presently I'm at liberty." Jerry flicked a streamlined Ronson lighter and it fired first snap. "Just hit town this morning. Chicago, I thought, now who do I know in Chicago? So I looked in the phone book and there was K. Ashton right up front. Aha, I said to myself, I bet that's my Kathy, so I grabbed a cab and come right on over."

Mom handed him a sour look along with the ashtray. "You'd have been surprised if your Kathy turned out to be Karl or Kenneth. With the phone in your hand you might have checked first."

Jerry's grin widened. "If I had, I lay you odds you'd be gone right now. Don't get all shook up, babe, I didn't come to start no fuss. This is strictly for auld lang syne, you know what I mean? Just one short cup of kindness yet."

Mike had never figured out what auld lang syne was supposed to be, but it always sounded friendly. No matter what Mom thought, playing piano for Tommy Dorsey was *fame*, man, *success*.

54

Swing musicians got their names in the papers, their pictures in magazines, movies, radio, jobs at swanky hotels and ballrooms and on the stages of big downtown theaters. Ask any kid in America who Bill Rhodes was; you'd find out. And if Jerry came back today wanting to patch things up with his long-lost family—boy!

But Mom didn't offer him any auld lang syne or anything else. From the look on her face she'd sooner patch things up with a skunk. After a minute she went and found herself another ash-tray, along with her own cigarettes and matches.

Jerry quirked an eyebrow. "Oh, sorry, I should have offered. I had no idea you indulged these days. My, the world's a changing place. Genteel womenfolk smoking the filthy weed and wearing pants and cleaning their own kitchens on Sunday yet. War is hell, it most certainly is. How about you, Mike, do you smoke now too?" He made a gesture of reaching for his pack again.

"Of course not," Mom said sharply, and Mike shook his head no. He'd tried once or twice, but she didn't know it; she didn't miss the few he'd swiped. Dumb habit anyway. They didn't even taste good.

"Yes, indeed, traditions are crumbling right and left." Jerry stretched back and spun a handsome smoke ring at the ceiling. "Broadway blacked out, can you imagine that? Horrible, it gives you the creeps. And gas rationing is going to kill business. When even the weather turned lousy, I couldn't take no more. Go west, young man, I said to myself. That's where the action is now."

"Not here," Mom said rather quickly. "You wouldn't like Chicago at all."

"Oh, I don't know." He launched another lazy ring. "No gas shortage here yet. Nor anywhere else really, from what I heard. Rubber, now, that's different, that's serious. I can foresee real acute personal problems if they go and ration our rubber goods, huh, Mike?"

"They already did ration tires," Mike said.

Jerry gave him the raised eyebrow and a grin that didn't mean tires. "I guess you're still more worried about losing your lollipops. What are you now, thirteen?"

"Fourteen. Fifteen next September." He caught the point now all right. But my gosh, what kind of crack to make with ladies present—in front of Mom, of all people! She hated dirty jokes with a passion. Like at the State-Lake stage show last year with Horace Heidt, the only live swing band Mike had ever seen in his life and it wasn't so great at that—when the comedian started telling some slightly blue jokes, Mom nearly got up and walked out. Mike looked over cautiously, but her face was noncommittal now. Maybe she missed the point too. He hoped she did. But still Jerry ought to know better. It seemed almost as though he'd done it intentionally to embarrass her, to rake up the past, to remind her that once upon a time they had— But they're divorced now, Mike thought angrily. They're almost strangers. He has no right to embarrass people with that kind of talk. That's a heck of a way to patch things up, dropping dirty jokes.

Mike tried to steer the conversation into safer channels, but every subject he launched kept running aground. School was good for about two sentences. Baseball covered a paragraph. Play much ball? Jerry asked him. Oh, some, not so much now. Who do you follow, Cubs or, uh, White Sox? Cubs, naturally; the Sox never win. Mike got in fast with the sixty-four-dollar question: "Who's going to take the Series this year?"

Jerry shrugged. "What Series? Way things look, they'll all be drafted." He fiddled with his cuff link for a while. "Well, what do you do with yourself besides school? Collect stamps or chase blondes or what?"

"Well, I play trumpet," Mike said cautiously. He had been itching to mention it, although he was scared to, being so absolutely amateur in the presence of a real professional. Jerry's face lighted right up at the news.

"Hey, how about that. Who with?"

"Uh, nobody, except just in the school band. I'm not so great at it yet."

"Let's see your horn."

When Mike went to get it, Jerry followed him. The bedroom was all messed up with junk he hadn't decided what to do with, pack away for the summer or throw out now. He'd been digging buried treasures out of his desk—tinfoil, golf balls, playing card collection, a Dick Tracy pin and a Willkie button and a Jack Armstrong whistle ring. The entire history of Michael Ashton's childhood lay spread out naked on the desk top for all the world to see and laugh at. He grabbed the most embarrassing item (a

1936 secret decoder badge of the Radio Little Orphan Annie club) and dropped an open comic book carelessly over the rest, wishing he had ditched it all yesterday.

Jerry didn't comment on the juvenile mess, but Mike caught the look on his face when he saw the trumpet. "How much did you give for that little gem, two bits and a Wheaties boxtop?"

"Twenty-seven dollars with the case and music stand. It was used, of course, not new. The cheapest gold one in the store was sixty-five. The man said silver trumpets play just as good, I mean as well, if you can't afford better."

"I bet Mama agreed with him in a hurry, didn't she? You were damn lucky to get *any* kind of horn out of her." Jerry clunked the valves dubiously a few times and handed it back. "So play something."

Mike swallowed and wet his lips and swallowed again. He knew better than to try any of the good Rhodes things; he could only mess up and look stupid. But "Blues in the Night" was low-range and slow with the same phrases repeated, not likely to trip him up. He played as far as he dared, up to the middle part, and quit without having blown any clinkers.

"Who's been teaching you?"

"I don't take lessons. Mostly I mess around by myself and learn from records and the radio."

"By ear? You can read, can't you?"

"Of course I can—" Mike began indignantly. "Oh, you mean read music. Well, sure, I can read the music we play at school, marches and waltzes and that kind of corn. But what I really like is Bill Rhodes. He's my inspiration. If I could play like him, boy, wouldn't that be the end of the world?"

Jerry was fiddling with an old plane model, spinning the propeller with the tip of his finger. "I thought that vibrato sounded familiar. So you think he's good?"

"Good! He's only the world's greatest trumpet player that ever lived, that's all! You take 'Flight of the Bumblebee.' He rips off three million notes a minute so fast it's one great big blur, so high, my gosh, clear off the top of the staff, and I don't think he breathes twice in the whole piece! He must have lungs like—like a hurricane. Or 'Carnival of Venice,' that's another great one. I've been trying for a year to learn it, but it's *impossible*."

57

"On that hi-yo Silverking horn of yours? You could bust a gut reaching for high C."

"You're not kidding. I'll learn it someday if I don't sprain all my fingers first, but that poor old record is getting pretty scratchy. It's the first in my collection. I bought it last summer right after I saw his movie, you know, that ice-skating thing? That's when I discovered him. You want to see my collection?" He took all seven records tenderly from the dresser drawer and passed them one by one for inspection.

"Rhodes," Jerry said. "Rhodes, Rhodes, Rhodes and Rhodes and Kay *Kyser?* How did he sneak in?"

"Oh, that. Mom gave it to me for Christmas. She thought I'd like it."

"You're strictly a one-band man, are you? Just Rhodes, nobody else?"

"Who else is there? I couldn't afford to buy more anyway; I'm broke all the time. Fifty cents apiece is a lot of dough. . . . Oh, hey, no, I wasn't hinting for— Well, thank you, thanks a lot!"

"So merry Christmas already," Jerry said. "Spend it in good health."

Mike put away the dollar and the records, and they returned to the living room. Mom looked eager to hand Jerry his hat, if he'd brought one, but he sat down unperturbed. This time he offered her a cigarette first. She refused it but took one of her own, which struck Mike funny because they both smoked the same brand. When she reached for a match, Jerry was right on the spot with his ever-ready Ronson, so she had to accept or start a forest fire. Jerry seemed to feel more at home now. He launched his own conversation, tales of life on the road with plenty of emphasis on "I says to TD and he says to me—" Mom looked skeptical, but Mike thought they sounded true and he read more band fan magazines than she did. If Jerry would just take a local job and stick around until Mom thawed out toward him, everything would be great.

Jerry talked while Mom went on looking skeptical, disapproving and bored. Mike began to feel hungry. He had done a lot of hard housecleaning on a very skimpy lunch. But Mom didn't make a move toward the kitchen. She was going to outlast Jerry if it took all night. Mike had just decided the heck with politeness, he would fix himself a cheese sandwich, when Jerry stubbed out his fifth or sixth butt and looked at his watch. "Hey, it's getting pretty late. How about we all go out for dinner? I'm in the mood for Chicago steak."

"Steak!" Mike said. "Sure, let's go. I'm so hungry I could eat a whole steak by myself!" It seemed to be the wrong thing to say. Mom glared and Jerry looked at him as if he had two heads.

"You mean to say you never did?"

Mike looked surprised in his turn. On the rare occasions when Mom cooked a steak, they divided it carefully between them. Eating a whole steak would be like eating a whole pie, pleasant but awfully greedy—and expensive. But in Jerry's world steaks apparently came one to a customer. "Well, uh, we don't go out to restaurants much." Still the wrong answer. Mom was really giving him the foot-in-mouth look now; he didn't know why.

"Well, go powder your nose," Jerry said. "You'll dine at the Blackstone tonight."

"Oh, no, we won't," Mom said quickly. "It's out of the question."

"Okay, where? What's the best place?"

"That's not what I— We can't go with—" She stumbled around, looking for a polite way to spit in his eye. Mike knew why now. If she wouldn't even accept a cigarette from Jerry, she certainly wouldn't accept an expensive hotel dinner. But *steak*—

"Aw, *Mom*—"

Jerry was giving the whole room a thoughtful look, sort of puzzled, as though something didn't add up right. "Your son is starving, Mrs. Ashton. Come on, live a little, let him eat steak. Once in his life won't poison him no matter who pays for it. He'll need strength to peddle his papers."

She sighed. "Oh, all right. But not the Blackstone. Not anyplace fancy."

"You can pick it yourself. Anything but One Lung Joe's chop suey palace. I've seen enough of them."

So Mike hustled into his suit, the 1938 Fraternity Prep model that the son of some lady in Mom's office outgrew before scarcely wearing—a pretty good fit now but no zoot suit. When Mom decided to unbend her pride and go, she went first class, dolled up in the new dress she had just bought for the trip. Jerry did a real double take when he saw it. His eyebrows slid clear up and he whistled. She got red and then mad, like for two cents she would cancel the whole party.

But Mike suspected that she enjoyed the dinner; she just wouldn't let on. And the steak was delicious! Kind of pink inside and so tender, not chewy at all, it practically melted in his mouth. All through the meal Mom looked worried, expecting him to lean his elbows on the table or make more stupid remarks to reveal his nonacquaintance with nice restaurants. She kicked him under the table when he ordered the chocolate sundae. Maybe he shouldn't have; it was thirty-five cents extra and his dinner already cost over a dollar. But what the heck. Like Jerry said, live a little. By the time he could afford to splurge like this again he would be too old to care.

When Jerry let the cab go and came upstairs with them, Mom looked fit to be tied. What was he trying to do, move in overnight to save hotel rent? Boy, would that be a scene. Maybe he was hanging around hoping to talk to her alone, but she obviously didn't want to talk to him. Mike wondered whether to give them privacy or stay and play chaperon. Funny situation to be caught in, chaperoning your own parents.

When the phone rang later, he answered, being nearest. "Mr. Hill for you, Mom." While she was talking, in a quiet and naturally businesslike way with her back turned, Jerry flagged Mike with an inquiring eyebrow. "Who's this Hill?"

"Mom's boss."

"On Sunday night? Business must be booming." He seemed to lose interest, but Mike knew he was eavesdropping. Suddenly his ears went up. "Passport? What does she need a passport for?"

"South America," Mike said.

"South A— Are you kidding? When?"

"Next week, right after school gets out."

"Well, I'll be damned. You've been sitting there three hours with your bags packed and nobody mentions it? That's what I call restraint. Or do you fashionable Ashtons take tropical cruises every summer?"

"Not me, I'm not going. Just Mom and Mr. Hill."

Jerry whistled up and down two octaves. "A business trip? Well, well. I thought something smelled funny. What kind of South American monkey business would this be?"

"Pan-American relations. Mr. Hill has business down there and he needed a secretary, so he's taking Mom."

"Is that all there is to it?"

"I don't know. Ask her."

"Ask her what?" Mom said as she hung up the phone.

"Ask her what's cooking south of the border," Jerry said before Mike could answer. "I hear that you're going to indulge in some fancy Pan-American relations with a gent named Hill."

Mom gasped, then turned practically red, white and blue. "If it's any of your business, which I doubt, yes, I am accompanying my employer to Venezuela." She began firing off statistics about shortages and priorities and synthetic rubber from Venezuelan petroleum while Jerry sat nodding and smiling agreeably—*uh*-huh, *of* course, *oh* sure, *ab*solutely essential, *I* see—until she ran out of steam and gave up, glaring at him.

"Nice work if you can get it," he said. "What happens to Mike meanwhile?"

"Don't worry, he's provided for. I certainly wouldn't go off for three months and leave him alone."

"So who's providing?"

"I've got a summer job at Lake Winnewashta," Mike said proudly. "Mr. Hill fixed it up."

"Hill again? That man is really on the ball. Where in hell is Lake Wishywashy?"

"In Wisconsin. The Johnsons' resort hotel has boats and diving boards and horses, real neat. I get to live there free all summer and wash dishes."

"Really? All this and pearl diving too? How lucky can you get?"

Mike laughed at Jerry's fake enthusiasm. "Well, they offered me the horse barn, but I picked dishes."

"It's just a small quiet family-type resort," Mom said before Jerry could make another crack. "The Hills used to vacation there. But his wife has passed on and the children are grown and married, so he hasn't stayed there recently."

"Grown and married," Jerry repeated thoughtfully. "How old is this gent?"

"Oh, about fifty. Middle fifties. He's been with Apex since forever; they couldn't do business without him. A very nice man to work for."

"Well preserved for his age, I hope? Good strong heart? Wears his own hair and teeth?"

Mom gave him another cold look. "To the best of my very limited knowledge, yes. I said fifty, not eighty."

"That's good. It could be real unnerving to wake up and find his teeth smiling at you from the bedside glass."

Mike laughed; to his mind it suggested a Halloween skeleton. Then he caught the rest of the implication and stopped laughing. It was his *mother* being smiled at, and what would she be doing in— Another dirty crack, even worse than the rubber shortage. Jerry could brag about his own private life if he liked, but he had no business suggesting that anybody else did it. Least of all Mom! She would never in a million years— Somebody should throw this guy out. He wished he was big enough to do it himself, just grab Jerry by the collar of his sharp sport coat and give him a swift kick in the rear of his cuffless pants.

As it turned out, he didn't need to. Mom stood up suddenly. "Jerry, I think you'd better—"

"Mind my own business and let you mind yours? Certainly, babe, if that's how you want it. It's been a real pleasure talking to you. You have set my mind at ease on several points. Now I needn't worry about anybody starving in attics, do I? I see you're taking care of yourself just fine. The good righteous young widow always wins out, doesn't she, after she meets the generous old benefactor who pays off the mortgage. You appear to have located yours. So I won't impose my presence on you no further."

He stood up and adjusted his shirt cuffs and flicked an ash off his trouser leg. Then he gave each of them a pleasant parting smile. He offered Mike his hand again. After a moment of hesitation Mike took it, not knowing what else to do. Jerry looked at Mom and made a faint gesture of extending his hand to her, just enough to make sure she refused it. "Well, so long," he said. "Be seeing you around." And left, whistling down the hall. Mike recognized the tune, of course, popularized just last year by Swing-and-sway-with-Sammy-Kaye. "Daddy . . . you wanna get the best for me."

Mom slammed the door and threw the double lock as though she expected to withstand a Nazi invasion single-handed. She had a funny look on her face. Mike couldn't tell if she was more mad or embarrassed or sorry or disgusted. "Auld lang syne!" she said under her breath. " 'See you around.' Not if I see you first!"

Then she changed back into working clothes and started scrubbing the kitchen again, banging things around and slamming every cupboard door she met. Mike decided that *auld lang syne* was French for stirring up s-h-i-t. Jerry sure knew how to do it. Mom was right after all. Under the smooth expensive front he could be a real nasty character.

It didn't take Mike one week to get his stomach full of Lake Winnewashta. A muscular lifeguard hero named Hackett nudged him off the dock on the second day, fully clothed of course, and managed to half drown him in the pretense of rescue. The lake was ice cold and the rowboats leaked and horseback riding was a literal pain in the rear. Another jerky college boy spent his kitchen time coaxing waitresses to go joyriding in the hotel pickup truck while Mike rassled with all the greasy pots in the state of Wisconsin. He felt like a buck private on perpetual KP without even twenty-one dollars a month or a weekend pass to town. After Hackett drowned him twice more and the other clown buried his wristwatch in the garbage can, Mike was ready to start hitchhiking to Venezuela. September seemed a million years off.

But then who should drop into the scene like Superman out of the sky? Jerry Riley in person, big as life behind the wheel of the longest, sharpest, reddest convertible that Buick ever built! Mike thought he must be dreaming. "What are you doing way up here?"

"Oh, just a small detour on my route west. Chicago's not for me. They say California is the new happy hunting ground, land of sunshine and starlets busting out of their bathing suits. I can't think of a likelier place to spend my reclining years."

Yup, it was Jerry all right. But Mike was so glad to see a familiar face that he could overlook anything. "Boy, that's some neat car. Did you just get it?"

"Couple days ago. I met a guy who happened to need quick cash in the worst way, and I felt a sudden wicked impulse to own a red convertible, so. . . . Jump in, sonny, see how she rides. The ice-cream sodas are on me today."

She rode like a dream around the lakeshore to town, and ice cream was cool on Mike's slightly choked-up throat. He didn't mean to act like a homesick baby, but when Jerry said "Well, how

63

do you like the pearl-diving business?" Mike couldn't hold back. He spilled the whole sad story, grease and garbage and drownings and all. The more Jerry heard, the less he liked it. "Sounds like a concentration camp. Your mother sure picked a great place to provide for you."

"It's not her fault. She never even saw it."

"Old Grandpa Hill then, the big executive fixer-upper, he should know. Personally I don't think I'd care to do business with that man. He was in one hell of a big sweat to ditch you someplace and catch the boat to dreamland. Serve him right if he drops dead in the middle of dictating an urgent me-mo."

"Yeah, well, he probably didn't realize Johnsons' had turned into a dump. It's not the place so much; it's those two big clowns picking on me all the time, swiping my watch and all that stuff."

"Listen, sonny boy, you don't have to take that shit. Tell 'em to shove it—you're going to California."

"Calif— Hey, do you *mean* it?"

Jerry looked unsure for a minute, then smiled. "Sure, why not? I'm driving and I can use the company. You want to hit the road with me?"

"Do I! Wow, I'll say! Let's get going, I'm ready right now." Mike couldn't believe his luck. He would have gone anywhere with anybody to escape from this crummy scene. But to *California* in a *convertible* with a *swing musician?*

He packed his bag in five minutes flat, told the Johnsons good-bye forever and had the ultimate joy of thumbing his nose at Hackett, who caught a slack-jawed mouthful of dust when the Buick roared out of the parking lot.

"Westward ho!" Mike said broadly. "Which way is westward?"

"You're the navigator. Aim us right or we'll wind up in Hoboken. Where's our first stop?"

Mike studied the U.S. map. Three hundred miles at sixty per, D divided by R equals— "Five hours. We'll make Des Moines in time for dinner."

Sixty was pretty hair-raising speed over paved but narrow roads with steep hills and blind curves and railroad tracks, old Ford trucks full of pigs to market, dogs running out to bark as they passed, chickens that crossed the road and a few that didn't make it. They bombed over a hill and found Farmer Jones' boy chugging his tractor dead ahead. Mike yelled, "Hey!" Jerry said,

"Jesus!" and slammed his brakes and then let them off and cut around fast, tires screaming. When Mike opened his eyes and looked back, the farm kid gave him a nonchalant wave.

Crossing the Mississippi at Dubuque, Mike thought of Huck Finn. No smooth upholstery on a raft, no radio, no steak dinner ahead with Hollywood at the end of the line. Tough luck, Huck. You never had it so good. But shortly after four o'clock he saw a mileage sign—DES MOINES 180 MILES. "What the heck? Something's crazy."

"Dinner in Des Moines, huh? Boy, your arithmetic stinks."

Mike couldn't believe it. Better than three hours to come a hundred miles? Well, they did waste half an hour getting gas and Cokes and maps and sunglasses, and all those fifteen mph Main Street towns must have slowed them down. "Don't sweat over it," Jerry said when he tried anxiously to explain. "Same difference wherever we stop. Any place with a bed and a bar will do."

"But it's two *thousand* miles to Los Angeles. At this rate it'll take weeks!"

"So what? Relax and enjoy the scenery. On a train or a bus it isn't real. What you see through the glass is just painted backdrop they unroll before you come along and take down after you pass. Mountains, rivers, trees, all that jazz, but what good is it? You don't touch or smell it; you just shoot by. This time I want to *feel* it. That's why I got me an open car, to be right outside with the world."

After steaks in Cedar Rapids they wandered around town and had just decided to see a movie when Jerry changed his mind. "Here, take the room key. I'll see you later." Mike watched the show alone, testing his pocket every few minutes to make sure the key was still there. Just a mushy love story; Jerry was smart to pass it up.

He felt funny letting himself into an empty hotel room in a strange town. The big overhead fan hummed as it ran, and the sheets rubbed his sunburn when he lay on his back. Still it was a million times better than croaking frogs and old Hero Hackett stuffing horse apples into his lumpy cot for laughs. Jerry saved his life, coming along when he did. Mom wouldn't like the idea of them traveling together, but she didn't understand the situation at all. Steaks, movies, hotels, the open road at sixty per with the wind in your hair, the radio playing swing music, Jerry telling

65

fantastic stories—what a vacation! Mom was having hers in Venezuela. Why shouldn't he enjoy one too?

Towns were fewer and highways flatter and faster as they crossed South Dakota, but it still took two full days. A fleet of bombers couldn't raise Jerry out of bed before 10 A.M. He did drive later into the evenings, though, saying that they might as well stir up their own breeze as sit in one-horse towns and feed the local mosquitoes. They spent a day sight-seeing in the Black Hills, gawked at the Presidential profiles on Mount Rushmore, picked up genuine souvenir Indian moccasins.

Mike's education took various, sometimes unexpected forms. West of the Black Hills they stopped for a long lunch. While Jerry pursued his own business elsewhere, Mike practiced pinball in the air-conditioned café. He became quite expert at racking up free games without lighting the Tilt sign, and nobody said, "Don't waste your money, Michael." Jerry handed out money as if he owned the mint. What Mom didn't know wouldn't hurt her for a while longer. No use writing on the road; she couldn't answer. In California he would tell her how great things were.

Outside the café the sun felt twice as hot. The car upholstery sizzled as Mike slid across it. Jerry took the winding mountain road a little too casually, squealing the tires on all the curves. When Mike said, "Hey, take it easy on the rubber," Jerry just laughed. "This car can do anything." Maybe the car can, Mike thought, but what about the nut that holds the wheel? They were stuck behind two slow cattle trucks on an upgrade until Jerry said, "Oh, bullshit," and cut around to pass. First time okay, all clear, so he rode his luck and tried it again. A car came at them over the crest and they just squeaked through.

"Damn roadhog farmers think they own the whole friggin highway," Jerry said. He was sweating, but he didn't seem very concerned about their near miss.

Oh, good night, Mike thought suddenly, he's drunk, really loaded. He must have been drinking all the time I was playing pinball. Drunk driving is no joke, man. People get killed that way. He's drunk and doesn't even know it, doesn't even care.

"Hey, how about letting me drive for a while?" The words came out before he thought; he couldn't take them back. To his

66

horror Jerry pulled over and stopped. Oh, man, now I did it. Now he's mad.

"Okay, take her, she's all yours. Any fool can make out with a no-clutch hyderamic. You treat her just like a dame, see. Shove in your key and give her the gas and she's off and running like a ten-dollar lay. Gimme your sunglasses, I seem to have mislaid mine somewhere, thank you." He pushed over to the passenger side, laid his head back and slumped down. "Wake me up in Casser."

Mike gulped. He couldn't drive, he didn't know *how*, he was too *young*. But he'd offered and Jerry thought he could. Maybe he could. He'd been watching across three states now; it didn't look so hard. If farm kids could drive tractors, he could drive this. Maybe. Learnin' by doin', his scoutmaster used to say.

He got in under the wheel and wiped his hands on his pants a couple of times. Breathing deep and holding tight, he inched the Buick onto the pavement, right foot light on the gas, left foot ready to hit the brake. Two pedals, two feet, that was okay. What he needed was four eyes, one for the mirror and one for the speedometer and two for the road ahead. Amazingly enough the car obeyed his cautious commands. When he turned the wheel left, the Buick went left and then sharply right as he jerked it back from the center line. When he pressed the gas harder, it speeded up, but thirty-five was fast enough for a beginner. He was sweating hard in the high afternoon sun, gripping the wheel with slippery hands but scared to let loose for a second to wipe them. He sat so straight he was practically floating off the seat. He felt as if he were soloing in a B-17 bomber a mile long and half a mile wide. God help him if he met another car—or a truck!

He knew the smartest thing would be to pull over quietly and stop, just sit and wait until Jerry had a good nap and felt like driving again. Wasn't that what you did for drunks, let them sleep it off? But Jerry said call me in Casper and maybe that's what he expected Mike to do, drive the car to Casper dead or alive. If he found himself sitting under a dry cottonwood tree in the middle of nowhere at dinnertime, he'd be mad as hell. Mike hadn't seen Jerry mad yet, and he didn't want to. Jerry was a pretty impulsive guy. No telling what kind of temper he might blow when things went wrong.

All things considered, driving was the safest bet. He might be an unlicensed beginner, but at least he was sober and in his right mind. If he ran into trouble, he could always stop, which was more than Jerry looked qualified to do right now.

So Mike drove on. He navigated his first curve and his first hill. He met his first car without catastrophe, just gritted his teeth and steered straight ahead, resisting the temptation to shut his eyes as they passed without a single scraped fender. He made it through his first little town, in one side and out the other at a decorous law-abiding fifteen mph and sweating bullets. Safe out of town he heaved a big sigh and speeded up again. No mountains now. Going thirty-five on a straight, flat, practically empty highway was just like standing still. He could drive forever and never gain an inch on the horizon. Fifty was about right and sixty better yet if he ever expected to get there.

On to Casper. On to California. California, here I come, right back where I didn't start from. . . .

Home, home on the range, where the beer and the canteloupe laaaay. . . .

Oh, give me a home where the buffalo roam and I'll show you a house full of. . . .

. . . *Deep in the heart* of Texas!

He looked down and saw the speed needle swinging cheerily at sixty-five and the gas needle quivering on the E-for-Empty. Suddenly he knew that he had driven far enough. Too far. He let off the gas and coasted as far as he could, a long way down the empty road to an easy gentle stop, and switched off the motor. Disturbed by the sudden silence, Jerry roused up and looked around, took off the glasses and rubbed his eyes. "Where in the everlasting blue-eyed hell are we *at?*"

"I don't know," Mike said.

"Anything wrong?"

"Nothing except we're just about out of gas."

"You're kidding."

"Unh-unh," Mike said. Jerry put on the glasses again and stared into the wide-open spaces. Not a gas pump in sight. Not a farmhouse, not a windmill, not a tree.

"Well, that is one hell of a lovely note. Why didn't you wake me up?"

"Because you said Casper and we haven't got there yet." Mike hung onto the wheel with both hands and tried to keep from shaking. "I didn't notice the gas until just now. I've been *driving*."

"I didn't tell you to drive the tank dry, you moron. I gave you credit for some smarts."

"Listen, I couldn't—"

"Like shit you couldn't. You'll be taking a long walk, sonny boy."

"I'm sorry," Mike said desperately. "Honest, I'm sorry. Besides, the tank's not clear dry yet. We might make it to the next town."

Jerry poked around for a map. "Wyoming?" He unfolded it and slapped it around a few times and finally got it right side up. "Casper, yeah, here. Did we pass through Douglas yet?"

"I don't think so. No, it wasn't Douglas. Something like Luck."

Jerry squinted at the map and drew lines with his finger. "Lust. *Lust?* Hey, what a name. Do you think they— Oh, shit, no, it's Lusk. Thought we had something. You turned west there, right?"

"The road went straight through, I think."

"The road went straight through all right, but you were supposed to turn west. Wasn't there a sign?"

"Yes, there was a sign. It said, 'Fifteen miles per hour, Streets Patrolled.' All I wanted was to get through Lust without meeting any curious cops. I didn't see any other signs."

"How long ago was this?"

"I don't know. Half an hour, an hour, long time ago. *I* don't know." He opened the door and nearly fell on his face; his legs wouldn't hold him. After sitting stiff and tense for so long, he could hardly move. He stumbled to the side of the road and watered a deserving weed, really gave it a cloudburst after the long hard dry spell and widely distributed because his legs were still shaking. Jerry was doing his bit for irrigation a few paces to the left. The crops should flourish. Mike zipped his pants with an unsteady hand and went back to the right side of the car.

"What's the matter, are you heat-struck or something? You look green."

"No, I'm all right. Can you— I mean, would you like to drive now?"

"Oh, thanks, how generous. Fifty miles down the wrong road with an empty tank and then he says, 'Now it's *your* turn.' Thanks a lot, pal. I'll do you a favor sometime."

"I'm sorry," Mike said again, shakily.

Jerry gave him a grin and a punch on the arm. "Forget it. It could happen to anybody. You did okay for your first solo flight. If we make it to a station, there's no harm done. And if we don't, guess who gets to take a walk with the little red can?"

Mike blew out a sigh of relief. That kind of walk he wouldn't mind. Even five miles across the hot desert would be fair enough punishment for a dumb dope who missed the turn sign and forgot the gas gauge. As long as Jerry wasn't mad at him anymore, he could take the rest of it. Drunk or sober, Jerry was all he had and he was one heck of a long long way from home.

The motor coughed and died just as they limped into a junction with an old shack store and one blessed gas pump, a place so remote from civilization that it still sold Hershey bars. Mike felt like saying, "Hey, dontcha know there's a war on?" They knew, all right; there was a blue service flag in the window. His Hershey turned out to be strictly prewar, so old and gray that he threw it out for the antelopes.

Instead of Casper, they stayed in Cheyenne and ate tough steak. "The fat ones go to heaven in Chicago," Jerry said. "These stayed home on the range and died lean and hungry. You'd better broaden your taste, buddy. There's more good things in this world besides steak."

After his headfirst baptism into driving, Mike took regular turns at the wheel. All day single-handed driving was a real lively pain in the ass, Jerry said, but now they could each do a half-assed job. Mike gained confidence rapidly. Once he took a curve too fast and swerved onto the shoulder almost to the ditch. Jerry only said, "Watch it, ace, you're flying too low!" He hit a pedestrian jackrabbit which made him feel bad for a minute. A million rabbits populated Wyoming, living dangerously and dying young, their carcasses splattered all along the highway. Only a rabbit, but he didn't mean to hit it. It could have been a dog.

They stopped to swim at a shabby little amusement park in Utah. Afterward they sat and ate popcorn on a green slat bench beside the merry-go-round. Between customers the music wheezed on, bass drum thudding and the calliope organ mangling the melody with repeated false notes that made Jerry wince. "F-*sharp*, dammit! Don't you have an F-sharp on that lousy keyboard?" He took a pull at his bottle of pop. "Hey now, would you look at that. Mike, do you see that horse right there, the little pink filly with the blond mane? Spitting image of an acrobatic dancer I knew on the Orpheum circuit. Hi there, Clarice baby, how's tricks?"

Mike had seen only one stage show, but he had seen plenty of musical movies. It sounded crazy, but Jerry was right. The wooden horse did resemble a painted dolled-up girl—big eyes, pink skin, a phony grimacing smile, long yellow hair streaming in the wind, legs stretched in midair like a dancer doing leaps and kicks.

"Yes, that's old Clarice all right, coming up fast on the outside and pounding down the homestretch. Attababy, go, girl, go!"

"Did you say a dancer or a racehorse?"

Jerry gave him a grin. "Well, she could give a guy a real good run for the money. Nymphomaniac, they call that type dame. It's like being alcoholic for sex, see. They're crazy for it, absolutely cannot get enough. Clarice did this wild routine with two men throwing her around. She could take 'em on and wear 'em out two at a time, vertical or horizontal. Very versatile performer."

Mike could feel his neck getting red. Funny kind of conversation to go on between father and son. More like behind-the-garage talk with the gang back home, only those guys didn't know anything for certain; they just snickered vaguely about bushwhacking and screwdriving. Jerry knew it all, no doubt, if anybody cared to listen. *Two* men?

But he didn't learn the details of Clarice's peculiar acrobatics. Jerry switched onto merry-go-rounds. "Lots of lights and mirrors flashing, all red and gold to attract the crowd and music to pull them in. Give them a show, give them a ride, a little pleasure to pass the time. You don't *go* nowhere on a merry-go-round. Don't learn anything, don't gain any ground, no farther along at the end than at the beginning. That's life in show biz, just exactly like that, swinging around the old circuit. You get what I mean?"

"You mean playing in a band is like riding on a—"

"Hell, no, not riding on it. You *are* it. You're the lions and the tigers and painted ponies that the customers climb onto and dig their heels in. Dancers, comics, sidemen, all galloping along full blast chasing after. . . ."

Mike tried to help him out. "The brass ring?"

Jerry shook his head. "No. That's what the customer gets, the

71

loud brass ring. Us, we're chasing after—oh, hell, lots of things. Money, top billing, applause, kids wanting autographs. You run like mad after success, but you never catch up with the guy ahead or escape from the guy behind. Take a good close look there, Mike. Notice how beat-up those animals are, dirty, smudgy, paint chipping off? That wild-eyed look is weariness, man, plain old dizzy exhaustion from high kicks and high notes. The riders climb on and they ride you and slide off. The music keeps playing and the drum keeps beating. Play to a full house, play to an empty house. Just keep grinding it out to the end, when they turn off the pretty colored lights and cover up the machinery and everybody else goes home. Hell of a stupid life."

Mike knew he must be exaggerating. "If it was really so bad, you wouldn't go on doing it."

"What's the choice? You're stuck right there, saddle-sore, shafted with a frigging brass pole through your guts. No place else to go except up and down and roundy-roundy."

It took them altogether two weeks on the road to reach Los Angeles, land of the ultimate Golden West. Mike heaved a long happy sigh and settled down to stay forever. But they hadn't been in town two weeks more when Jerry went out one day to check the music situation again and came back humming bugle calls. "Pin a rose on me, Mama—I just signed up with Uncle Sam!"

Mike dropped his mystery book and fell off the bed. "You just *what?*"

"Enlisted for a twenty-week hitch with USO Camp Shows Ink to entertain our brave boys in uniform. That outfit doesn't fool around, man. They grab you today and ship you out tomorrow at dawn, clean laundry or no clean laundry."

"Ship you where? Overseas? Alaska?"

"No, not this unit. They'll just play bases in the Western states, nothing more exotic than San Diego and Camp Pendleton. You might as well start packing."

"Awww, heck." Mike kicked his paperback across the room. "What'd you go and do that for? We just got here. I don't want to go back yet." What a gyp. Things had started out so great, too. Jerry had bought him some sharp Hollywood threads—a zooty plaid sport coat, high-waisted pants, a couple of bold ties—and a really good trumpet, a gold Holton with a complete set of profes-

72

sional mutes, a hot hockshop bargain worth double the fifty bucks. They checked out the sunkist beauties on the beach and the band at the Palladium; Jerry promised to go again when Rhodes played there in August. But now the summer was ruined. What was worse, he didn't know where he could go back *to*. Not Johnsons' Wishywashy Resort, but where else? Mom wouldn't be home until September.

Jerry didn't seem concerned about Mike's future. "I was probably nuts to take it. It's a pretty cruddy-looking group, just some vaude acts and a chorus line, and they don't pay half what I could get in a band. But it's all for Uncle, strictly patriotic, and no hassle with the union. What are you pulling that long face for? Aren't you anxious to make time with fourteen beautiful girls fourteen? Some of them aren't hardly older than you—sixteen, seventeen, real live jailbait."

"Me? You mean *I* get to go along? You signed me up too?"

"Sure, why not? I didn't exactly sign you up, but they can always use a brack boy. Somebody has to hustle all that gear."

The USO certainly had gear, mountains of it. Eighty-seven trunks, a PA system, a set of footlights and eighty hand props— tomtoms, rubber balls, hurdles for the trained dog act—with only two paid men to wrestle it all from train to truck and from truck to stage and back again almost daily on the complex circuit of military camps up and down the Pacific coast. Mike was the unpaid brack boy, the go-fer, the supernumerary stowaway that everybody knew about but pretended to overlook. Twenty-five performers, nineteen of them young to middling-young females, were delighted to let him carry their luggage and run for their coffee, aspirins, newspapers. Mike fetched and carried willingly, anxious to earn his keep any way he could. He had to stay in good. He didn't even have a stowaway's security. One false move and they could dump him overboard at any station stop and let him sink or swim for Chicago.

He made his false move on the third day out. While the rest of the troupe was rehearsing cues for the evening show, Mike took a little walk across the Army base to get a better look at some fighter planes he had noticed from the bus window. Suddenly he was staring straight down the muzzle of a large .45 in the hand of a nervous guard. Mike smiled and said, "Velly solly please," which was apparently not the password of the day because the guard hauled him in. Then he got cussed out three separate times, first by a tough security officer, second by the troupe manager ("military secrets; we aren't supposed to see or hear *anything* inside *any* military installation") and last and most juicily by Jerry. "Listen, you moron, you're my kid and I'm responsible, see? No more messing around. You get me in trouble and I'll beat the living shit out of you, you understand that?"

Mike said, "Yes sir, I sure do."

After that he was scared to stick his nose outside the door of the base theater. He supervised each rehearsal and performance, paying close attention to the music. The troupe carried no band of its own, only Jerry on piano and Maestro Roy Edwards, who had to whip together a temporary pit band of Army musicians at each new camp along the route. Some of the former dance-band sidemen now in khaki could play anything in sight, but the amateurs had a rough time. One hundred and forty music cues to learn in one afternoon and play the same night! The first show was always ragged, full of clinkers and late entrances, but the uncritical GI audiences laughed at the comics, clapped for the dog act and raised the roof with whistles and cheers for the sexy singing sisters and the fourteen beautiful girls fourteen. On the second and third repeat shows the music smoothed out. Then the troupe moved on to start all over at another camp with another fresh new band. Maestro Edwards lived on Alka-Seltzer and yelled at everybody, at Mike and the soldier musicians and the chorus girls and Jerry. He kept begging the L.A. office to send him a couple of permanent lead men or at least a drummer. So far, no luck. Sorry, pal, there's a war on. Things are tough all over.

From constant exposure Mike could hum right along with every brass section cue, note for note. He could have played first trumpet any night they let him—or second or third at least, his high notes still being a little troublesome. Of course they wouldn't let him. He didn't dare suggest it. The only time he could touch the music was when he did librarian duty, arranging the folders on the stands before each show and picking them up afterward. If he tried to sneak a glance at the first or second trumpet score, somebody always started yelling, either Edwards or Jerry, whichever felt crabbier that day.

Youthfulness was his biggest handicap. Who wanted a four-teen-year-old sideman? He did what he could to mature more rapidly, growing his hair longer and combing the sides back with plenty of grease the way Jerry did. He lit up Camels at strategic moments and let them burn gracefully between two fingers à la Bill Rhodes in the magazine ads, with now and then a cautious mouthful and quick exhale, but never for cripes' sa .e *inhale* because it singed his lungs and made him cough and ruined the entire effect. Cigarettes cost him nothing after he switched to Jerry's brand. Jerry, a two-pack-a-day man, never missed a handful or even a whole pack as long as it didn't empty the carton.

But smooth haircuts and sharp clothes didn't convince the company of his manhood. No matter how bold his neckties or how well draped his slacks, they all knew Mike Riley was no threat to the morals of the chorus. Nor did he want to be. If he held a perfectly innocent conversation with one of the friendlier girls, just passing the time about bands or movies, Jerry and the senior wolf pack moved in afterward to give him the business. "How about it, Mike, you looking for a piece of that? Better get it there quick before she gives it all to the soldiers. But check with your old man first; he covered her territory thoroughly just the other night, didn't you, Jere?"

"With map and compass," Jerry drawled, "and damn near lost my alpenstock. Lay off that one, she's no good. Play with somebody your own size."

Mike just gave a nervous smile and eased off the scene. He didn't want to play that game yet. He didn't think he could and he wasn't about to make a fool of himself proving it. Faking around with cigarettes was one thing; faking around with girls was something else. When it came to the place that separated the men from the boys, Mike knew perfectly well which side of the line he stood.

He hustled the baggage and ran the errands, helped walk the trained poodles, delivered goofy messages from soldier boys to chorus girls and back again. Between times he played solitaire and read paperback mysteries. Through train windows and bus windows he saw a lot of painted scenery, mountains, redwoods, deserts, fog-bound Pacific coast. He sweated on Monday in Bakersfield and shivered on Tuesday in Monterey—in August, yet, real crazy weather. How did Californians tell if it was summer or winter? But hot or cold he knew that September

75

would follow August, and September meant Chicago, home, high school and the end of the long long road.

He held his breath well into September, daily expecting a horde of G-men and truant officers to come for him. Or at least a furious telegram or call from Mom. Suddenly he realized he had never even taken the time to write her. Maybe she didn't know where he was. With offhand carelessness he checked with Jerry one afternoon. "Heard anything from Mom yet?"

Jerry was sacked out with a copy of *Down Beat* and a hotel water glass half full of straight bourbon, the bureau-drawer bottle close at hand. "Not a word."

"She must be back by now, huh? I wonder if she enjoyed it?"

Jerry shrugged. "She never enjoyed it with me, but maybe old granddad's brand is easier to take, more genteel. Just so she got what she went for, that's all, the signed contract."

"For petroleum?"

"For marriage, sonny boy, marriage. The fur-lined guarantee. Underneath the spell of the old tropical moon plenty of gals wouldn't hold out for that. But knowing Kathy, I'd say she would keep her legs crossed and her eye firmly on the dotted line. She might not even let the poor guy in for a free sample before she had the ring on her finger." Jerry looked over at Mike and then laughed. "Oh, come on, don't look so stricken. Would you begrudge your poor mother some soft luxury after all those miserable years? Besides, think of the future. How else could she possibly send you to Harvard Law College?"

Mike gasped. "Me! *Harvard!* Are you crazy? I wouldn't ever go to— Listen, you've got it all wrong. She wouldn't marry anybody, not for any reason. She likes living alone and she hates men, and Mr. Hill, my gosh, he's old enough to be her father! How could she—"

"Exactly her type. Fatherly old gents don't expect a lot of high-powered sex action, see. Don't worry, she knows what she's doing this time. She has had ten lean years to figure all the angles. Security, yes, sir. Sex, heavens, no, keep away from that nasty stuff. All she ever wanted from me was to carve my soul out of my body and lock it up in a little square box bounded by breakfast, lunch, dinner and payday. But in bed she— where are you going?"

"Out," Mike said. A walk around the block, standing on the corner and counting cars, anything would be better than listening

76

to Jerry's filthy lies. Drunk or sober, he had no right to talk that way about Mom.

Jerry laid a hand on his arm and sat him down again. "Stick around, sonny, you may as well hear the truth of it. All these years she's been telling you what a rotten, selfish SOB your old man was, what a dirty deal I gave her, right? Right!"

Mike stared out the window. "No, she didn't talk about you much."

"I'll bet." Jerry poured himself another shot. "There's plenty she never mentioned. She never mentioned all the presents I brought home, did she? Nice stuff, beautiful expensive stuff that nobody appreciated. Anything nice I gave her she only bitched how much it cost, said I was wasting money, what did she need with fifty-dollar earrings, where did she ever go out? And you, same way. I brought you the nicest electric train set, and you took and knocked the cars right off the track."

"I did?" Mike said, startled. He couldn't remember any train and he strongly doubted if there ever was one.

"You sure as hell did. Your mother said it was too dangerous, you'd electrocute yourself, so she put it up. I finally gave it to some guy for his kids, I forget who. Real nice Lionel train, headlight and whistle and everything."

Mike wished that they had saved it until he was older, eight or ten. He'd have appreciated it then all right. "I'm sorry. I guess I was too little."

"Yeah, maybe. Remember the stuff I brought you from the nightclubs, you know, paper hats, horns, balloons, clackers? You had a ball with them."

Yes, that triggered something. A whole room full of balloons. . . . But was it a real memory or just a dream like the bear in the bedroom? His clear memories began with the train trip to Chicago when he was five. Before that was only fog with occasional meaningless glimpses—a shade flapping against an open window, all those balloons, a long dark flight of stairs going down—and the feeling of worse things hidden in the fog that he'd rather not find. *Bears.* A big shaggy bear jumping on the bed at night to bite and hug and eat them up, Mom first and then—"Did we—did we go to a zoo?"

"The Bronx Zoo? Oh, sure, we must have sometime. I took you on the ferryboat to Staten Island once, I bet you recall that."

Mike shook his head. "It's funny. When I see pictures of New York in books, like the Empire State Building, for instance, I try to remember it. But it's just pictures. I don't really remember."

"Man, *I* remember that boat ride. Cold windy day, you got mustard on your shirt and wet your pants and bawled and caught a cold after. Kathy gave me forty kinds of hell for taking you. Trying to be nice, that's all. Tried to be nice, but nobody ever appreciated it." He reached for the bottle again. "Like that goddamn 1929 Essex. I knew it'd be a headache, but she had to have a car, had to take drives in the country, had to show little Michael the moo-cows."

"What's so important about cows?"

"Exactly what I said. She swore you'd grow up warped otherwise, so we bought the damn thing. Trouble, nothing but trouble. Stinking traffic jams even worse than nowadays, dusty roads, flat tires every other mile. Then I loaned it to a pal of mine; he met a telephone pole coming slap at him sixty miles an hour on the road to Atlantic City and pow!—that finished the Essex. I never owned a car again till the Buick. . . . But I tried, Mike, so help me I tried. Not my fault that musicians keep lousy hours, work nights, sleep days, if anybody can sleep with a vacuum cleaner and a baby bawling. She knew it when she married me, she knew it, but she had this crazy notion she could change things. She wanted a little vine-covered cottage in Hoboken, grass, picket fence, Ford flivver, square husband working eight to five, *days*, not nights. She thought she could nag me into it. Almost did, too. I tried the pit orchestra of the Paramount to finance her classy genteel apartment on the west side of the park so you could play on nice clean grass. Hell of a grind that was, four or five shows a day, the same crappy classical music thirty times over every week. Oh, sure, it was good money and it was 'respectable' and finished by midnight, she liked that. Only I generally went uptown afterward for some decent jazz to wash out the Paramount taste. She said I went to Harlem to get drunk and fool with the colored gals. I tried to tell her what a jam session was, but she didn't understand, she didn't care. So I thought what the hell, I'll get blamed anyway, why not enjoy it first?"

So now he admitted it. Mike knew it must have been that way, no matter how Jerry tried to wriggle out or shift the blame. Obviously it was his fault. Just look at both of them, how they

78

lived, the kind of people they were. Anybody could see what caused the divorce. What Mike couldn't see was, what caused the marriage? How could two such totally incompatible people get together in the first place?

"I wasn't the man for her," Jerry said, almost as if he was reading Mike's thoughts. "Her kind grow in the cornfields of Illin*oise* and populate all the little hick towns west of Jersey. She could have married a hometown joe and lived happily ever after. But no, she had to rush off to seek her fortune in New York and fall for a born night-owl musician—and then waste five good years trying to turn me into her idea of the perfect square husband. I should of tipped my hat and rode away when I had the chance. Plenty of guys would, I'll tell you that. But I loved her and I married her, not that half-ass companionate way but legal as all hell, right there in City Hall on the coldest damn day of the year. Nobody can say that Jerry Riley didn't stand up to his responsibilities. I did my share. I paid the rent and I bought your shoes, buddy boy, and I got damn little back in return but excuses. Not now, not now, it's too early, it's too late, I'm tired, what will the neighbors think, and sh, don't wake the baby. Seventy-three ways to say stick it elsewhere, buster, I'm not interested. So I did and what happens? She raises the roof because I'm unfaithful. Shit, you can't win. Well, I just hope to God she gets what she wants *this* time. A sweet old sugar daddy, mink-lined security, and sonny's college education prepaid—for all that she shouldn't begrudge spreading her legs for ten minutes once a month maybe."

Mike sat with his jaw clenched and his ears closed. Lies, lies, dirty lies from a slob whose mind always lived in the gutter. Mom was right about him all along. She said Jerry was a drunken bum and she was absolutely one hundred percent correct. If he'd been smart enough to believe her, he wouldn't be here now, stuck two thousand miles away from Chicago with no ticket home. They'd say a guy was crazy to choose home and high school against show business. Well, sure, if he were really part of the show, playing trumpet in the band, that would be different. But nobody needed him that much, just a volunteer go-fer doing errands to keep busy and out of trouble. Jerry was sick of him and he was sick of Jerry. . . . But if Mom married Mr. Hill and didn't want him back there either— Holy cow, what a mess!

79

*　　*　　*

Late in September the home office finally sent three experienced musicians to join Jerry as the permanent core of the pit orchestra—one trumpet, one sax, one drummer. What a difference! Edwards quit screaming and tearing his hair. Jerry shrugged off the weight of the show and devoted more time to the serious pursuit of chorus girls. Naturally Mike started right in to study the new trumpet man, George Miner, a good solid brass man who had done time in West Coast bands. George showed Mike one useful gimmick, how to hit high notes à la Rhodes without blowing his brains out. But he didn't seem to appreciate Mike hanging around or asking eager questions. "Whatcha doing, kid, trying to steal the job I just got? Get lost, you're standing in my light."

The sax man Cohn was just a sax man; Mike ignored saxes. But the man at the drums was Russ Kelbert, skin-beater extraordinaire. Russ made those soldier-boy drummers look like the Spirit of '76. His layout covered half the pit: not three or four but *six* dazzling pearl-finished drums—bass and snare, floor toms and ride toms—five gold cymbals, plus a handful of special effects—and Russ himself on his throne in the middle, going to town as if he had eight arms. He livened up the show music with plenty of hot licks, pushing the beat faster, making it swing. He added subtle sound effects to the other acts, footstep echoes, pratfall thuds, a dramatic roll and crash to accent a dancer's kick or the poodle's clever flip. Mike thought it was a shame to bury such splendor in the pit. Russ ought to be right up onstage, front and center for all to see and admire.

He might be just nineteen, but he had really been around, in and out of half a dozen bands, in and out of the Navy too. He showed Mike convincing proof: the tattooed anchor on his arm ("Old Popeye Kelbert, they called me in them days") and a snapshot of himself and a buddy in boot camp whites, leaning cockily on opposite sides of a San Diego lamppost. "Dig that Navy issue haircut—two inches long, but it waved like the good old Pacific Ocean." Russ carried no proof of his big-band career, but the names he mentioned sent Mike straight through the bus roof. "Bill Rhodes! You actually know Bill Rhodes!"

"Sure I know him. I worked for him once."

"Hey, maybe you're on some of my records."

80

"No, I never cut any with him. I wasn't there long, only a couple of weeks."

Mike was too tactful to ask why. Great as Russ was, the Rhodes band was greater. "How is he to work for?"

"Bill? Oh, he's swell. But I'll tell you who's a real SOB, though, and you'd never guess it from looking at him. . . ." Russ knew the inside dope on all the famous names, the details of stories Mike had seen hinted in movie magazines. If Russ knew them, they must be true. Mike couldn't believe his own incredible fortune. A friend in the troupe at last, a real friend willing to spend time with him, to talk to him and listen to him and treat him almost as an equal. Russ let him help set up the drums and pack them around from place to place—but gently, tenderly. "This is fragile cargo and *expensive*, man, you'd better believe it. Five hundred dollars this set of skins cost. You can't go rolling them around like beer barrels."

"I wanted drums once," Mike confessed. "A kid up the street had this Swing-King set—just three-piece, nothing really. I knew we couldn't afford it, but I drove my mom nuts begging for it for Christmas."

"Did she come through?"

Mike grinned. "No, she gave me a bicycle. Couldn't afford that either, but I guess she thought it was quieter—and less dangerous."

"What's dangerous about drums?" Russ asked, but Mike didn't explain. In return for his help Russ taught him to hold the sticks and do a few basic beats. Sometimes they jammed together, trumpet and drums, Russ shooting off percussive fireworks while Mike blew himself dizzy faking what he could remember of "Sing Sing Sing" and similar jungle classics. He couldn't ad-lib worth a nickel, but he could fill the spaces with high-level blasting. Thanks to Miner's high note trick, he could toss off high C's now without getting red in the face. Jam sessions lasted only until some party pooper hollered, "Shut up, dammit, knock off that racket! Why don't you two clowns go join a drum and bugle corps?" Russ would stop obediently, wait until the echoes died down, then sneak in one last cymbal smash to prove that the man at the drums always has the final word.

While Jerry and Miner and the other older men spent their backstage and travel time in poker games and endless discussions of horse racing and girl chasing, Russ and Mike played gin rummy and drank Cokes and talked about bands. Russ didn't drink liquor, not even beer. In the first place he couldn't get it. Nobody would sell it to him. "Bartenders take one look at my face and say, 'Get lost, sonny, we don't serve children.' In the Navy I could get it sometimes with a fake ID card; they're not so touchy about servicemen. But now that I'm a hairy old discharged veteran, unh-unh, nothing doing. That's all right, though, I don't care. Frankly I wouldn't waste money on the stuff. It's not worth it."

Mike agreed. "It sure makes a mess out of Jerry. You should try rooming with a guy who comes in gassed every other night—slings his clothes all over and mumbles and snores and then stumbles into the john to throw up, yechhh, it's awful. One night he didn't even get there and I had to— And hung over in the morning, grouchy as hell, throws shoes at a guy for the slightest little noise. And always bragging how the girls spread their legs for him and arch their backs and beg for more, a real dirty blow-by-blow description. If all the girls in the U.S. were laid end to end, Jerry Riley is the guy who did it. It makes me sick."

"He tells *you?*" Russ sounded shocked. "Boy, he must be warped or something. You know what they say about guys like that? Any man who spends all his time screwing girls and bragging what a big he-man he is, he's just trying to prove something to himself, something he isn't sure about. If he was perfectly normal, he wouldn't need to keep proving it. That's really disgusting. I don't see why you put up with it. Me, I'd move out."

"Me, I got no choice. He's my dear old dad and he's paying my bills on this trip. I guess it's better than going home to school and Mama."

A whole lot better, Mike thought, now that somebody cared. If only he didn't have to share hotel rooms with a drunken slob. He wished he could change that. He got his wish granted very suddenly one day when he went up to get a handkerchief and walked straight into a torrid scene. The girl shrieked and Jerry swore and Mike shut his eyes and backed out fast but not before he'd seen too much, two sweating bodies and the tangle of legs in raw profile. Seeing was definitely believing and the naked truth was as ugly as he pictured it. They could have hung out the Do Not Disturb sign. Sure the door was locked, but he had a key. It was

82

his room too, wasn't it? He lived there too. How should he know?

One good result came out of it. Jerry might enjoy bragging of his conquests, but he didn't enjoy interruptions. "Why don't you room with Kelbert from now on? You two boy scouts can sit around your campfire and tie each other in knots."

"Sure, you bet," Mike said. "That's a great idea."

With Russ' prompt agreement he switched rooms the same night. From then on it was downhill all the way. No muss, no fuss, no interrupted sleep or grouchy mornings. Russ was the ideal roommate. Mom would approve if she knew him. He was a very clean guy who took lots of showers—an old Navy habit, he said—and shaved about twice a week oftener than he needed to. Although he might not pass for twenty-one, anyone taking a closer look would know he wasn't a schoolboy. He wasn't tall, not over five seven, but he had a good athletic build with muscles all over his arms from banging the drums. Popeye the Sailor, sure enough. When Mike looked at those bulging biceps he felt like a string bean, the ninety-seven-pound weakling with sand in his eyes. The show girls really went for Russ and his blend of cuteness and muscle. They fell all over themselves playing for his attention. He would grin and kid around with them, but somehow it never led to anything. Mike enjoyed watching the neat way Russ could raise a girl's hopes and then just drift away uncommitted and leave her there pouting. Those wild-eyed painted ponies sliding up and down the brass poles—a guy could live just fine without them. There must be better ways in life to get your kicks.

"Sure there are," Russ said. "I know several if you're man enough to handle them. When you're looking for kicks, you want kicks, not a hangover or a case of the clap. I've got something here that will kick you right up through the ceiling and hang you on a cloud, man."

Mike gave the reefer a cautious look. "They're, uh, sort of habit-forming, aren't they? You get hooked and can't quit?"

"Hell, no. You're thinking about hard drugs like heroin. I wouldn't touch any of that stuff; it's really wicked. But tea is perfectly safe. You can take it or leave it any time."

"Are you sure it works? I mean cigarettes are supposed to satisfy, but they don't do anything for me."

Russ laughed. "Naturally not, the way you pussyfoot around with them. Listen, these babies cost fifty cents apiece and they're meant for kicks, not looks. You can't light it and hold it and pose for your picture with a satisfied expression and a curl of smoke rising up. If you don't mean business, forget it. Just keep on sucking your chocolate Camels and leave tea for the experts."

Fifty cents for one smoke! "You're sure, huh? Kicks and no habit?"

"Trust me."

Mike swallowed. "Well, here goes nothing."

He choked on the first drag and started to cough, but Russ grabbed his wrist and kept him from putting it down. "Go on, man, keep going! They burn fast, you can't waste it. Inhale, dammit, *in*-hale, in, in, in, that's it, that's the way." Mike kept going the best he could, inhaling bitter smoke that scorched all the way down. He couldn't quit now, not with Russ right there watching and coaching and cheering him on as if he were running for the winning touchdown—go, man, go; fight, team, fight. If Russ said it would work, then it would work. Russ knew everything and he never lied, absolutely George and the cherry tree honest and the most beautiful marvelous person in the world because he knew and shared the secret of success that Mike had been hunting all summer. Here it was, grass from the Garden of Eden, the knowledge of good and evil rolled up together in one neat cylindrical package, evil going down but so good afterward. Who else but Russ would do that for him? Nobody else cared.

"That's how they all are, you know," Mike said confidentially. "Selfish, purely selfish."

"Women?"

"Women *and* men, adults, parents, every damn body over twenty-one. Selfish. They have it all and they know it all, but they hate like hell to spread any of it around, they hate to share the wealth. Leave a guy ignorant forever, that's how mean they are. You know what it is, don't you? It's a conspiracy."

"Sure, that's it. Conspiracy."

"A secret conspiracy, like it's this secret club they have for adults only, see. Sign on the door, No Minors Allowed. You can't get in till you're twenty-one years old with hair on your chest like old Jerry. *Then* they let you join the team and learn the secret passwords and code and all the signals. When you're a full-fledged card-carrying member of the Adults' Union, then it's perfectly legal for you to do everything, smoke and drink and cuss and gamble and screw all the girls."

84

"Screw 'em all, man," Russ said agreeably. "If that's your pleasure."

"Not mine. Jerry's. That stupid jerk couldn't live through the day without two packs and a fifth and a piece of tail for dessert. He can have it. I don't need any of that stuff. This right here is good enough for me."

He wasn't fooling around with it; he took it seriously and with respect. The knowledge of good and evil was no laughing matter. Like Adam's famous apple, it stuck in the throat going down. Life was simpler before he found out. Now he was stuck with the knowledge and responsibility, stuck with making the choice every time. Should I or shouldn't I? I'm not supposed to do it, but it feels so good. It's not a habit. Nobody makes me do it. I can always decide not to. But since I can take it or leave it, I might as well take it, what the heck, why not?

Not a habit, not a daily occurrence. Just now and then for a special treat when Russ was willing to share with a pal. He never sold them to him, always refused the money when Mike offered to pay. "That's all right, forget it. You can do me a favor sometime." Mike would have done unlimited favors anytime, would have cut off his arm up to here or waded through blood if Russ had said the word. Nothing was too good for a true friend. But Russ asked nothing but the pleasure of his company. Of all the people he might have picked, he chose Mike to share the secret ride, the long, lazy, private float into space on a joint apiece or maybe one shared between them, passed quickly from hand to hand before the ash burned down to nothing. Then the corners of the room went cockeyed like the tipsy house at an amusement park and Bill Rhodes' trumpet was absolutely past belief, recorded superlatives, sweeter and higher and better than best. Mike knew that *he* could play just like that, exactly like it. Whatever Rhodes could do, he could do. Just pick up his own horn and out it would come: "Two o'Clock" or Russ' favorite "Stardust" or "Flight of the Everlovin' Bumblebee," note-perfect Rhodes, easy as falling off a bed. But his horn was clear across the room, miles away, too damn much trouble and bother to walk way over there to get it. Who needs a trumpet? He could play the notes inside his head and sound just as good if not better. Save the effort of fingering, save his breath for other occasions. What a marvelous invention, the Riley built-in trumpet. Convenient, cheap, portable; no musician should be without one. Very clever of him to invent it. Russ said,

85

yes, he was very clever. As clever as the man who invented the repeating phonograph arm, which was another fine laborsaving device. No need to get up and change the record every three minutes. Just put one on and let it go, beginning to end, click-click, up and back and begin again, Stardust Stardust Stardust to the infinite ends of everlasting infinity. . . .

Until the cockeyed roof fell in.

It crashed like a slamming door and showered down in a slow-motion nightmare. Jerry yanked Russ up off the bed and slugged him right in the mouth, yanked him up and slugged him again. Russ never had a chance. He didn't know what hit him. He was just lying there nicely stoned and minding his own business, enjoying the beautiful trumpet Mike and Bill Rhodes were play-ing for him when zap! pow! all bloody hell broke loose, a crazy Irishman cussing a blue streak and trying to knock his teeth out.

"Leave him alone!" Mike yelled. "Damn you, leave him alone!" He grabbed Jerry's arm and Jerry backhanded him. Mike stumbled backward and went down hard, hitting his head on the frame of the bed. He sprawled there too dazed to get up, tears in his eyes from the knock he'd taken. He couldn't believe any of it. It couldn't happen, Jerry never hit anybody. He got mad and cussed a lot, but drunk or sober, he never risked his hands in a fight. He always said it himself, laughing—I'm not a fighter, I'm a lover. But here he was clobbering the bejesus out of Russ, ham-mering him right and left like he meant to kill him. And Russ couldn't or wouldn't fight back but took it all limp, his head flopping back each time Jerry hit him again.

When Jerry finally dropped him, he went down like a rag doll, not out cold but gasping, blood on his face and the front of his T-shirt. Jerry looked contemptuously at the anchor on his arm.

"Not enough spinach, Popeye," he said. "Stardust" was still playing. When Jerry jerked the tone arm up and the needle screamed across the record, Mike felt as if he'd been slashed with a knife.

"Fifteen minutes," Jerry said. "If you're still in town, then I call the cops. Got the picture?"

Russ sat up and wiped his hand across his mouth. "For what? Assault and battery?" That's telling him, Mike thought. Who started this anyway?

"For possession and contributing, to start with," Jerry said.

"Then we check into that service discharge and see what it was the Navy didn't like about you."

"It was medical," Russ said, but he looked sort of green.

"Like shit it was. Fifteen minutes, sweetheart."

To Mike's astonishment Russ didn't argue. He stood up dizzily and started throwing things into his suitcase. Not much to be thrown; they were due to move on in the morning. "My gear's at the station."

"Lucky for you. You can catch the next train to anywhere. Or plane or bus or friendly camel caravan. It's no skin off my ass which way you travel. Just take your little drum and beat it before I lose my temper."

With the room key in his pocket Jerry thought he had settled everybody's hash, but he was wrong. While he was seeing Russ grimly off the premises and recovering himself in the hotel bar, Mike packed his own bag and split down the fire escape faster than Huck Finn on the lightning rod. He'd have slid down knotted bedsheets if he had to, but the fire escape was handier. He caught up with Russ at the Greyhound station. "Wherever you're going, me too."

"Why?"

"Why not? We can start a combo like you mentioned once."

"No, thanks."

"Aw, Russ, please. You gotta take me along."

Russ gave him a funny look and touched his tongue to his split lip. He had washed off the blood but his bruised face was starting to swell, one eye darkening. "You got any money?"

"About ten bucks."

"All right, listen. I'm not taking you anywhere, see? But there's a bus to L.A. in half an hour. If you should happen to be on it, that's your own business."

They got off the bus in Los Angeles and walked straight into the arms of the law. In spite of his fifteen-minute promises, that rat Jerry had blown the whistle on them.

The authorities tossed Russ in jail, but Mike, being a minor, was left to swing his heels in juvenile solitary. And when they turned him loose, what then? He wouldn't live with Jerry again for a million bucks, and certainly Mom wouldn't want him after all he'd done, reefers and running away and a jail record.

Mike never did learn what happened to Russ. When Jerry

showed up at Juvenile Hall later in the day, hot and sweaty and grim from a sleepless bus ride across the desert, the authorities handed Mike back to parental custody. And Jerry politely resigned the job. He made a fast phone call and stuffed Mike on board the first train to Chicago, so thankful to be shut of him that he didn't even bother to cuss him out. He only warned him to behave himself this trip. "Give my regards to Mama. Tell her I wish her all the luck in the world."

"Luck? Is she married?"

Jerry shook his head. "Nope. I guess her big scheme fell through. You'll have her all to yourself again, sonny boy. I'm sure you should both be very happy together."

III

A year of lessons in Connor City had jelled Mike's Saturday mornings into firm consistency. He slept as late as his mother would let him, went over to Paul's place for ten o'clock scholarship, then downtown to catch the best noon movie at one of the two first-run theaters, the State and the Cornhusker. Today the pattern slipped a little. Mike was in great shape, never better, but Paul felt flu-ish and cut the lesson short. That put Mike downtown half an hour too early for the show, but he knew where to kill his time.

He left the bus at Fourth Street and walked three blocks south and around the corner into Hoffman and Franks Music Store. On his left, the record shelves, enlarged photos of the Columbia giants smiling down from on high, Bill Rhodes second from the left. On his right the case of instruments, guitars and rebuilt saxes topped by the crown jewel, a fabulous two-hundred-dollar Bach trumpet. Straight ahead the record booths where the new discs were auditioned to death by kids without a dime in their pockets. And wrapping it all up, the crazy quilt of music in the air—Stokowski against Sinatra, somebody testing a piano, kids' Saturday morning lessons upstairs, beautiful discord. Mike inhaled with both ears and felt his soul expand.

Mr. Hoffman nodded to him from behind the counter. "Hello there, how are you today?"

"Fine," Mike said. "The new *Down Beat* come in yet?"

"I think so. Help yourself." Hoffman was a real prince. He understood that a young musician struggling toward professional sidemanship on a buck-a-week allowance couldn't afford to buy everything he read. A guy could hang around here studying the trade magazines and new music all day, as long as he didn't wrinkle the merchandise or absentmindedly slip any under his jacket. Which Mike wouldn't, of course, no matter how badly he wanted it. He didn't dare risk losing his free library privileges. Paul lent him old stocks to practice, but he had to keep current, ready to jump when his lucky break came. When and if. Even after a year of lessons Paul wouldn't commit himself on Mike's professional competence. He just said vaguely, "Oh, you're coming along," and changed the subject. Mike felt pretty ready. The only sure test would be to play a real job.

He glanced through the new *Beat*, watching automatically for certain names. "Bill Rhodes," said page three, "finished his third smash week at the Palladium." That was no news to Mike, he'd caught their late radio show last night. "Bill's current vocalist, lovely little Linda Page, made a big hit with the West Coast fans. . . ." Current is right, Mike thought. He fires a girl singer every other month. They may score with the fans, but they strike out with old Bill every time. And he's definitely in a position to pick and choose his dames or sidemen or anything else he wants.

No mention of Jerry anywhere, there never was. No telling where he might be by now, playing piano for TD again or flat on his face in skid row. Who knows, and who cares? No mention of Russ either. He was probably still serving five to ten in Alcatraz, poor guy.

Mike returned the *Beat* neatly to the shelf, then started browsing through the rows of stock orchestrations. There was a new one, "GI Jive" by Johnny Mercer. He began humming the first trumpet part to himself, beating time with one foot. Pretty complicated, this one. Sort of like boogie piano rhythm, right-hand triplets against walking bass, ra-da-da *dee* day-o, da *dee* day-o. . . .

"Excuse me, please," Mr. Hoffman said gently, and Mike, still humming, drifted three feet to the north. "That's all right, don't let me disturb your studies. This gentleman just needs some music."

The cash customer looked over the rack and picked up half a

90

dozen orchestrations. Now who's this cat? Mike wondered. He was Paul's age or a bit older, heavy-built, thinning hair, ordinary gray business suit. Pretty square-looking gent to be playing the stock market. Maybe a manager? He and Hoffman moved away and Mike returned to "GI Jive." Ra *deet* d'lee-a-da *deet* d'lee-a-da. . . . Reading stocks was pretty simple now that he knew the language. But ad-libbing a good original solo was something else.

"How is business at Roseland, Jack?" he heard Hoffman ask. Well now, how about that? Mr. Square Double-breasted must be Jack Herron, Paul's sometime boss. Couldn't have guessed by looking at him. Funny, Mike thought, that he had lived in Connor City more than a year and never yet come face to face with its only respectable dance band. Well, not so much funny as pathetic. He had no money to take a girl dancing at Roseland Gardens—no girl to take or inclination to find one—and Mom wouldn't let him go out there just to hang around. Even when Herron's band played for the ROTC Ball last spring, Mike didn't stay to hear them; Mom made him come home right after the cadet concert, a ten o'clock Cinderella. If she thought the sound of Jack Herron's band would contaminate him, she was really out of her head.

"Just fair," Herron said. "Between the war and the weather and half the town sick, you can't expect much. I caught that damn bug myself last week. Now my second trumpet is coughing his head off and I can't find anybody to fill in tonight."

Mike dropped "GI Jive" and scattered fifteen double pages of music over the floor. He squatted to gather them up, reaching without looking, his eyes and ears on Herron. Second *trumpet?*

"You've tried Paul Kessler?" Mr. Hoffman asked.

"I just did, but he's sick too. You happen to know of anyone else available?"

Mike stood up. "I am."

He waited for the ceiling to fall on his head, but not even a chunk of plaster dropped. Mr. Hoffman smiled at him encouragingly. Herron gave him a long appraising look, as if able to judge his playing ability by the size of his ears or more likely the shape of his lip. Mike stood tall and looked as professional as anybody could in dirty cords and a windbreaker jacket.

"Oh? How old are you?"

"Seventeen," Mike said firmly.

"Union? Who you been working with?"

Dammit, he would ask that. Mike thought fast. "Nobody around here, but I was on the road with a band in California."

"Yeah? I need a second. Can you ad-lib?"

Dammit, dammit, all the wrong questions. Mike crossed his fingers. "Sure. Want to hear me?"

Herron looked thoughtful. "I guess. You don't have your horn here, do you?"

"Well, as it happens, I do." He couldn't think of any reason why he should have, apart from the lessons which he wasn't going to mention, but Herron didn't question it. They went upstairs to the practice rooms. A kid was playing Italian fandangos on a 120-bass accordion; an alto sax beginner honked out scales as though he had a split reed and didn't know it. Herron opened up one of his stocks, handed over the second trumpet sheet, and Mike smiled. "Lonesome Doll," a slow sad ballad, the flip side of the Rhodes record he had bought not two weeks ago. Linda Page— no, not lovely Linda, it must have been recorded before the ban, back in '41 or '42—another of Bill's ex-chicks sang it, brave through her tears; you ditched me for a new love but I'm a sucker for punishment, come back any time and we'll try it again. *Yechhhh*—like those dopey chorus girls who fell into bed widespread for Jerry. But forget the words; the tune is all that counts now. Slow four, nothing tricky, just sock those figures as they come along.

Herron stopped him halfway through, took it back and gave him another. "Take it from Letter C."

Oh-oh, trouble. Lettered chords with cued notes over them, a hot solo to play if you couldn't ad-lib your own. "Uh—as it's written?"

"No, whatever you want."

Mike twiddled his valves and looked it over carefully. Well, it was straight twelve bar blues, the standard pattern. He knew something to fit it, a sort of memorized ad lib he had worked out and polished up. Herron wouldn't know he wasn't inventing it right off the top of his head. He took a breath and socked into it, loud but not too loud. The phrases linked together nicely, two-bar chunks of a hot jigsaw puzzle that sounded quite a lot like Rhodes. Well, it should.

When he finished, there was a little silence. The accordion and sax had stopped in respect for the quality of the competition. Herron looked thoughtful again. Mike held his breath. Don't call us, we'll call you? Thanks, but no thanks—come around in five years if you learn to play your own solos?

"Eight o'clock tonight at Roseland Gardens," Herron said. "You need a ride?"

Mike's breath sizzled out slowly and, he hoped, silently. "I could use it."

"Okay, where do you live? . . . Pick you up on the corner then, about seven forty-five, right? Wear your tux."

"Sure," Mike said. "I'll be ready."

He had the job, he had the horn, he was ready to travel. Almost. All he needed now was a tuxedo.

It fit him pretty well. A little generous in the waist and shoulders, a little stingy at the wrists and ankles. But cuff links were supposed to show and behind a music stand nobody would see his socks. The loose waistband worried him most. He would certainly panic Roseland Gardens if he stood up to take off a solo and lost his pants instead. But you don't look a gift tuxedo in the fly; you take in a grateful hitch with safety pins and hope for the best.

He straightened his tie and studied his reflection—Riley the composite well-dressed man. The tux and suspenders and clip-on tie were Paul's, lent without questions. Jerry in a moment of half-gassed generosity had given him the cuff links, a gold-plated memento from some tarnished romance. The shirt and shoes and winning smile were Mike's very own. No contribution from Russ. The only things Russ ever gave him were long gone up in smoke, except memories.

He ran the comb over his hair again. Just the right length now, so of course Mom was screaming get it cut, get it cut, you look like a starving artist. His skin had cleared up nicely, hardly any zits left, and being pale gave him a sort of natural nightclub pallor.

He picked up his overcoat and left the bedroom quietly, hoping he might escape unnoticed. No luck. Mom was reading in the living room and she looked up the minute he walked in. "Where in the world did you get *that?*"

"What?"

"The tuxedo!"

93

"Oh, this?" Maybe if he kidded around, she wouldn't be so suspicious. "Looks neat, huh? I bought it at Goldman's this afternoon. On sale."

She nearly flipped. "You did *what?* With what money?"

"I just charged it."

"Michael! You didn't!"

He saw the joke had gone wrong. "No, I didn't. Of course I didn't, Mom, how could I? I was just kidding you. I borrowed it from Paul."

"Oh." She relaxed in the middle of an indignant sizzle. "Oh. Well, I *thought* you had more sense." But she still looked puzzled and worried. Financial questions apart, she smelled something funny. He couldn't possibly tell her the truth, she'd go straight through the roof. But maybe a sort of halfway truth. . . .

"There's a dance tonight."

"A school dance?" She looked surprised now. "You're going to a formal dance?"

"They call it the, uh, Winter Wonderland." He cast around quickly for helpful details. There was a dance like that recently, he had seen the notebook stickers and the write-up in the school paper. "It costs a dollar fifty per couple and they crown a snow queen or something."

"You might have mentioned it sooner."

"I—uh—I did mention it." He crossed his fingers. "Don't you remember, the other morning, but you said never mind, you were late?" It was a pretty safe gamble. She was never too sharp early in the morning, half awake, grabbing breakfast, pushing him off to school and herself to work. "I can't help it if you forgot, but you said it was okay then and it's too late to call it off now."

"I didn't say it wasn't all right. I'm just surprised. Who are you taking?"

"Oh, a girl."

"Really? I thought you would take a trained chimpanzee," she said. "A real live girl?"

He grinned with relief. "Yeah, the chimpanzees were all spoken for. Jean Harriman in my Spanish class, she's blond, about so high, good-looking. Smart, too, gets straight A's." True, quite true. She was in his class.

Mom brushed a speck off his jacket and gave him a sentimental proud mother look, sad but happy. "You should have told me you needed a tux. We could manage it somehow."

94

Wow . . . the brass ring falling right into his hand. "I didn't like to ask. I know they cost a lot." If he could get a steady job with Herron, he could support himself and ease her load, buy her some nice things too.

"You have a good time now. Do you have your key? What kind of corsage did you order?"

"Corsage? Oh, uh, gee, I forgot. I guess it's too late now, huh?"

"You'll have to stop and pick one up. White carnations are nice. Just a minute, you'll need some money."

His conscience couldn't stand any more. "Never mind, I've got enough. I gotta go catch my ride. Bye, Mom." He ducked out fast before she could think of anything else. His trumpet was already hidden downstairs, ready for a quick getaway. White carnations for his nonexistent girlfriend, good Lord, how complicated could it get? Why couldn't he just look her in the eye and say, "I'm going to play in Jack Herron's band tonight!" Because she'd scream and fall dead, that's why. He didn't want to lie and sneak out, he really didn't want to, but what else could he do?

Mike's nerves were jumping when he took the stand at Roseland. For the first few sets he sat on the edge of the chair and counted everything with both feet. He missed a few entrances, bad enough once to draw a funny look from the boss. Nervousness tightened his throat and squeezed the juice out of his high notes. On his first ad lib he sounded thinner than old Roger Peterson wringing the neck of the "Double Eagle."

When the band took their first break, he was ready to pack up his horn and start walking back to town. Even if Herron didn't can him now, he'd never survive the whole evening, dry and winded as he already was. His intermission cigarette left him coughing his head off while he dodged and faked his way through awkward offstage conversation with the sidemen. When they asked where he'd been playing, he spun a yarn about a hot young band in the L.A. area, just beginning to be known when the draft blew half their men into service and scattered the rest. Herron's boys seemed to buy the story. When somebody mentioned the union, Mike took another coughing fit and went to find water. But they didn't doubt he was seventeen, the magic age, old enough to work but too young for the draft. And they liked his playing. A couple of them said he sounded like Rhodes.

Inspired by their compliments, he returned to the stand in

better shape, caught his second wind and played the rest of the night in an easy breeze. He read those stocks like do-re-mi and fired off some good variations on his favorite twelve-bar blues theme. By sheer good luck he didn't have to ad lib anything absolutely unknown. By one o'clock he was dog tired, but he wasn't blowing clinkers.

Though Herron didn't say much, what he did say was beautiful. "Nice going, Riley. Come back tomorrow night, okay?" Mike floated home rich and happy, ten dollars in his pocket and the world on a string. He knew it was just one more night, another single gig for the absent Evans, but it proved he could play without disgracing himself. If Herron liked him once and twice, why not permanently? Sidemen got drafted right and left; holes opened up all the time.

He couldn't sleep when he got home but lay with his stomach tied in knots and trumpet music echoing in his ears. Those ad libs—pretty cruddy, most of them, they barely got by. He should be playing first trumpet, not second. Must be the coffee keeping him awake. He wasn't used to coffee anytime, let alone one o'clock in the morning.

When he woke up again, he knew what the trouble was. Not the coffee and not the ad libs. He had the job for tonight all right, but how could he get there? What could he tell Mom this time? The formal dance story was great, but it wouldn't go around twice in two nights.

"Well, how was Winterland?" Mom asked when he came into the kitchen.

He drained the glass of juice and shuddered. Grapefruit, *canned* grapefruit. "Winter Wonderland, like the song. It was okay. What's that, scrambled eggs?"

"Omelet."

"Hey, neat, that's all right. You're a good cook." Flattery never hurt, and it wasn't flattery. She could cook when she bothered to. Usually she came home worn out from work and just opened cans and fried hamburgers, but Sunday mornings they took their time with something special like pancakes or waffles. He ate the omelet and sweet rolls while he pondered tonight's escape. What was that excuse in the funny papers? *I have to sit up with a sick friend.* No. *Jean Harriman wants me to play my trumpet at her church youth meeting.* Till one o'clock in the morning? No.

96

"Was there a band at the dance?" Mom asked. He choked on a crumb and grabbed for milk to wash it down. But she didn't sound suspicious. She was only discussing his new social life.

"Jack Herron. He plays at Roseland practically all the time. It's a good band too, not Mickey Mouse. Paul plays with them sometimes. He thinks Herron is a real fine guy. If Paul said Herron was a good man to work for, you'd believe it, wouldn't you?"

She shrugged. "Mr. Kessler can work for anyone he cares to; I really don't—" Suddenly she caught the drift. "*Who* wants to work for Herron? *What's going on?* Mike, did you— Last night, you didn't ask—"

"Don't get rattled," Mike said quickly. "Take it easy, let me tell you." He began talking fast, hoping to beat the explosion. He told it just the way it happened—Hoffman's, the audition, Roseland, and—

She didn't let him finish. "You told me you were going to a dance!"

"I did go to a dance."

"A school dance! You said you had a date. You lied about the whole thing!"

"What else could I do? Herron hired me to play for him for money, real money, ten bucks, see?" He pulled out his wallet and flashed the bill, the first honest cash of his life. "That's what a sideman gets for one night's work, just four hours. How much do *you* earn by typing four hours? After I took a whole year of lessons to get ready, do you expect me to turn it down?"

"You lied to me," she said again.

"What the hell, am I the first guy in the world that ever told a lie?"

Silence hung between them. Mike was breathing hard, his fists clenched on the table. His mother looked at him and then down at her plate, blinking back tears.

"No," she said very softly. "No, Michael, you're not the first."

He knew what she meant and he felt sick. Jerry. Lies and blarney and smooth talk to charm the birds out of the trees. "I'm sorry, honest. I didn't tell you because I didn't want you to worry. Here, you take the money. Buy yourself nylons or something."

She waved it away. "Oh, Michael, no! Don't you understand? Taking the job was bad enough, but lying about it was much,

much worse. When people can't trust each other, they just don't have anything. Lying and cheating and sneaking around, trying to make up afterward with phony presents, pretending to care when you don't care, that's the worst thing of all. You can't be like that too. Promise me you won't, Mike, please promise."

Mike swallowed. "I'm sorry. I just thought you'd be happier not knowing. I guess I was wrong."

It wasn't a promise, but she accepted it. "The truth is always best, believe me."

Okay, he thought, here comes the truth. "I'm going back again tonight."

Her coffee cup went down with a crash. "Oh, no, you're not!"

"Yes, I am. He hired me."

"Hired you! To play trumpet in a *dance hall?*"

"Not permanently! Just tonight, just this one night. He's counting on me."

"Well, he can stop counting because you may not go. I forbid it and that's final."

"Why not? Give me one good reason."

She looked at him as though he must be insane to ask. Then she took a breath and started. "It's Sunday, for one thing. It's a school night, for another thing. Roseland Gardens is a dance hall where they sell liquor and you are a minor child just sixteen years old; it's illegal for you to work in such a place. And entirely apart from all *that*, even if it was Saturday afternoon at the public *park*, you may *not* play your trumpet in a . . . swing band!" The gap was long enough for several sizzling censored words. She wouldn't say them aloud, but Mike could read her mind. "Not tonight or ever!"

"Oh, come on, Mom, you know it isn't that bad. Nothing evil happened to me last night. I didn't get sick or drunk or turn blue, did I? There's no law against a guy my age working in a band. Ask Paul, he'll tell you there isn't."

"Paul?" She looked suspicious again. "Did he put you up to this?"

"No! He had nothing to do with it. I never even mentioned his name for a reference."

"But you borrowed his tuxedo. He must have asked why?"

"Yes, but I—" Mike stopped short. "He didn't know."

"Oh? I think I'd like to hear him say that. What's his phone

98

number?" She didn't wait but grabbed the book to look it up.

"Honest, Mom, he didn't know. Don't jump on him, it's not his fault. Anyway you shouldn't bother him today because he's—"

Too late. She silenced him with a look while the phone rang. "Katheryn Ashton, Mr. Kessler. I hope I'm not disturbing you—"

"You are," Mike said. "He's sick."

"—but something serious has come up. Do you happen to know where my son went last night in your tuxedo? . . . A DeMolay dance! Is that what he told *you?* Oh, for heaven's sake!" She looked at Mike accusingly. He gave her a sheepish smile and walked over to look out the window while she poured the whole story into Paul's unlucky ear. ". . . He seems to think he's going to encore the performance tonight, though I told him flatly that he can't. Would you have the goodness to come pick up your tuxedo and pound some sense into his head while you're about it? He won't listen to me, I'm only his mother. . . . Yes, fine, any time, thank you, thank you very much."

"You shouldn't have done that," Mike said. "He's sick, remember? He was feeling rotten yesterday, that's why he cut my lesson."

She looked a little taken aback. "Oh. Well, he didn't sound sick and he said he'd come. He could have said no if he didn't want to. Now pick up those papers and take that Coke bottle off the radio. You don't want people thinking we live in a pigsty."

"Don't worry, he's used to messy houses. Those Jansky kids leave their junk all over his studio. Every time I go for a lesson I crunch down on toy cars and Army men."

"Well, little children can't help it, but we can." She began batting at the cushions and gathering dirty ashtrays in a housewifely manner. "Come on, help me straighten up here. This is all your fault, you know."

"*My* fault? I didn't invite anybody to—"

"You know what I mean. You began it with that awful job and lying to everyone, disgraceful, I'm so ashamed of you, Michael, I really thought you would never do such a sneaky thing to me. I thought I could depend on you. . . ." And on and on, first ending, second ending, and take it again from the top.

"Yes, Mom," Mike said at intervals. "I'm sorry. I *said* I was sorry. What should I do, cut my throat? Look, I'll wash the dishes and you can get dressed. Unless maybe you want people thinking you live in the pigsty in your bathrobe?" That cut her short and she scuttled off to dress.

By the time Paul arrived the apartment was decent and Katheryn was fully clothed. But the look in her eye still spelled trouble and she barely let Paul through the door before she started in.

"Will you please tell this boy that—"

"Listen, she thinks Roseland Gardens is—"

Paul looked from one to the other, opened his mouth and closed it a couple of times, then gave them both a cautious smile. "Look, if it's all the same to you, I just dropped by to pick up a tuxedo."

"You can't, man, I'm going to use it tonight. Herron needs me bad."

"You are not going to use it tonight, Michael. Don't make a foolish scene about it, just get the suit and give it back. There's been trouble enough already."

"Listen, Paul, she thinks Roseland is full of sin and corruption and naked dancing girls. Sit down and explain to her what kind of nice clean decent place it is, will you, please, huh?"

Paul looked doubtfully at Katheryn. She made a slight gesture toward the couch, with a look that said talk if you like, but it won't make any difference. "Take off your coat, Mr. Kessler, it's warm in here. I'm awfully sorry to have bothered you about this. Mike told me you were ill, but I'd forgotten. A cold?"

"Flu, I guess. Nothing serious, just a bug. My sister's kids were all down with it last week."

"I know, it's all over town. Half our office staff has been out. So far I've been lucky." She rapped the end table, with a smile for such superstitious precautions. Mike caught Paul's eye and mouthed the word "Roseland" again.

"Yes," Paul said. "Well, as far as I know, Roseland Gardens has always been a well-run place with a good class of customers. It's just a ballroom, not a nightclub, no floor show or entertainment as a rule except the orchestra for dancing. Both the high schools hold formal dances there, with no trouble I can recall hearing of, except maybe Morton kids trying to crash Bryan's party or vice versa. Nothing serious."

She didn't look convinced. "I'll bet they sell liquor."

"Beer and soft drinks," Paul said. "No beer to minors. I guess

100

it's tougher to enforce that law now on the boys from the air base, but they try to keep it legal. I honestly doubt there's anything there for you to worry about."

"That's what I *said*," Mike said. "Now tell her Jack Herron isn't a dope fiend or white slaver or anything."

"Never mind the testimonials," she said. "I don't care if he's a deacon of his church. It's Mike's health and education I'm most concerned about."

"Oh, Mom, be reasonable. How could one night hurt my health and education?"

"You've had one night. If you go tonight, it's two nights. Next week it's three or four, and where does it end?"

Mike grabbed at the little crack of weakness in that word "if." "Don't worry, I'm not that good. He probably won't ever ask me again, but he does need me tonight and I promised."

Mom looked at Paul. "What do you think?"

Paul rubbed the back of his neck. "I don't know, it's up to you. The union might raise a stink if they found out, but I guess that's Herron's problem."

"Union!" Her face seemed to stiffen. "Musicians' union, you mean. I'd forgotten all about that."

"We don't have many union men in town, but Herron's band is. The local can be touchy about jurisdiction. If Mike keeps working, he'll need to join. There's an initiation fee and dues, and one thing and another, hardly worth the hassle unless he—"

"Oh, no," she said quickly, shaking her head. "No, he can't do that. Not *professionally.*"

Mike glared at Paul, figuring he damned well knew what he had said. A dirty word like *union* killed everything on the spot. Sitting in for a night or two was one thing, but joining the union, turning officially pro, was a different kettle of fish.

"No, that settles it, of course. Call Mr. Herron, Mike, and tell him you won't be there."

"Mom, I've got to. He's counting on me. He doesn't care about the union, he never said—"

"Shall I call him?" She reached for the phone book.

"Oh, for Pete sake, no! *You* can't."

"Then you do it."

"If you'd just be reasonable, nobody would need to—"

She leafed through the book. "Herron. One 'r' or two? Never

mind, here it is." She began to dial. Mike let out an anguished groan and took a step toward the phone.

Then Paul reached out and stopped the call. "Wait a minute. Nobody needs to phone him. I'll fill the chair tonight so he won't be stuck without a man."

Mom gave him a very grateful smile. "Oh, would you? That would certainly save a lot of trouble."

"I thought you were sick," Mike said sourly.

"I'll survive." Paul didn't look at all eager, so now there were two men unhappy because one stubborn woman wouldn't listen to reason. No fair, no fair at all.

Grudgingly he handed Paul back the traveling tuxedo. "Give my love to Jack and the boys now, y'hear?" he said with heavy sarcasm.

"I'll do that." At the doorway Paul added in a quiet voice, "Sorry how this worked out, but—" He ended with a shrug.

"Yeah, I know," Mike said. "Them's the breaks. You can't win 'em all."

Three weeks later he was blowing his horn in Roseland again, but it was a strictly half-assed victory. The band was nonunion, the uniform of the day khaki, and the music was concert, not stocks. In short, the eighth annual Military Ball, high point of the Bryan social year. High point of the ROTC Band, too, its only chance to shine in a formal concert of musical smorgasbord— cornfed Yankee marches, Vienna Wiener schnitzel, one tough chunk of Beethoven, a Latin-flavored olio called "Pan-Americana" and assorted tidbits for dessert. The closest they came to swing was "Sophisticated Lady," postponed from last year, and for Mike's money she was still suffocated. Cadet Captain Kenny Blair, braid and medals and crew cut to the bone, directed part of the concert and Paul took the rest, his blue pinstripe looking lonesome against all the khaki background. The band wore white shirts with their uniforms, slick and beautiful, buttons and horns polished to a dazzle. Anybody who showed up without shined shoes and a fresh haircut needn't bother to return.

All the noncom promotions were announced. Roger Jerk Peterson got a stripe for sucking up to Kenny ever since September. But Michael the Horn Riley got a whole fistful of stripes for nothing but honest talent. Three above and one below, staff sergeant, the only junior to make the rate. He was startled at first, but on second thought he felt he had earned them. He didn't act off in band; he kept his nose clean and his uniform tidy. His lacquered horn shone like a beacon day and night, no sweat about polishing it. And everybody knew he played ten times as much trumpet as anybody else in the section, including seniors. If things kept moving in that direction, he'd be captain himself next year.

After the concert there was a little lull while the ROTC Band cleared their chairs off the floor and Jack Herron's orchestra set up to play for the dancing. Kenny and the other officers and their girlfriends hustled off to form the Grand March, big suspense feature of the evening, all the crowd breathless to see who would be commissioned lieutenant colonel of the battalion. Mike packed up his horn and wandered over to say hello to Herron and the boys, hoping they would remember him.

Herron didn't, not right at first. He gave him a real blank look before it registered. "Oh, hi, Riley, how are you? I didn't recognize you in the soldier suit. You belong to Kessler's outfit too?"

Mike could have kicked himself into the Roseland Gardens swimming pool. The ROTC uniform was a dead giveaway of his schoolboy status, almost as bad as telephone calls from Mama. Oh, well, he'd done it, so make the best of it. "I'm helping them out tonight," he said carelessly. "How about that concert—gruesome, huh?"

"Oh, not so bad for school kids."

"You hear them botch up the Ellington, though? Man, that was awful. They never even came close. How's everything with you?"

"So-so. I guess you heard the Army got Evans. They discovered he was still breathing, so they swore him in, poor guy. Too bad you weren't available—I could have used you."

"Available!" Mike yelled, and a couple of the sidemen looked at him. "For second chair? Who told you I wasn't available?"

Herron looked surprised. "Paul Kessler did. He said you were still in school and your folks wouldn't let you join the union yet. That's right, isn't it?"

"At the moment it is," Mike said through his teeth. That rat. that dirty double-crossing miserable rat. Some real loyal blue-eyed friend he turned out to be. Filled a guy's chair and knifed him in the back. "But things could change."

"Well, let me know if they do. We might get together if I still have a band left."

"Thanks a whole bunch," Mike said. He pushed his way out through the ring of crowd. Half a dozen bandboys waited by Paul's car, mostly sophomores, younger kids without dates who needed rides home. Paul was juggling instruments, trying to fit a couple of baritones and a dozen other horns into the trunk unmashed. When Mike came up he pushed a trombone case at him.

"Take this for a second, will you?"

"You take it and shove it right up your frigging ass," Mike said. "Crosswise." Paul almost dropped the horn on his foot. He stared at Mike and then went red in the face. "What's eating *you?*"

"Don't pull that crap. You know what's eating me. You can't pull a shitty trick like that on me and get away with it, you bas—"

"Shut up, Mike," Paul said. He didn't say it loud, but his tone chopped the word in two and left Mike holding the back half. "Save it, understand? We'll discuss it later."

"You're so damn right we will discuss it." Mike stalked around the car and thumped down in the back seat beside a popeyed Roger Peterson.

It was a very quiet ride back to town.

Paul delivered the other kids to their doors, one by one, until Mike was the only passenger left. He drove on another block and stopped the car, lit a cigarette and leaned back. "Okay. Now tell me."

Mike let him have it loud and clear. ". . . Who are you anyway, my agent? You want ten percent of my earnings? Ten percent of nothing is nothing, man. Why in hell don't you mind your own business? *You* don't want to work for Herron, so why kill *my* chances?"

"You had no chance. You know your mother wouldn't let you do it."

"I could have talked her into it if you hadn't butted in. You weren't trying to help me. She's the one you're out to please, not me. Well, you can save your energy because it won't do you no good to butter her up. She doesn't play around with anybody, man, nobody a-tall. If you think—"

"All right, that's enough," Paul said sharply. "Now I'll tell you something. If you ever use foul language to me again in front of the band, I'll knock you cross-eyed, you understand that? You

104

think I won't, just try it and find out. Anything you want to say in private is your own business, but in public you speak civilly or you don't speak."

"I don't speak, period. I'm all done speaking to you. If you want to do me a real favor, just leave me alone. No more private lessons, I'm through with that crud. And another thing—those sergeant's stripes—you can shove those too. I don't take bribes."

"Bribes! What are you talking about?"

"You know. You fixed that promotion because you had a guilty conscience."

"Mike, that's not so. The band officers decided that, not me. If they say you earned it, you earned it."

"Yeah, well, I don't think so. Why don't you sew your stripes on Peterson's ass? He'll make a real keen suck-up sergeant. In fact, he'd be so grateful that I bet he'd let you—"

"Mike—"

"—screw his mother," Mike finished. He grabbed his horn and opened the car door. "Never mind seeing me home, Mr. Kessler. I'll walk it from here. I'm a big boy now. I get to cross streets all by myself."

He had learned his last lesson from Paul Kessler and he had learned it good. Never Trust Anybody Over Twenty-One. That's the enemy, man. Don't trust anybody, don't tell them anything. Loose lips sink ships and also dreamboats.

Time dragged more slowly with nothing to break the monotony, nothing to anticipate but June vacation. Take a day, any day. Take, for instance, Thursday, May 4, 1944, a date destined to go down in history without a splash or ripple. He loafed through English and doodled through biology—held the trumpet section together in Band—stood fifteen minutes in line for cafeteria horseburgers with seven minutes to choke them down—burped through American government and siestaed in Spanish. Jail dismissed, he escaped across the street for a semilegal smoke and Coke in Ernie's drug. Here the big wheels revolved after school—ROTC officers, lettermen, sweater girls, the Hags and Decs of the underground clubs. Mike knew their names and reputations; they didn't know him from Adam's off-ox. He was just another peon now. But his turn would come. When he played featured solos at the Hollywood Palladium and cut big Columbia records, *then* they would recall his name. "Mike Riley? Oh, sure, I went to school with Mike Riley, the famous trumpeter!" They would come backstage and beg for his autograph then. Maybe he would give it to them. Or maybe he would just spit in their eye.

He caught the bus home just before the student price went up to adult fare. Late afternoon was the best time to play his horn, before the working folks returned. None of the other three families had lived in the building longer than he had, possibly a left-handed tribute to his trumpet. With the Ball concert behind him and no Saturday lessons ahead he didn't have much to practice, but he messed around for an hour, trying out ad libs, playing along with records. He had to keep his lip in shape, though for what God only knew.

Around five thirty Mom blew in and they ate a quick dinner of boiled hot dogs and spinach and canned pears. "No candlelight and wine tonight?" Mike asked, meaning to be funny. Once when she gave him the electric bill to pay he had stuck it in his jacket and forgotten it. The next week darkness had descended right in the middle of Waring's Pennsylvanians, and Mom had let go with a few choice words. "If you're going to be the man of this house then act like it, remember your responsibilities. If I can't trust you, then I'll do it myself." It wasn't fair. She expected him to be the man occasionally. But when he wanted to get a job and earn real money for them both, suddenly he was just a helpless little child.

After dinner he stayed in his room, pretending to study with the radio turned low. At ten o'clock the bands began to play half-hour air shots from the big hotels and ballrooms. He cruised along the dial from one to another. A very dull bag tonight. Blue Barron and Henry Busse and Tick-Tock Tommy Tucker Time. Finally at midnight he caught Tommy Dorsey for a while, but the distant station kept fading out. Thursday the fourth was definitely not his day. And Friday the fifth would very likely be no better.

May 5 was not, but May 19 turned out something more his style. That night they let him blow his horn in the Bryan Varieties of 1944, featured soloist and lead trumpet of an otherwise un-

106

talented cadet dance band. Of course the band was a mess, even after two weeks of rehearsal on three stock orchestrations with Kenny Blair fronting, Paul shoving hard from behind and Mike dragging the brass along with him through "Blue Moon and "In the Mood."

The rest of the show was a rickety roller coaster of ups and downs. At the downmost point a tap dance team in Western garb clippity-clopped to a record of "Don't Fence Me In," and an amateur Sinatra clung to the microphone, forgot his lyrics and should have been booed off the stage. But some of the comedy skits were good, and the well-stacked blond singer in black sequins carried a husky torch. Then the ROTC Crack Squad snapped through their silent drill, fifteen white-glove white-pants toy soldiers, poker-faced and mechanically perfect, thump, smack, click, spin. Mike watched from the wings while a small knot of panic tightened behind his belt buckle. Those guys were too damn good. Nobody, least of all an amateur swing band, ought to follow them. However, that was how the program ran. Kenny's Crew scuffled through "Blue Moon" with a few goofs and gliches and set the stage for "Stardust."

When Mike stood up in his blue spotlight, fear caught him right behind the knees. He had played this piece a million times but never under a spotlight before, never facing a full house audience. He grabbed a good deep breath and spun out the first three pickup notes, three long clear threads of blown glass stretched across deep blue silence. Then he slid into the chorus and the saxes came in behind him with slow fat chords to cushion the melody. He played it the right way, Rhodes' way, simple on the first chorus with variations laced in the second time, starry clusters of notes, sparkling blue grapes on glass stems, too fragile to touch, too perfect to mess with. Russ always said "Stardust" wasn't composed; it was discovered. Nobody could compose a piece of music like that, not sit down at a piano and figure it out coldly note by note, choosing this chord to follow that one. Somewhere it had always waited, ripe and ready, hanging in the eternal void until Hoagy Carmichael wandered through with a pencil and manuscript paper.

The Bryan audience went wild. They clapped and whistled and shrieked for Mike as if he were Rhodes at the Palladium. He took four bows before they let him sit down. They wanted an encore, but he couldn't give them one. For Mike's money, nothing followed "Stardust."

As soon as the final curtain closed, fame broke over him like a wave. All the cast and crew crowded around, pounding his shoulder, shaking his hand, dripping barefaced admiration on his sleeve. "You were great, Mike, you really knocked 'em dead out there, better than Rhodes any day!" He stood there with stardust in his hair and a silly grin on his face, saying, "Well, thanks, glad you liked it, it went pretty good, didn't it?" When he tried to ease offstage, they wouldn't let him go. He was good, but to say he beat Rhodes was pure nonsense. He slid out into the hall where boys were waiting for their girlfriends, parents coming to collect their kids. He set his case on a windowsill and reached for the polishing rag. Those backstage idiots had smudged their fingers all over his horn.

"Congratulations, Mike—"

"Thanks."

"Really sounded nice—"

"Thanks."

"Good show—"

"Thanks."

"You Mike Riley?"

At last, an intelligent question. Mike looked up. "Yeah, that's me." Three boys in this gang, strangers. One big, one middling, one smallish and crew-cut. The three bears.

Middle-sized Mama Bear led off. "That stage band—where did you find such sad musicians, man?"

"Under a rock, I bet," the big guy said before Mike could think of an answer. "There never was no talent here. You could lump all the talent in Bryan together and stick it right in your eye without noticing. I don't see why you guys bother to attempt a show. Compared to our Roadshow, this thing was so corny—"

"Sorry you wasted your money," Mike said. Actually he was inclined to agree, but he didn't like Papa Bear's snide tone. Or his looks either—too handsome, too greasy, too many waves in his hair. This trio must come from Morton, pretty hard up for bragging material.

"As a matter of fact, you sounded pretty good," Mama Bear said. "I mean you personally, in spite of the backing. Very good, in fact. Who do you work with besides them?"

108

"Me? Well—" Mike hesitated. "I was with Herron at Roseland for a while."

"See, I told you," the big guy said. "Union. Skip it, Johnny, let's go."

"No," Mike said. "I'm not union."

"Then you're a liar," Papa Bear said flatly, "because Herron is. Come on, you guys, this place is knee deep in bullshit. No wonder they named it Barn High. I told you we wouldn't find nobody here."

By now Mike knew he was talking to musicians who knew the score. "I did play a gig with Herron, but it was only one night, substituting. He wanted to hire me permanently later, but I didn't go. That's no bull, it's the truth. If you don't believe me, you can ask him or Paul Kessler. Right at this moment I'm at liberty, and who are *you* with?"

Papa Bear thrust a pocket advertising card under Mike's nose. THE JOHNNY DEAN ORCHESTRA it said in well-smudged purple print, with phone numbers in both lower corners. They offered more confusing identifications. Papa Bear was Dean or Dino Castagnola (he spelled it out; it sounded like Castanyola), front man, vocals, hot tenor sax. Mama Bear was John Schultz, drums and manager. Crew-cut and hitherto silent Baby Bear was Mel Taylor, piano. Mel was a junior at Morton, the others recent alumni.

"It's a real good band," Dino said. "The name is new since I reorganized it, but me and some of the guys was together before. You remember Weidel's band in the '43 Roadshow? No? Made this one look sick, I'll tell you. Anyway, that was us. It busted up when Weidel got drafted. I just reorganized in March. We got all kind of good jobs lined up, like, for instance, a girls' club dance for fifty dollars guaranteed. That's pretty near union scale."

"Not when you split it nine ways, it isn't," Johnny corrected him.

"Eight ways without Al."

"Even eight ways it isn't. Don't go exaggerating it all up in the sky again, for Christ sake. That's how you lost Al, promising what you couldn't deliver. Listen, Riley, I'll level with you. We're just getting started. Next Saturday is our only firm booking just now, except for our stage shows."

"Stage shows! Where?"

Johnny's grin broadened. "You ever attended a Saturday matinee at the Royal?"

"Matinee? You mean you play along with two Westerns and two cartoons and chapter seventeen of *The Lone Ranger Rides Again*? I bet the kiddies throw popcorn at you."

"Better than throwing eggs. No, actually they love it, you'd be surprised. It's good publicity, and we get a free place to rehearse, not to mention free passes. But we really do have a paying job next week and we need a first trumpet."

Free kiddie matinees and five-dollar dances, Mike thought. Very small potatoes. For all their bragging these guys could be foul. But an audition wouldn't commit him to anything. "Okay, I'll come around."

Getting there was easy; he told no lies whatsoever. While Mom was busy vacuuming her bedroom, he looked in and hollered, "I'm going to the Royal Theater, okay?" She nodded and he walked out free and clear, horn in hand. He would tell her the absolute truth about his job, right after he checked it out. No sense discussing it before he knew all the facts. If they turned out sour, he wouldn't join, so why cross bridges?

It wasn't his side of town. He didn't know the territory, so he missed the right bus stop and had to walk back two blocks to the little business district. The Royal sign stood tall, overruling the corner drug and the friendly neighborhood grocer. The box office and lobby were deserted. Mike rattled both pairs of glass doors, banged the last one vigorously and waited. Today the posters promised him Greer Garson in *Madame Curie*, but that would be the evening show, not the bubble gum matinee. Grade-school kids demanded, and got, Gene Autry shoot-'em-ups where the hero kissed only his horse.

Mel Taylor came at last to let him in. They crossed the lobby in three paces and went down the side aisle of the house. Mike had never noticed the Royal's stage; he had just assumed a brick wall behind the curtained movie screen. Now the screen was raised and the Johnny Dean Orchestra sat behind the blue cardboard fronts monogrammed JD in silver glitter paint. Mike gave the setup a quick professional eye. Four saxes in the front row; one trumpet, one trombone, one empty chair behind them on a riser; piano to the left side and drums finished in champagne sparkle—bass,

110

snare, floor tom and three cymbals. Adequate, nonunion adequate. Johnny Schultz was riding a conventional beat on the high-hat behind Casaloma's "Body and Soul" tenor.

Dean didn't lift body or soul from his chair when Mike came up, but Johnny shook hands in a very welcoming manner. "Hi, glad you could make it. Do you know these guys?" He hit the introductions a little too fast for Mike to follow. Lead alto sax Dick Frye, the rest of the section a delicatessen of tongue-twister names.Second trumpet Sammy was working hard on a mustache to disguise his zits, and the guy on trombone looked too short to reach past sixth position. Mike took the empty chair and warmed up with some high Rhodes licks for effect. He leafed through the library of mixed first and second trumpet parts. Only about twenty pieces but more than half swing classics, "In the Mood," "String of Pearls," "Two o'Clock," "King Porter." Any dance that this gang played for should really jump.

"Okay," Johnny said from behind the drums. "Cut the messing around, you guys. Put up 'A Train' and let's get going."

He kicked off the beat and the band socked right into it, good solid unison saxes on the melody, brass hitting the figures. First and second trumpets split the solos, Sammy taking the muted one and Mike the open. They rode all the way to Harlem without a hitch, no flubs, no failures, nobody falling off. Very good for openers, Mike thought. It could be their best number, though, one flash in an otherwise empty pan. But "In the Mood" was even better. Dino and Frye tossed the alto and tenor breaks back and forth like jugglers swapping tenpins, never fumbling a note. Mike, playing second, gave them the ad lib he'd used in the Bryan show, none the worse for polished practice. When he climbed out of the well at the end, Sammy was right behind him, pushing, not being dragged, but just from habit Mike faked the last five high notes. Sammy went along, but he gliched the D and dropped back to B-flat.

"That high part is written for first trumpet," he said diffidently, as if he thought Mike might possibly not be aware of it.

"I know," Mike said. "Sorry, it was habit. I've been playing it because nobody else could." And you can't either, bud, so don't get antsy about it. But Sammy played a good solid second with interesting ad libs. One high note artist in the section was enough.

111

By the time they finished "Two o'Clock" Mike knew for sure he was in the right place. Popcorn or no popcorn, these guys played his language. He was home.

They practiced about an hour, then broke for lunch. Over drugstore hamburgers and milk shakes they lined up the matinee program and discussed future plans. "Don't let this kiddie show discourage you, Mike," Johnny said. "We really do have prospects."

"Oh, hell, yes," Dean said broadly. "Mel's Uncle Albert's ballroom in Lanville could hire us steady this summer."

"Don't hold your breath," Johnny said. "We'd have to invest in a lot of new music. Those farmers won't listen to swing all night. They want *dance* music, waltzes, polkas."

Dean held his nose. "That crap makes me sick. We need more ballads, though."

"Yes, Frankie. What we need worst is paying jobs. How are your commercial connections, Mike? The different clubs at Bryan must hold dances."

"Sure they do," Dean chipped in ahead of Mike again. "Those richbitch frats and sororities throw parties every week, real wild orgies, everybody getting stoned and screwing like mad. That's my kind of job, man. I'll entertain them cute sorority chicks any old time, dirt cheap, just let me in there. Hey, Johnny, remember that redhead with the big knockers like Rita Hayworth, the one I—"

Johnny started laughing. "Dirt cheap is right. Honest to God, Mike, you wouldn't believe what this clown tried to pull. It was our first job, see, the very first one. This gal wants us for her club dance. Old Dino takes one look at her sweater and starts howling. 'Sure thing, honey, you bet, happy to oblige.' He sets up the whole deal, time, place, everything except the money, he clean forgets money. So I tell her fifty bucks is standard—"

"Is it?" Mike asked.

"Well, no, but I figured start high and come down if necessary. She says they can't afford fifty. Dean says, 'For you, sweetheart, forty.' She looks real worried. Would we take twenty-five? That's not even three bucks apiece and we need everything, music, PA system, so I told her she'd better rent a jukebox. But Dean says, 'Oh, don't worry about the money. We wouldn't dream of disappointing you lovely ladies. I know an arrangement that could work out mutually pleasing to the girls in your club and the boys in my band,' he says. 'Why don't me and you get together privately and discuss the details, hmmm?' very significant, looking her up and down. She sort of gasps and says, 'Well, I really don't—' and then I bust in, 'Okay, sis, twenty-five dollars cash, it's a deal!' and I grab Dino and drag him out fast. I swear to God, Mike, this crazy nut wanted to play free and take it out in trade, the whole band, and he was going to tell that to the president of Damma Phi! That's his idea of good business. Sheeesh!"

Dino was grinning broadly as Johnny told the story. "Best idea I ever had. See, Mike, what JJ here doesn't know is that me and Madame President got cozy after the dance anyway. I made out like a burglar, man. But those other poor suckers played all night for two dollars apiece and some lousy Kool-Aid punch. If they'd listened to me, everybody could have enjoyed a lovely evening."

Mike didn't know whether to believe him or not. The look on Johnny's face was half-cynical, half-amused, shrugging it off as par for Dino's course, but it didn't warm Mike's heart at all. This joker reminded him too much of Jerry, the big bad wolf bragging his conquests. Dino Casanova, the famous front man—all front and no back. Trust him to know all about "the wild orgy parties of Bryan High" which Mike had never heard of. What a crock. Everybody knew it was *Morton* where that kind of jazz took place, kids getting drunk and into trouble.

At the matinee, they waited behind the closed curtain, listening to the babble out front, kids chasing up and down the aisles, rattling the tip-up seats, yelling at their friends, impatient for the show to start. Then Johnny kicked off the theme and the theater manager, doubling as stagehand, hauled the curtain open. The bandshell did not slide forward; it vibrated in six directions and threatened to collapse. The microphone did not ˙rise automatically from a little trapdoor in the floor; it was carried out and adjusted by hand, whistling feedback. No blue spotlight shone on Mike's solo, or even a white one. If the Royal had a spot, the projectionist was too cheap to turn it on. But Mike didn't need a spotlight. He could play "Stardust" by flashlight or candlelight or the flame of a burning match. When he stood up and socked the first three pickups, the kiddies stopped kicking the seats and snapping their gum and rustling the popcorn bags. They sat

113

quietly and listened, enchanted as the children of Hamlin. The Italian delicatessen fed him a background of chords so beautiful he nearly forgot to play. Blue stardust fell from heaven, sparkling on Johnny's drums and the monogrammed music fronts. The kids hollered and whistled and shrieked fit to split, ten times the ovation they gave Dean for his Swoonatra solo.

Mike soon realized that juvenile applause came cheap. The real hit of the show, the real panic maker, was "Mairsy Doats." The band stood up and yelled out the words against rhythm background. "Ooooooooh—Mairsy doats and dosey doats and liddle lambsy divey, a kiddely divey too, wouldn't you-oo?" Hardly the Pennsylvanians or even the Nebraskans—Mike's gray sport coat, Sammy's horse-blanket plaid, third alto in shirt sleeves with his silver sax. But the kiddies loved it. They gobbled up two choruses and screamed for more, still screaming as the curtain closed, the screen thudded down and Popeye the Sailor flashed on to a blast of hornpipe.

The bright sun startled Mike when he stepped through the fire door into the alley. He had lost all track of time, couldn't believe it was only two in the afternoon. They stood outside for a while, leaning on the wall, smoking, talking it over like sidemen taking a dance intermission. Mike thought of Roseland and felt quite professional until Johnny handed him his afternoon's pay—two pink personal passes to the Royal Theater, admit one any night except Saturdays, Sundays, or holidays, not negotiable, not transferable, and subject to ten cents' service charge plus U.S. defense tax.

He read all the fine print and started laughing. "What's this thing worth in cold cash?"

"Two bits," Johnny said, "but you can't cash it. Don't worry what it says, though. They'll let you in any time. You can bring your girlfriend tonight."

"Haven't got any."

"Oh, come on, get off it. A good-looking guy like you? I heard those Bryan gals screaming last night. I bet you have to beat 'em off with a club."

That'll be the day, Mike thought, but he let it go without comment. Not a bad idea to use them tonight. Maybe Mom would enjoy *Madame Curie;* she liked soppy films and highbrow ones. Of course he would have to explain how he got the passes.

114

But he had to tell her anyway, and this time he'd tell the truth, whole and nothing but.

He went straight home and told her in one big burst of straightforward sincerity. And of course she squawked. "I thought we settled all that. No swing bands!"

"But listen, this is nothing like Herron. These are kids like me, nonunion. They hardly ever get a job; half the time they don't get paid. It's almost like the variety show band at Bryan, except better. 'Mairsy Doats' for the little kiddies at the Saturday matinee—now if that's professional, then I'm Bill Rhodes!"

Already he could see she was softening. "Just schoolboys, all of them? You're sure?"

"All but two. Dean graduated in January and Johnny last June." He didn't name their alma mater. Morton's reputation wouldn't help his case at all. And he'd better make sure she never met Dino. Johnny and Mel should pass her standards of clean teen decency.

She looked confused but still stubborn. "It will interfere with your schoolwork."

"Mom, vacation starts in two weeks. It's so boring to sit around all summer. You're at work all day; I've got nothing to do. If I earn a couple of bucks in the band, I can use it for swimming. Come on, please say it's okay."

She weighed it for another anxious moment. "Well . . . I suppose it can't really do any harm . . . in vacation."

115

IV

Use it up—wear it out—make it do. . . .

By the fall of '44 Bryan High squeezed full patriotic mileage out of its auditorium. It started each morning in low gear as Senior Homeroom, shifted up to three periods of instrumental music, became a lunchtime study hall, then cruised through the afternoon with drama and choric speech. The seniors stayed barely long enough to warm up the seats while announcements were mumbled and war stamps sold, hot rumors exchanged and wrong answers compared. It was an impossible place to sleep, Mike had already discovered, and a bad place to finish homework. Writing in the lap came out scribbly. A knee-balanced notebook sometimes shed its leaves before the first frost. A pencil dropped in row R could roll clear down to row A and fetch up against the orchestra pit if nobody offered a foot to stop it. If it had a good eraser, you could kiss it good-bye forever, and if it was a Parker pen, you'd better offer a large reward.

The seats ran alphabetically, and so did the seniors for easy roll taking, Aberson to Zorad. If he had stayed an Ashton, he would have had a front-row seat and possibly heard the announcements when they were read aloud. He would also have been under the teacher's eagle nose and first at bat all day for every oral quiz. Thanks, but no thanks. He'd rather be Riley, comfortably back in the crowd with plenty of time to rehearse his smart answers. If there were any vital news today, he'd catch it in the Bryan *Bugle*,

117

hot off the biweekly press. Items like RED CROSS ELECTS OFFICERS; HOMEROOMS PICK REPRESENTATIVES. DEBATE COACH SELECTS SQUAD . TRIMBLE COMMENDS STUDENTS—for buying war stamps instead of hot dogs.

Mike's alphabetical neighbor, Joyce Reynolds, looked over as he turned the page. "How do you like the new record column?"

"Where?" He hunted through the jumble of editorials, interviews, movie news, fashions and hyphenated gossip—Mac-and-Sal, Mutt-and-Jeff or who's goin' steady already. Here it was, "Platter Chatter." "Hiya, moosic lubbers! We're back to good old B.H.S. once again, so how's about dustin' off the shelves and seeing what's new in the line of some strictly torrid boogie-woogie—" *"Yechhh!* Who wrote this crap?"

"Somebody signed A. Hepcat. Isn't it awful, all that phony jive talk?"

"Not only that, it's full of mistakes. Look, he says 'We'll Get It' for 'Well, Git It' and misspells saxophone with an 'a,' and he talks about 'this brand-new Bill Rhodes platter' that was actually recorded in 1941, which any fool but him would know because Rhodes had fifteen other girl vocalists since Jane Baker, and *no* band has cut *any* Columbia records since September, 1942. This jerk thinks it's new because *he* never heard it."

"Yes, I thought that was wrong. Do you think anyone else will notice?"

"Not around here. I've got friends who would wet their pants laughing if they saw this, but then we're professionals."

"Who are you professional with?"

He offered one of the business cards with phone numbers all over it, Johnny's in one corner, Dino's in another, and his own penciled in for good measure. No booking would slip past the J-D Orch for want of a ready phone connection. "We play all kinds of jobs. We were on the road quite a bit this summer." He liked the sound of that phrase; it suggested a big trailer bus and one-night stands in union ballrooms. No need to mention that they traveled in Dino's rattletrap Model A and Johnny's dad's Plymouth or that the out-of-town customers were 4-H Clubs and Junior Water Buffaloes on a thirty-dollar band budget. By the time they paid for midnight hamburgers and black-market gas, they were lucky to come home richer than they left. He took the newspaper clipping carefully from his wallet, pretty battered from constant

118

unfolding. "This was taken at the USO center last July. The faces don't show up much, but that's me right there and Johnny at the drums."

Joyce studied it with a puzzled look. "Then who's this leading the band?"

"Dino. Johnny Dean is just a made-up front name. It gets confusing when somebody comes to the stand and says, 'Hey, Johnny!' We don't know who should answer, Johnny Schultz, or John Mann, the trombone player, or Dino, who's supposed to be fronting, only half the time he doesn't. Once at the Royal a couple little girls asked him for his autograph and he was so surprised he forgot and wrote 'Dino' and they thought he couldn't spell his own name, which I doubt if he can, Castagnola, Jesus, it took him a whole extra year in second grade to learn how. Actually the band is a partnership, they own the equipment fifty-fifty. Dino thinks he runs it, but it'd fall apart in ten minutes if me and Johnny didn't do all the work. . . . No, you keep the card. This friend of Johnny's who takes printing class at Morton ran us off a million free copies. If you know anybody who needs a good band, give us a call. We're playing at the USO again tonight."

"What about the football game? Doesn't the ROTC Band have to march?"

"Yeah, I'll be there first. When you see a streak of light shooting out of the stadium just past half time, that'll be Riley's Comet taking off."

Joyce smiled and tucked the card into her purse. "Good luck, Mike."

It took luck, but he made it. As right guide of the fourth rank he marched smartly to a fast drum cadence and paid his respects to Old King Cotton. When the band left the field, he ducked out to meet Johnny, who waited on the corner with his motor running. "Man, you're late!"

"Don't throw a pageant. They won't start the dance without us. Pardon me while I do my striptease."

While Johnny barreled downtown, running all the orange lights and cussing at the red ones, Mike traded his uniform for a hangerful of civvies. It wasn't easy, cramped among drums with Dick Frye humming "Take it off, take it off" and making snappy comments on his underwear. Lucky they didn't have a girl

119

vocalist on board. Dino kept talking about it, but so far no action. Mike was glad they didn't. Just another person to split the meager profits. He leaned forward to knot his tie.

"Remove your fat head from the mirror," Johnny said. "I gotta watch for cops."

"You better slow down then. A speeding ticket would shoot hell out of tonight's profits."

"What profits? This job is for free, a patriotic salute to Our Brave Boys in Uniform, and don't you btch about it either. We could have gone to Lanville for fifty bucks if you hadn't been doubling in brass with your schoolboy cadets."

"I couldn't help it. If I miss a home game, my commission goes right out the window."

"Oh, that's right, you're bucking to become a wheel. Yes, sir, Lieutenaı Riley, sir. Big deal."

"You're just jealous because you never made it."

"I never tried. Dean did, but he couldn't get past corporal. At Morton they don't hand out commissions on platters. I bet all that you guys have to do is kiss up to your director. Nobody kissed up to old Danielson, man. He's strictly cold as an iceberg."

"Nobody'd want to," Frye said. "I'd sooner kiss a pig."

They started the dance only ten minutes late, playing the first set with loosely assembled drums and a minimum of tuning up. Mike, metamorphosized from sergeant to sideman in one easy crosstown jump, fell into his natural habitat with a welcome splash. He didn't care who won the football game, though he did hope that Paul hadn't missed him in the second half. ROTC Band with its dozen trumpets could spare him easily in the stands, but here he was fifty percent of the section and desperately needed. Fifty percent? Hell, ninety percent. Sammy couldn't begin to carry it alone. Who would thrill the crowd with Mike Riley's immortal "Stardust?" It was practically his theme song nowadays; he played it at least twice (by request of course) at every job. All alone, out of silence, *taaa . . . taaaa . . . taaaa . . .* three stair steps to the stars and then the band coming in behind him. Mike Riley and His Stardusters.

All the marching and blowing and chasing around town had given him an appetite. At Walgreen's during intermission he bought a chocolate sundae. For no reason at all Dino started razzing him. "Yeah, you'd better eat. You're skinny as Sinatra.

120

That's why girls scream when you play 'Stardust.' They think you'll bust a gut on those high notes and faint from sheer exhaustion. It'll take more than chocolate to put hair on your chest. You wouldn't know what to do with a girl if she came at you bareass naked in a locked room. The only thing you can raise is your trumpet, and you sure as hell can't screw 'em with that, son, it just won't fit."

"The kind of girls *you* date, it would," Mike said nastily. Dino turned red and everybody laughed. They all knew his rooster reputation, the classy chicks he pursued and the tough ones he generally caught.

"Don't worry about *my* sex life. *I'm* normal. You're the one who needs to worry. Hey, Frye, you know what this character did all summer? He kept house for his mama. He scrubbed the floors and washed the undies and cooked dinner every night. He's a real handy-dandy little housewife, no bull. Me and Johnny stopped by one day and found him in his apron surrounded by pots and pans whipping up a double chocolate frosted delight layer cake."

"What it was," Mike said to keep the record straight, "was one lousy little box of chocolate pudding. I don't see what's so damn funny about it. You'd cook too if your mom went to an office instead of waiting on you hand and foot all day."

"Not me, man. That's woman's work. Any guy who likes to cook must have something wrong with his balls."

"I don't like to cook. I just like to eat, and peanut butter sandwiches get boring."

"Sure, cookie, we know how it is. You guys better watch out, I'm warning you. Be ready to defend your virtue in case he starts making passes at you. I sure wouldn't room with him on the road."

"No chance," Mike said. "You're not my type, big boy." It was the wrong answer; it got a laugh but not a very sympathetic one. Well, what was he supposed to do, take a swing at a guy who outweighed him by fifty pounds? It was a pretty stupid joke, that's all he had to say, calling him a queer just because he didn't go around cocked up all the time and panting after every pretty girl he saw, like Dino, like Jerry did. A real stupid joke. Asinine. He could find himself a girlfriend any old time he cared to look around.

*   *   *

So when Joyce Reynolds smiled at him in homeroom Monday and asked if he reached the USO on time, Mike smiled back and told her all about the job. She seemed to be very interested. They ate lunch together on Wednesday and danced at the Friday after-school mixer. That's all it took. When the next edition of the *Bugle* hit the streets, *Mike-&-Joyce* were old news in the gossip column.

Going steady kept him busy. Along with regimental parades and pep rallies before school and extra marching drill after, football games, homework and weekend jobs with Johnny, now he had Joyce to fill in the cracks with social security. They met every morning at her locker before homeroom, ate lunch together and revolved in the circle of her big-wheel friends, who welcomed Mike as a rising star of local show biz and a potential ROTC flat hat. He felt as if he were juggling four or five raw eggs, but he managed to keep them all airborne for two whole weeks until the ROTC commission list came out. Then the first egg slipped through his fingers and crashed.

At first he thought it had to be a misprint, but Paul confirmed the bad news. "I'm sorry, Mike, believe me. You passed the test and I recommended you, but they consider other things too—leadership potential, your grades, your office record—"

"And whose ass you kiss. My grades are okay, I never flunked anything, and I haven't had office trouble for years. Is old Trimble still nursing his bomber-plant grudge on me?"

"I doubt it. You weren't turned down. They just chose the other two first."

"Big difference," Mike grumbled. "Smitty's okay, but that clown Monroe, Jesus, he doesn't know middle C from third base."

"He's sharp on the military part, though, really aced the test."

"Oh, sure, he would. That eager beaver shouldn't be in Band at all, let alone officer of it. He belongs in a regular company where he can play war games with the GI Joes. You watch, he'll have us all crawling through obstacle courses and doing KP instead of playing music."

He hated to let his disappointment show, even to Paul. Why should it matter if he made rank or not? Meaningless, really, no talent required. Any clown who passed the garbage test and kissed Trimble's ass could get a commission. Who needed it?

But it soured things slightly between him and Joyce. She sympathized and agreed it wasn't fair. She tried to pretend it didn't matter otherwise, but Mike knew she was disappointed. She expected to be an officer's lady, socially elite, honored in the Grand March at the Military Ball. He had practically promised it. Most of the guys in her crowd made the list. They swaggered through the halls with jingling brass; their girls flaunted silver pips on well-filled sweaters. All the world could see who rated around Bryan High and who didn't. A whole sleeveful of top sergeant stripes didn't mean a thing socially. Joyce couldn't wear his stripes.

He went downtown and bought the biggest gold trumpet pin at Hoffman and Franks, realistically proportioned and gold plate, not enamel to chip off or brass to turn green. Three dollars, but well worth it. When he pinned it on Joyce's sweater, she almost cried; for a minute he thought he'd jabbed her. "Oh, Mike, it's beautiful! Nobody in school has anything like this." Which was true enough. She was pinned to Riley the Horn, the best trumpet in Bryan High, probably the best nonunion trumpet in town. If she wanted more glory than that—well, he couldn't do everything.

He couldn't, for instance, take her every place she wanted to go. Going steady meant automatic dates to every school dance and to many private parties. But Johnny's band, rapidly rising in popularity, worked nearly every weekend. When Bryan held the Fall Frolic, Mike was playing for the Morton M-Club. When the Decs held their Friday-the-Thirteenth hayride, Johnny's band went to Lanville for a fifty-dollar DeMolay dance.

But when the Hags threw a Halloween party, Mike knew he'd better be there. Joyce was a Hag. (Some people said it stood for Highly Active Girls. Others said Hot-Assed. Nobody knew and the girls weren't telling.) Johnny didn't work that night, so Mike was finally able to drag his Hag to a genuine Bryan part, which could have been a Sunday school picnic for all the benefit he gained. Joyce loved to dance, even with a left-footed clod who never took lessons. He could dance, naturally. Any guy with a sense of rhythm could put his arm around a girl and shuffle his feet to the music. But something was missing. It didn't send him out of this world. He spent two hours cheek to cheek with Joyce, and all he raised was a sweat.

It wasn't all his fault, though. She didn't encourage him to get too cozy. Some steadies were making out madly in parked cars outside the dance, but that's the type of kids they were, passionate neckers with a bad reputation. Joyce expected Mike to behave like a gentleman and he certainly did. He danced with her till his feet burned, drank Kool-Aid punch till he floated, escorted her home on the bus and kissed her on her doorstep at midnight, one short, clean, careful good-night kiss. He could have been kissing his mother.

But Dino believed in the myth of Bryan High orgies, so Mike fed him a wildly jazzed-up report the following night. "Oh, man, what a blast! No chaperone—all the spiked Cokes we could drink—guys passing out right and left—every bed in the house in constant use. Jeez, it was fantastic!"

"Yeah? How'd you make out personally?"

"I was doing great until Joyce made me take her home about two o'clock. She was afraid the neighbors would call the cops. Her folks are strict, see, they wouldn't approve if she wound up in jail."

"Uh-huh," Dino drawled. "Take me along next time. I'll believe it when I see you in action, cookie. In fact, I doubt if you've got a girl at all. Why don't you bring her around so we can meet her?"

"Hell, no, not you slobs. She thinks I have good taste."

"You're scared to. You know what would happen. Bring her around any time, man. I bet you five bucks I'll have her pants off in fifteen minutes from a standing start. When I'm through with her, you can have what's left."

"Go blow it out your B-flat tenor," Mike said.

He took Joyce to the Sunday show, one of those sappy wartime romances, all sad partings and tender reunions with violins throbbing in the bushes. . . . *Wait for me, darling, I will return to you, though it be ten thousand miles.* Strictly a waste of money. Mike leaned back and prepared to enjoy it as best he could. *Oh, yes, John* (violin tremolo), *I'll be waiting for you* (clarinet run). . . . Then Joyce jabbed him right in the ribs. "Quit it!"

"Huh? What's the matter?" Quit what, for Pete sake? He wasn't even holding her hand.

"You were *snoring*," she hissed in a voice purple with embarrassment.

"Who, me?"

"Yes, you."

"Sorry."

Two minutes later she was jabbing him again. "Cut it out, that isn't *funny*."

"Who's trying to be funny?" Mike asked. He shook himself awake and tried to concentrate, but the combination was too potent—two late nights, the dark theater, dull dialogue and violin lullaby. His series of jaw-cracking yawns bothered Joyce almost as much as the snores. When they came outside, the fresh air woke him up and he felt fine, but Joyce rode home on the bus in silence that was louder than words.

The next weekend he played two more jobs and spent Sunday afternoon arguing on Joyce's front porch in thin November sunshine. "The whole trouble is that you don't respect my band jobs; you don't take them seriously. If I worked nights in a store or theater, you wouldn't expect me to take you dancing."

"But every single weekend, every single dance and party—it's just not fair."

"Any time you want to go with somebody else, go right ahead, it's perfectly okay with me."

She looked startled. "You know I can't, unless we break up. Is that what you want to do?"

He uprooted a dead flower stalk from the garden bed and began snapping pieces off and throwing them away. "It's a crazy system, going steady. It's as bad as being married or something. I mean what the heck, you want to go to a dance and I can't take you because I'm working, but nobody else can take you either, unless we have a big fight and say good-bye forever. It's stupid. I don't want to fight with you."

"You wouldn't mind if I went out with somebody else?"

It sounded like a dangerous question, but he gave it an honest answer. "Not if you wanted to."

"But I don't want to! I want to go with you, Mike. I understand about your band, I know it's important to you. I wouldn't ask you to give it up—"

He tossed the remains of the flower away. Give up the band! No chance. No girl in the world could ask him that.

"—But it seems like we could manage something. You don't really have to work every single night."

"I don't work lots of nights."

"Sure, weeknights when we can't go out anyway. What about

November twenty-fourth, are you booked for *that* night?"

"Not as far as I know now. What's happening?"

"The Turkey Trot at Roseland. It's a vice-versa so I guess I have to ask you. Will you go?"

Mike spread his hands in a questioning gesture and slapped them down again on the step. "Who knows? If we have a job, I have to play it. That's the way it is." The words stirred an unhappy echo in his head. Had his mom and dad ever argued this way? *Can't you ever come home at a decent hour? Do you have to go on the road again? Of course I do, dammit, it's my job. You want to eat, don't you?* Somewhere deep in the New York fog there were echoes of bitter quarrels, of sarcasm and tears, doors slammed late at night, a piano pounded with vicious chords. How did Jerry say it once? . . . *"She wanted to lock up my soul in a box made of breakfast, lunch, dinner and payday."* . . . That's what women always wanted—promises, commitments, your heart and soul on a plate. And the Bryan social system favored the girls' demand for faithful security: We go steady or we don't go, period. It was rough on Joyce, missing all the fun. She had a right to complain. Maybe he could skip just one job to make her happy. . . .

"If you really want to go to the Turkey Trot—" Mike said slowly, and then stopped.

She looked at him eagerly, waiting for the magic promise that would make their future safe. Guaranteed security in a box. "Yes?"

He sighed. "You'd better ask somebody else."

So that was it, the end of the line. They didn't fight or call each other names. They parted friends, which was almost worse. She gave him back his trumpet pin and he went home feeling pretty low.

It was all over, a six weeks' romance dead and buried. Sergeant Riley blew "Taps" over the grave on Armistice Day, his trumpet echoing sweetly in the Bryan halls. Mike-&-Joyce declared themselves formally unhyphenated. She asked some other wheel to roll with her to the Turkey Trot. Just as well, too, because Mike couldn't have gone; the band booked a job for the twenty-fourth. Joyce was much better off without him. Why should she waste her whole senior year on a guy who couldn't give her anything she wanted or deserved—a slot in the Grand March, a guaranteed

126

Saturday night or even a kiss that would raise her temperature? That was funny. You'd think, wouldn't you, that if anybody could kiss up a storm, it would be a professional trumpet player. But if his good-night kisses thrilled Joyce, she certainly never let on. Maybe she was afraid to arouse the beast in him. What beast? It didn't make sense that he could date a nice, pretty, companionable girl, spend hours in her company, kiss her good-night and still feel like a brother to her.

Unless Dino was right and he—

Oh, jeez, no, of course not. How could he be queer and not know it? Dino was just trying to stir up shit. That fool thought if a guy wasn't a ravenous howling twenty-four-hour wolf, then he must be the extreme opposite. Dino was cracked on the subject of queers; he saw them everywhere. He would probably even claim that *Russ*— Russ! Old Popeye-the-Sailor Kelbert, built like an All-American quarterback with muscles bulging all over his arms. If *he* was queer, Mike was queen of the May. But Dino would overlook the perfectly plain evidence of normality and whip up something from thin air to prove his dirty insinuations. Russ didn't chase girls night and day. Russ took plenty of showers and combed his hair a lot. Russ was sort of cute and young-looking for his age. Well, so what? He couldn't help his looks. A dimple in your cheek was no worse than a slot in your goddamn chin.

Mike started to laugh, remembering. After one of those twenty-minute slow-dissolving showers Russ was standing in front of the mirror in a bath-towel kilt, combing his wet hair and agonizing over a very small zit and wondering whether he ought to shave again this week. "Hell, you've got more beard than I do." That was a polite exaggeration; Mike had nothing yet but the merest shadow of fuzz on his upper lip. "Don't worry," Russ said. "You will before long, you're the type that does. A year from now you'll be shaving daily with sideburns down to there just like your old man. Look at him and see yourself in another ten years."

Mike made a face. "Not if I can help it."

"Why not? He's a good-looking bastard, you could do worse."

"He's a bastard all right." Mike went over to stand beside Russ and study his own face in the mirror. "Do I really look like him?"

"Look at your chin, you certainly inherited that. If we stuck a nickel in that slot, a Coke bottle would drop out of your navel."

Mike nearly fell over laughing. Funniest thing he'd ever heard.

"No, that's not where it comes out. That's where you pry the bottle cap off."

"My mistake," Russ said. "Hey, let's give it a try, see what happens." He found a nickel in his change on the dresser and poked it at the slot, but Mike was laughing so hard he dropped it and it rolled away.

"Sorry, you're too late. I'm all sold out. Come back next week."

Two years later it didn't seem quite so hilarious. Mike quit laughing. Could Dino make something out of that? Yes, he could and he probably would, something downright nasty too. He'd say you couldn't tell by looking at them. They didn't always lisp or mince or wave handkerchiefs. You might room with a guy for a month and suspect nothing until one fine day when he suddenly made a pass. Was that supposed to be a pass? Hell, *I* was the one who said—

He'd say Russ was working up to it by stages, taking his time, and the reefers were a come-on to make it easier, softening me up, buying my cooperation. *You can do me a favor sometime.* And I would have, dammit. I'd have done anything Russ asked me to.

Anything?

Well, almost anything. Not that.

Then you do admit he had it in mind?

Hell, I don't know what he had in mind. He never said anything to me. He never made obscene advances, whatever an obscene advance may be. I think this is a bunch of hogwash, that's what I think. Russ wasn't a queer, he couldn't have been. My gosh, he was in the *Navy.*

And he was discharged out of boot camp. Why, huh? What caused that?

A medical discharge, that's what he said.

Medical, hell. Jerry guessed it. He smelled something funny, that's why he dropped on you and broke it up so fast and called the cops afterward to make sure. It was more than reefers that scared him. He suspected Russ and he suspected you, and *how do you know he wasn't right?*

Mike started sweating. I don't know, dammit. I don't think so, but I can't prove it.

Cautiously he took stock of himself, adding up his assets and liabilities. He couldn't see anything wrong that twenty or thirty pounds and a few years wouldn't cure. His voice didn't squeak.

128

He shaved occasionally. He was thin, certainly, lean and sardonic like a detective hero. Not athletic. He felt no desire to get his brains scrambled on a football field. Too smart to shed his blood in fistfights if he could talk his way out of trouble. But nobody could call him a sissy. A sissy is a mama's boy who runs home for protection whenever things begin to look a little bit tough. He'd never done that.

Not that Mom wouldn't have let him. She always did fuss over him too much, all his life; she worried unnecessarily if he stayed out after dark or rode his bike too far from home. He knew why, now, looking back on it. He was all she had left after she divorced Jerry. Just the two of them, they needed each other. He used to get scared sometimes, wondering what he would do if anything happened to her, if she got run over by a streetcar or caught pneumonia and left him a Norphan in blue denim and lumpy oatmeal. Well, so he was a dumb little kid in those days; he read too many comics and saw too many movies. No disaster occurred. Mom survived and so did he with nothing more fatal than winter colds. He was never clobbered by a truck or lost in the wilds of downtown Chicago or kidnapped by an evil stranger with a bag of candy. Unless you count Jerry? Or Russ?

It always seemed to come back to Russ.

Well, even if Russ *was* funny—and thinking it over, Mike had to admit the faint possibility—even if Russ was, it didn't contaminate *him*. *He'd* never done anything like that or felt like wanting to. Maybe girls didn't turn him on, but boys didn't turn him on either.

When you came right down to it, the thing that turned him on was kissing a trumpet. If that was a sexual abnormality, it was a new one on him. Hey, look, doc, I'm a *hornosexual.* I'm queer for a horn. There's this beautiful golden-blond Bach trumpet imprisoned in a glass cage down at Hoffman and Franks for two hundred dollars' ransom. I dream of riding in there on my white charger, see, cash in hand, to rescue that lovely doll and carry her away where we can make beautiful music together. Just let me get my hands on her, man, and I'll show you how a musician makes love. I'll bust high C open and climb to the stars all night long, all night and every night in showers of stardust, like nothing old Dino ever did with any dame. The whole world will hear the news when I go steady with that lovely, lovely horn.

Fat chance of it happening, though. He might as well dream of marrying Rita Hayworth on his income of three-, four-, five-dollar weekend jobs. If he hoarded up every cent, if he never bought another Coke or record or movie ticket, he might save two hundred dollars in a year. By which time he would be out of school and drafted, probably dead in the Pacific, while the Sleeping Beauty would be long gone into the hands of a quick cash customer. He wanted her *now*. He wanted it so bad he could taste it, so bad that he dreamed about it nights and woke up sweating, literally hard up for a goddamn horn.

Queer? Fantastic. If the doctors heard this he'd make medical history. They'd have to rewrite the psychiatry books.

The band practiced Monday nights now at Johnny's house. Thanks to another Dino blunder, they had lost their lease at the Royal. When the manager shone his flashlight into the back row one night and found his own fifteen-year-old daughter pantsless on Dino's lap, he kicked Dino into the street and fired the band without notice. "I don't know what he was so sore about," Dino said innocently. "I was just using the thing he gave me. Hell, was printed right on it—'Personal pass, admit one any night.' She admitted me just fine, no service charge or nothing. It's a gyp, man. I got a whole bunch of them pink-ass tickets left, but he said he'd shoot me if I ever showed up there again."

Nine men and a set of drums fit the Schultz living room like sardines in a can. Mike squeezed between the sax section and the sofa to reach his chair in the brass. When he sat down, Johnny's high-hat practically rested on his shoulder, ready to bite his ear if he leaned two inches farther left. Lucky that the band was no bigger or somebody would be playing in the front hall.

The rehearsal started off bad and kept getting worse. Every number Dino called up was strictly for his own benefit, featuring either a Frankly Sinatra vocal or a sour sax solo. His singing wasn't so bad, but his takeoffs were terrible, honk honk honk for sixteen bars on the same two notes. Finally Mike couldn't stand it. "Somebody went to lots of trouble writing these arrangements. They'd really sound good if everybody just played what's written."

"Not on the solos. Those are only cues. If I prefer my own, I can play it."

"Yeah, and stink up the whole number. You think you can ad-lib it better than Vido Musso did?"

"Well, I can try, which is more than you do. I never heard you play an original note in your life, just that cruddy secondhand Rhodes."

"That's because I'm smarter than you are. I happen to know that I can't improve on perfection, so I don't waste my time trying."

"Perfection, shit. You think Rhodes is Lord God Almighty, every note out of his horn was handed straight down from heaven. Why don't you go join his band if he's so wonderful?"

"Listen, I would if I could. Don't think I stick around this town because I love it here. Two minutes after graduation I'll be heading west so fast you won't believe it. And in the meantime, I'd like to play with a band that sounds at least half-assedly decent, so why don't you quit murdering those stupid takeoffs and concentrate on reading your music?"

"Don't tell me how to play, cookie. I'm boss of this band, not you. I make the decisions. Any time you don't like it you can get lost, see?"

"So make a decision," Mike said. "Play something. Don't keep us squashed in this sardine can all night. Let's rehearse and go home; I've got better things to do."

"Oh, I know you do. All them socks to darn and a whole basket of ironing. Mondays are really terrible, aren't they, dear? A woman's work is never done. Don't be cross, Michael, we understand those nasty washday blues. Or is it the wrong—"

Johnny burst into sudden fireworks, double paradiddles and repeated cymbal crashes that rattled the windows and made Mike's chair bounce. Grateful for the interruption, Mike lifted his horn and began jamming with him, "Sing Sing Sing" on a drum and bugle kick, right off the record, but so what? He couldn't improve on perfection. He took a couple of well-known choruses and then let Dino have a turn to call the hogs in his own inimitably miserable manner. Let him blow his meanness out his horn and forget it.

After five minutes of free-for-all jamming they settled down to work in better spirits. The practice ran almost smoothly through three numbers. Then the doorbell rang. They stopped cold and looked at each other nervously, the same thought written on every face. *Oh-oh, somebody called the cops.* It was bound to happen, Mike thought. Sooner or later he knew some nasty neighbor would turn them in for disturbing the peace on Monday nights. In the business block of the Royal nobody noticed or cared, but Johnny's street was quiet. God damn Dino anyway. If he hadn't screwed things up with the manager's daughter. . . .

"Answer the door, Dino," Mike said sweetly. "You're the boss of this band." He thought Dino would fade out and let Johnny take the rap, it being his house and neighbors. But surprisingly enough Dino got up and went to deal with the problem, while the others sat still and held their breaths.

But what Dino let in wasn't cops at all, unless they were plainclothesmen disguised as two high school girls, one blonde, one brunette, in raincoats and headscarves. Very well disguised down to the sweaters and plaid skirts and saddle shoes. Beyond that point Mike couldn't testify, but they looked like girls to him and they certainly had Dino fooled because he was sniffing around eagerly like the old wolf hot on the trail.

"Hey, great, you made it. I thought you'd never get here. Have trouble finding the place?"

"Within two blocks we couldn't miss," the blonde said, and Mike grinned to himself. That's what he kept telling them right along, but nobody listened to him.

Dino helped the blonde out of her coat and left her friend to struggle alone. "This is Darleen Verbeck, you guys," he said as though he thought he owned at least ten percent of her. No sweat guessing which ten percent. It would be the blonde area generally enclosed by silk panties. "She's here to sing with the band."

Oh, wow, Mike thought disgustedly. That's all we need, man, a *vocalist.* A little yellow canary to perch on the stand and snatch a share of the profits for her off-key warbling. Casanova goofs again.

"All right, let's get on with the audition," Dino said, flaunting his Fearless Frontman authority. "What would you like to sing?" He offered Darleen the folder and she picked "I'll Walk Alone." Maybe she could sing alone too, but not against competition. The band drowned her out completely. When Dino said, "Hey, that was great, you really put it over," even Darleen didn't believe him.

"The music was too loud. I'm sure nobody could hear me on a dance floor. I could hardly hear myself."

132

"Oh, well, the acoustics are lousy in here. It's totally different in a hall with a PA system. You'll knock 'em dead. What do you say guys, isn't she great?"

"Let's try it again with mutes," Mike said.

"Oh, hell, she's fine, you heard her."

"All I heard was horns. Now I want to hear *her*. That's the purpose of an audition."

The muted brass still drowned her. On the third try, backed only by rhythm, she finally came through. Not much of a range, some trouble with high notes, but she put out a fair delivery with some of the husky sexy tone that helped to sell a song. With practice and a PA she might not disgrace them. But Mike couldn't see any reason to sign her to a lifetime contract. He turned to Johnny and muttered, "Don't call us, we'll call you." Johnny nodded. Before Dino could make any rash proposals, Johnny cut in tactfully. "Thanks very much for coming over. We'll let you know our decision in a few days."

Darleen said, "Sure," in a very unconcerned voice. She didn't seem to care if she got the job or not, which struck Mike as odd. If she didn't care, why bother to try out? Big waste of everybody's time.

"Stick around, I'll drive you home," Dino said. Darleen and her still anonymous girlfriend sat down on the sofa while Dino called up the best "Body and Soul" type sax number in the book and kicked it off too fast, standing up and looking important. As soon as he sat down, Johnny eased to a better tempo. Dino honked to his heart's content, surpassing himself in mediocrity, eyes shut, cheeks puffed, lip loose and tone gravelly. While his eyes were shut, Darleen and friend rose and let themselves quietly out the front door without saying good-bye, though Darleen did pause on the threshold to give them all a parting smile. Mike nearly cracked up, but he managed to keep on playing. When Dino looked around for applause and saw the empty couch, Mike let out the big laugh.

"Your canary bird has flown, man. She couldn't stand your lousy ad libs either."

Dino's face was red from blowing; it went still redder. "Well, that little—" He broke off and shrugged. "Oh, well, I'll see her later."

After practice Mike, Johnny, and Dino stayed to discuss the

vocalist question. "Forget it," Mike advised. "We don't need her. She can't sing."

"Sure she can sing," Dino insisted. "She was nervous tonight, her first time with a band. But she's just what we need. Every professional band has a girl singer, you know that. She'll give us some class. That kid is loaded with sex appeal."

"She didn't appeal to me."

Dino snorted. "Of course not, cookie, she's the wrong sex for you. She appeals to *me*, and that's what counts."

"Yeah, I'll bet. You promised her a singing job so you could get into her pants, and now you have to pay off."

"That's a lie! I never promised her nothing. I can make it with Darleen whenever I care to, no promises necessary."

"Then screw her on your own time and leave the band out of it. We don't need more people."

"Oh, hell, don't be so greedy. Splitting ten ways instead of nine makes it easier to figure. And she lives right up the street from me. I can pick her up easy for practice and jobs. Look, Johnny, how about it? I say yes, Mike says no, so what do you say?"

Johnny was sitting a little bit out of it, tapping soft cadences on his snare while Mike and Dino battled it out. Appealed to at last, he offered his thoughtful opinion. "We could let her try with us next Saturday. If the customers like her, we can sign her up. I think we owe her that much chance."

"You're making a mistake. You're asking for trouble. That dame will bust the band wide open."

Dino grinned. "She's got just the bust to do it with, man. Wait till you see her dressed up."

Saturday night they met at the Schultzes', as usual, to consolidate into two cars. Johnny, the dispatcher, had established a tidy system: five people in Dino's Model A, four plus drums in the Schultz Plymouth, same people in same car every time for maximum black-market mileage with minimum fuss and nobody left behind. It had worked fine up till now. Tonight the Plymouth was loaded, all sidemen present and ready to go, only waiting upon the arrival of Fearless Frontman and his new pet canary. Uh-huh, Mike thought, I knew it. That's how it'll be with a girl in the band. Everybody stands around freezing their balls off while she spends an hour to curl her eyelashes.

When the Ford showed up a good ten minutes late, Darleen jumped out and rushed over to Johnny. "I'm riding with you. He drives like a maniac and his heater is broken, it's twenty below zero in that car."

Dino came charging after her. "You're cold? Hell, baby, I can remedy that problem single-handed. Come on."

"No, thanks! I don't trust single-handed drivers and I wouldn't trust your driving even with three hands on the wheel. I ride with Johnny or I don't go."

Johnny looked confused. "Well, listen, we've already got a load. You'd better—" Dino gave her an angry look and stalked back to his car, where his other regular passengers were boarded and waiting. He slammed the door and gunned the motor.

"Hey, *wait* a minute!" Johnny yelled too late. The Ford was off in a blast of steamy exhaust. "Oh, hell, now what do we do? We can't put five in here."

"See, what'd I tell you?" Mike didn't bother to lower his voice. "Trouble already. Leave her home, we don't need her."

"I can't do that, not now."

Mike shrugged. "You figure it out then." He climbed into his established place, front seat shotgun, and left Johnny and Mel and Frye to solve it among them. They asked for trouble, they got trouble. Anybody could see there was only room for three guys in front and one in back with the drums. The trunk was full of horns and stands. Everything fit with shoehorn accuracy, no room for a temperamental excess blonde.

The other four stood looking at each other, waiting for inspiration. Suddenly Frye and Mel seemed to reach the same conclusion. They both made a jump for the back seat; Mel won. "Sorry chum, better luck next time." Frye climbed over Mike to straddle the gearshift.

"You could go around," Mike said.

"You could move over."

"Like hell I could. This is my place, I always sit by the window." The next thing he knew, Darleen plunked herself right down on his lap. "Hey! What's coming off here?"

"What's the matter, Mike?" Mel said. "Would you rather hold the bass drum instead?"

Well, he just as soon would, but he knew he couldn't say so. Anything he said would be playing right into the hands of the dirty jokesters. But what timing, what an unfailing instinct for troublemaking this girl had. The only guy in the band who didn't particularly want her, he was the lap she picked to land on for a ten-mile ride. Thank God she didn't weigh much. She was just a little thing, quite a bit smaller than Joyce. But even a hundred pounds of cute little petiteness radiated a lot of heat in a closed and crowded car. When he tried to open the window, Darleen complained immediately. "Don't do that. It's freezing outside and the wind will mess up my hair." She put her hand over his on the window crank and they squabbled a bit before he grudgingly closed it.

"Oh, we certainly can't have our petite little new vocalist arrive at the dance looking windblown, can we? Better that our old first trumpet should arrive drenched in sweat. *He* doesn't matter, nobody ever looks at him."

"Well, you could take off your overcoat if you're that hot."

"I could if you let me move my arm."

She slid forward on his knees while he struggled with the coat, not an easy job with four people in the seat and no room to maneuver. Then she twisted around to help him. "Raise up and I'll pull it out from under you." How in the heck could he raise up with her on top of him? In spite of her help, he finally wriggled out and threw the coat back on Mel and the drums.

"There, now are we all comfy?"

She might be, but he wasn't. He was hotter, if anything, after those silly acrobatics. Ten more miles of this? Usually he loved out-of-town jobs; they seemed so much more professional than Girl Reserve dances and the Teen Canteen. This ballroom tonight wasn't the Hollywood Palladium, obviously, or they wouldn't be booking the Johnny Dean Orch, but it was a real commercial place.

"You're right," Darleen said suddenly. "It is warm in here. Would you mind—?" She gestured for help with her rat-fur jacket.

Then she proceeded to snuggle back against his chest (and she just complained she was hot?). She wiggled around trying to

136

make herself comfortable. And there Mike was, trapped, with her upswept blond curls tickling his cheek and her perfume rising in waves strong enough to knock him out. First time in his life a girl on his lap, and what a girl to start with, radiating sex appeal out of a low-cut strapless green formal. Dating Joyce was *nothing* like this. He never saw Joyce in a formal, but he could bet it would have puffed sleeves, or at least shoulder straps, and a full skirt with layers of net over a lining. Darleen's dress was slinky green fish scales all over and it fit her like a mermaid's tail with hardly greater coverage, very low in back and dangerously low in front. He could look over her shoulder and right straight down the slot if he cared to; the way she was sitting he couldn't help it. With those bare white shoulders pressed back against his chest and the mermaid tail slithering around on him and the waves of heat and the perfume and the curls and the view down the cleft, and no place to put his arms except around her ... well, holy Jesus Christ, what else could you *expect?*

Boiiinnggg.

He sat there hard up with steam coming out of his ears, uncertain whether to laugh or cry. Jesus! He always knew he was perfectly normal. He knew it no matter how Dino and those wise guys tried to scare him. He knew he only needed the right girl to turn him on. Well, he'd just met her. Darleen Verbeck turned him on but good. Dino should see him now. It settled the old question once and for all, but it raised a hoard of new ones. Like, for instance, how in hell could he survive eight more miles of this car ride?

The suspense was killing him.

The next question, did this gal know what she was doing to him? He thought she did. He was, in fact, pretty sure of it. She was doing it deliberately, teasing him and laughing because what could he do about it, trapped in a car with three other guys and a set of drums on the way to a job? Jesus, what a girl. No wonder Dino promised to let her sing. For this kind of come-on he'd promise her the world on a string, anything, anything to get her pants off.

By the time they reached the ballroom Mike was ready to take a flying dive into the nearest snowbank. He survived the first few sets in a sort of stupor, dropping mutes and missing entrances.

137

Dino said, "We have a request for Thirty-seven," and Mike asked "What number is Thirty-seven?"

" 'I'll Walk Alone.' "

"Yeah, but what *number* is it?"

"Thirty-*seven*, dumbhead."

"Oh, okay," Mike said. Then he caught on and grinned, sheepishly, while Dino gave him a hopeless look and everybody laughed. Darleen's voice carried nicely over the PA. How well she sang didn't seem to matter so much anymore because she looked like a million bucks in that slinky formal with her hair piled on top of her head, a sexy pinup girl for the boys to dream about. She walked alone with a soulful throb in her voice, lonely but true-blue to her absent lover. *You will like hell walk alone*, Mike thought as he punctuated her vows with cup-muted figures. *Not you, doll, it couldn't happen.* But every air base soldier on the dance floor believed she was singing straight to him personally, saving herself for him, promising him her everlasting devotion. They applauded her song and some of them whistled. She gave them all a big toothpaste smile as she left the microphone and sat down beside Dino's end of the sax row.

Two unattached fly-boys began hanging around the band-stand. At intermission they wanted to buy Darleen drinks and teach her how to navigate by starlight. She kidded with them and might have gone further, but Dino broke it up. "Sorry, men, you can't handle the merchandise." Since he was bigger than either of them, they wandered off making sarcastic remarks to each other. "This is what we're fighting to protect? Gee, I wish I was a four-F musician." Dino took Darleen into a corner and talked to her earnestly. Mike couldn't tell if he was advising her about band-stand etiquette and customer relations or reminding her whose girl she was supposed to be. Well, there wasn't any ring on her finger. Vocalists were supposed to charm the customers. Darleen could smile at anybody she cared to, soldier, civilian or sideman, and if Dino didn't like it, he could go screw himself.

Mike had his own private plans in that department, if Darleen's cozy traveling tactics meant what he thought they did. He was cool now, able to play right and think straight, and he tried not to anticipate the trip home because he didn't want to start aching again. But every time he looked up from the music there she was just a few feet away from him, ahead and to the

138

right, just out of reach, the smooth white neck and shoulders and back merging into the V of shiny green fish-scale sequins. She didn't sing many numbers, which was smart, not having rehearsed them. Mostly she just sat and looked at the crowd, flashing a smile when anyone glanced her way, a special smile for anyone in khaki. It must be kind of boring for her, Mike thought, but she didn't look bored. On the jump numbers she tapped her silver sandals and moved a little as if she would rather be dancing than sitting them out. Like Joyce . . . but nothing like Joyce otherwise. Darleen was a thousand times sexier than Joyce Reynolds ever dreamed of being.

When Mike stood up for "Stardust," she turned around to watch him. He looked down once and almost gliched a note, then pulled his gaze sharply away and stared at the ceiling. A big glass ball hung from the center of the roof, turning slowly while a hundred little mirrors scattered stars around the walls and ceiling. That's what stardust looked like. And this was how it sounded as it drifted slowly down, warmer than snow, softer than rain, sweeter than a shower of spring apple blossoms. Powdered memories of what he once had, of what he never had, of what he might someday be lucky enough to have—a beautiful Bach trumpet and a beautiful mermaid girl, both of them built to be held in his hands and kissed and caressed and made love to the best way he could, with heart and soul and body and breath. He might have been slow to realize it, but he knew what he wanted now. Just two things, two lovely things—Darleen and the Sleeping Beauty. Either one was not enough. He would get them both somehow or blow his brains out trying.

After the dance he pitched right in to help Johnny load the Plymouth. It was hard to fold down music fronts and carry out drums while Darleen was bidding fond farewells to the troops and fooling around with Mel at the piano, playing four-handed "Chopsticks" and "Heart and Soul." But he had to do it because it fit his plans. He personally took care of the back seat arrangements, making sure to hollow out a private little nest among the drums, just room enough for two to be as cozy as one, with a little maneuvering space and no sharp cymbal edges to slice his ribs during the long, lovely, continuous, uninterrupted ten-mile necking session. It would be a tight fit, but so much the better; that's just the way he wanted it. If he put a foot through

139

Johnny's snare head he'd pay for the damn thing. It'd be worth it. Mel could ride shotgun to fend off the Indians. Those three clowns could keep their eyes on the road and talk about the weather, or if they wanted to eavesdrop it was okay with him, he didn't care. He'd give them something new to joke about. Nobody would call him cookie after this trip.

And Darleen would find out what kind of dynamite she was fooling with when she teased Mike Riley. If she'd never kissed a trumpet player before, she would learn the facts of life tonight but fast. He might be a long, skinny drink of water, but he had muscle where it counted, the best-developed embouchure *she'd* ever puckered up to. Embouchure, man, embouchure, the method of applying lips and tongue to the mouthpiece of a wind instrument, or what every good trumpet man knows. He could kiss the hell out of a trumpet and he could kiss the hell out of Darleen Verbeck with lips and tongue and any old way she liked it, sustained for as long as she wanted it. Long notes and high notes, he had them both, with vibrato and fast fingering if it came to that—as it easily might if she let him and the trip lasted long enough. He was all warmed up and ready to give her consecutive hot choruses for the rest of the night. By the score or ad lib, any way she wanted to play it.

"Come on, get in," Johnny said. "You going to stand here talking to yourself all night?"

Mike pushed down a small shudder of anticipation and wet his lips. His stomach felt funny, the way it did just before he stood up to play a hot takeoff, wondering how it would come out, how it would sound, would it succeed or fizzle away? Mel was sitting in the middle front seat, leaving the shotgun position open. Mike looked quickly around the empty parking lot. "Where's—everybody else?"

"Frye's coming in a minute, he went to the can. Darleen left with Dean. We'll have plenty of room going back."

"With Dean!" Mike yelled, and felt his stomach start to dissolve. "She said she wouldn't ride with him! She couldn't stand his wild driving and his busted heater."

Johnny shrugged. "I guess she changed her mind. Woman's privilege, like they say. She's a pretty good singer, huh? Those soldiers really liked her. What do you think, should we hire her permanently?"

"I don't care."

"Well, you were the one against it. Did you change your mind too?"

Mike cleared his throat and spit into the snow. "I said I don't care. Suit yourself. Take her if you want her."

V

EVERYBODY said that little Dorothy Lee Verbeck ought to be in the movies. She was such a darling with her big blue eyes and bobbing yellow curls as she pouted through a chorus of the "Good Ship Lollipop." Personally Dorothy Lee detested and despised Shirley Temple. Those cutesy songs made her want to throw up, but doting relatives were generous with dimes, ice cream and birthday presents. Every Saturday morning from age six she took tap and ballet at the Rainbow Dance Studio, upstairs over the grocery across from the Royal Theater. At ten she was a thoroughly bored Rainbow Junior Rockette in pink rouge and lipstick and star-spangled tights, scheming how to switch to the accordion or at least baton twirling. She liked the dance costumes and makeup, but recitals occurred only once a year while Saturday morning came around every week. She knew better places to waste it than a stuffy dance studio. In the drugstore, for instance, reading movie magazines. She never bought them, but sometimes her older sister did, and passed them on to her later with all the Nelson Eddy pictures cut out. Dorothy Lee thought Nelson Eddy stank. She preferred rugged brunet men like Clark Gable.

She was going on eleven and coming home from school one afternoon when Dino Castagnola whistled at her as she passed his house. She didn't stop walking, but she sort of slowed down because she was so surprised.

"Hey, Dorothy Lee, where ya going?"

She said pertly, "Crazy, want to come along?" Her sister, Margaret, was fifteen and she knew all the answers to give to boys who whistled. But Dino must be kidding her. She knew she wasn't anywhere near whistleable material yet, not in school clothes anyway. In Margaret's old formal and high heels and lipstick she looked pretty sexy in the mirror, but nobody else would know that, including Margaret, and certainly not Dino.

He got up off his porch steps and came over to meet her. "Pretty smart, aren't you? I got something you'd like in my garage."

"No, you don't either. What?"

"Something real nice. I wouldn't show it to just anybody. You probably never seen anything like it in your whole life."

"Bring it out here then."

"I can't, you have to go in there."

"Unh-unh."

He shrugged. "Okay, suit yourself," and started to walk back up the driveway.

"Is there really something in there?"

"You'll never know if you don't take a look." He kept walking away slowly.

"I bet it's just a car."

"You'll never know."

Curious now in spite of herself, she followed him up the driveway. A car in the garage would be Dino's idea of a joke. On the other hand, it could be something interesting, newborn puppies or kittens. Or rabbits or white mice for all she knew. Dino was one of the big guys, the eighth graders who played ball in the street and hung around the front of the drugstore making smart remarks when a girl walked by. Big girls, that is, not fifth graders of the hopscotch-and-paper-doll set. He'd never given her the time of day before.

She followed him inside and he shut the door again behind her, probably so that whatever it was wouldn't escape. There was no car, just a big black oil spot on the floor where it ought to be, and all the other usual garage stuff, bicycles, lawn mower, stacks of old newspapers, boxes and paint cans. No puppies or interesting animals. Well, she knew all along he was kidding.

"So where's this great thing you've got?"

144

"Right here," he said.

"Oh." She took one startled look and started to walk out, but he stepped in the way of the door.

"I told you it was something like you never saw before."

"I've seen them before," she said without much confidence. She had and she hadn't. She had seen little boys peeing in bushes and she had seen pictures of statues with and even without fig leaves. But Dino's equipment looked awfully big and ugly, not hanging down limp like a statue but sticking out sort of swollen and angry red like an infected sore. He seemed to be proud of it. "Touch it," he said. "Right there."

She shook her head, revolted but fascinated. It was like seeing a run-over cat in the street—she didn't want to look, but she couldn't help looking.

"You want to see something else interesting?"

No, she thought, but she said, "What?"

"Take your pants off."

"No, unh-unh." She didn't need to see what *she* had; she'd seen it. Or hadn't, rather, because there was nothing to see, certainly nothing to compare with this.

"Oh, come on. I showed you, now you show me, that's only fair. I'm not going to do anything. I just want to see if you're old enough to, uh, join the club."

"What club?"

"You know, the big kids' gang. We play some real neat games. I bet you'd like to play with us."

Wouldn't she, though? The big kids on the block played out almost every night until after dark, kick the can, punch the icebox and other games that she knew less about, the whole gang scuffling and giggling inside a locked garage or someone's basement with the lights off. Margaret told her about one good game with a make-believe killer and victim and a detective to solve the crime. "You mean like murder?"

"Better than that, lots better. I'll teach you how, but first you have to show me that you're grown-up enough to play."

She knew there was something wrong about this. Nice girls didn't show anybody their underpants, let alone what was inside them. Margaret never mentioned any games like *that*. But of course she wouldn't, would she? Margaret knew a lot of things she wouldn't tell, like about brassieres and Kotex and what f——

meant, and she was awfully stingy about letting anybody try on her clothes or use her perfume or even bath salts. Later, she always said. Later, when you're older. You're too young now.

But Dino thought she was old enough and he wanted to let her join the gang.

"Come on, please, just try it once. I bet you a dime that you'll like it. Here, see—here's the dime. The name of the game is, uh, Screwdriver. If you play it with me and win, you win the dime. In fact, even if you lose, you can have the dime after, just for trying, okay?"

A dime would buy two double-dip cones or three Hershey bars or a movie magazine. And she had it either way. Win or lose, she still got the dime if Dino kept his promises.

"Sure, come on, that's it. Take 'em off and let me see. It's just a game, I'm not going to hurt you or anything—"

She froze. The word "hurt" was the tip-off. She had heard that line so many times before, in the dentist's office, the doctor's office. When grown-ups said coaxingly, "This won't hurt a bit, now open your mouth—" or "Hold your arm still—" it *always* hurt, you could bet on it every time. "Open your mouth for the medicine, it doesn't taste bad—" but it always did, ugh, horrible. They always coaxed and lied when they wanted to get something into you, a tooth drill or a doctor's needle or a spoonful of castor oil. Dino was pretty grown up and he had already lied once. If *that* nasty thing was what he figured on sticking into her somehow, after she took her pants off for him—"I'm not going to *do* anything, I'm not going to *hurt* you—" then of course it would hurt. She knew it and he knew it too, that's why he was coaxing and lying with that funny guilty smile on his face. She didn't know how he thought he could do it or why, it didn't even sound possible. Inside her pants? Like an enema? Ugh. What kind of crazy game would this be? All she could think of was dogs, two dogs on the street climbing on each other and Margaret saying don't look, it's nasty. Suddenly she knew exactly what Dino's game was going to be, and she knew he wasn't going to let her go home until she played it. He could make her do it. He was as big as a man, fourteen or fifteen years old, too old for eighth grade because he'd flunked a year, everybody knew that. He picked on little girls half his size when he couldn't find anybody else willing to play his game. How much would it hurt? she wondered. Worse

146

if she fought and he knocked her down on that oily concrete floor. But maybe. . . .

She took a breath. "All right. I'll play if you give me the dime first."

He handed it over.

"Now you shut your eyes just a minute while I take them off."

And while he stood there like a big stupid idiot with his eyes shut and his dirty eager smile, she ducked for the door and jerked it open and ran. He yelled, "Hey, wait!" but she didn't wait. She was clear down the driveway before he could get his pants buttoned up, and across the street before he started chasing her. She knew she was a fast runner. He yelled, "Hey, wait a minute!" but he couldn't chase her all the way to the drugstore.

She spent the dime for a chocolate soda. She stayed an hour and read all the movie magazines for free and then walked home on the other side of the street.

In sixth grade she changed her name. "Dorothy Lee" was so dumb and childish; it sounded like the Wizard of Oz ("Please sir, which way to the Emerald City?") But "Darleen" sounded like Hollywood, exotic and glamorous like gardenia perfume and Stop Red nail polish. Miss Darleen Verbeck sent twenty-five cents to Kotex to learn about growing up in a plain wrapper. The wrapper was plainer than the story inside. It hedged quite a bit and left out the most urgent and interesting facts, like how long did it take to do it, and how did it feel, and what did sperms and eggs have to do with letting boys kiss you but not unhook your bra in the movies (and she herself almost twelve years old with neither bra nor boyfriend!)? But she figured out the relevance of Castagnola's garage. She knew what Dino was trying to do, though she didn't suppose he wanted a baby any more than she did, and she didn't even like dolls. But he sure picked a dumb approach, offering her money and scaring her half to death. She wouldn't do it with him now for a dime or a dollar or a hundred thousand dollars. Not him.

In seventh grade she got the brassiere, with a little moral support from Margaret ("You'd better, Mother, she needs it") and started using Kotex privately and Tangee lipstick publicly. In eighth grade she took the social dancing class, much more fun than Rainbow Studio, and dated boys to movies with two strict parental limitations: only eighth-grade boys and only Saturday afternoon movies. Her mother didn't forbid unhooking bras, of course; how could a mother mention that? She just said, "Behave yourself," which Darleen did, one way or another. Nobody could possibly get into trouble at the Royal matinee, where the biggest dangers were flying popcorn and gum on the seats. She also played kick the can and murder with the twilight gang. While hiding behind garages and under backyard bushes, she got kissed a few times unexpectedly, but nobody tried seriously to take her pants off.

In ninth grade she went to Morton High, where Dean Castagnola was a flunking senior with a robin's-egg-blue Model A car. When he offered her lifts at the bus stop, she just laughed. She wouldn't be caught dead in that clunky old car or anyplace else with him. Everybody knew the kind of girls he dated. Darleen dated freshmen and sophomore boys who seemed pretty childish to her, more fond of football than dancing. She envied Margaret, nineteen now with a job and lots of pretty clothes and dates with soldiers, but still very stingy about sharing any of the wealth.

She was fifteen-going-on-twenty in the summer of '43 when she met Tex. She went to the downtown show one afternoon with her best friend Carole, feeling very romantic in a sexy low-necked blouse of Margaret's. Tex and his buddy moved in a flanking maneuver from opposite sides—"Pardon us, are these seats taken?"—and the girls were delighted to say no, they certainly weren't. It was any girl's patriotic duty to be nice to a man in uniform, particularly an Air Corps fly-boy, especially a cute corporal with a Southern drawl who even turned out good-looking by daylight. They drank Cokes at Walgreen's after the show and Tex spun long slow stories of his fantastic war experiences, although so far he hadn't been any nearer to fighting action than Darleen had. Someday he would go, she knew, and it was only right that he do his living and loving first, tomorrow being so uncertain.

Carole's soldier faded and was never seen again, but Tex and Darleen met at the show regularly for two months, sitting well back in unfrequented parts of the balcony. She halfway saw and halfway heard a lot of movies that she couldn't have described clearly afterward, while Tex taught her how to kiss and french-kiss Southern style and neck as heavily as possible within the

148

limitations of adjacent plush seats. He didn't actually get her pants off, but he got them far enough down to make it interesting. Darleen discovered sensations that she never suspected to be within her and Tex wound up cooling his ardor in the gentlemen's lounge. But he was no daring fly-boy, only a ground crew mechanic with more patience than fortitude. When his squadron moved in August, he had to say good-bye without ever once getting off the ground.

Having discovered the pleasures of patriotism, Darleen and Carole became volunteer USO hostesses, lying valiantly about their ages and wearing high heels and plenty of pancake makeup to look as old as they claimed to be. In the nonalcoholic, well-lighted, chaperoned service center they danced and played ping-pong with some very nice lonely boys. Nothing prevented them from going elsewhere afterward or making dates to go elsewhere another night with boys just as lonely but not quite so nice.

Darleen's favorite elsewhere, Roseland Gardens, was much more than just a ballroom. A big, privately operated park on the outskirts of town, it boasted a swimming pool and picnic grounds and a special woodsy area for nature lovers, variously known as the Virgin Timber and the Cherry Orchard. On her second trip out she dated an Air Corps lieutenant, twenty years old with fortitude to burn. Amid the soft grass and chirping crickets and the distant orchestra weaving "That Old Black Magic," Darleen was more than eager to take up her recently neglected education and compare necking techniques. Charlie kissed nicely, she thought, with a slight flavor of spearmint preferable to Tex's strong Dentyne. And he had nice hands, very skillful. When her pants slipped clear off, she never even noticed, but the cool grass felt nicer than theater plush and gave them much more room to maneuver. Just when the first real shivers began to follow his hand up and down the inside of her legs, he stopped. She was about to tell him that he needn't quit yet, when she realized that he hadn't. Long before the point where Tex always excused himself to make a dash for the men's room, leaving her with a tingling suspicion that life could be beautiful, Hotshot Charlie just climbed into the cockpit and revved his throttle, switch off, contact and into the wild blue yonder. Well, of course he couldn't do *that*. But she was flat on her back at forty thousand feet and he was right on top of her and inside of her, holding her arms so she

149

couldn't move and kissing her so she couldn't yell. She wriggled and tried to pull away, but that didn't even slow him down. By this time it didn't matter; he had zeroed in on target and she was going down in flames. She knew she was trapped and she might as well give up. No sense fighting the inevitable, they always said. Relax and enjoy it.

Some time later she got up off the grass and pulled her dress down and hunted around for her underpants in the dark, wondering where they could have flown to or if she'd have to go home without them. She found them hanging on a bush and put them on while Charlie pulled himself together and put on his uniform jacket. Then they walked back to the ballroom, where the orchestra was playing "He Wears a Pair of Silver Wings." She knew her dress was all over wrinkles and probably grass stains shouting to the world where she'd been if it didn't show plain enough on her face. But neither of them felt like dancing now, so they soon left. He rode with her as far as her stop but stayed on the bus to continue downtown and transfer out to the air base. Buses ran pretty seldom after ten o'clock and God knows when he would have caught another; he couldn't be late on his pass.

She had only a couple of blocks to walk alone. Under the circumstances it seemed silly to worry what might happen to her on the way home from the bus stop. And just as well that Charlie didn't get off; she couldn't be seen coming home with a soldier. Her folks thought she was at Carole's tonight, just as Carole's folks thought *she* was at Darleen's, and heaven help them if anybody started comparing notes. She wondered if Carole was still dancing or if she'd found a different spot to count stars. That would be pretty funny, wouldn't it, both of them on the same night? But Carole wouldn't have done it. Carole would be shocked if she knew. "Boy, that was a dumb thing to do! Why'd you let him? What if you get—you know, or what if he had some awful disease and you caught it? Oh, boy, Darleen, you shouldn't have let him, you should have stopped."

Yes, I *know*, she said to the absent Carole as her heels clicked anxiously along the last block. High heels scared her, always off-balance, tilting forward, ready to twist an ankle and fall on her nose. But she had to wear them, flats were childish. . . . Yes, I *know*. It's easy for you to say why didn't you stop. Just try stopping a soldier sometime. It's just as easy as getting off the roller coaster

150

halfway down the first slope. First you don't want to stop and then you can't stop and then it's all over. Done is done, over the bridge and under the dam so forget it.

Well, she lucked out, beginner's luck. She didn't catch anything and she didn't get caught, but it scared her into caution. She stayed in the clean bright lights of the USO center and refused all dates to Roseland while the grass grew green in the Virgin Timber. She never saw Charlie again. He probably got shipped out, like old Tex, who still wrote occasional sloshy, illiterate letters. But there were other soldier boys in need of dancing partners. Some danced as if they were driving an Army truck across the battlefield, damn the artillery, full speed ahead! Some couldn't dance at all, but they didn't know it; they muttered, "Sorry," as they stepped on her aching feet. Some danced by remote control, holding her like spun glass and blushing to the roots of their crew cuts if her breast should touch their jackets in the course of an innocent turn. There were the Fred Astaire hotshots who jitterbugged wildly on fast tunes and broke into exotic tropical tangos on the slow ones. And the wolves in GI clothing who danced every number in a close tight clutch, pasting themselves against her all the way from shoulder to knee, cheek to cheek and breathing heavily in her ear, reminding her with their eager bodies that dancing was only the vertical indoor prelude to Charlie's horizontal maneuvers on the Roseland grass.

As time went by and memories blurred, her good resolutions began to soften. She thought of Roseland's big smooth dance floor, the soft colored lights and live professional music, a much lovelier place to spend an evening. Safe, too, if you kept your feet on the floor and stayed out of the Virgin Timber. She was older and wiser now. She'd lost it, but she knew the score. She could take care of herself with any man now.

Soldiers were glamorous, but civilians made better dates. They had more free evenings, more money to spend, and best of all, they owned cars—cars with radios and heaters and comfortable seats, a place to sit privately when Jack Herron's band took its long intermission and the ballroom was smoky, the outside air a bit too crisp and the grass buried deep under snow or mud. In a car she could sit and sip beer and listen to Dorsey or Rhodes on the radio and neck as much as she felt like necking, depending on how nice the guy was and how worthwhile he made it. If the outside temperature grew too cold or the internal passion too hot, she could quit right there—cool it, friend, I'll see you later—and go back inside to dance again, keeping it clean and vertical.

The ride home sometimes got pretty sticky. A guy who had been dancing too close for too long couldn't help wanting to express himself. If he insisted on driving way out into the country to park on a deserted road—no fooling now, baby, put out or get out—well, ten miles through the snowy night is too far for a girl to walk home. And what, after all, did she have to lose? Some men went to a lot of trouble and expense to pave the way. It really seemed heartless to turn them down, ungrateful after such a pleasant evening. It wasn't much trouble to give them what they wanted. Especially when she had no choice.

The nicest civilian she ever met was Ernie Stanton, a welder with a dark blue 1942 Hudson, the last model off the prewar line. He was pretty old, at least twenty-five. Not the handsomest man in the world, on the short side, broad-shouldered and strong as a wrestler. But Ernie had unexpected class; he really knew how to give a girl a good time. On the first night they met they drove clear to Omaha and ate dinner at the Paxton Hotel, danced there and again later at a nightclub west of town where he bought her real whiskey highballs, much nicer than beer. They wound up in a classy motel. Then Darleen realized for the first time why people get married—for inner-sprung smooth-sheeted comfort and the complete privacy behind a locked bedroom door. No scuffling around with zippers and bra hooks and pulled-down pants, furtive hole-and-corner necking that anyone might see through a car window. No hurry, no worry, just all the way up the long winding path to cloud nine. Ernie had something that Tex and Charlie and the young 4-F's and fly-boys lacked. He had patience *and* fortitude. He took about an hour at it and he really rang her chimes. It was like following chalk arrows drawn on the sidewalk, at first plain white and then longer and fancier and drawn with prettier colors—this way, this way, don't get lost, keep coming, but not too fast, it'll wait for you, this way, around the corner and straight ahead to reach the buried treasure chest, the pot of gold at the end of the rainbow. She didn't know if it was Ernie or the bed that made the difference, but she approved the combination wholeheartedly.

Going out with Ernie twice a week undetected was only a slight

152

problem, nothing she couldn't manage. Everyone in her family was working now, her father on day shift and her mother and brother on swing; Margaret had married a soldier and moved out. In the general coming and going and clanking of lunch pails, Darleen's own movements went largely unnoticed. She and Carole had been living in each other's houses for eight years, providing ready alibis for all occasions. Her folks thought she went to the USO on Friday nights and stayed overnight with Carole afterward to avoid coming home alone. Sometimes she actually did that. But Friday was usually Ernie's night for the first-class trip, dinner in Omaha or Lincoln, dancing or a show and always the cloud nine finale.

Once a week wasn't enough. On Tuesdays they met for a shorter encore in a friendly tavern, then on to the Riverbend Motel, their handy home away from home with carpeted floors and bathroom glasses wrapped in sanitary tissue "for your protection." They could take their time and undress completely like proper married people on a honeymoon. Ernie looked at her admiringly and told her what a beautiful body she had, so slim and lovely, such nice skin, until she began to shiver with anticipation before he even touched her. Then he turned off the light and made love that was really love, not just selfish what's-in-this-for-me but real passionate honest-to-God love, as if his only concern was to make her happy. It was beautiful while it lasted.

But she couldn't relax and fall asleep in that comfortable motel bed. They always had to get up and go back to town in the cold dark night, divorced before their wedding night was half over. If Ernie had proposed to her after one of those cloud nine sessions, she would have been tempted to say yes. She knew she was awfully young to think of marriage—only sixteen, with years of fun ahead of her—but he was such a sweet guy and so great in bed that she just might consider it. So he was ten years older than she was, so what? He didn't know she was sixteen and she certainly wouldn't tell him yet in case it made him nervous about taking her into bars. Lots of girls faked their ages to get a drink.

It turned out, actually, that Ernie also had faked his age a little bit. He was really thirty-two and told her twenty-six because he thought she'd like it better. She could forgive that. Who cared, as long as they loved each other? But that wasn't the only thing he'd lied about or carefully neglected to mention. His last name wasn't Stanton, it was Stanislaus. And he was married. *And* the father of three children. *And* the youngest child was exactly ten days old at the time all these news flashes came off the press. What's more, he dearly loved his wife and hadn't the faintest intention of leaving her.

Darleen just about dropped dead. She couldn't believe it. She could not believe that any man could be that sweet on the surface and such a thoroughly downright rubber heel inside, to cheat so wildly on his wife and deceive his girlfriend and then claim it was done out of loving consideration. When he finally decided to confess, he confessed all very frankly. He said that on the night he met her he'd had a minor spat with Mildred, who was at that time eight months pregnant, big as a house, exhausted with cares and touchy as hell to live with just then, although generally as sweet and lovable a woman as you could ever hope to meet. Millie more or less told him to get lost—not really meaning it, you know, just feeling overwrought by circumstances—and Ernie, who had had a bad day at the plant, stomped out to cool off and met Darleen instead. One thing led to another and there they suddenly were in bed, where Darleen could give him everything that Millie temporarily couldn't and wouldn't. Being only human, he followed through. But he liked Darleen so much that he couldn't tell her how it was because he knew she would tell him to get lost too. It was all his own fault, he admitted it frankly. His fault entirely, a rotten lousy thing to do and he was sorry now, sorry as hell, ashamed of his weakness. But she saw how it was, didn't she? He really loved Millie and always had; nothing could ever come between them permanently. She'd had a rough time delivering her third, nearly scared him spitless. Now that the baby was born (another girl, three girls in four years, he couldn't seem to father a son), he wouldn't dream of cheating on her any longer and of course he didn't have to. He hoped Darleen could understand and forgive him, but in any case she'd have to forget him because he couldn't see her again.

It made her sick, the whole business. What if he'd gotten *her* pregnant too, as he might well have? My God, three kids in four years, he was pretty good at hitting the mark. Suppose she had to marry him and couldn't, a fine mess that would be. Luckily she needn't sweat over that nasty possibility, because she was having the curse just last week when dear Millie was delivering her third and poor old Ernie couldn't find himself a lay anywhere then, tough luck for him.

She understood all right, but if he thought he could weasel out so easy, he was crazy. When she told him how old she really was, Ernie turned green and nearly passed out. "*Six*teen! Christ, you can't be!" Then she knew how to fix his wagon. With him so very married and her so very underage and all those motel keepers to give evidence, she could really put him through the wringer. All she had to do was tell her folks or, better yet, tell Mildred where good old Ernie had been putting in his big fat overtime on Tuesdays and Fridays. That would fix him. He would end up divorced and disgraced and maybe in jail. . . . But what good would that do her? *She* didn't want to marry him. She wouldn't touch him now with a ten-foot pole. And by "telling all," she might incriminate herself on five or six counts because she had gone with him perfectly willingly; he hadn't enticed her or anything. Better to keep quiet and chalk it all up to experience. But she hoped that he sweated good and hard for a while, waiting to see what she would do.

She knew all about men now. Men were all alike. Soldiers, welders, high school boys, whether they were tall-handsome-and-conceited or short-sweet-and-married, they all wanted into her pants and they'd do just about anything to get there—lie, cheat, sweet-talk, offer money or push her down and shove it in. But if Ernie did one good thing for her, it was to raise her minimum standards of sex. She wouldn't do it in parked cars and bushes anymore. From now on, any man without enough class to take her to a nice motel—well, he could just forget it. She wasn't a gold digger. She wouldn't demand expensive dinners and dances and drinks (though they were nice), but a decent bed was an absolute must, a clean bed and a locked door. And not to share with just anybody, either. She would pick and choose very carefully to her own taste. Even if a guy had a Cadillac and a million bucks in his pocket and he offered her diamonds and a mink coat, if she didn't like his looks, forget it. He could take his Cadillac and stuff it.

In fact, she might just give up men altogether, period.

Her romance with Ernie began and ended in the spring. Through summer and fall she concentrated on the USO center as the best place to have fun. She knew how to handle soldiers. She could dance with them, tease them and lead them on all evening, making them jealous of each other, fighting for the chance to buy her Cokes. They knocked themselves out to coax her onto the fire escape. If she liked the guy's looks, she might go, because absolutely nothing dangerous could happen to a girl on the USO fire escape unless she fell off and broke her arm. They tried every trick to persuade her elsewhere. Out for a soda? Out for a drink? The movies? Swimming? How about Roseland for a nice floor and a real band, not this corny volunteer combo?

No, thank you, Sarge. Thanks a lot, but no thanks, not tonight.

Could the sergeant see her home? No, he couldn't, thanks so much. Little Darleen's new theme song was "I'll Walk Alone." When he asked why, she said she was engaged to a sailor overseas, saving herself for Jim. Sometimes she said she was engaged to a soldier who died in Italy, a real hero to whose memory she would always remain true, although she felt that working at the USO and cheering up other lonely boys in a platonic way was her patriotic duty and poor dear Bob would be the first to agree. A touching story, the sergeant thought. He kissed her more respectfully.

One night in late November she Walked Alone to the bus stop because Carole had gone home early with cramps. Darleen knew the schedule and caught her bus just right, with minimum exposure to wolves and chilly winds. Two blocks later who should get on but Dean Castagnola, rigged out fit to kill in a zooty-looking suit with a flower in his lapel and a tie to put your eye out, green and blue and purple splashes. There were twenty empty seats, but of course he sat down sociably beside her.

"What's the matter, did your car break down again or did you lose your license?"

"Neither," he said comfortably. "Just saving gas for my more essential purposes." She knew what his essential purposes were, driving girls into the country and coaxing them to put out. Ding-Dong Dino, the hot-rod expert—*he* thought. His rod was permanently hot, but he couldn't seduce a normally intelligent girl if the instructions came printed right on her pants. What he had to offer was nothing so special after all, nothing to brag and show off. Probably not even as big as it had once looked to her shocked inexperienced eyes. Nothing too big for her to handle now if she cared to, but she didn't care to. In fact, if Dino Castagnola were the last man on earth and she were the last woman, civilization would perish.

But he did have something new to brag of, or so he claimed. He had his very own dance band.

"Where do you play?"

"All over. School dances, the teen canteen, USO—"

"That's funny. I go to the USO a lot and I never saw you."

"Well, you must have missed us because we played for them four or five times since last summer. Maybe you didn't recognize the name Johnny Dean? That's my professional name, see. It's a real great band. . . ." He went on talking and bragging and probably lying about their wonderful past and future prospects. Poor old Dino, always trying to thrill the ladies with his hot rod and his hot sax and his clunky old turquoise blue car. So now he had a dance band. Biiig deal. ". . . Now that we play in such classy places, I been thinking of adding a girl vocalist. I sing ballads myself, of course, but a good-looking girl dresses up the band. Would you be interested, maybe?"

"Me? Well, I don't know, I never thought of it before—" She *had* thought of it occasionally. She could sing as well as most girls on the radio and plenty of guys had told her she was pretty enough to be in Hollywood. Not that she fell for that hairy old line—as if anybody in Connor City could promise her a screen test. She wasn't born yesterday. "I guess I could sing if I wanted to."

"I'll bet you could. If I like your style, I can hire you, but naturally I can't make no offers till I know how you perform." He let his hand drop carelessly on her leg for just a second, just long enough to be no accident. A big hand, thick-fingered, with a Morton senior ring. "Whaddaya say, shall we hold an audition?"

Ho, ho, ho. She recognized that pitch from somewhere else. It was the old dirty song with new cleaned-up lyrics for broadcasting. Hold an audition or join the club, it came to the same thing in the end. "Where?" she asked sweetly. "In your garage?"

Dean jerked as if he'd been kicked in a sensitive spot. She saw his mouth twist as if he wanted to say something nasty right back, but he thought better of it and smiled, pretending he didn't know what she meant. "No, at Johnny Schultz's place. That's where we rehearse now, Monday nights. I'll be happy to drive you over."

"That's all right. Just give me the address and I'll get myself there. If I decide to come, that is. I'll have to give it some thought."

She thought about it over the weekend, kicking the idea around in her mind, maybe yes, maybe no. Any band Dean led couldn't amount to much. If it were any good, she would have heard of it before at school. But singing with a band might be fun. A change, at least, something new to try, a chance to dress up in a sexy formal and give the boys a thrill without letting them paw the merchandise. Glamor and spotlight attention with no unpleasant aftertaste.

She could see the possibilities. Dean might think she would hand him her pants out of sheer gratitude for such a lovely chance—singing with your *dance* band! Oh, my goodness, I'm so thurillled! But she had news for Dean. Prices had gone up now, way waaaay up. Before she was finished, he would change his tune from bragging to begging, real down-on-his-knees-and-hard-up begging, but it wouldn't do him any good. Civilization would still perish. Let him find out the hard way, though. She outsmarted him when she was ten years old and she could still outsmart him any day of the week and twice on Monday.

VI

MIKE went shopping on the eve of Christmas Eve. Last chance for this year; the stores would close on Sunday, and Monday was Christmas. He saw that he had cut himself a little too close. The shelves were practically empty everywhere except for really hideous junk—flimsy rayon nightgowns, watered-down cologne, plastic kitchenware. But desperate husbands and boyfriends were grabbing it up and paying ready cash from their well-stuffed doubletime-overtime wallets. That was one of the horrors of war—plenty of money to spend and nothing good to spend it on.

Even Mike was flush today with thirty bucks in his pocket, his entire bankroll saved from band jobs. He might splurge five or even ten on a really nice present for Mom if he could find one. She never got anything else for Christmas except maybe a fifty-cent scarf in the annual office gift swap or a small box of candy from the boss. Those high-powered executives who showered Chanel No. 5 and nylons on their secretaries sure didn't try such wolfish tactics on Kathy Ashton; they knew they'd be wasting their time. But she deserved a decent gift, and this year, for a change, Mike could afford to see that she got it.

After examining a lot of crap that he wouldn't have taken home on a bet, he finally found a nice jewelry set of diamond pin and earrings. Fake diamonds, of course, for five dollars but classy, not glassy and gift-boxed too. Mom could wear them with her black dress when she went out reveling with Paul on New Year's Eve. *If* Paul asked her, that is, and *if* she accepted. Though where they could revel was another question, since she wouldn't drink and he couldn't dance. At the midnight movie, probably, after dinner at the Charles and music by Mickey Mouse and his orchestra.

The whole situation was very iffy; Mike didn't quite dig it. Paul seemed to be trying to promote himself gently from friend-of-the-family up to Kathy-Ashton's-boyfriend and maybe even eventual second husband, but no one could accuse him of whirl-wind tactics. As far as Mike knew, it all began last summer at the Sunday-night municipal band concerts when Paul shared the Ashtons' hillside blanket for the community sing afterward, chaperoned by Mike and/or half the population of Connor City. A courtship launched in this Gay Nineties atmosphere—white duck pants and Sousa marches, "Oh, My Darling Clementine," sulfur in the socks to discourage chigger bites and ice-cream cones on the homeward trip—could only be termed genteel and gentlemanly. Which, come to think of it, was exactly Mom's cup of tea. In the fall they fell into a habit of Saturday-night movie dates—unchaperoned now, Mike having his own fish to fry—with now and then a high school drama or church organ recital thrown in for variety. At the highest point of the season, their most bold and thrilling adventure to date, Paul drove her down to Lincoln to attend a symphony orchestra concert. Jerry would have split a gut laughing. Mike just grinned quietly to himself and let the old folks enjoy their little fling. At their advanced age, both pushing forty, who expected passion? Paul had probably forgotten what it felt like and Mom had forgotten for sure, no serious man in her life for more than ten years.

But Mike could have told them a thing or two about feeling passionate. He knew. Oh, man, did he know. Since the night Darleen Verbeck dropped into his life, he had learned one hell of a lot about aching guts and frustrated desires.

Darleen. Jesus, she could drive a guy straight up the wall! So sweet one minute, cozying up as if she really meant to let him in. And then turning right around to ignore him while she did the same for some other jerk, Dino or Mel or any soldier on the dance floor. At last night's job, the YW Snowball dance, a bunch of mistletoe decorations caused constant uproar as guys tried to

160

maneuver their girlfriends underneath. Nobody could coax Darleen to that spot; she didn't fall for it. But when the dance was over and the crowd all gone, just the band left to pack up, she deliberately stood on the fatal spot and said, "Form a line, gentlemen." They did, naturally, skidding across the waxed floor with whistles and wolf calls, Dino knocking everybody down to be first. She distributed kisses like Christmas candy canes, one to a customer, same identical treatment for everybody from big bad Dino straight down to little Johnny Mann, the fourteen-year-old trombone, who turned red as a beet and started giggling. Mike was so disgusted by this wholesale post office game that he didn't bother to fall into line. He kept on knocking down the music fronts until Mel called, "Hey, don't you want your Christmas present? She's got one left." Mike didn't answer, but Dino said, "Oh, hell, give it to me. Mike doesn't kiss *girls*."

Ho *ho*, Mike thought to himself, little do you know. He strolled over as if it didn't matter to him and gave Darleen a careless brotherly peck on the cheek. Then she flung her arms around his neck and really planted one on him, a real burner square on the mouth, ten times as much as she'd given anybody else. He responded as if he were shooting for the F above high C and held it until he ran out of breath. It was just exactly like trying for an impossible note seventeen ledger lines off the top of the staff, only this time he had hit it and it was beautiful, man, just beautiful.

He came out hot and dizzy with his ears ringing. Darleen looked at him dazedly like *wow, where did that come from?* The other guys were whistling and making cracks, and old Dino absolutely purple with envy because he only got a lousy penny candy cane while Mike walked off with the five-pound box of chocolates. Mike could have told him it was his own fault for studying the wrong instrument, learning to chew on a mouthpiece instead of kissing it properly. But he felt too good to start a fight. He reached up and took the mistletoe down—being ten feet tall, he could reach it easily—and put it in his pocket for future reference on the way home. But Darleen crossed him up again. She went off in Dino's car and left Mike with hot balls and ringing ears and a pocketful of dead leaves.

There was a beautiful gold necklace in the store jewelry case that would look great on Darleen, perfect with her mermaid dress and high hairdo. She would love it. But $19 was a fierce amount of money to spend on a girl. It would pretty nearly wipe out his bankroll and it might set a dangerous precedent. With inflated ideas of her own value Darleen would expect more little trinkets from him which he couldn't possibly supply. What would he do for an encore?

On his way to the bus he dropped by Hoffman and Franks to pay his respects to his other flame, the Bach Sleeping Beauty. Two lovely dolls in the world for him, two beautiful golden blondes, and both of them so expensive, so far out of reach that it broke his heart thinking about it. Neither of them would wait forever. The store was almost empty, just a couple of girls buying each other Sinatra records for Christmas. Mr. Hoffman always liked to hear the news of Johnny's band. Mike mentioned the Snowball and their terrific out-of-town booking for New Year's Eve. "A hundred-dollar job, would you believe it? That's *ten* apiece—minus gas, of course, and hotel money. We're staying overnight because it's sixty miles and Mr. Schultz won't let Johnny drive back so late with the drunks on the road. But a hundred-dollar job, isn't that great?"

"Yes, it sounds fine. Keep it up and you'll be able to buy the Bach before you know it."

Mike threw a wistful glance at Sleeping Beauty's cold glass coffin. "Not before *I* know it. I've been waiting too long." He wanted to ask for another chance to try her out, but he hardly dared. Hoffman knew how he felt. It would be ridiculous to pretend he hadn't made up his mind. And in a way he didn't want to touch her again until he was ready to pay the ransom and carry her off. Until he did, anybody in town could ask the same favor—hey, let me try her out, man, let's see what she can do. Any damn fool could walk in off the street and pick her up, stroke the engraved scrollwork along her bell, press his sweaty fingers on her pearl tits and blow his germy breath into her and *break her in.* Jesus! Mike felt sick thinking of it. That lovely virginal brand-new trumpet, straight from the factory, never owned, never played except in the politest sort of audition while Hoffman, the diligent chaperon, permitted not the slightest disrespect. She was waiting for *him* and nobody else should lay a hand on her first. He didn't even trust himself with her now. He wanted her too badly; he might get carried away and go too far, make love before the wedding night. Wait for me, baby, please wait.

162

Hoffman looked toward the two giggling girls in the record booth and then at his watch. "Business is slow today, I might close early. Make me an offer on the Bach, Michael."

It was almost a bad joke under the circumstances. But what the hell, what could he lose? He opened his billfold and spread all his cash on the counter, every cent down to the loose change. "Twenty-five eighty-seven and I walk home."

Hoffman pretended to give it serious consideration. "What have you got for a trade-in?"

That was easy. "My Holton. It's a very good horn, perfect condition, should be worth, oh, seventy-five bucks."

Hoffman thought a minute. "Why don't you bring it in one of these days for me to look at? Maybe we could work out a deal."

Mike grabbed the edge of the counter with both hands. "You're kidding, aren't you? My Holton and twenty-five bucks for a two-hundred-dollar Bach? This is Christmas, but you're not Santa Claus."

Hoffman smiled. "Well, no, not quite. But maybe you could pay the rest in installments next year, if your band is doing so well. I know you want it and I'd like to see you get it before you're too old to hit high C anymore."

"You're serious? You're not kidding me or anything?"

"No, seriously, I think we can do business. Bring yours in sometime and we'll see."

Mike gulped. "Sure, okay, I will." He pocketed his money in one big wad and was almost out the door when Hoffman called him back. He'd left his package on the counter. "Oh, yeah, my mom's present, I can't lose that. Uh, Merry Christmas, Mr. Hoffman. I'll see you later."

He went straight home and grabbed his horn and caught the next bus back downtown—the same bus, in fact; he recognized the driver—praying all the way that Hoffman wouldn't renege. It was like a miracle after all those aching months. He had figured on a trade-in, of course, maybe fifty dollars, but it never occurred to him that Hoffman would be willing to trust him for most of the balance too—him, a two-bit high school kid who couldn't even afford to pay for the *Down Beats* he read. The Christmas spirit must have really overcome Hoffman to provoke such a generous offer. . . . Christmas, oh, Jesus, the last shopping day and what time was it now, four thirty already? Hoffman might close early like he said, go home to his family, and after Christmas he'd regain his senses and cancel the deal.

He ran the three blocks from the bus stop, dodging through the last-minute crowd like a juvenile shoplifter eluding the law. He skidded around the corner and gasped with relief—the door still open, lights on, and good old Mr. H. tidying up the shelves. Not a minute too soon. "Let's—talk business."

To his private surprise Mr. Hoffman agreed to allow seventy-five dollars on the Holton. Mike didn't tell him that Jerry only gave fifty for it in L.A. two years ago, secondhand then. Instrument prices had gone up and a dealer should know its value. Hoffman wrote up the contract of sale and Mike signed his name with a handsome flourish—"Michael B. Riley" in black ink, though he would gladly have used his own blood—and it was done, square, honest, legal as a marriage license. The Sleeping Beauty was released from her glass coffin and tucked into a plush-lined carrying case, the lid closed gently, locks snapped, key turned. Mike pocketed the key—a real Yale key, not one of those silly little two-pronged things for a kid's piggy bank—shook Mr. Hoffman's hand, and picked up the case. He felt like a bridegroom leaving the church. Somebody should throw rice.

Next step—break the news to Mother. She couldn't have been more shocked if he had eloped to Reno and walked in with a brand-new bride.

"But you have a perfectly good trumpet already."

He tried to make her understand by comparing the difference between a used '38 Chevy and a new Cadillac if there were such a thing, wartime restrictions permitting. But the only aspect she caught was the money. She didn't know trumpets, but any fool could guess that this one cost more. When he told her how much more, she nearly fainted. "Michael, you must be out of your mind! No trumpet in the world could possibly be worth two hundred dollars, not even if it were solid gold and encrusted with jewels! How could they let you take such an expensive instrument home on approval? Suppose something happened to it?"

"It's not on approval, Mom," Mike said gently. "I bought it. I signed a contract. . . ."

She began to sizzle at the word "contract" and exploded in blue flames when he named the terms. "Time payments! Contract! That's ridiculous! It's—it's criminal! You were cheated,

164

Michael, just plain cheated, and I won't stand for it. You'll return it first thing tomorrow and get your money back or I'll—I'll sue somebody."

"Tomorrow's Sunday."

"Well, Monday then—no, Tuesday, you'll take it back Tuesday. And don't touch it until then, either. He might claim you damaged it or something. Crooks like that will pull any shady trick. Terrible, it's just terrible how people will try to take advantage of— I don't think that contract is even legal. Minors can't sign contracts, can they? If it is, we'll get it canceled somehow."

Mike's stomach was twisting into knots; he felt as if he wanted to cry. "Mom, listen, you don't understand. Nobody cheated me. She—I mean it's worth two hundred, it honestly is. Bill Rhodes uses the same kind and you know he wouldn't have anything but the finest. It will last me all my life. I could play it in any band in the country."

"Well, you won't. You're not Bill Rhodes and the horn you had is perfectly good enough. That's selfish, Michael, selfish and irresponsible. Two hundred dollars is more than I earn in a whole month, more than it costs us to live! Could I take my next month's pay and buy myself a fur coat just because I happened to like one I saw in a window? How would we eat next month if I did? How would we pay the rent? You know I couldn't."

"No, but you could pay twenty-five down on a coat and the rest in installments if you wanted to, like I did. It's not fair to talk about your money. This is *my* money. I earned every cent I put down, and the horn I traded was my horn; Jerry paid for it, you didn't. I'll earn the rest to pay it off. You never expected me before to pay the food and rent out of what I make with Johnny, but I'd do it if you asked me to, I'd be perfectly willing to do it. If you would let me go union, I could buy you a fur coat and anything else you want."

She gave him an exasperated look. "I don't *want* a fur coat! Don't go dragging fur coats into this argument."

"I didn't, you did. You said it first."

"Well, I'm sorry, it was a slip of the tongue. I only meant it was something expensive and utterly unnecessary, like a new trumpet. And I don't expect you to support me either. Your only job now is to go to school and prepare to support yourself later on and support your family when you're grown up and married. That's all in the world I expect from you, Mike, that you should grow up into a good responsible person who can take care of himself. But indulging yourself with foolish things is wrong, even if you think you have the money for it. Your father did that all the time. He spent money like it grew on trees; he didn't give a damn about tomorrow or next week or where the rent would come from. And that's why I left him—one reason why, not the only one—because I couldn't stand to have you grow up like that, hand to mouth, feast to famine. Is that the kind of man you want to be? Selfish, careless, out to please yourself and damn the rest of the world. Is it?"

This is no fair, Mike thought helplessly. No fair at all. "No, of course I don't. I swear I'd never be like him, never. But— You just don't understand about this horn. It's not some little whim I happened to see in a window. I've been saving for months to buy it, ever since, oh, jeez, I forget how long, way back last spring. I couldn't get anywhere because our jobs never paid enough. I would have gone on saving however long it took, years maybe. But Mr. Hoffman knew how bad I wanted it, so he let me have it before somebody else came along." His voice started shaking when he thought about that. "It's not hurting you in any way, is it? You just said you didn't need my money or want it, so why can't I buy the one thing in the world I really want? Don't you want me to be happy?"

"Oh, Mike, what a question. Of course I do. But you can't— it's not— there's more than—" She looked at him helplessly. "Does it really matter so much?"

Does it matter! He wanted to tell her how desperately it mattered, but how could she understand? So it's a luxury, so it's selfish, I can't help it. Maybe I'm as nutty as a fruitcake, but I love that horn and I'm going to keep it. Weren't you ever in love? Didn't you ever want something enough to sell your soul and go to hell for it? No, I guess you never did. You're too cool and smart and sensible. That's Jerry's side of the family in me, wanting something and grabbing it quick, never mind what it costs. Women don't do that, but men do. Don't tell me I'm wrong, don't reason with me, just leave me alone. I know what I'm doing. If I'm going to hell, then I'll go there my own way.

She couldn't hear any of the words, but she must have read the look on his face. "Well, I guess we can't do anything about it now.

166

The stores are closed until Tuesday. We'll think about it some more. Maybe you're right. It's your money, as you say. Maybe I can't tell you how to spend it. If it means so much. . . ."

Mike grabbed her and kissed her, something he hadn't done for years since he was a little kid. He was getting to be quite a gay blade, kissing madly right and left, Darleen last night, Mom today. He pretty nearly kissed old Hoffman this afternoon, just busting out with Christmas spirit, goodwill toward everybody. But he knew what he really wanted to kiss—his beautiful bride who waited in her purple plush bed, waiting for the touch of his lips and trembling hands. He'd won her like an honest man, signed the license, paid the fee, and good old Mr. Hoffman pronounced them man and wife. With his mother's reluctant blessing, nothing stood in the way of true love.

He picked the Sleeping Beauty up and carried her over the threshold into his bedroom and shut the door behind them.

Now.

It was a beautiful, beautiful honeymoon. Saturday night and all day Sunday he stayed in his room and made love to the Bach over and over, playing through surge after surge of emotion, resting on his bed between times, lying there looking at her and holding her and fondling her until new passion rose in him and he had to play again. He couldn't get enough. The most ardent girl in the world couldn't have kept pace with him. He would have exhausted the flesh of the most willing bride, but not this one. The Bach was always ready for more, eager to try another chorus. Take me again, darling, I'm yours, all yours. Her valves responded feather-light to his touch, closing and springing up instantly without a whisper of friction. When he kissed her, it was like heaven, like nothing in the world could ever be. Songwriters talked about love that made beautiful music, but they had it backward. It was music that made beautiful love.

Sheer pride of possession drove him to explore further into her. It seemed almost indecent to unscrew the valve caps and pull the slides. He did it as gently as he could, anointing them with careful strokes, fitting them smoothly back. Her valve oil was Chanel No. 5, the polishing cloth soft as a bridal blanket. She didn't need to be polished, but he couldn't keep his hands off her gleaming golden flanks, engraved with the most delicate tracing of scroll-

167

work leaves and flowers. A tattooed lady, my God, even Jerry never had anything like that. One in the eye for you, Dad. I've got me a gal who never quits. She cost a fortune, but she's mine, all mine for a lifetime.

He stayed in his room almost all day Sunday, coming out only for occasional simple necessities like the bathroom or a drink of water. He had never put in so many consecutive hours with a horn before—never had the reason to, the desire to, the overwhelming urge. He felt a little dizzy when he walked to the dinner table, a trifle light-headed, but his lip was just fine, not the least bit sore or tired. He could have gone on indefinitely, night and day forever to the final blast of the Last Trump—and played that too, the Archangel Michael announcing Judgment Day. Who cared about Judgment Day? He was in heaven already.

He could have gone on, but maybe he'd better not. There was such a thing as overdoing it, taking too much out of yourself. Men had been known to kill themselves on their wedding nights, although they had problems of a slightly different nature. His heart and lungs could stand it, but maybe his mother's ears couldn't. No sense antagonizing her. She might get mad and make him take it back after all. Which would be like—oh, Jesus, like breaking up a marriage, like exiling his bride to Siberia after a two-day honeymoon. He couldn't, he wouldn't, he'd rather die. But Mom didn't know and she'd never understand, she'd think he was clear off his head. He'd better go easy and let her accept it gradually. She would. She'd come around when she realized how happy he was. Besides, tomorrow was Christmas. He owed her some consideration then, at least.

Christmas morning was—well, Christmas for about ten minutes and then just plain morning, like any nonworking day. They splurged on waffles and sausage for breakfast and then opened their presents. Mom was delighted with the diamond pin and earrings. She said they were beautiful, just what she had always wanted, excellent taste, not a bit too flashy. When she put them on, they did wonders for her old flowered bathrobe. She gave Mike a collection of mystery stories and a red and white ski sweater covered with a blizzard of snowflakes and piebald reindeers fore and aft.

"Oh, gee," he said with a big grin. "I bet you knit it all yourself."

168

"But of course. Every day while I rode to work, standing up in the aisle of the bus. Does it fit?"

It fit fine, made him look like a big athletic dude from Sun Valley. And that was just about it, for gifts. The old lady across the hall brought over a box of homemade fudge. He ate five or six pieces while he was reading the first mystery story. His nose began to feel hot, then his ears and then his whole head, the combined effects of waffles and fudge and a heavy ski sweater over his shirt and about eighty degrees of heat in the apartment, Good King Wenceslaus, the landlord, treating them to a sudden generous burst of Christmas fuel.

He felt like a stupid schoolboy sitting there reading and eating and sweating as though he didn't have good sense. But it sort of seemed like the polite thing to do. Mom didn't have *any* Christmas toys to play with. He wished he had sprung another twenty-nine cents for a jigsaw puzzle. That used to be his idea of a real fine gift, back in the days when he did his shopping at Woolworth's on a two-bit allowance. It would give her something useless to do to pass a long dull holiday and he could put down this silly book and go play his horn without feeling so damn guilty.

She sat and fidgeted for a while, picked up a magazine and laid it down, touched the pin on her robe and tilted it a little to admire the sparkle when it caught the light. "This is lovely, Mike, it really is."

"Too bad it's not real," he said. "You could hock it to buy a fur coat and then we'd both be happy."

She gave him a sharp look. Suddenly she laughed. "This is silly. I'm going to clean in here and vacuum. You can get out of my way. Go practice or something."

She didn't need to ask him twice. He was into his bedroom like a shot and peeling off his sweater, stripping for action. Look out, beautiful, here I come. The Sleeping Beauty welcomed him and then he was lost in love.

About one o'clock he and Mom went out to Sutherland's Café for the Christmas special, turkey and Ivory soap dressing, a teaspoonful of cranberry sauce, pumpkin pie with cardboard crust. When they left the restaurant, there was still half a day to kill. "We could go downtown to the show maybe?"

"No, I don't think so. But you go ahead if you want to."

Mike couldn't, actually, because he was broke, only fifty cents

169

left to his name. But he couldn't admit that he had mortgaged himself to the literal eyeballs for that horn. He hadn't asked Mom for money since he started getting band jobs and this was no moment to admit poverty.

So he went home with her and sat around some more until the doorbell rang and—surprise!—it was Paul. So that's why she didn't want to go to the show and why she vacuumed the living room maybe. Well, company would be nice, anything to break the monotony. Paul came bearing gifts, too, a nice two-pound box of chocolates (Mike eyed them uninterestedly, being full of dinner and fudge, but he knew they weren't for him anyway) and two flat squarish packages that looked exactly like record albums. *Scheherazade* for Mom, longhair stuff suited to her square taste, and for Mike four practically priceless old singles, two early Rhodes and two even earlier Wilson when Rhodes was in his brass, all four out of print and rare as rare can be. Collector's items they were, in fact, right out of Paul's own collection with his name stamped on the labels. Mom looked a little underwhelmed with the idea of secondhand records as a Christmas gift. Mike didn't try to explain to her why his were fifty times more valuable than her new straight-from-the-shop album. He knew and Paul knew; that's what counted.

Paul had just escaped from a family gathering, a bunch of Jansky in-laws gathered for Helen's turkey dinner, and pretty hectic it was, he said, with Huey-Dewey-and-Looey fighting the Battle of the Bulge with toy machine guns supplied by some idiot relative. He was wearing an unbelievable Christmas necktie, red and green lightning bolts on a sky-blue ground. "Guess who picked that out? That's right, a committee of three."

"I made out better than you did." Mike posed with his muscular sweater.

"Did skis come with it?"

"Where would you ski around here?"

"The municipal golf course makes great coasting for the kiddies."

While Mom was in the kitchen making coffee, Mike gestured at the ceiling light fixture where he had thoughtfully attached the dry sprig of mistletoe from the Snowball. "Did you happen to observe our yuletide decorations?" Paul looked and grinned but made no comment. Then Mike said, "Wait till you see what else Santa brought me," and unveiled the Sleeping Beauty.

170

Paul's jaw dropped. "Good God, where did you get that?" He took a closer look at the engraved trademark. "Is it Hoffman's?" When he heard Mike's story, he gave a long envious whistle. "Wow, did you luck out. I guess he decided nobody else in town would ever come up with the cash. What does your mother think?"

Mike made a warning face. "She's reluctant, v-e-r-y reluctant. Maybe you could talk to her real tactfully about it later on, huh? But don't say anything stupid because I've got to keep it, man, there's no other way."

He put it away before his mother came back with the coffee. They all sat listening to her *Scheherazade* album. Parts of it were almost good. Mike could imagine it in swing like Miller's "Volga Boatmen" or the Les Brown Bizet, saxes kicking a unison melody around while the brass punched in sharp figures. Not bad, not bad. He thought the yuletide decorations were long forgotten. But when Mom started across the room to change the record Paul said, "Wait," just sharply enough that she stopped and looked at him. Then he came out of his chair, moving pretty fast for a man with a stiff leg, and caught her right on the spot. She was startled for a second, but she didn't dodge; she kissed back. She made a tentative motion to put her arms around his neck and then thought better of it and finally broke it up. Not looking angry, just a little confused, *this is nice, but enough's enough and not before the children.* Mike felt embarrassed. He had hoped to start something, but he didn't expect quite so much.

"Merry Christmas, Kathy," Paul said softly.

Mike cleared his throat. "I'm going to take a walk around the block." Nobody tried to discourage him. When he left, Paul said, "Don't hurry back," but he said it kiddingly, not urgently. He was back in his chair drinking coffee and listening to the music.

A nice sunny afternoon was slushing the snow a bit, perfect weather for little kids to test their new sleds on three-foot terrace slopes or to pass new footballs or pitch new baseballs on cleared driveways. Mike remembered the year he got his bicycle; he nearly died waiting for the streets to clear. That was seven years ago. Jeez, he was getting on. The California trip with Jerry had drawn a line right across his life, a big deep ditch between Michael Ashton, the square schoolboy, and Mike Riley, the show biz musician. He couldn't cross back and he didn't want to. After one more boring school semester he would be a hundred percent professional, working in a real union band. Six months till June. With the Sleeping Beauty for company he could stand it, but Darleen's company would be welcome too. Making love to a trumpet was slightly one-sided, like jerking off. There had to be more. He knew what was missing, all right, but getting it was another story.

Now why the hell did he stir up *that* subject?

Cold fresh air and exercise didn't help at all. The drugstore was open, so he went in and phoned her, risking a wasted nickel. He could hardly hear her over the background noise at her house, a record playing, kids talking and laughing. "What's going on?"

"A party!" Darleen said. "Come on over, why don't you?"

"Who's there?"

"Oh, everybody. Mel, Dean, a bunch of kids from school."

Mel's voice cut in on the line. "Hey, old buddy, you should be here. Her folks are gone and the joint is really jumping." Then he started laughing and said, "Hey, cut that out—" Mike could visualize Darleen fooling around with him, messing up his hair or tickling him or blowing in his ear, the silly teasing tricks she knew to drive a guy up the wall. So he said, "Oh, shit," and hung up. He wanted to see her but not that way, not a mob scene with Mel and Dino and every other stud in town. She could wait. Only she wouldn't.

He hung around the store as long as he decently could, drinking a Coke slowly and reading magazines until the manager started giving him dirty looks. It was five o'clock when he left, the sun going down behind a bank of clouds, the air colder, wet sidewalks starting to freeze again. The new sweater felt good under his jacket as he walked home. Paul's car was still parked in front. Mike went upstairs whistling "On Top of Old Smoky" and fumbled around with the doorknob a little in case they needed warning. But they were still sitting more or less where he'd left them, half a room apart, talking in a friendly way. Well, they'd had their chance. If they wasted it, tough luck for them.

Paul began to talk about leaving, but he didn't go. He stayed for grilled cheese sandwiches and said they were just right, the one thing he could face after that big Jansky turkey. After supper Mike played a couple of his records, which precipitated a heavy discussion about Bill Rhodes' style, 1937 vs. 1944. Paul said he thought Rhodes was better then, freer and more honest. Mike said no, the newer sides were far better. "Like 'Stardust.' That solo is perfect, just out of this world perfect. You couldn't change a note anywhere."

"Why not? He invented it, he ad libbed it. What happened to get cut in wax that day was just one version out of a hundred possible tries. It's not sacred. God didn't engrave it on stone tablets and hand it down immutable forever to be worshiped. A record is just a record."

"But it's a classic, a masterpiece. There's no point in anybody else fooling around with it. Heck, if you had a great painting by Rembrandt, would you try to touch it up, change the colors and move the people and add a pig in the corner? You'd just ruin it."

Paul smiled. "For a kid who hates longhairs, you certainly have literal standards of interpretation. All right, so you have an original Rembrandt. Are you going to spend your whole life trying to hand-paint perfect reproductions of it? Any fool with a camera can do that with one click and no effort. I can buy a good Rembrandt reproduction for a few dollars. I can buy a good Rhodes 'Stardust' for fifty cents and listen to it any time I like. Maybe there's a certain thrill in copying something so well that you can fool a few people with it. Some people make nice reproductions of ten-dollar bills and pass them around the country. But will that be your whole career, Mike, turning out counterfeit Rhodes solos? Who are you going to fool?"

Mike felt confused. "Oh, hell, forget it. I know what I'm doing. If it's good enough for him, it's good enough for me."

"Okay, have it your way." Paul picked up the evening paper, a very skinny holiday edition with war on the front page, peace-on-earth ads in the back. He looked very comfortable in the easy chair, smoking in his shirt sleeves, collar open, the goofy li'l-nephew necktie pulled loose. The radio was playing; Mom sewed a button on one of Mike's shirts. What a homey scene. Only things missing were a crackling fireplace and a shaggy dog on the hearthrug. Mike wished it were true. He wouldn't mind having Paul in the family. Paul needed some loving; he was obviously lonely, even in that cheerful Jansky household. Mom could quit her job and cook for him and sew *his* buttons and fuss over him when he had a cold. And when Mike graduated and left town, they could hold hands together into the sunset.

173

But he couldn't tell Paul to come down off Old Smoky and propose before he was too old to follow through. Maybe Paul didn't even want to. Maybe Mom wouldn't take him on a silver platter, a man with a scarred face and limping leg. Maybe she didn't want any man ever again. Those were their problems; they'd have to work them out. Mike had his own urgent problems to solve. One romance at a time. Darleen first.

The band left home late in the afternoon New Year's Eve, drove sixty miles over fairly clear highways and checked into their hotel before the job. The guys traveled in their tuxedos, a very classy professional-looking crew tonight, but Darleen had to change and comb her pincurls into the sexy upsweep. All the hotel rooms were five-dollar doubles and the band needed six, since Darleen flatly refused all generous offers to go halvsies. Nine into five left an odd man out and Mike grabbed it to avoid the wrong company, snoring or dirty socks. *He* knew about roommates. He'd been on the USO circuit when these clowns were schoolboys.

"Yes, we'll all sleep easier if you room alone," Dino said meaningfully and got the usual laugh. Mike just grinned to himself. He had plans for company later, but Dino didn't need to worry.

The Bach did him proud from the very first set. He always sounded good, but tonight he sounded marvelous, superb, out of this world. Everybody said so—Johnny, Sammy, the customers; even Dino gave him grudging praise. The crowd was very appreciative at first, making requests, applauding all the solos. Mike played "Stardust" twice in the first half and they were still asking for it. Little by little the mood grew louder, more restless, more competitive. Half-gassed soldiers lurched around the floor slinging serpentine and handfuls of confetti. They hoisted each other up to pop balloons. They serenaded the band with paper horns and blowout whistles, yodeled off-key vocals, launched wolf calls whenever Darleen stood up to sing.

By intermission Mike was fed up. "For two cents I'd let them provide their own music. The next idiot that throws confetti into my horn will get a bust in the mouth for auld lang syne."

"Don't do it," Johnny said. "You'll start a riot and we'll lose our money sure. Now you know why they pay so high for New Year's Eve."

Since nobody seemed to care, the band indulged themselves with all their loud fast favorites. After six consecutive jump tunes the manager came to complain. "They're breaking their legs trying to dance to all that hot stuff. Can't you play waltzes?" So they held their noses and waltzed through one whole slow set, *boom* da da, *boom* da da, hoking it up, the saxes sloshing in Lombardo vibrato. Mike played an entire chorus of "My Buddy" in the wrong key, a full step higher. The band collapsed laughing, but no one else noticed. In fact, one couple said it was just beautiful. Dean swallowed his grin and said, "Thanks, glad you liked it."

At midnight they accompanied an orgy of wholesale kissing while confetti swirled in a multicolored blizzard and balloons popped steadily like the Fourth of July. Mike looked around for someone to kiss, but Darleen was out of reach. Not out of Dino's reach, unfortunately. He nailed her for a good hearty buss and clinch while the crowd whistled and applauded, figuring it was part of the show. Suddenly the lights went out, provoking laughter and shrieks and a few insulted slaps and scuffles around the floor, but the band played on regardless. Who needed light to fake "Auld Lang Syne"?

From then on it was murder. The lights flicked on and off erratically, sudden blackouts leaving them stranded and unable to read in the middle of a chorus. The crowd was stupidly staggering drunk; the decorations drooped in torn paper strips and shreds of burst rubber. Mike gave them one last "Stardust," pearls before swine, then "Two o'Clock Jump," screaming down the upper octave chromatics with the greatest of ease. Then it was *one* o'clock, praise the Lord, time to fold up and quit with a chorus of their "Blue Moon" theme and the final two-bar chaser. They shook the confetti out of their horns and unwound the serpentine from the cymbals, packed up, yawned and stretched and went out for hamburgers.

Six of them crowded cozily into one booth—Johnny, Mel, Mike, Darleen, plus Dino and a girl who had been hanging around the stand all night. She had applauded Mike's "Stardust," but every time Dean gave out with a Swoonatra ballad she started to sigh and wriggle and melt like a sunburned snowman—

ooooh, Frankie, you *send* me! Dean caught the message fast and returned it, aiming his songs straight at her, clutching the mike and letting his long notes sag with heavy passion. *It's all for you, baby, you alone, so wait for me after, okay?* And believe it or not, the chick waited. She said her name was Veronica. Mike doubted it, but no sweat to him what she called herself or how old she was either. She might be anywhere from fifteen to twenty-five, but she had what Dean liked best, a well-developed chest expansion under a tight blue dress. If she was out alone on New Year's Eve and playing kneesie under the table with a sex-mad sax man, she must be up to the age of consent. When Dean said, "No onions on yours, baby," she said, "Of *course* not," with obedient delight. Mike grinned. The chick was really asking for it.

They all went back to the hotel together, tiptoeing past the sleepy desk clerk to hold a private party in Dean and Johnny's room. "This was the last fifth in Connor City," Dean said proudly. "I hunted all over hell for it." His heavy dark Italian good looks had fooled bartenders and liquor clerks for years; now he was almost old enough to drink legally. He poured a generous shot into a water glass, looked at it thoughtfully, doubled it, sloshed in a little ginger ale and handed the finished product to Veronica. "Here you go, baby, happy new year and all fondest regards. Let me know if it's too weak."

She tasted it and gasped, then covered up with a smile. "It's fine, just fine."

Mike drank his first highball cautiously, unsure what to expect. Not so bad. Only an expert like Jerry with a galvanized throat could handle straight bourbon, pure raw flaming cough medicine. One tentative sip from the old bureau-drawer bottle had cured Mike's curiosity about that. But he was younger then, much younger. Bourbon mixed with ginger ale went down easier. Not bad at all. The second one was *good*. Smooth, man, very shmeuuuth.

Mel chickened out after half a drink and left just before Darleen arrived with freshened makeup and her own empty glass. "Where's the ice?"

Dean gave her an exasperated look. "Where do you think you are, the Stork Club? Listen, I furnished the liquor and the mix, so take it or leave it. If you want ice, you can get it yourself." He wrapped a cozy arm around Veronica, sitting beside him on one

176

bed, and gestured broadly with his drinking hand. "I'm very busy and it's cold outside."

"Hey, that's an idea," Mike said suddenly. He went to the window, opened it, and stuck his head out to look up. Their third-floor room was right under the roof. A row of icicles hung along the eaves not more than three or four feet above the top of the window.

"Hey, close the goddamn window. You're freezing us!"

If he climbed out and stood on the sill and held onto something with one hand while he reached up with the other and broke off an icicle— *Voilà,* ice cubes. Well, why not? If he happened to slip, it was only about thirty feet straight down to sudden death on the concrete. But old surefooted Riley never slipped. Any man who could bust F above high C wide open and hold it seventeen seconds without falling over dead could do anything. If they strung a tightwire from here to the opposite building, he could cross it with the greatest of ease, umbrellaless and blindfolded, stupefying the crowd below.

"*Close* it, shithead, before I come over there and split your lip!"

He measured the distance with his eye. Just crouch through and stand up and there he was. Easy as pie for him, insanity for anyone else. Dino couldn't do it. Old Dino couldn't push his fat 4-F butt through the window, let alone perform daring one-handed acrobatic feats on the sill and capture an icicle for Darleen's drink or a sparkling handful of stardust for her to wear in her hair.

He caught the window frame lightly with both hands and put one foot on the sill. Johnny grabbed him from one side and Darleen from the other and they dragged him back before he could raise the other foot. "What in the name of everlasting hell are you *doing?*" Johnny demanded. "Trying to kill yourself?"

"Just getting Darleen some ice," Mike said.

She looked at him gratefully, admiringly. "No, never mind, that's all right. But thank you anyway." She clung to his arm as if to prevent another attempt. But he was safe. No thirty-foot fall could kill him tonight. Fearless and indestructible, faster than a speeding bullet, able to leap tall buildings at a single bound—look, up in the sky! It's a bird—it's a plane—it's RILEY, man!

They sat down together on the side of Johnny's bed with their backs to the rest of the party—Johnny flaked out and pretending to snore, Dean and Veronica necking up a storm on the other bed, still more or less vertical but sagging. As Darleen went on rubbing her hand along his sleeve, Mike could feel his biceps developing right under her fingers. Muscles were bulging out all over him, rippling steel-bending muscles with Charles Atlas power. *All* over him, man, everywhere. Little did she recognize Superman disguised as a mild-mannered trumpet player. But he could show her, dammit, he could really show her if she just gave him the chance. A week of one-sided fantasy marriage to the Sleeping Beauty had raised an unbelievable pitch of longing for flesh-and-blood satisfaction. He was hot as a firecracker. He had to make love tonight or explode in a million aching fragments.

This wasn't the world's most private place, but so what? If Dean could neck here so could he. He kissed Darleen without benefit of mistletoe. She not only let him but welcomed it and gave it back double, eagerly. It turned into a kissing version of Bill Rhodes' "Carnival of Venice," theme and variations on a couple of long-winded breaths, chorus upon increasingly complex chorus that wound up in truly virtuoso triple-tonguing, or should he say double-tonguing. That piece had frustrated him for years, but tonight he could play it perfectly, every last blessed note.

What Bill Rhodes couldn't teach him, Darleen could. She seemed ready and willing to continue the lessons, but Mike felt a little bit wary. He knew what a horrible tease she was, how easily she could raise a man's blood pressure to aching heights and then laugh in his face and walk away with somebody else. If she did that to him tonight, he couldn't bear it. He would open that window again and dive straight out, Superman or superfool.

The room was getting awfully hot, as thick with passion as the wet sweet air inside a greenhouse. Mike sensed vaguely that he wasn't the only one feeling it. After two or three sturdy drinks and a lot of heavy necking Veronica was clinging to Dean and practically begging to be screwed. All of me, like the old song said, why not take all of me? Why not indeed? Too many damn spectators, that's why. Johnny was lying there looking very bored, the one single man surrounded by panting passion. Mike and Darleen were busy but not too busy to notice a display of serious intercourse right under their noses. Old Dean was really up the creek without a paddle. What a terrible fix for an eager stud—a pliable, well-oiled, thoroughly willing girl on his hands and *no place to lay her.*

He detached himself finally, said, "Hold it just a minute, baby," and tapped Mike on the shoulder. "I gotta talk to you, it's very important."

"So talk."

"No, over here." He pulled Mike into the most private corner and spoke in low urgent tones. "Swap rooms with me, will you?"

Mike gave him a straight answer. "Get lost."

"No, listen, man, I gotta have that single room right now, or I don't know what I'm going to do."

"Go screw yourself," Mike said simply with considerable pleasure.

"Come on, Mike, be a pal for once. You don't need that room and I do. I'll give you five bucks for the key and you can sleep here free."

Mike shook his head.

"Six bucks?"

"No, thanks." He wondered how high the bidding would go. Dean was in bad shape, sweating hard and just about ready to split his pants.

"Seven . . . and a bust in the mouth if you don't take it," Dean said with sudden agony. "Oh, Jesus, you can have it back in an hour."

Mike was about to tell him where he could put his seven bucks when he saw Darleen sending signals. "Excuse me," he said politely, and left Dean sweating.

"What does he want?" she asked.

Mike wasn't sure he ought to tell her, but why not? "He wants to pay me seven dollars for the key to my room."

"Take it."

"Are you crazy? Listen, *I* want that room, don't you—" He faltered and stopped with confidence leaking away. If she was telling him that he didn't need it on her account—after that lovely promising "Carnival of Venice" prelude—then he might as well jump out the window and get it over. "Aren't we—" He couldn't ask outright, it sounded too crude.

"Sell him your key, you dope. I've got a room too."

Mike inhaled confidence to new proportions. *Well*, now. Now we're cooking. "Right," he said, and went back to Dean, who was purple with frustrated passion. Mike dangled his room key between them. "Seven fifty, did you say?"

"Yes," Dean said through his teeth and grabbed it.

"Cash down," Mike said.

"Later!"

"Now."

Dean groaned, but he paid it. "Never mind the receipt." He swept Veronica up and out without farewells. "Bon voyage," Mike said. He hoped they made it in time. It was five doors away and Dean might not stand up to the trip.

He went back and kissed Darleen again to make sure things were all right on the home front. They were. He wasn't feeling desperate yet, but he thought it would be well to take her down the hall pretty quick before anybody changed their minds or ran out of courage.

Courage.

There was a little whiskey left in Dean's bottle but no more ginger ale. Mike poured himself a shot for luck and gulped it straight down like a tough cowboy in a saloon. Then he stretched out a hand to Darleen and said very gallantly, "May I see you to your room, Miss Verbeck, ma'am?"

She smiled at him and said, "Yes, Mr. Riley, sir, you surely may." They both bid Johnny a fond farewell.

Johnny said, "Jesus, it's about *time*," and rolled over as though he meant to sleep with his clothes on, too weary to move. Alone, poor guy, all alone.

So they modulated down the hall to Darleen's door, where Mike ran into all kinds of trouble at the last change of key. She handed it to him, an old-fashioned long-barreled skeleton-type key on a brown tag, twin to the one he had sold Dino. The great big clumsy thing looked as if it would open every door in the hotel. But it wouldn't open hers because he couldn't get it into the lock. He could hardly see in the dim hall light and the keyhole kept blurring and drifting around and his hands were shaking so bad that he dropped it. They both started giggling. "Go on, Michael," she said, "open the *door*, I'm *waiting*."

He picked the key up and tried again, jabbed at the lock a few times, getting impatient because the damn thing wouldn't stay focused. "Hold still, dammit!" He gave a shove and suddenly it went in clear up to the hilt, right straight through and out the other side of the door, wiggling impotently. He thought, jeez, it isn't possible. Darleen was in absolute hysterics by this time, hanging on his arm and laughing fit to split. He was laughing too because it was so ridiculous and almost crying because it was so frustrating. What's the matter with you? What happened to Superman? What kind of clumsy eager idiot are you? If you can't put the key in her goddamn lock, how are you going to open her goddamn door? We'll be out here all *night.* Shove it in or break it down, man, one or the other.

Then Darleen put her hand on his and together they pulled the key back a little and turned it and click! it worked, easy as pie. All it took was simple cooperation. He stood there red in the face and looking stupid, feeling stupid. At this point it wouldn't have surprised him if she slid through the door and slammed it in his face because he had to be the most stupid, inept, clumsy, fumbling guy in the world, the world's number one jackass who couldn't do anything right, not the simplest thing, couldn't even unlock a girl's door with a skeleton key, let alone perform when he got inside. She knew everything, but he didn't know anything. She would laugh him straight out of town.

She opened the door and took a step and stood waiting. Then she took hold of his hand and practically pulled him through, impatiently but gently as if she almost understood how he felt.

So there he was inside her room, virtually in like Flynn but not quite. Between virtually and actually is a long long mile when you don't know what the hell you're doing except stumbling around strictly ad lib. Ad libs were always his weakest point. But some things had to come naturally, learnin' by doin'. Nobody ever taught him how to drive a car, did they? He picked it up all by himself, first time he tried. Like Jerry said, any fool could make out with a "hyderamic" drive. You just shove in your key and give her the gas and she's off and running. With a little more luck and Darleen's cooperation, he had it made.

They drove home on New Year's Day in the morning, pretty stiff and sleepy but otherwise undamaged. Mike chewed mints all the way, and tried not to breathe in his mother's face as he told her about the job. He described the pretty decorations, the hilarious crowd, how great the music sounded—and that was all. Absolutely no details after 1 A.M.

School began again on Tuesday, same old drag, same old rat race. Nothing new added except a new date to remember to write on his papers, A.D. 1945. The only date he cared about was a date with Darleen. He was afraid she might not speak to him again. Not that he'd done anything to her that she didn't *want* him to do. It was her idea just as much as his. But you never could tell how a girl might react. The excitement of the occasion, everybody looped on highballs—she might be sorry now and mad at him for following through.

He waited a couple of days, doubtfully, then called her up. She wasn't mad at all. She said, "Why don't you come up and see me sometime?" in a sexy Mae West voice.

Mike said, "Like when?"

She said, "Like now."

It took him an hour by bus, two buses with a long cold wait at the transfer point, riding past the Royal Theater neighborhood and farther east through snowy wastes of unexplored territory. When he finally found her house, Darleen said, "What took you so long?" and seemed amazed at his answer. "You don't have a car? Not your folks either?" It was like confessing that he lived with kerosene lamps and outdoor plumbing. Everybody in the civilized world had a car. No gas or tires for it, maybe, but they had a *car*. What kind of Young Lochinvar came riding out of the west on a *bus*, for Christ sake? No class at all.

The evening never did go right. Darleen's mother was out at a neighbor's, but her father was right upstairs, either sleeping or reading the newspaper, which made for an uneasy living-room scene. They drank Cokes (unspiked, her old man kept his liquor locked up) and tried to dance to radio music. Mike wasn't a good dancer under the best waxed-ballroom-floor conditions and worse yet on a rug amid furniture. They shuffled around like kids working up static to strike sparks on each other's noses. When he kissed her, it struck sparks all right, very nice ones, so they sat down on the couch and started necking. But Mike couldn't concentrate worth a damn. He thought of her father upstairs and her mother likely to return any minute. It cramped his style to keep one eye on the front door and the other on the stairs and both ears straight up for the sound of footsteps. If anybody came in and saw them, Jesus! He'd be out that door and into a snowbank headfirst. Darleen said her old man was a truck driver. Mike could just picture him, seven feet tall, two fifty, hands like hams and no patience for any punk kid who messed around with his darling daughter.

Worse than that, Mike realized that he really had no style to cramp. They had sort of leaped over the necking stage the other night. First they were sitting in Johnny's room kissing, and suddenly they were in bed together in the dark, no transition between. He knew there should be a lot of pleasant intermediate steps, things they could do without going all the way. But he didn't know exactly what Darleen would let him do now or what she expected him to do. He kept on kissing her and sliding his hands up and down the back of her sweater and then under her sweater against the back of her slip and up to bare skin around her shoulders. He wondered if unfastening her bra would invite a sock in the eye. He didn't know, he just didn't know. And she didn't tell him anything, dammit, nothing he could depend on as a stop-or-go signal. He couldn't go on stroking her back forever like he was petting a damn pussycat, nice kitty, nice kitty. It felt very nice and smooth, but it wasn't getting him anywhere. After a while he found himself stroking in time with the Rhodes record on the radio. A good solid jump tune with a terrific brass chorus, the whole section carrying a very complicated harmonized melody, very bouncy in cup mutes, dah d'lee-a DAH doh, dah *dee* dah, rahtadahta . . .

Darleen pulled away and gave him a very fishy look. "*What* are you doing, if I might ask?"

"Huh? Nothing."

"That's just what I thought," she said. She went and turned the radio off and came back, but the spell was broken. He'd lost the beat completely, lost his place in the score and couldn't get back into the chorus. It all petered out in sour notes. When he decided it was time for him to go home, Darleen didn't coax him to stay longer. So he left without having the doubtful pleasure of meeting Mr. or Mrs. Verbeck. He wandered four or five blocks through the pitch-black night and stood waiting at a bus stop until his balls froze solid and dropped off, which they might as well do because what else were they good for? He was no kind of lover. New Year's Eve was only beginner's luck, a fluky happenstance that couldn't occur again in a hundred years. He might as well stick to kissing his horn and forget about kissing girls.

Monday night at practice Darleen treated him just the way she usually did, hot and cold, sweet and nasty, keep 'em guessing. So he returned the same to her, criticizing her singing and being generally disinterested and professional. Nobody would guess there was anything special between them. He felt like standing up and saying, "Hey, you guys, guess what happened New Year's!" But only clods like Dino bragged about their sexcapades. Besides, it took more than one lucky screw to hold a hot romance together. His news might not be very big news. The others might say, "So what's so unique? Welcome to the club, comrade."

What he needed, what he needed most of all, was a chance to make love under better conditions with no fear of interruptions. If he just had a car. She'd have to cooperate then. He'd be in the driver's seat and she'd have to make love or walk home in the snow. But he didn't have a car and he couldn't borrow one and that was that. Too cold in a car anyway, this time of year, and probably too cramped and crowded. They'd catch pneumonia bareassed in a back seat. Forget it.

And then he had it. The whole scheme sprang to his mind in one bright flash, stunning in its simplicity. Easy, easy as pie. Easy as catching a cold.

He cornered Darleen at the end of practice and told her what he had in mind. He thought she might spit in his eye—oh, no, not again—but she liked it just fine. Great, she said, the smartest idea you ever had. Then she patted him kindly on the cheek and left to ride home with Dean. Straight home, he hoped, but there was no telling.

Tuesday he simply skipped school, a ridiculously easy thing to do. Mom left for work at seven thirty, so she couldn't possibly know that Mike didn't leave at eight. He waited for an hour, anxious and itching, wondering what was keeping Darleen. Maybe she forgot or couldn't sneak away. It would be harder for her, having to start for school at her regular time and then transfer north unnoticed. So much harder that she might have decided not to bother at all, dammit, and there he'd be stuck alone at home all day with nothing to do but suck his thumb.

Just when he was about to give up hoping, she came, muffled to the eyeballs and breathless with cold. "God, it's thirty below zero out there! Some gallant Galahad you are, making me come clear to the North Pole in this weather while you stay home in your toasty little apartment." She peeled off her gloves and coat and scarf, fluffed up her hair, then flopped into a chair and extended her feet. Mike took the hint and pulled her boots off—her shoes too, as it happened, everything together. "Gee, your legs are cold."

"That's not all of me that's cold. I swear I stood twenty minutes waiting for your stupid bus. Oh, brrrr! Warm me up, Mike, I'm freezing all over."

"With the greatest of pleasure," Mike said. "Pardon me just one small minute." He made sure the front door was locked, the curtains closed, everything looking normal to the outside world. Then he came back and took her in his arms. He hadn't the slightest doubt in his mind now what to do or how to do it or whether she would like it or not. She was cold, literally ice cold and shivering, and he was going to warm her up with his hands and his lips and his body until she glowed all over as hot as he felt himself. You have to warm up a cold horn before you can play it, breathe your breath into it and coax it into readiness or the music will be flat and sour. Anything you can do to a horn you can likewise do to a girl if she wants to play or be played on—played with?—no, played on was right, correct the first time. When a horn is ready, it tells you by its tone and feel, the way it responds. So does a girl. When her skin feels warm and smooth as polished brass but softer, much softer, and the nipples of her breasts spring erect like mother-of-pearl valves under the touch of your fingers and her lips open to your most skilled tonguing attack, then you know she is ready to make beautiful music. The bell of a horn will accept a straight mute. A girl's flared thighs will accept a hand and invite it to find the source of the music. A whisper of silk slips aside to reveal the place where heaven begins and the simile ends, because even the finest custom-built horn in the world is only cold empty brass tubing inside its bell, not warm, living, pulsing flesh to be stroked and explored and entered. Vincente Bach made beautiful trumpets, but God made beautiful women.

And that was only the introduction. When neither he nor she could wait any longer, they moved into his bedroom and into the first chorus—a higher key, an increased tempo, dynamics swelling multo crescendo to the double forte climax of the first ending.

185

Then they lay out for sixty-four measures of rest, side by side and pleasantly crowded. He wished his single bed were wider, but it would do; he was lean and she was small and they didn't need much room. They rested and then began all over from the top of the page. Letter B—second chorus, sax chorus, warmer, fuller, richer and sweeter than the lead of eager driving brass. Two in a single bed while the Sleeping Beauty slept alone, cold in the closet, unaware that Prince Charming was cheating her blind with another golden blonde. What a rake, what a Don Juan he turned out to be. Two weeks married, gloriously unfaithful and not the least ashamed. The Bach could echo whatever emotion he put into it, but only as an echo of empty brass. Darleen was warm and soft and real. She cradled his whole body and took his entire love, doubled it, strengthened it, harmonized it in ways he couldn't invent or begin to dream of. The song of love could never be a solo.

After the second ending they took a long intermission for lunch, a romantic meal of milk and peanut butter sandwiches. He had to laugh because Darleen looked so cute in his bathrobe, barefoot, the sleeves flopping over her hands and the hem almost dragging the floor. They started scuffling around and he peeled the robe off and of course she didn't have anything on underneath so there was nothing to do but go back to bed and try a third chorus for luck. Letter C, third chorus, generally featuring clarinets or a trombone solo. With Darleen's inspiration Mike could do anything, be everything, the virtuoso of a one-man band. His personal trombone extended at full thrust to reach eighth position which was deep enough in any man's band, deep enough to make Darleen gasp and shudder and rake her fingernails into his back. She was crying and he thought he must have hurt her, but she said no, no, he hadn't, no, he couldn't hurt her that way ever, never ever.

Darleen dressed slowly while Mike lay on the bed and watched her, too loose and happily spent to lift a hand to help or hinder her as she covered her wonderful woman's body with layers of schoolgirl clothes—underpants and bra, slip, blue plaid skirt, blue sweater, white ankle socks. She hunted around for her shoes until she finally remembered they were still inside her boots. Mike got up and put on his pants and saw her to the door like a good host. He helped her on with her coat, watched her wiggle her feet into the white rubber boots and stamp the heels down, watched her knot the heavy headscarf under her chin, button her coat and turn up the collar, fumble in her pockets for her gloves. He kissed her good-bye gently, with the last whisper of passion in him. She picked up the schoolbooks that she had to bring—for camouflage, for the day she should have spent at Morton—and she smiled at him and left. "See you, Mike. Be good."

"You be good," he said. If you can't be good, be careful, he thought vaguely. Of course they would be careful. They would guard their sweet little arrangement with their very lives and no one else would ever hear a whisper of the silent secret music. Three choruses, man, three choruses and out. Pretty damn good performance for a beginner. He was pooped, beautifully gloriously pooped, so limp he couldn't even take a shower. He just fell back into bed and went to sleep with his pants on.

When he woke again, he didn't know what time it was, morning or evening, or even what day; he was completely fogged out. His watch said five o'clock. Then it registered. *Five o'clock*, Jesus, Mom due home any minute and the whole place littered with incriminating evidence, the bed a mess, rumpled sheets pulled out, lipstick on the pillowcase. He jerked the blankets up and threw the spread over everything but he'd have to do something about that smear, wash it somehow. Twice too many cigarette butts around, more than half of them lipstick-stained. A reddish purple smudge on the rim of an extra milk glass in the kitchen. That goddamned lipstick branded everything with a Purple Passion that Mom would know instantly could never be hers. On his face too, he noticed just in time, and lathered it off fast. He couldn't wash off the fingernail marks on his back, couldn't do anything except pull on a shirt to cover them. Mom wouldn't see them. A lucky thing too, because he couldn't explain them away in a million years. *I was scratched by a cute little blond blue-eyed kitten, Mama. I was just petting her and she scratched me. But not because I hurt her. She said I could never hurt her no matter what I did. She followed me home, Mama, please can I keep her?* . . . Fat chance. This time he needn't ask. He was a big boy now and he could write his own arrangements.

And he did. Not once, not twice, but again and again and again. Darleen returned on Friday by popular demand and they

187

sailed through three more sensational choruses. But the next week she said no. At first Mike thought he'd overdone it, gone too far, worn her out or disgusted her with his eager appetite, a kid turned loose in a candy store and wanting to grab while the grabbing was good. But then he realized why she wouldn't. It was all right, more than all right because it relieved his mind completely. Couldn't, not wouldn't. He didn't need to worry in that department. Darleen was much too smart to let anything go wrong. That little kitten would always fall on her feet.

They booked two more dates as soon as she could. Everything came off smooth as silk—the same simple arrangement to skip school, the same cozy day together, the same beautiful music, Tuesday with a Friday encore. But two choruses satisfied Mike on Friday, the second ending weaker than the first. He guessed he couldn't expect it to keep on improving forever, or they would go spiraling right off into the clouds. Even happy married couples got used to it, didn't they? After the novelty wore off, making love could become an automatic habit, the thing people did on cold January nights. Or February mornings.

So here they were being cozy again, snug in their nest while howling wind and snow buried hopes of an early spring. What a life. Other men must plow through that god-awful weather to make a living, while he stayed home and made love. Thank God he needn't sweat any married problems, bills and babies and broken washing machines, the seamy side effects of sex. He had enough problems elsewhere right now—trying to persuade his mom that occasional weeknight jobs with Johnny wouldn't threaten his health or sanity, trying to con his teachers out of midyear grades he hadn't earned. And ROTC Band was in a big flap over the sudden departure of Lieutenant Gung-ho Monroe. The crazy idiot had gone and *joined the Army.* Enlisted, voluntarily signed up! Mike always knew he was nuts. With the war practically over Monroe swapped his safe cadet brass for a regulation GI suit and rushed out to win genuine medals for bravery. Medals, hell. He'd get his ass blown off with a grenade, that's what he'd get. . . . He left a hole in the ROTC chain of command, a gap Mike might be asked to fill. But Mike wasn't holding his breath. He didn't go wild any more at the thought of pink officer's pants and a saber. Kid stuff. He already had a good built-in saber and Darleen's pink pants were enough to excite the living hell out of it.

188

On occasion. Not so much today. He didn't feel so brisk about executing saber-dance maneuvers this morning. One chorus was plenty.

"I think I'm catching cold or something."

Darleen giggled. "You're kidding. A real cold now after all those phony ones? The school office won't believe it."

"Those dopes will believe anything. Six absences in three weeks and no two days together, Jesus, how gullible can you get?"

"That's because I forge such beautiful excuses for you. Yours aren't bad either. The secretary looked kind of sharply at the one I turned in yesterday—you know, where you spilled the Coke on it? I told her it was cough medicine. It's lucky we don't go to the same school. They would notice something fishy if our illnesses always matched."

Mike sneezed again. "If you catch this, we'll keep right on matching."

"Well, don't walk around barefoot, silly. Honestly, Michael, what would you do without me to take care of you?" She kissed him comfortingly. "Yes, you do feel hot. Is that fever or passion?"

"I don't know. It feels kind of cold in here to me."

"If you can't tell, it must be fever. You put your bathrobe and slippers on and I'll cook your lunch, how about that? I feel very domestic today."

"Domestic, my ass. You wouldn't know which end of a can to open."

"Certainly I would. I'm an excellent cook, you have no idea. Wait until you taste my creamed tunafish à la Rice Krispies."

"Jeez, no, never mind. Sandwiches are okay."

"No, I'm going to cook you a nice hot meal," she said with stubborn sweetness. So she did, playing house in the kitchen as if it were her own little honeymoon cottage. She spilled crumbs on the floor and splattered grease on the stove and burned the hell out of Mom's favorite saucepan. "Well, I couldn't help it. I'm not used to electric stoves, we have gas."

The stuff she cooked wasn't so great either, barely edible after he scraped off the burned parts. As a newlywed bride she could cause a guy some bad indigestion. "Now I really am going to get sick."

"Well, I like that!" She pulled an anguished face and she really did look a little bit hurt—embarrassed, probably, that she'd messed it up. She turned on the radio carelessly, a blast of noon-

189

time polka music. Mike leaped to turn the volume down. "Hey, watch out! The neighbors will hear it."

"So what if they do? You're home sick with a cold, aren't you?"

"At Bryan I'm home sick. At home I'm in school like a good little boy."

"Where are you right now, what class?"

"Oh, let's see. Fifth hour, I guess. I just ate lunch and went to history."

"That's a coincidence. I'm taking a test in government this very minute. What a bore. Can you name all the Cabinet members in order of succession after Roosevelt?"

"Last year I could. State, Treasury, War and I forget the rest."

"Me too. It's silly anyway. How could the President and Vice President and six or eight other people all drop dead at the same—"

The phone rang right at Mike's elbow and he jumped a foot. He hesitated, started to lift the receiver, but Darleen grabbed his arm. "Don't, stupid, leave it alone!" They both sat watching while it rang itself to death, six or seven rings before it quit.

"Maybe I should have answered."

"No, of course not. Who'd be calling? Your mother wouldn't call an empty house, and nobody would call her here while she 's at work, unless it was a salesman or a wrong number."

"Maybe the school to check if I'm really home sick like I keep saying I am? I bet that's who it was, dammit. And now they'll know I was ditching."

"Don't worry, it's all right. If they never called before, they won't start now." She sat down on his lap and put her arms around his neck. "There's nobody here but us chickens." She nuzzled up against him and started to mess with his hair, but he didn't feel like necking now. After a while she realized it and gave up, looking hurt again. "Party pooper. Let's do something. Let's go downtown to the show."

"Unh-unh, it's too cold out."

"It's cold in here too. Come on, let's go. It's a good show and I want to see it."

"Go see it, then. Go ahead, who's stopping you?"

"You are, party pooper. I didn't ditch out on a very important government test today just to go to the movies by myself. I did it for you, but if you don't want me here just say so. That's all you have to do, Michael, just say so and I'll know how you feel about me. *I* can tell when I'm not appreciated."

"Oh, hell," Mike said. "Shut up and let's go to the show."

The weather was rotten, but the movie was good, so good they sat through it twice. Mike got home late and had to hustle to clean things up. No telling what souvenirs Darleen might leave behind these days, butts or books (with her name all over the cover and six inches high) or long blond hairs in the bathroom sink. Today there was the mess in the kitchen, grease and crumbs and the saucepan burned black and practically ruined. Domestic, ha. He was still scrubbing at it frantically when Mom walked in.

"What happened there?"

He thought fast. "I was fixing myself a snack after school and, uh, forgot it. I'm sorry. I'll clean it up."

She looked surprised and for good reason. He had been cooking for years without burning pots. "You look feverish. Are you catching a cold by any chance?"

"Yeah, I could be. But I doubt it," he added quickly, remembering that the band had a job Saturday night. He couldn't afford to be sick.

"I don't doubt it. Everybody else I know has one. Germ warfare—they cough and sneeze in my face all day long. You're not taking care of yourself, that's the trouble. You don't get enough rest."

"Sure I do." He knew where *that* argument would lead. Too many band jobs, not enough sleep for a growing boy. She would be surprised if she knew how much time her growing boy spent in bed these days. . . . But he *was* catching a cold. A genuine juicy old cold in the head, just in time for the weekend. Nuts. Playing trumpet with a stopped-up nose was hell; it really loused up his breath control. Damn Darleen and her passion for movies. He should have stayed home in bed, with her or without her.

When Paul came by after dinner, Mike was feeling so runny-nosed stupid that he almost told them there was a good picture at the State they would enjoy. Just in time he remembered he couldn't have seen it yet.

"Oh, Mike, by the way," Paul said suddenly, "your commission came through today."

"My what?"

"Third band officer. Congratulations, buddy, you're a big wheel at last."

"I'll be damned," Mike said. "No kidding, huh? It's official?"

"Straight from headquarters."

Well, now, and how about that? Big wheel at last, after all hope was dead and buried. Lieutenant Mike Riley would march grandly across the stage of Roseland Gardens with his proud saber outthrust (no, no, not that one, the metal one!) and his lovely lady fair upon his gallant arm. What lady fair? Could he take *Darleen* to the Ball? Technically he could. A few guys dated Morton girls, and she would love to go. But in their case, Jesus, it would be risky.

Paul was looking at him oddly, as though he expected a more wildly excited reaction and maybe some gratitude. He might have engineered the whole deal himself. Gung-ho Monroe had never been Paul's choice. "I figured you'd want to hear the news. I tried to phone you at noon, but I didn't get any answer."

Mike saw the puzzled look on Mom's face and rushed in fast. "Oh, was that you? Yeah, I heard it ring, but I couldn't come. I was, uh, in the bathroom."

"When?" Mom asked. "At noon *today?* Here? You weren't in school?"

Oh, Jesus, he thought, and started babbling. "Yeah, well, you know, my cold. You wouldn't want me sneezing germs all over the school to start epidemics, would you?"

"No, of course not. But you didn't tell me that you stayed home. I thought you said—" She wasn't buying it. He had slipped up somewhere in his story. But he had the cold to prove it. He blew his nose and tried to think.

"No, it's important to take care of yourself," Paul said. "I've been worried about you missing so much school lately. An infection that hangs on for weeks can be dangerous. Maybe you should see a doctor."

Mom looked more bewildered. "But Mike hasn't been sick. He hasn't missed a day since before Christmas."

Paul stared at her. "Hasn't been sick! Today, and Wednesday, and a couple of days last week and— Five or six times last month at least! *You didn't know?*"

Oh, Jesus, oh, Jesus, oh, Jesus. Mike shut his eyes. When he felt Mom clutch anxiously at his arm, he swallowed hard and opened them.

192

"Michael! Were you staying home sick when I didn't know it? Tell me right now, Mike. I have to know."

He blew his nose again, stalling for time. Not an excuse in his head, not a glimmer of thought. Trapped. Trapped like a sneezing rat.

"I—I missed a couple of days."

"Paul said five or six."

Paul has a goddamn big mouth. "Yeah, maybe, I guess it could have been."

"They were excused absences." Paul shafted him deeper but oh, so casually. He knew damn well those notes were forged, and he wanted to make sure Mom knew it too.

"Michael?"

He pushed his hair back from a hot sweating forehead. He was burning up right under their eyes and they had him on the spit with flames below. No fair, dammit, no fair to pick on a guy when he was sick, *really* sick. "I wrote the excuses. I didn't want to worry you."

"Worry me! Mike, how could you? Don't you think I have a right to worry when you're sick?"

"If he was," Paul said half to himself, but loud enough.

"Yes, that's right, *if* you were. It's very funny you could be sick six times without me noticing it. Which days exactly did you miss?"

"I forget." He couldn't have told her today's date right now, he felt so rotten and guilty. "Wednesday."

"And you played a job Tuesday. I'll bet every one of those absences came right after a band job, didn't it? You weren't sick. You skipped school to sleep late because you were tired. Weekends were bad enough, but now it's school nights too. You just can't do it, that's all. It's ruining your health and it's probably ruining your schoolwork. When do midyear grades come out? Or have they come already and I didn't know about that either?" She looked ready to accuse him of burning his report card or forging her name there too.

"Today," Paul said. "He wasn't there to get his."

"Yes, but I'm not flunking anything. My grades are perfectly okay. They'd have to be or I couldn't get the commission, isn't that right Paul?"

Paul nodded rather unwillingly. Mike could swear he was enjoying this scene. *Thanks,* dad, I'll do you a few big favors

193

sometime. You can take your goddamn commission and stick it up your ass. And don't come sniffing around here trying to catch Mom with your two-bit candy boxes and Friday nights at the movies. We don't need you here. I warned you once before but you ignored the hint. Get lost, man, get lost.

"Even if your grades are straight A, you still can't skip school to sleep," Mom said impatiently. "Suppose I stayed home from the office that way, what do you think would happen?"

"You'd be canned."

"Exactly, and my work wouldn't get done. You have responsibilities too, Mike, don't you realize that? They just made you an officer of the band. And your other classes are equally important whether you like them or not. You're a graduating senior! Your education is the most essential part of your life. . . ."

She was warming up to a really square lecture when the phone rang. Mike grabbed it—anything to escape the Education-Above-All routine.

"Hello, tiger," Darleen said in her sultriest movie-star voice. His temperature shot up five degrees, not so much from passion as from panic. Oh, Jesus, what a night! Everything coming down on him at once when he couldn't even think in a straight line. Darleen on the phone and Mom and Paul standing right there hearing every word he said.

"Hi," he croaked.

"How's the cold, lover boy? You sound worse. Was the trip to the movies too much for you?"

He cleared his throat. "I'm fine, thanks. How are you?"

"Just fiiiine. But lonesome. There's nobody home at my house tonight but little old me, just sitting here in my peekaboo nightie and wishing for company."

He cleared his throat again. "Uh, well, I've got some right here."

"Some what? Oh, you mean company? Like your mother, maybe?"

"Among others. *Right* here."

"Oh, and you can't talk. I get it. Okay, answer yes or no. Did I leave my lipstick there today?"

He choked and started coughing. "Where?"

"That's what I'm asking you. Under your bed or in the

194

bathroom or someplace. If it's there, you'd better find it before somebody else does."

"I'll say. I'll, uh, check into it and let you know."

"It's a brand-new tube and I don't want to lose it. Bring it to the job tomorrow if you find it, okay?"

"Yeah, if I'm there."

"Why wouldn't you be? You're not *that* sick."

"It's, uh, uncertain at the moment. Things are— Well, I've got a bad cold, see, and I stayed home from school today—"

She giggled. "I know that, dopey. I stayed home with you, remember?"

"And my mom may not let me work tomorrow night."

Darleen paused to think this over. "Is she still listening now?"

"Yes."

"And she *knows* you skipped today?"

"Yes."

"Oh-oh. Is she mad?"

"Yes."

"Just today, though? I mean not all the other times too?"

"*Yes!*"

"But she doesn't know *why*, does she?" Darleen's voice rose in panic.

"No."

Her sigh of relief almost blew the receiver out of his hand. "Sheeeesh! Oh, did you have me scared! Listen, you find that lipstick and bring it tomorrow or Monday or whenever you can. And don't say another word to *anybody*, understand? That wasn't very bright, you know. Very careless, I'd say."

"Same to you," Mike said and hung up. Everybody was picking on him tonight and he couldn't even defend himself, he was *sick*. But he'd be sicker if Mom found that lipstick. He rushed to the bathroom, letting them think he was about to heave or crap his pants or something. He didn't care what they thought as long as he found it first. And there the damn thing was, a little gold tube right in plain sight on the floor where anybody could step on it. Jesus, she had a nerve talking about carelessness. She might as well have written her name purple across the mirror— "DARLEEN WAS HERE."

He dropped it into his pocket and flushed the toilet for effect and then took two aspirins for real. He must have 105° fever. If anything else went wrong tonight, he would die.

Mom and Paul were putting their coats on when he came back, so it looked like a lull in the storm. "Enjoy yourself at the movies," he said politely. "I'm going to bed early."

"You do that," Mom said. "I'll talk to you tomorrow." She would, too; he knew she would. She had plenty of lecture saved for three or four more installments.

"Take care of that cold," Paul advised him in a friendly, almost fatherly voice as he left. "I'd like to see you in school Monday."

"I feel sure that you will," Mike said. I'd like to see you in hell Monday, you bastard. But don't bust your stiff leg on our icy sidewalk like the man who came to dinner, because we don't have any extra beds here. Nobody wants to sleep with you, man. But nobody.

VII

IT was a cold night at the Lanville Skyline Club, cold inside and out. Johnny Dean and His Band sounded like nine refugee penguins huddled on an iceberg. The saxes were all flat. Sammy had a sore lip and gliched notes right and left. Mike's "Stardust" echoed lonesomely through the half-empty hall. *He* was okay tonight, recovered from his cold and feeling fine, but he couldn't carry the whole band on his back. Considering the puny size of the crowd, they could all have stayed home in bed. Bill Rhodes himself might have trouble drawing a crowd tonight, let alone a sour semipro band that Lanville had never heard of. They stayed away in droves.

" *'Oh, I'm packing my grip . . . and I'm leaving today. . . .'* "

Mike played the muted figures behind Darleen's vocal without bothering to count the rests between. Of all the rotten times to book a percentage job, midweek on a stormy night! Johnny should have known better, even if it was Mel's uncle's place. If the attendance didn't improve fast, they could really get shafted.

" *'Taking a trip . . . California way. . . .'* " True, man, true. He'd sell his soul for the San Fernando Valley right now, golden sunny land of orange blossoms and romance. Nebraska winters were six months long. It was winter before he met Darleen, and still winter three weeks after they broke up housekeeping. What a season he'd spent—December in pursuit, January in bed, half of February

197

recovering. He still missed her, but by no means badly enough to commit suicide in a snowdrift. There were other chicks around. . . .

. . . Like that cocktail waitress tonight in the little black dress hardly more than a bathing suit, lo-and-behold at the top, ass-high at the bottom. If a customer dropped a ten-dollar tip on the floor, she wouldn't dare bend over to pick it up. Her dangly earrings went jingle-jangle-jingle as she switched her hips past the bandstand and she smiled at Mike each time she passed—smiled at him personally, he could swear it. The sight of all those drinks going by made him thirsty, so he flagged her down. "Hey, beautiful, bring me a Coke next time, okay?" She winked at him and jingled away.

"Bet she won't," Sammy said.

Mike shrugged. He doubted it too, but no harm asking. And two numbers later there it was, a glass of Coke delivered right to the back of the bandstand, service with a glowing smile. "Hey, thanks. How much?"

"It's on the house if you play 'Stardust' again."

"Well, sure, that's my pleasure anytime." He took a swig and almost choked because it wasn't what he expected, not straight Coke but spiked. Heeey now, how about that? If he went to the bar and ordered a Coke-high they would laugh in his face. But now it came free without asking, just because the waitress liked his trumpet style. He set the glass down beside his chair and took a gulp each time the brass laid out. Drinking on the stand wasn't exactly cricket. It made him look like a boozehound who couldn't wait for intermission. But it tasted good and it warmed his chilly soul, just what he needed, a dose of fizz and bottled well-being.

His second "Stardust" sounded ten times better than the first. Sammy looked envious. "What was in that Coke?"

Mike just smiled. "Talent, pure talent."

From then on the evening warmed up. He drank two more stiffly spiked Cokes and paid for them with two more splendid trumpet solos—"Velvet Moon," "You Made Me Love You" —while Miss Jingle-Jangle stood by the stand watching him, letting her ice melt, letting her customers die of thirst, letting the other girls steal her tips. If that wasn't appreciation, Mike never saw it. She was no dumb little bobby-soxer either, but grown and mature, at least nineteen and plenty wise. Working in a ballroom,

198

she must hear trumpets every night, good and bad ones. She could recognize talent.

When the dance ended at midnight, Mike let the other peons load up the gear. The Great Riley would sign autographs and chat with his admiring public, whose name was Angie. She really thought he sounded like Rhodes—which he did, of course, tonight as never before. He knew it, and it warmed his heart to know that other people thought so too.

But his warm expansive Riley-the-Great balloon burst when Johnny handed him his share of the take home pay. Three bucks, three lousy bucks for four hours of the most superlative trumpet playing the Skyline Club had ever heard. *Three lousy stinking dollars!*

"Tell Uncle Albert to take it and jam it!"

"You tell him," Johnny said glumly. "I tried and Mel tried, but it's no use. We agreed to play for percentage and that's what we got."

"Shafted is what we got. An icicle right up the ass we got, and after we mushed our dog sleds thirty miles across Siberia to play in his lousy igloo." Mike turned indignantly to Angie. "How can you stand to work for such a penny-pinching bastard? Does he pay you a salary or do you survive on tips?"

She apologized for her cheapskate boss and offered some after-hours consolation drinks for Mike and his closest friends, who turned out suddenly to be Johnny and Darleen. The others went home loaded to the roof of Dean's car, unaware that the leftover trio planned to stay and get loaded on the spot. For almost an hour they sat at a table near the supposedly closed bar, drinking, talking, kidding with Angie, who doubled as their hostess and barmaid. Mike had a good head start, three under his belt already but no intention of quitting. Darleen and Angie kept up pretty well, but Johnny nursed one drink along in a lazy manner. "It's a long trip and I don't know, the roads could be pretty bad."

Mike was playing footsie with Angie and only half listening. "What? Rhodes could *never* be bad! How can you cast such scurvilous remarks about the world's finest living or dead trumpeter?"

"I didn't say Rhodes, I said roads. R-o-a-d-s. Streets. Highways. Pavement."

"Oh. I thought you meant going to Omaha to see Rhodes. You said long trip. But it'll be worth it, man, you know it's worth it."

Angie looked interested. "Is Bill Rhodes coming to Omaha, really, in person? At the Orpheum?"

"No, it's a one-nighter. He never plays stage shows anymore."

"Are you going?"

"Goddamn right I'm going. I'll crawl on my knees through the snow if necessary, but I presume Johnny's going to drive us, aren't you, old buddy?"

"If I have the gas, old buddy."

"I'll steal you the gas personally. Jeez, I was scared when I saw the date. I thought March fourteenth was the Military Ball, but it's the sixteenth. That would absolutely tear me apart if they both hit on the same night. I have to make the Ball, but I been waiting my entire life to see Rhodes."

"I don't see why," Darleen said in a sarcastic voice. "You're every bit as good as he is, aren't you? Maybe even slightly better?"

Mike winked at Angie. "Well, yes, now that you mention it, maybe I am. But his *band* is better." He knew what was itching Darleen tonight. But how could he help it if another cute chick liked his style? When a man became famous, the girls always followed him around, begging for autographs, snatching his shirt buttons, offering him their delicious ass on a plate. Mike already knew Darleen's flavor—butterscotch ripple delight and very tasty too. But Angie would be something else. Hair and eyes like rich dark chocolate sauce, fresh strawberry lips, double scoops of smooth vanilla rising from the lo-and-behold neckline. Everything right there but the cherry and who needed that? Not that he'd get around to it tonight, probably, but *he could if he wanted to*. And Darleen was jealous as hell. She thought she still owned him, but he had news for her. Riley the Great signed *no* long-term contracts, but he could make a lot of cute chicks happy on a one-night-stand basis. Jerry's old philosophy—lay 'em and leave 'em.

He had to leave this one unlaid, though. Johnny insisted they must hit the road. "One o'clock, let's go. I have to get up in the morning."

"So what? I do too." Mike shed a tear for the sweet bygone days of sleeping late. He couldn't risk a thing at school now, not even minor tardiness. Paul would find out and rat straight back to headquarters. "Well, good night, Angie. I certainly do hope that you have the extreme pleasure of meeting me again in the near future," he said grandly. "Though I personally would not play another job in this lousy cheapskate hall if you gave me one-hundred-and-*ten* percent of the gate."

Three in the front seat for warmth and company, drums and equipment filling the back, they drove across sleepy Lanville in the black-and-white night. It was snowing again, and no chains on the Plymouth. Johnny hadn't wanted to clunk thirty miles over cleared highways, but now the streets were turning slick. "We should have started sooner."

"That's all right," Mike said comfortably. "We have the utmost confidence in your considerate driving skill. Don't we, honey?" He wrapped his arm around Darleen's shoulders. She unwrapped it and handed it back to him. "S'matter, honey, are you peeved about something? Tell Johnny how much we trust his con-conspishuous skill."

"Well, I don't trust these tires," Johnny said. "This could be a hairy trip."

"Who's Harry Tripp? Any relation to old Slippery Rhodes the famous Eskimo trumpeter? He's coming to Omaha on the sixteenth, remember. We have to be there in person."

"You mean the fourteenth," Darleen said.

"Fourteenth, sixteenth, any old night except Ball night, when I am previously engaged. Without me they couldn't even *give* their stinking concert, that's how essential I— Goddammit, man, what are you— Hey, watchit, *watchit!*"

Johnny hit the brakes too late for the stop sign. The car kept right on going, skating on the icy corner, slithering in a slow crosswise skid onto the highway and square into the path of the only oncoming car in half a mile. He wrenched the wheel uselessly; the other car swerved, but they met fender to fender in a crunching thud and a tinkle of shattered glass.

There were two stunned measures of rest before Johnny caught his breath and started swearing. Mike removed his head from the glove compartment and straightened up cautiously, dislodging Darleen, who clung to his back like a knapsack.

"And so much for your consumptive driving *skill*. Jesus, what happened?"

"Ice. I *told* you those tires—"

The man from the other car rapped anxiously against the window. "Okay in there? Anybody hurt?"

Johnny cranked the glass down. "I guess not."

"No," Darleen said in a small shaky voice.

"Yes, goddammit!" Mike clapped a hand suddenly to his face where he felt trickling wetness. "My nose! Oh, Jesus, gimme a handkerchief somebody, quick, I'm bleeding like a pig." He couldn't see the blood, but he could feel it on his hand and taste it in his throat. "You broke my nose, you sonuvabitchin' roadhog bastard!"

Darleen gasped and began to cry.

"Now, just a minute! You were the ones who ran the stop sign and plowed into me!"

"Didn't run it," Johnny said. "Skidded it. Ice on the street, I couldn't stop."

"Don't tell me, sonny. Just stick around and explain it to the cops."

Johnny went to inspect the crumpled fenders, but Mike sat where he was, nursing his nose, until Lanville's lawman arrived at the scene of the crime. Disgruntled by being brought out on a night like this, he listened and questioned and slowly wrote down copious details. Darleen sobbed and shivered. Mike soaked through two handkerchiefs and began on his shirttail.

"Listen, dammit, quit horsing around all night. Why don't you just arrest the bastard and let us go home?"

"Shut up, Mike," Johnny said out of the side of his mouth. "It's all right."

"No, it's not all right! I got a broken nose, man, I need a doctor."

The cop gave him a look of sudden interest. "Let's see your nose."

"Don't touch it, dammit, it's fractured."

"Umm-hmmmm." The cop handed him a new handkerchief and made more notes in his little book. "How did it happen?"

"I hit it on the dashboard when this friggin' roadhog creamed into us going seventy down the wrong side of the highway."

"Who was on the wrong side?"

"*He* was, stupid, who'd you think? Jesus, do I have to bleed here all night while you write a book?"

"No, bud, you sure don't. Get in my car and we'll go see to your medical attention."

202

"No, no, that's all right," Johnny said quickly. "I'll take him."

The cop ignored him and turned to the Ford owner. "If your car is still running okay, you can drive to the station and file your complaint now, or in the morning will be all right. Okay, you three, come along."

By the time a weary doctor came to the police station to inspect Mike's nose the bleeding had stopped. He poked it a bit and gave his casual professional opinion that no, it was not broken, only slightly bent. "But you could get an X-ray tomorrow to make sure."

Mike touched it gingerly. "Thank God it wasn't my lip."

"Why?"

"I play trumpet for a living, man. My lip is valuable."

"Nothing seems to be wrong with your lip," the cop said sourly. "Plenty left."

The desk sergeant looked thoughtful. "Trumpet, you say? Swing band? Where were you playing tonight?"

"Shylock Club."

"Skyline Club," Johnny said.

"What I meant. Shylock's the guy who runs it, Uncle Albert Shylock the well-known three-dollar miser. Never catch me playing *there* again, believe me."

The sergeant exchanged significant glances with the doctor and added another note to the report. "You just may not get the opportunity. How old are you, Riley?"

"Twenty-one."

"Draft card?"

"Seventeen, so what? Is it a crime to be seventeen in Lanville?"

"When you're drunk in a car at one A.M., it is."

"I wasn't driving."

"Be thankful that you weren't, bud. You'd have worse than a bloody nose now. Your pal here fixed you up pretty well anyway. Well, there's none of you in shape to drive around the block, let alone Connor City, so I think we'll just keep you here until morning."

"Morning! You can't do that! You can't hold us unless you arrest us. You got to arrest us or turn us loose, one or the other."

"Shut *up*, man!" Johnny said in an anguished voice.

"Shut up, hell. I know my rights. I want a lawyer. What's the charge?"

The sergeant looked disgusted. "Do you really want a charge?

203

Let's see—running a stop sign, speeding, reckless driving, disturbing the peace, threatening an officer . . . and who did you say sold you that whiskey?"

Mike finally got the picture and subsided.

"Tell you what. You can be our guests tonight, or you can all go home as soon as a responsible adult comes to pick you up. Which one wants to call your parents?"

They looked at each other for a while. Then Johnny cleared his throat respectfully. "Well, sir, I would, but they couldn't come because I have their car. That's what we got wrecked in, see?"

"How about you, trumpet man? I think I'd like to meet *your* folks."

Mike touched his swollen nose. "Tough luck. My mom doesn't drive."

They all looked at Darleen, who started sniffling again.

"Well?"

After another long silence Mike sighed. "Well, gimme the phone, dammit. I know somebody I can call."

Paul struggled to the surface of sleep and realized that the sound which his dream had symbolized as an insistently ringing telephone was, in fact, a telephone ringing insistently. He rolled out of bed onto the wrong leg; it buckled and sent him sprawling against the doorjamb. Cursing, he limped to the desk to strangle the phone. At this hour what else could it be but a wrong number, some sociable drunk wanting to chat with good ol' pal Charlie.

There was a brief word or two he didn't catch and then Mike was on the line, far-off and uncertain. "Paul? Uh . . . are you awake?"

"No!" Worse than sociable drunks, it was schoolboy humor. "What in hell do you want?"

"Help, man," Mike said. His voice was blurry, almost as if he were crying. "Can you come? We had a —wreck . . ."

It hit him with a physical blow, a lead-pipe smack in the stomach that knocked him off his feet and into the desk chair, doubled over and gasping. Mike was still talking but he couldn't hear a word. *No, oh, God, no not again, it can't happen again, not twice, not to me. . . .*

He choked on the words before he got them out. "What—is—is she all right?"

Silence on the line, or his heart pounding so hard he couldn't hear. "Mike, for God's sake you have to tell me—*is she hurt?*" *God, no, please not again. . . .*

"Darleen?" Mike said vaguely.

"*What?*" The old nightmare took a terrifying new twist. *Somebody* was hurt in the car. Someone screamed for help, but he couldn't help her. He couldn't move while he lay pinned under the wheel, his leg twisted in agonizing pain and blood running down his face. Blood pouring into his eyes and he couldn't see who was crying beside him, Beth or Kathy or . . . *Darleen?* Who in hell was Darleen? Nightmare dissolved into reality again. Sweat on his face, not blood. A telephone receiver gripped in his hand, not a steering wheel. He wasn't trapped, he could move, and the ache in his leg came only from collision with the dark doorframe. He took a shuddering breath. Darleen. Mike. "Where *are* you?"

"Lanville."

Paul took another breath as the fog began to lift. Lanville, of course. A band job, another weeknight date. So Kathy was safe at home. Only a trick of sleep-fogged memory had put her into a hideously wrecked car. But there *was* a wreck.

"Are you all right?"

"No," Mike said. "We're in jail."

"Jail! What'd you do?"

"Nothing. We didn't do a thing, but this dumb squarehead cop won't turn us loose till somebody comes. You gotta bail us out, man."

"Oh, no, I don't." Panic gave way to relief, and relief to anger. Mike couldn't do that to him, wake him up at 2 A.M. babbling about accidents and pushing him back across three years into nearly forgotten horror. If Mike was safe in jail, he could damn well stay there till morning. Best place for him. Teach him something.

"Hey, listen, this is no joke! Johnny has to go to work tomorrow and Darleen won't stop crying and it's colder'n hell in here. Come get us, Paul. Please."

It would be a tough lesson for scared kids, cold and shaken up, while their parents waited at home, wondering whey they didn't come. Kathy waiting and listening for Mike. . . .

"All right," he said. "Sit tight, I'm coming."

*   *   *

It took him nearly an hour to drive it in the foul weather, but he found the Lanville police station without difficulty, the only lighted building in town. A sleepy sergeant sat behind the desk and three kids waited in the corner, Mike and Johnny slouched side by side on a straight wooden bench, the girl huddled miserably in a chair.

Relief washed over Mike's face when he saw Paul. "Jesus, what took you so long?" The words were blurred. There was blood on his chin, spatters of blood on the front of his white shirt, dried to an ugly reddish brown. He stood up fast and then swayed dizzily. Paul grabbed him, gripping his shoulders hard, steadying himself as much as Mike.

"*What happened to you?*"

"Nothing," Mike said thickly. "Nosebleed. Not busted. S'only a damn bloody nose."

Then Paul smelled the whiskey. He looked from Mike's foolish smile to Johnny, flushed and half asleep. Drunk, both of them. Drunk enough to wreck a car and risk themselves and the lives of any poor fools unlucky enough to cross their path. He released Mike with a sudden shove. Mike backed into the bench and sat down hard. Paul fought down anger as he looked at them— Johnny unmarked, Mike bloodstained, the sniffling bedraggled girl who had to be Darleen. The band vocalist, presumably, and a sad little canary she was now—blond curls disheveled, makeup streaked with tears, dark smears of mascara under her eyes, wet muddy stains on the hem of her green formal dress. But no blood on her or on Johnny, and not very much on Mike. Fools and drunks were always spared; only the innocent suffered.

Paul turned away abruptly and went to talk to the desk sergeant. "What's the story?"

He felt sicker as he heard it. But it could have been worse, so much, much worse. Four people shaken up, but no serious injuries and only minor damage—a crushed fender on the innocent Ford, fender and headlight on the guilty Plymouth, both cars able to drive away. "They couldn't have been moving too fast when they hit," the sergeant said. "Schultz said he skidded through the stop sign and God knows the streets are slick enough tonight. He's had a couple, but he's not too drunk to remember. They came out lucky, that's all. Another bunch of idiot drunk kids had a head-on collision here at Christmas time—wrecked both cars, killed two people, three more still in the hospital. A girl younger than that one there lost her arm, torn right off, Jesus, and they say her face is messed up for life. Nice Christmas present, huh? They'd been to the same place, too, that damn Skyline Club. Somebody is awfully generous with underage liquor out there. But what the hell, these kids nowadays all carry false ID cards. If they don't buy it in bars, they drink it at home. I tell you we've had more juvenile trouble in this town in the last two years than everything else put together. They get drunk and swipe cars and throw rocks through windows and shoplift and fight and the parents don't know what's going on because Papa's working days and Mama's working swing while the kids run wild day *and* night. Little six-year-olds left alone at the show till midnight, would you believe that? Cheaper than hiring a baby-sitter. Which of these three did you say is yours?"

"None of them exactly. My name's Kessler; I'm a friend of Mike's—well, a family friend, you might say."

"Oh, yeah, the hotshot with the valuable lip." The sergeant made a disgusted face. "Now that one I wouldn't mind locking up for a few days. Has he been in much trouble before?"

"No, not really."

"He will be. He's working on it, believe me. I've seen a lot of his kind in here, mister. They think they're too damn smart to get caught. Well, you can take them home now if you want to. I don't imagine anybody's losing much sleep worrying about them, but you never know. If you want to do them a favor, make sure the parents hear exactly what happened. They won't thank you, but they ought to know."

No, they won't thank me, Paul agreed silently as he turned to face the dejected trio in the corner, still frozen as he had left them—Darleen curled up in her chair, tearstained and sniffling, Johnny dozing openmouthed, Mike staring vacantly straight ahead, touching a tentative finger to his swollen nose. "Okay, come on, let's go."

Mike nudged Johnny awake with his elbow. "Come on, man, we're blowing jail. Good old Uncle Paul sprung for bail and he's taking us bye-bye."

Paul's hands clenched into fists. Nothing but the sight of the blood on Mike's shirt kept him from swinging. I'm not your uncle, you crummy punk. Not your uncle or your father and I'm going to do something for you that your own father was afraid to do, afraid and ashamed. I'm going to take you home to your mother and watch her heart break when she sees you.

It was a long thirty miles in the cold dark night, headlights cutting a narrow path through falling snow on an empty highway. The car heater didn't work right, had never worked right in three years. The boys in back slept huddled in their overcoats. Darleen shivered in the front seat, her cheap short jacket clutched tight around bare shoulders. Suddenly she began crying again, desperate uncontrollable sobs. Paul thought vaguely of shock and internal injuries. "You're sure you're all right? You're not hurt?"

She shook her head, but she didn't stop crying. The poor kid, Paul thought, scared to go home and face her family at four in the morning. The boys hadn't been drinking alone; she'd had her share. Maybe sequins and painted-on glamor gave her the right to explore adult kicks, but now she was scared and sorry. Or, on the other hand, maybe not. Maybe her tears fell only for a wet stained dress and muddy silver shoes.

Connor City lay silent and unconcerned. Sleepy traffic lights blinked at deserted streets. Darleen's house was dark when they found it. Paul thought about the Lanville sergeant's last request, but he couldn't follow through. He didn't have the guts to wake those people and try to tell them where their daughter had been tonight or what had almost happened to her. If they weren't awake and worrying now, they didn't deserve to know. Facing Kathy would be bad enough, let alone any drowsy bewildered strangers, likely as not to leap to false conclusions and blame *him* for the whole mess. Darleen would just have to take care of herself. In spite of her despairing tears, he had a hunch that she could.

No lights at the Schultz place either, but he didn't worry about Johnny escaping punishment. By the time Mr. Schultz had ridden the bus to work for a few days and gone to Lanville to recover his car and argued with insurance men and settled for two damaged front ends he wouldn't be likely to forgive or forget.

Mike was asleep when they reached the apartment, asleep or faking. Paul reached over and shook him hard. "Come on, snap out of it. You're home." Mike looked around vaguely, then picked up his horn (still with him through thick and thin, though Johnny's drums had stayed in Lanville) and opened the car door. "Thanks, man. Real frienna need. See ya round."

"Not so fast. I'm coming up with you."

"You don't needa do that."

"Oh, yes, I do," Paul said. But he was the one who had trouble on the stairs, dragging his stiff leg and holding the railing while Mike went up light as a bird and waited at the top, leaning lazily against the wall, yawning, trying to look as though there were nothing wrong with him that a good night's sleep wouldn't cure. When Paul reached for the doorbell, Mike grabbed his arm.

"Don't. No sense wakin' people *up*. I got a key."

Paul hesitated. It would be so much easier that way. He had done everything now that a friend in need should do—answered the midnight summons, driven sixty miles through the dark winter night, bailed the kids out of their trouble and delivered them home to their doors, safe and virtually unharmed. Now their parents could take over, listen to the excuses and mete out the punishment, if any. He had no responsibility for Mike, no right to force an issue. Let Mike use his key and sneak in unannounced. Let him gargle to cover his breath, let him invent lies to explain his bloody shirt in the morning. He could do it. Kathy would fuss and weep and lecture. Mike would say, "Sorry, Mom, give me another chance," and go on to bigger and better crimes, finer and fancier heartbreak.

Paul took a deep breath and pushed the doorbell. Mike said, "Aw, hey, man—" and trailed into silence, waiting.

They didn't wait long. Kathy must have been waiting too, tense and listening in the dark. By one o'clock Mike could have been home, by two he certainly should have been and now it was after four. Long hours of waiting and wondering, imagining every possible kind of trouble, listening for the key in the door that meant safety or the ring of the phone that meant danger.

In less than a minute Paul heard her coming, so anxious that she didn't even stop to check who it was, a simple precaution that years of living alone must surely have taught her. You don't open your door to the unknown that way, not in Chicago, not in wartime Connor City, certainly not if you are a woman alone at night. Not unless you are half out of your mind with anxiety.

"Did you forget your—" she began, just a touch of impatience in a voice warm with relief. She saw Paul and stopped, bewildered. Then she saw Mike and gasped. Barefoot on the rug in a flowered robe, her hair tousled from a restless night, her face wiped clean of makeup and startlingly pale, she looked at this moment as old as Paul felt, a frantic parental forty, and he loved her more than he ever had before.

And then she was sobbing against Mike's bloodstained chest, her arms tight around him, as if by clinging fiercely enough she could protect him retroactively from the dangers he had faced. "Mike, Michael, you're hurt—what happened to you—how did it happen—"

"Jesus Christ, another bawling dame," Mike said. "They're drowning me tonight."

Paul could have knocked him down for that. But he kept his clenched fists at his sides and waited for the rest of the scene. Almost blinded by her tears, Kathy saw only the obvious marks of suffering, the dried blood and swollen nose. "Were you in a fight?"

"Yeah," Mike said vacantly. "Oughta see the other guy."

Paul didn't have to refute the lie. Kathy smelled alcohol at last, and her sympathy turned instantly to horror. "You've been drinking!"

"Nothin' but good old Cola-Cola. They never sell highballs to minors at the Shylock Club. I mean Skylark Club."

She stared at him silently, too stunned now even to cry. It isn't true, her shocked face pleaded. This sodden young stranger reeking of liquor can't be my son. I don't know him. *I don't know him. . . .*

Mike leaned against the closed front door, tall but slouched, his deep red hair a tangle of oily strands, his eyes half-closed in smudgy shadows, mouth drooping, the slot of his chin marked sharply in dried blood. In the musician's working clothes—tuxedo, stained shirt and cockeyed bow tie— he too looked older, much too old and much too wearily wise. Kathy stared at him and her face went even paler, numb with a sort of horrified recognition. Paul knew what she was seeing. He saw it too, though he had no basis for comparison but a single casual glance at a USO group photograph. But she had known the original far too well, far too intimately, had seen him too many times in the same clothes, the same condition. She couldn't deny it now, however desperately she wanted to. Take a good look, Paul thought. This kid is not your baby, Kathy. He's Jerry Riley's boy too, and I think it's time you remembered it.

She knew it now. "That settles it. You'll quit that band right now!"

Mike shook his head with lazy confidence. "That's what you think."

"That's what I know! This is it, Michael, the last straw, the very last straw. I thought so before but now I'm sure. You're through, do you understand? *No more bands!*"

"Like shit I'm through! I'll play in any band I like and you can't stop me!"

"Oh, yes, I can!" Her white face flushed with sudden anger. "Give me that trumpet!" She grabbed the case out of Mike's hand before he realized what she wanted. He grabbed back at it, lost his balance and almost fell. "We'll see whether or not I can stop you!" She flung the case onto the table and fumbled to open it. "We'll just see!"

"Hey, what are you trying to *do?* Dammit, leave my horn alone!"

There were tears of rage in Kathy's eyes as she struggled with the resisting catches. "I'll smash it, that's what I'll do! Take a hammer and smash the goddamned thing to smithereens!"

"You do and I'll smash you!" Mike lunged to protect the case or strike on its behalf, but Paul caught him by both arms and held on. "Let go, you bastard, who do you think you're shoving around? Smash you both, goddammit!" Paul tightened his grip. Mike struggled for just a moment and then slumped back in sudden relief. "It's locked. Oh, Jesus, it's locked."

"Give me the key," Kathy said.

"No!"

"I can break the lock open, you know."

"And I can break your head open! You lay just one finger on that horn and I'll kill you, so help me I will! I warn you, don't try it, I warn you—"

They were both crying now, shouting and crying in hysterical fury, Kathy balked by the locked case, Mike by Paul's restraining grip. Then she realized what they were doing, what horrible things they were saying. She said, "Oh, *no,*" in a strangled voice and covered her face with her hands. Mike quit struggling; Paul turned him loose as Kathy's rage subsided in a flood of helpless tears.

Paul thought the crisis was past. No horns would be hammered tonight and no more blood shed, thank God. Kathy could flash a frightful temper, but she couldn't back it with sustained strength. All her emotion blew up in fireworks, loud and bright but quickly burned out and forgotten. And Mike was much the same, quick to blow his top and swear violence but equally quick to smooth down. If Jerry Riley was another Irish hothead, no wonder their family life exploded.

Paul wanted to take Kathy into his arms, to hold her and comfort her until the anxious storm had passed and she could sleep the rest of the night in peace. But he couldn't. "It's late," he said stupidly, stating the obvious fact and omitting everything that mattered. "Can't you talk it over tomorrow when you're both—feeling better?"

Kathy wiped her eyes with the sleeve of her robe and looked at him as though she had forgotten he was there. As he shouldn't be, of course. No one had invited him into this heartbreak scene. Mike called for help and he answered the call, but good old Uncle Paul's bail-bonds-and-taxi-service ended at the front curb. He had no right to force himself into a family battle that began years ago and might go on for a bitter lifetime. He couldn't even take sides in it because he saw both sides too clearly. Kathy was right and Mike was right and they were both wrong. He could only stand and watch them struggle for the upper hand, hurting themselves, hurting each other, tearing him apart with divided loyalties.

"No," Kathy said wearily. "No, we'll settle it now. I won't smash the trumpet." Paul heard Mike's sob of relief. "We'll just sell it."

"No!" Mike yelled. "You can't! It's my horn and you can't touch it, you got no right, it's *mine*."

"It's not yours by any means; you've nowhere nearly paid for it. That was a ridiculously overpriced deal to begin with—two hundred dollars for a trumpet—insane! And nothing but trouble since the day you brought it home. Back it goes to Hoffman's tomorrow, do you understand, first thing tomorrow. If he wants to return the cash you gave him, that's fine. But it *goes*, and no other trumpet comes into this house either, not the old one, not any one, not ever again. If you don't take it, I will, *but it goes*."

Mike started crying. No more curses or threats of violence, only the tears of a heartbroken child. "No, don't, you can't do that,

212

please, Mom, don't, don't make me, please, you can't, you don't understand. I'll quit the band, I'll do anything you say, but don't make me sell my horn. I can't, I can't—"

Not the angry tears of a child denied candy before dinner or punished with the loss of privileges ("If you can't take better care of your bicycle, I'll lock it up for a week!"). Not tears of sadness for a misplaced teddy bear. Not even tears of pain for a badly skinned knee. In three years with three little boys Paul had heard all kinds of tragic wails, but only once like this. Huey had cried this way when his dog was run over—genuine frantic inconsolable grief for the lost beloved. Paul had cried this way in the hospital after Beth died—or he would have cried this way if grown men could. Could a seventeen-year-old boy feel such desperate grief for a *trumpet?*

"Anything you want, Mom, anything, I promise, *anything*—" Mike was ready to fall on his knees and crawl and lick dirt for that horn. Paul felt sick watching him, sick and a little bit scared because it didn't seem rational for any kid, drunk or sober, to break his heart over a lifeless coil of cold brass tubing. Maybe Mike was slightly off his head. But in any case it would be too cruel a punishment to part a musician from his instrument forever.

He looked at Kathy and shook his head. She looked from him to Mike and back again with a bewildered face. *Then what should I do?* her helpless look asked. *Tell me what to do.* He couldn't tell her because he didn't know. If Mike were his son . . . he still wouldn't know. If Mike were his son, Mike would be a different sort of kid, less volatile, less talented and certainly less practiced at conning his mother into giving him his way. But it was seventeen years too late to worry about that. The damage was already done. Kathy was the one who must decide now whether to be heartlessly cruel for Mike's own good, if good could come from cruelty, or to back down weakly and let worse disasters follow.

She knew she had to decide alone. "All right," she said finally. "We'll settle it tomorrow."

"Let me know," Paul said.

"Of course. Good night. And—thank you for—bringing him home." He realized then that there were a lot of things she still didn't know—the wreck, the police station, how Mike bloodied his shirt, Johnny Schultz driving drunk and Darleen crying her black-lashed eyes out. But she didn't have to hear them now. She had suffered enough bad news for one night. Mike wouldn't tell her, you could bet on that. By tomorrow Mike might not even remember where he'd been.

Maybe she didn't have to know at all. *They won't thank you.* Parents don't want to find out when their children get into trouble of their own making. They'd rather go on hoping for the best and denying the worst. Other kids might be juvenile delinquents, but not *my* child, never. He would have to tell her, but not tonight.

"Good night, Kathy."

It was five o'clock when he went to bed and then he couldn't sleep. Early cars were beginning to pass on the street before he finally dozed off. When the alarm blasted at seven, he felt like rolling over and ignoring it, telling Helen to tell the school he had the flu or something. He had something, all right, a jangling headache that aspirin wasn't going to cure. A sympathetic hangover? He hoped Mike felt twice as bad.

But he hadn't missed a teaching day all year and he wouldn't miss this one. The headache would pass off in time; he wished he could say as much for the rest of his problems. So he got up wearily and went to school, prodding the orchestra through halfhearted Beethoven, dragging Junior Band through their eternal Dick-and-Jane marches, woodshedding concert music for the ROTC Ball. He half expected Mike to be absent, but that guess was wrong. Mike was right on the spot in first chair fourth hour, without his uniform but with his horn, definitely with his beloved horn. Pretty quiet and subdued today, no lip, no wisecracks, sitting still and keeping his mouth shut between numbers except for frequent jaw-cracking yawns. His nose might be a little swollen but not bruised enough to cause comment. His music, though ... something wrong there. Not sour, no false notes, the execution as faultless as ever—but spiritless too. Mike was playing school music like a schoolboy who didn't care how it sounded. He just didn't give a damn.

Hung over, all right, Paul thought without sympathy. Live and learn, bud; you'll find out about the night before and the morning after. It isn't worth it.

At the end of the hour when most of the cadets deployed and charged full speed for the cafeteria, Mike packed his horn away slowly, taking time to give it a loving rubdown with the polishing flannel. Something about his manner gave Paul a sudden scare.

214

Could Kathy really stand by her threat to sell? Paul's stomach turned over when he realized the full import of what that meant. Mike would lose his trumpet and *he would lose Mike.* Without Mike's music as the connecting link he would have even less excuse to see Kathy, even less hope that they might ever reach something better and more real together than living-room conversations and the everlasting Friday-night movies. He couldn't blame her for being cautious. Once burned, twice shy, and her marriage to Jerry Riley must have been a hellish mistake. Internal scars could be as painful and lasting as visible ones. If movie dates and small talk were enough for her—well, he wouldn't push it further. Be grateful for small favors; God knows he hadn't much to offer.

Mike snapped the locks down and turned the key with an awful finality. But instead of leaving the stage, he walked over to Paul and held out the case.

"Okay, Mr. Kessler," he said. "Here it is."

Mr. Kessler, Paul thought dully, wondering how long it had been since Mike had called him that. It was always "man," "Listen, man, you gotta hear this," or "Paul" or a flippantly meaningless "dad"—"Don't throw a pageant, dad, I'll get around to it."

Paul stared at the polite young stranger who stood before him in Mike's red-and-white ski sweater and held out Mike's Bach trumpet case. "Here what is?"

"My horn. You're supposed to lock it up in the band room until tomorrow."

"I'm *what?*"

"Lock it up in the instrument cupboard so I can't get it," Mike said tonelessly, reciting a carefully learned lesson.

"Is this your mother's idea?"

"Whose else do you think, man? I had to crawl through shit to get that much. I can use it at school, but I can't ever bring it home. Here, take it, will you, I gotta go to lunch." Mike pushed the case at him with the desperation of an unwed mother on a sheltering doorstep. Paul took the baby because he had to, no choice offered. But when Mike started to detach the key from his long zooty pocket chain, Paul protested. "No, you keep that. I don't want it, I'd probably lose it."

"Take it or the deal's off, that's what she said. She thinks I'd sneak it out after school if I could open the case. Either you keep the horn and the key or else—you know. *Take* it, man, *please*." Mike thrust the key into Paul's hand and turned away fast, but not before Paul saw the tears in his eyes. He wasn't drunk now, but cold sober and miserably grateful for the crumb of comfort left to him. They locked up his beloved darling, but they granted him visiting privileges, forty-five minutes a day five days a week. With possibility of parole?

"How long does this go on?" Paul asked.

Mike was already walking away; he didn't turn back. "I don't know. Forever, I guess."

Now Mike knew how an amputee felt, a crippled veteran trying to live without a vital part of himself. Days of strained, off-balance slow motion, nights in a hot sweat, wiggling fingers or toes or valves that weren't really there. Dreams of desperate frustration— Oh, Jesus, if I just had it back again, what beautiful incredible things I could do—run a ten-second mile, knock home runs around the world, play "Carnival of Venice" standing on my head. How can I live without it?

An hour a day at school was just a tantalizing taste to whet his appetite. He could only play ROTC music then, concert stuff, dishwater—fairly dirty dishwater too, when he couldn't take it home to practice and clean up. He had heavy responsibilities in the concert, two solo passages plus playing first in a novelty trumpet trio with high notes nobody else in school could touch. And he himself was having trouble with them now, thanks to that lousy hour-a-day restriction. He could hardly get warmed up before he had to quit. Before long he would lose his lip altogether, and wouldn't that be a hell of a note?

Mom wouldn't care. She wouldn't care if his lip dried up and turned sky-blue. Jeez, but she was mad at him, really pissed off. Once when he was a kid, he did something else wicked—rode his bike too far from home and came back hours late for dinner. She had blown her top and grounded him for a month, but relented after only a week because he was so miserable. This time she showed no signs of relenting. He tried to butter her up by working hard at school, doing his homework and going to bed early. What else could he do nights without a horn or a job or a chance to get out of the house? But it didn't help. After two endless aching weeks he was still as grounded and dehorned as ever, and getting mighty fed up with looking at four walls and a radio.

On just one point Mom relented. Cinderella could go to the Ball, not just the concert but the whole affair. She didn't care how many jobs he missed, but she wouldn't deprive him of his one big night of square glory, the officers' Grand March and formal dance. So Mike had to find himself a date. That was easy enough. Even though the best girls were tied up by the ready-steady system, a bachelor officer *never* went hungry at Ball time even if he waited until B-day-minus-two to make his choice. Mike knew which chick he wanted if she wasn't already booked solid. Surprisingly enough, she wasn't.

"Are you sure *you'll* be able to go?" Joyce asked a bit doubtfully. "No jobs to play on a Friday night?"

Mike made a face. "This time there is absolutely no doubt. They couldn't hold the concert without me. Paul would slit his throat and mine too if I didn't show up." He didn't tell Joyce that he'd lost his job with Johnny. That painful subject was none of her business. Let her think she was competing for his Friday-night favors—it might make her more appreciative. He'd learned a lot about women recently; he wasn't the clumsy rube beginner who couldn't get to first base with Joyce last fall. He knew the whole score now, thanks to Darleen, but he sure wasn't losing any sleep over *her*. Darleen was great for kicks, for giving a guy a good roll in the hay and making him feel ten feet tall, but that was her only talent, the only tune she knew. He got fed up with that kind of sticky sweet jazz in a hurry. Joyce was different, she had real class. Funny that she wasn't going steady with anybody else now. Maybe she liked him better than she let on.

Things were beginning to look up, just a little. The longest, coldest winter in history seemed to be just about over. The snow looked old and thin and tattletale gray with mud and dead grass showing through. An unbuttoned jacket kept him warm enough as he walked home from the bus stop, no cap or gloves needed. He still felt unbalanced, though; a load of books didn't compensate for the comfortable weight of his horn. The house key hung lonesome on his chain, nothing to jingle against as he pulled it out to open the apartment door.

He let himself in, dropped the books, shed his jacket, made a sandwich, turned on the radio and started to pace. Six strides

217

covered the length of the living room with a problem to match every step. Money for the Ball tickets ... money for Joyce's flowers ... money for the Bach's March payment. That was one hell of a note, payment due on a horn he couldn't even touch without express written consent from headquarters. God knows when he would get a chance to work again, maybe not until June. He couldn't work without a horn, he couldn't keep the horn unless he paid for it, he couldn't pay for it unless he worked. Around and around and *around*. Maybe Paul would lend him ten bucks. ... The Ball situation was under fair control but things looked bleak for the Rhodes one-nighter. He didn't even need to ask, he knew Mom wouldn't trust him to ride around the block with Johnny now, let alone eighty miles to Omaha and back after midnight on a school night. No use telling her how much it meant, how long he'd waited, how urgent it was. She wouldn't understand. Bill Rhodes was just a name to her, a swing bandleader, famous, loud, but otherwise unspecial. She wouldn't—

The phone rang. "Guess who?"

"I was expecting Veronica Lake," Mike said. He sure wasn't expecting Darleen Verbeck. He hadn't seen or talked to her since the world blew up two weeks ago, fifteen days it would be now, fifteen horrible trumpetless days.

"How've you been, Mike?"

"Lousy. What's new with the band? Any good jobs?"

"Nothing much, but. ... Listen, there's something— Something's come up that you would be interested in knowing about."

"I doubt it. The only thing I'm interested in right now is getting my horn out of hock and getting some money. Anything else, forget it."

"But—" She hesitated. "This is about money. There's a—there's a man who wants to talk to you about a job."

"In a band?"

"Yes, sure, what else would it be? A job in a good band. He came by asking for you the other night, last night I mean, and I said I'd tell you so you could meet him today."

"What's his name?"

"I don't remember, but he's a leader, a big leader, union. He heard you play and he wants you."

218

"Well, Jesus Christ, why didn't you say that in the first place? Where am I supposed to meet him, what time?"

"The drugstore by the Royal as soon as you can get there. I'll be there to introduce you to him."

He was out of the house almost before he hung up the phone and running for the bus stop with his jacket over his arm. With any luck he'd make it to the Royal and back before Mom got home from work. Even if he didn't, so what? This was his *chance*. The big breaks came that way, straight out of the sky when least expected.

Luck rode with him all the way. The bus came two minutes after he reached the corner. He transfered without a wait, off one bus and onto the other, across town to the Royal and into the drugstore. Same old drugstore, unchanged from last summer, same greasy oniony hamburger smell, same three booths across the back where the band used to eat lunch and argue which tunes to give the kiddies besides their inevitable "Mairsy Doats."

Darleen was sitting alone in the last booth. He slid in opposite her. "Where's the man?"

"He's not here yet. You made good time."

"Yeah, the buses came quick for once. Tell me what's with this guy? Are you sure he really wants me, I mean me specifically, not just any trumpet he can find?"

She looked a bit uncertain. "Would you go if he hired you?"

"Would I *go?* Are you kidding?"

"Before June? I mean quit school right now and go to work?"

"That depends. Why can't you remember his name? If he's anybody, you ought to know it. I'm not signing with some slob who plays German polkas on the accordion. But a good band, sure, I'll go tonight if he wants me. Hey, you got an extra cigarette on you? I left mine home." Actually he had none to leave; he'd smoked the last and was too broke to buy luxuries. He lit up and puffed nervously, drumming on the table. "That's how Mitch Wesley joined Rhodes, you know that? He was seventeen years old in Ohio, playing with some little two-bit band like Johnny's, you know, and Rhodes came through and heard him and bingo!—just like that, hired him and off to New York he went, featured trombone. Or maybe it was somebody else who heard him and told Rhodes, I forget exactly, but he ended up famous no older than me right now. I could name you ten guys like that, all working with big-name bands. When you've got enough talent you always make it. What's keeping that guy? You sure he's going to come here?"

"I don't know. I guess so."

"You don't *know?* On the phone you said he was."

"Well, then he is." Darleen looked as anxious as Mike felt. "But he might not—hire you. I mean you can't absolutely count on everything working out the way you expect it. Sometimes things don't. Sometimes they go all haywire and there's nothing you can do."

"Don't I know it," Mike said, thinking of the last two weeks. And he still wasn't out of the woods. Even if this guy hired him *today*, he'd still have to fight it out with Mom and get his horn back somehow. Jesus, how could he manage that? Hit Paul with the news first, maybe, talk him out of the key and then . . . brother. Things were still sticky. . . .

"Mike?"

"Mmmm?" Better if he could graduate first and then go to work. Neater that way, fewer people left unhappy.

"Mike, I— There isn't any man coming."

"What?"

"There's no leader looking for you. I—I just said that so you'd come, because—"

"No leader." He stared at her stupidly. "No— What the hell did you say it for, then? That's a shitty trick, you know that? Getting a guy's hopes up for nothing! A real shitty trick. What's so god-damn important that you couldn't tell me on the phone, I have to come clear over here to hear it? Listen, I'm in trouble enough right now without you pulling any fast ones on me—"

"So am I," Darleen said. And stopped, as though that was the end of the message.

"Not like I am, man. I got grounded and busted out of the band, and they stole my horn and locked it up where I can't even touch it. You couldn't be in anything *like* the kind of mess I'm in."

"You want to bet?" she said.

The way she said it made the hair start crawling on the back of Mike's neck.

"*What* kind of trouble?" he said very softly—hoping, praying he wasn't reading the message right.

"*That* kind," she said, also very softly. Mike shut his eyes and

220

counted to ten. But when he opened them, nothing had changed. She was still sitting there, looking at him.

"You're kidding."

"I wish I was."

"You're wrong, then. It's a mistake. You counted wrong or something. Listen, how could— We haven't even— The last time was *January*."

"February second," she said, as if she'd been living eye to eye with the calendar. "And I should have come on the fifteenth and I didn't and I still haven't. That's three weeks over, three weeks, almost a *month* . It's no mistake. We've got to get married right away, Mike, and I mean *right away*."

"Oh, no, we don't! Maybe you do, but I don't. Not me. You can't con me that way. If you want to get married, you can find yourself another sucker."

"Mike! You've *got* to!"

"Get lost!"

He grabbed his jacket and slid out of the booth and took off fast. She called after him once more, "Mike!" in a desperate rising voice, but he didn't look back. He kept right on going, out the door and down the street, running, following the bus route but not stopping to wait until he was out of breath and long out of sight of the drugstore. Jesus!

He went home and waited for the ax to fall.

And waited.

Thursday night.

Friday after school.

Saturday, all day long Saturday, a day seventy-two hours long with the telephone holding its breath, ready to burst out ringing any minute and Mom right there to answer it.

Sunday, doubletime overtime Sunday. Bells always rang on Sunday. Church bells, wedding bells, telephone bells, doorbells. He began to think it was going to be the doorbell. Hey, Mom, guess who's here to see you, the Verbeck family, Papa Verbeck with his shotgun and Mama Verbeck with outraged tears and their darling little pregnant daughter, Darleen. They've got news for you, Mom, big news. There's going to be a wedding, and guess who gets to play the supporting lead part of bridegroom? Your son, Michael, that's who. He's the lucky winner who rang the bell and hit the jackpot. Shall we try to bluff out a church wedding or just whip down to Kansas tomorrow for a quick civil ceremony? Making it legal, that's the most important thing. Lock the barn door with the baby inside and hope that the neighbors and relatives can't count as far as nine. Oh, Jesus.

Sunday, Sunday, all day Sunday. Why didn't they call or come or do whatever they meant to do? Why keep him sweating like a nervous groom in a Turkish bath anticipating his joyful wedding day? He'd *had* his wedding day, five or six of them, in fact. They were very joyful, but he'd had them and the honeymoon was over and that was all the married life he wanted, thank you very much. He didn't and Darleen didn't either. They were just fooling around having fun, enjoying each other's bodies without the slightest intention of making *babies*, absolutely the last thing in the world either of them wanted or needed right now. Or ever.

Monday. He went to school on Monday like a square carefree schoolboy. He saw Joyce in homeroom and they talked about flowers, what color flowers he should buy to match her formal. Flowers! How could he be calmly discussing formal dance flowers with one girl while he trembled on the brink of shotgun marriage to another? He sat through his classes in blinding fog. Then he went home and paced the floor and looked at the telephone. It sneered back silently.

Ring, you goddamn bastard, come on, ring and get it over with. I can't stand this waiting. Darleen must be scared to tell her folks. But she must tell sooner or later. As sure as God made little green apples, babies don't go away for the wishing. Once they're started, that's it. They start small and grow bigger every day, from cell to speck to clot to tadpole, up through all the evolutionary stages to living squalling human beings. How long could she wait? The longer she waited, the worse it would be for him, for her, for everybody when the news came out. Tell them, dammit. Tell them and get it over. Drop the other shoe. Let the ax fall before I die of fright with my head on the block.

Tuesday. He got up in the morning and looked in the mirror for gray hairs, but they remained still handsomely reddish-brown. His face didn't even look older. He looked seventeen or eighteen and he felt like thirty or forty—husband-to-be, father-to-be, workingman-to-be, an early nongraduating casualty of the Class

222

of '45. The .45 was a wicked-looking gun that soldiers carried. He'd looked down the muzzle of one once, in a slight misunderstanding with a GI guard who thought he was a Jap spy. If Mr. Verbeck leveled a gun at him, he wouldn't offer any resistance, he'd come along quietly. Even marriage to Darleen was preferable to getting his head blown off with a .45. Jesus, he was losing his *mind.*

He sat in the living room Tuesday night watching the phone, daring it to ring, praying it would, praying it wouldn't, praying there was another way out of this mess but knowing there couldn't be.

It rang.

His heart took a leap up into his throat, flipped over twice and came down pounding twelve to the bar in galloping triplets. But he couldn't answer it. He couldn't get up or move or reach out a hand. Ask not for whom the bell tolls. He knew goddamn well for whom it tolled and what it told, but he couldn't do a thing.

On the fourth ring Mom came out of the kitchen, soapsuds to her elbows. She gave Mike a disgusted look as she lifted the receiver. "Hello . . . yes . . . just a minute. It's for *you.*" She held it out to him impatiently (my God, what a lazy lout, he sits right *there* while I—). Mike took a tremendous breath and pulled himself to his feet and took the wet receiver from her sudsy hand.

"Yeah?"

"Hey," Johnny said, "what about tomorrow night, man?"

Mike fell back into the chair with a flop that pulled the base of the phone off the end table and nearly took the lamp and ashtray with it.

"What the *hell*'s going on?" Johnny demanded after the crash. "Who's getting killed over there?"

"Nobody," Mike gasped. "It's okay. The phone fell off the table. What's tomorrow night?"

"Are you kidding? Rhodes! Rhodes in Omaha, man. You *can't* have forgotten."

He couldn't, but he had. In all the turmoil and panic of the last five days Bill Rhodes went straight out of his head, overwhelmed by urgent priorities, sunk to the bottom without a trace. "Oh, yeah, that."

"What do you mean, oh, yeah that? All I've heard from you in the whole last year is how desperate you are to see Rhodes alive in person, how you'd crawl fifty miles over broken glass to shake his hand. Now the time comes and you say, oh, yeah that. What did they *do* to you besides lock your horn and ground you? Did they cut your balls off too?"

Too late for that, Mike thought with a panicky laugh, too late. "No, it just sort of slipped my mind for the moment. I've been—occupied elsewhere. Tomorrow's the fourteenth, huh? You're driving?"

"No, Dean is. You're not the only one with personal problems, man. My driving is strictly essential these days, no out-of-town trips. But Dean's going, he'll take us."

"Not me. I can't go."

"Can't go! You gotta go, Mike, this is *it*."

"I know, but I can't. I am so damn grounded you wouldn't believe it. My mom won't let me go to the corner drugstore without holding her hand."

"But that's three weeks ago. She can't keep you locked up all the rest of your life, can she?"

"She can try." Mom was back in the kitchen now; he could hear dishes clattering in the sink. "No, honest, you might as well forget it."

"Oh, ask her anyway. Maybe you can con her into it. Listen, we're leaving six o'clock from my place, so if you can make it you meet us here, okay?"

"Don't hold your breath," Mike said.

Wednesday morning he exercised his brief daily visiting privileges with the Sleeping Beauty. What a farce to be sitting there solemnly rehearsing concert music. For other people the Ball mattered. For him it was a big hollow joke. If his doom didn't fall in the next two days, he would play his music at Roseland Friday night. He would squire Joyce through the Grand March, trying not to trample the hem of her lacy skirt. They would dance politely to the music of Jack Herron. He would deliver her to her doorstep at midnight with a ten-second kiss, if she let him, while Paul and Mom watched from the car to make sure he kept it clean. And by this time next week he'd be married to Darleen and working at the bomber plant, pushing a broom or lugging motors or whatever they let unskilled teen-agers do. They'd be living God knows where—with her folks maybe or in some crummy furnished room. Not at his place anyway, not with Mom; he couldn't face that. He'd never escape. He'd never play in a big-name band, never travel, never make his mark in the world.

Well, but why couldn't he— Hope rose for a moment as he saw a way out. Then it died again. No, he couldn't marry her to legalize things and then hit the road with a band to escape her company. That wouldn't be fair to anybody. Married meant *married*, not living it up with the boys and pretending to square his conscience with a monthly check to the wife and kid back home.

There was no way out. When he married Darleen, he would be trapped, stuck in the box forever.

His heavy thoughts intruded on his playing style. He messed up the trio music, goofed an entrance and even fumbled a few high notes. The other guys razzed him for it. "What's the matter, Mike, would you rather play 'Stardust'?"

"No, he's thinking about the Grand March. He's scared he'll stab himself with his sword or run it up somebody's ass."

"Go to hell," Mike said. He shook the spit out of his horn and put it away for another day. Good night, baby, see you tomorrow if I live so long.

Paul came over looking worried. "What's wrong with you today? You're supposed to know that music forwards, backwards and inside out."

"Well, what do you expect? How am I supposed to keep in shape without a job? Half the time I can't find high C with both hands anymore."

Paul knew what could happen to a neglected lip. "Two more days to Friday. You really could stand some practice. You'd better take it home tonight."

Mike stared at him. "Can I?"

Paul hesitated and then smiled. "Oh, sure, go ahead. You're a big boy now. Take it easy, though, don't go on an all-night playing jag to catch up."

"Thanks, man, thanks a lot!"

He took the Sleeping Beauty to lunch, held the case while he stood in line, held it while he juggled the tray to the table, held it in his lap while he ate. Be my guest, baby. It's so nice to have you back again. Stick close to me and tonight we'll make music together, sweet, sweet music. Not "Trumpeters Three" but just us two, shooting the moon with "Stardust."

But tonight was Bill Rhodes in Omaha, and he could go if he liked; he had a ride. How could they punish him for that? Add six months to his life sentence? Oh, hell, what a choice. Break jail to go see the Great Man in person, or stay home and be great in his own bedroom with his own horn. Either way for the last time as a free man, before Darleen blew the whistle and nailed down the lid on the square box of marriage from which there was no possible escape. . . .

No possible escape?

Oh, yes, there was. *Oh, yes there was.*

He sat and stared into the bowl of congealing chili while the thoughts raced around in his head. The Sleeping Beauty nestled in his lap, waiting for Prince Charming to pick her up and ride off with her into the sunset. He could do it. He could do it *now.* As long as Paul held her locked up hostage, he couldn't do a thing. Yesterday he couldn't move. Tomorrow might be too late. But today, and today only, he had the horn and the key and a wide open gate to freedom.

The horn and the key and a ride out of town. Wrong direction, actually, east instead of west, but any direction would do if it got him out of the box. All he had to do was ride as far as he could and then start running. Run like hell and keep on running, fast and straight and far without ever stopping or looking back. Better to be an escaped musician on the run than a stupid square serving out a life sentence for a small slip of sperm. Who would benefit from that?

Well, Darleen would. He guessed she would. Of course she would. She was caught in the same trap, wasn't she, with no way to escape from her share of the mistake. It grew right there inside her, bigger every day, inside for nine months and then outside, but still her baby, her mistake, her shame to live with all her life. No more her fault than his, but she would have to suffer no matter what he did. If he ran out, she would suffer alone. If he stayed she would have something—a legal husband, a paycheck to support her, a father to help bring up the kid.

A man could do that much. Like it or lump it, a man had responsibilities when he got a girl pregnant. He shouldn't run out. Even Jerry did that much when—Mike swallowed. He wasn't supposed to know about that. But he could add two and two now and guess why those two incompatible people had married each other, not from choice but from desperate necessity. Jerry was a lousy crumb, but *he* stood by, he got married, he didn't ditch out before the event or even after. Mom left him, finally; he didn't leave her.

If a no-good bastard like Jerry Riley could face the music. . . . so could Mike. He could even do it *before* Darleen started yelling, before she raised the big fuss that would enrage her parents and break Mom's heart. If he borrowed a car and took her to Kansas today, they could tie the knot and come back hitched with no embarrassing explanations, just a bold announcement. People might suspect, but so what? He was headed for the square box anyway. Why not make it easier on the rest of them? He could climb in with his eyes wide open and close the old lid down himself. No picnic, but more honorable than being shoved in headfirst with the business end of a shotgun.

So get with it, man. Get up off your schoolboy ass and start to behave like a man.

Kathy climbed the stairs with a small sack of groceries from the bus-stop corner market. She picked up the newspaper and let herself into the apartment. No radio playing, no sign or sound of Mike in bedroom or bath. That's funny, she thought absently, where would he be at this hour? She hung up her coat, then took the groceries into the kitchen. Bread, milk, hamburger meat, apples, nothing in the least exciting. Was there one new way under the sun to disguise half a pound of hamburger? Mike liked plain patties, but she got more mileage with rice or noodles and tomato sauce, always and everlastingly tomato sauce. Let Mike name his poison tonight. Where *was* Mike? He must have gone up to the corner for something, cigarettes or notebook paper, maybe to pick up his uniform from the cleaner's.

Breakfast plates from the drain rack became dinner plates on the table. She opened the paper and glanced at the headlines with a faint feeling of something awry. She didn't usually open it. Mike brought it in when it came (at four o'clock? five?) and read it backward, first the comics and theater listings and radio schedule, later the sports and war news. Where was he when it came today? No corner-store errand could take that long. Where in the world was he now?

There was no reason to *worry*, for heaven's sake. But he ought to be home. Six o'clock, dinnertime, three full hours after school let out. He had come home from school, hadn't he? With a nagging itch of concern rising, she looked around for proof. Nothing said he had; nothing said he hadn't. No schoolbooks on his bed or desk—but he didn't always bring books home. No fresh cigarette butts—but he didn't smoke as often as she did, sometimes not all day. No snack remains, crumbs, milk glass, apple core—but he wasn't a kitchen messer-upper; he could even cook and leave things tidy. He hadn't brought in the newspaper. What about the mail?

She went down to look in the mailbox—empty, but that again was not unusual; they didn't get much mail—then glanced up and down the street. Not even sunset yet, spring evenings were longer. She laughed at herself for such foolish concern. This was like years ago, calling him in from neighborhood play. She couldn't yell, "Yoohoo, Miii-chael, dinnertime!" to a high school senior.

But where was he?

Should she start fixing dinner now, assuming that he would arrive any minute with a reasonable excuse? Yes, she should. Mike knew it was dinnertime. On the other hand, hamburgers and canned vegetables took no time to cook. She didn't feel hungry, so it would be silly to eat alone. . . .

She wouldn't mind a bit, really, if she just knew where he was. She didn't want to keep him locked up, for goodness' sake. He should be able to lead a normal boy's life with normal freedom for his age to come and go around town, to eat downtown or with a friend if he liked. If she could just trust him always to behave sensibly and stay out of trouble. . . . Well, if she could, he wouldn't be grounded now and they'd both be a great deal happier. No one should need to force a boy his age to use normal common sense and keep decent hours. He ought to do it naturally. He had a good brain; he was brought up right with good habits. He knew what was good for him and what was not. He could behave if he wanted to. Why didn't he *want* to?

At six thirty she gave up waiting and started dinner. He would have to show up soon. If he didn't—well, he could just eat cold food and be grateful for that much. He would have to come with a mighty good excuse, too. She couldn't think of *any* acceptable explanation for such deliberate carelessness. He must know that she was worrying. If he really had to be late, he could at least

228

phone and tell her so. Just pick up the phone and— Well, so could she, for that matter, if she just knew where to reach him. Where could he possibly be at this hour? Not at school. With Joyce? Yes, of course! Yes, almost certainly with Joyce, making plans for their date to the Military Ball, and Joyce's family had invited him to stay to dinner. Very nice of them, but still he could phone home and ask if she minded. Of course she didn't mind. Joyce was a lovely girl, or seemed to be anyway, just the sort of girl Mike ought to date, a good influence. . . .

She found the number underlined in the phone book and dialed quickly, leaving the hamburgers sizzling in the pan. Mike might not like being checked up on, but if he couldn't behave more responsibly he would have to suffer the consequences.

". . . No, Mrs. Ashton," Joyce said politely. "Mike isn't here. I haven't seen him since this morning at school."

"Oh." She had felt so sure of finding him there; the negative answer left her at a loss. "Oh, he's not. Would you have any idea where he might be then?"

"No, I'm sorry, I don't. Is it something important?"

Of course it's important, Kathy thought almost angrily. My son's whereabouts is always important to me. "No, nothing really urgent. I just— He isn't home and I wondered—" She couldn't say, "He's half an hour late to dinner and I'm *worried*." Mike was seventeen years old, not seven. Joyce probably didn't even know that he was supposed to be grounded. "If you see him, please ask him to call home."

"All right." Then as an afterthought, "Couldn't he be playing a job?"

"No. No, he couldn't be. Thank you, Joyce. I'm sorry to have bothered you."

She rescued the slightly charred hamburgers and the madly boiling pot of green beans, dished up servings for herself, sat down alone to try to eat, but anxiety left no room for food. Silly to worry. Ridiculous to worry. Mike wasn't a baby; he was an almost grown young man, ready to graduate from high school. Nearly old enough to be in the *Army*, for heaven's sake, and next fall he very well might be. If she felt anxious over a little thing like this, how could she ever stand it to know people were shooting guns at him and dropping bombs on him? Well, they probably wouldn't. The war would be over by then, pray God it would be.

229

Mike would never have to fight, perhaps never serve at all. He'd be safe in college, where she wouldn't need to worry. . . .

She dropped her fork on the nearly untouched plate and went to the phone again.

"Paul? Do you— Do you know where Mike is?"

"He's not there?"

Not the brightest response in the world. *Obviously* not, or why would she be asking? "No, he isn't. I don't think he came home from school at all, and I— I thought you might know why, some explanation why he'd be so late. Something to do with the Ball, maybe? Officers' practice, or—"

"No practice that I know of—*Practice?*" Paul's voice was almost a gasp. "Oh my God, he didn't— Are you *sure* he hasn't been home?"

"Why, what—?"

"Stand by," Paul said urgently. "I'll be right over. Don't worry, just—stand by."

She couldn't stand. She paced from phone to door to window and back with rapidly rising hysteria. Paul knew something that she didn't, something too serious to discuss on the phone. Something terrible had happened to Mike. But what? *What?* In ten minutes' time she reviewed an appalling list of possibilities before Paul came to tell her which awful truth was true.

"He's hurt, isn't he? You can tell me. I knew all along it must be something like that; he wouldn't have stayed out without— Where is he? What happened? Was he hit by a car or—"

"No! No, for Pete sake, no. It's nothing like that. He's all right, he's not hurt." But Paul's anxious face belied his words. She couldn't believe his reassurances.

"Don't try to cover it up, Paul. I'm his mother, I have a right to know. Where is he?"

"I don't know," Paul said. And then, quickly: "But he's okay, I'm practically sure he's okay. There's no reason to imagine that he's not."

"But you don't *know?*"

"No, but—"

She grabbed for the phone. "I'm going to call the hospitals. That's got to be it whether you say so or not."

Paul caught her hand and replaced the receiver. "No, wait, wait a minute. Stop and think. If he were hurt leaving school, the hospital would have called *you* long ago. Or police or somebody, they'd let you know. Let's rule out some other possibilities first. You asked Joyce?"

"Yes, but she hadn't seen him."

"No ideas?"

"She thought he might be playing a job, but of course that's impossible. That's the one place I'm sure he's not, with his horn locked up at school. But I think—"

"It isn't," Paul said.

"What isn't?"

"Isn't locked up at school." Paul swallowed. "I gave it back to him today."

"You what? Gave it—"

"I had to. He was messing up the concert music something fierce, so I told him to take it home tonight."

"Oh, Paul, no! Why did you do that? It's the only real control we had to keep him out of trouble. How could you be so careless?"

"Careless! That's not the problem. I got sick and tired of sitting on that horn and watching the kid crack up right under my eyes. Mike's a fine player, but even an expert needs to practice. His lip was starting to bother him; that's a very bad sign. Your punishment may have been practical, I don't know, but it went too far."

"It wasn't a punishment."

"No, for Mike it was more like slow torture. There's a limit to what a kid can take without cracking up."

"Don't exaggerate," Kathy said sharply. "You make him sound neurotic, as if he couldn't live without it."

"He's always been a little bit nutty about that trumpet, you know that. Remember what happened when you threatened to get rid of it?"

"He was drunk." She felt her stomach tighten at the words. "He wasn't himself that night."

"He wasn't himself today either. He's been jittery as hell all week. I don't think he's hurt or anything like that, but Lord only knows where he is or what he might be trying to do."

In a car, on the road, moving with a purpose in mind, Mike felt one hundred percent better. That waiting around was murder. Arguing with himself all afternoon—should I, shouldn't I, yes or no—was even worse than waiting for Darleen to settle it for him.

He kicked it around for hours, during school, after school, wandering around downtown in a dazed state of mind. Every way he looked at it the future was so scary that it stood his hair on end. But finally he said to himself, "Well, are you a man or a mouse, dammit?" And then he knew what he had to do. The only possible thing to do. The only thing a man could stand to live with for the rest of his life.

It wouldn't be easy. He might be sorry later, but that was the chance he had to take. People would say he was wrong, but he couldn't help that. When a man's whole future hangs in the balance, he can't be stopped by what other people think. He must go ahead and do what he has to, no matter what. They'd just have to understand, that's all. He had to do it.

"It's going to be a great night."

"Yeah," Johnny said. "Glad you could make it. But how come you brought your horn along?"

"Oh, hell, that's obvious," Dean said. "He's planning to audition for Rhodes' brass section tonight. He thinks old Bill will hire him so he won't never have to go back to school again. Right, Flash?"

Mike grinned. Wouldn't that be a neat solution, though? A job and transportation west, all in one lovely package. Have horn, will travel. "Sure, man, that's exactly my plan. I'll drop you a postcard from the Hollywood Palladium next week."

"If anybody could, you could," Johnny said. "When did you get the horn out of hock? I thought you two were locked up in separate dungeons?"

"We're out on parole. I'm supposed to be practicing my recital piece—I mean the ROTC Ball music. A real knocked-out trumpet trio, you should hear it. Wins first prize at the state fair every time."

"Oh, wow," Dean said. "That should be some great show. Triple-tonguing trumpets and officers clanking around in their armor making crossed-sword arches for the big-ass brass to pass through. Like a military wedding. Hey, you don't suppose—no, I guess not. They don't do that for sergeants, do they?"

"Not in Kansas," Johnny said. "Quick and dirty is the procedure down there. I do, you do, kiss the bride, pay the preacher and run for the nearest bed. They don't even throw rice."

"Yeah. That's too bad. I mean it ought to be nicer than that, wouldn't you think? Kind of a crummy beginning."

"Well, if that's how they chose to get married, it's their own business. Nobody made them do it. Do it that way, I mean."

Mike in the back seat began to feel itchy. Why this sudden strange interest in Kansas weddings? They couldn't read his mind, could they, to know what he had almost done? No, of course not. Coincidence, just coincidence. People often popped over the state line when they couldn't wait for blood tests or second thoughts. Eager girls, soldiers on leave—it happened all the time. Not even worth talking about. . . .

He didn't want to discuss the Bryan Ball either. Just kid stuff, tin soldier games, but pretty nice in its way. He'd be sorry to miss it. Some other people would be even sorrier. Paul, for one, caught without his soloist and trioist and first chair section leader. And Joyce caught without an escort, stood up once more in favor of a band job, stood up for the last time. She would never trust a sideman again. And Mom would never see her tall, handsome son clanking a saber—or wearing a cap and gown either—or any other symbol of square success. . . . And of course Darleen would feel worst of all, caught without her shotgun husband. Caught indeed, very very caught. She waited too long to nail down the lid, and her rabbit slipped out and ran like hell for the tall timber. Too bad, too bad. It was a lousy rotten evil thing to do, the crummiest kind of dirty trick, but he had to do it. He had to.

Funny to realize he would never be talking to Johnny and Dean again, unless they met by chance on some distant bandstand. But neither of them seemed likely to turn professional. Dino lacked the talent and Johnny the ambition. A kid band for kicks suited them fine, but making a living was something else. Turning pro took real guts. Guts and talent and maybe a good swift boot in the rear to get him onto the road.

They were passing Boys Town, almost there, ten miles to go. "Did you hear if anybody else from Connor is coming tonight?"

"Sure to be some," Johnny said. "Couple guys at work mentioned they might if they had the gas. Fluid is the big problem."

"Darleen would have liked it," Dean said. "She was a big Rhodes fan, wasn't she?"

Oh-oh, Mike thought. That was a nasty angle he hadn't considered. Suppose she— No. There'd be a huge crowd, hundreds of people. Even if she came, he probably wouldn't see her. What could she do anyway?

"Don't be silly," Johnny said. "She's got better things to do nights then gawk at Bill Rhodes."

Mike had managed to keep his mouth shut so far, but now that her name was mentioned he couldn't resist. "Uh—how's she doing these days? I haven't seen her in weeks." It was a perfectly natural-sounding remark from an old friend and fellow musician. Nobody could suspect it. But there was an ominous pause before Johnny answered.

"Okay, I guess. Nobody's seen her since the wedding."

"Since what wedding?"

"Hers, man, whose do you think?"

"What?" Mike yelled it so loud that Dean jumped six inches and the car swerved almost off the road.

"Watch that! Don't bellow in my ear like that or you'll kill us."

"Darleen got *married?"*

"Sure," Johnny said. He turned to give Mike a funny look. "Didn't you know?"

"Married! Jesus! Who the hell *to?"*

"Oh, some guy. Raznik, Roushek, something like that. Soldier at the air base."

"Rusika," Dean said. "Technical Sergeant Elton Rusika."

"Yeah, that's it. Very, very sudden, a whirlwind romance, just like in the movies. Way I heard it they were out on a date last Saturday night and decided it would be nice to get married, so they just zoomed down to Kansas and tied the old knot."

"Saturday," Mike said faintly. *Saturday,* when he was climbing the walls waiting for her phone call. "Married. I can't believe it."

"They surprised a lot of people. We probably wouldn't know yet, but Dean heard it on the neighborhood grapevine, all the old biddies clicking their tongues. The betting is about fifty-fifty whether they were drunk or whether they had to, right, Dean?"

"She didn't have to marry him," Dean said heavily. "Not *him.* Hell, if I knew she was so hot to get married, I'da married her."

"With some other guy's kid maybe in the oven? You're crazy."

"That don't matter, I would of anyway. I don't care if she was in a mess or not, I'da married her. She didn't have to go marry that damn sergeant."

"Maybe she wanted to, ever think of that? Darleen's no sap. She knew what she was doing."

234

I'll say she did, Mike thought, and laughed out loud with dizzy relief.

"What's so funny?"

"You are, man. You wanting to marry Darleen. Jesus, you don't know how funny that is."

"Not *that* funny, dammit. Stop laughing, shithead, or you'll take a split lip to your big ball concert."

At the risk of his lip Mike couldn't stop. Jesus, Jesus, off the hook at last! *Find yourself another sucker,* he said, and she *did.* She grabbed the first soldier who gave her the eye and *boom*—over the state line and home free. Good luck, Sergeant Rasputin, you'll need it. The cute little kitten knows how to scratch. She knows how to grab a guy by the balls and pull him straight through the wringer, man. Like hanging him five days and nights by his fingernails from a cliff waiting for her to push him all the way off. Five days of sweating hell when *she didn't even need him.* She left him dangling over the chasm while she calmly went off and married another guy. Didn't even bother to let him know afterward. Dangling until he was so crazy scared that he took off and ran with nobody chasing him.

Nobody chasing him!

Oh, hell, now they told him. Eighty miles up the road to freedom with all his bridges burned behind him, *now* they told him he needn't run. Plenty of other guys were willing to assume his responsibilities. Dino gladly would have, but the sergeant got there first. Oh, shit. What a stupid crummy mess-up. A mess-up because too many women trying to push him around, trying to tell him what to do and how to feel, trying to make him into whatever they thought he ought to be, and every one with a different idea. Mom wanted a mild-mannered, obedient, scholarly son to go to Harvard Law. Joyce wanted a gallant, ready-steady dance escort with officer's pips. Darleen wanted a breadwinning lover-husband. But he couldn't be any of those things. He couldn't please any of them. All in the world he wanted to do was to go and blow his own horn. And he would, by god. He was on his way to do it. All the bossy, scheming, pleading, crying women in the world couldn't stop him now.

Mike was gone and his trumpet was gone, AWOL together. That was all they really knew. Where, why, how, for how long were questions left to Kathy's frightened imagination. But she

235

tried hard to swallow her fears. "He's all right then, isn't he? You agree he's all right and he'll come home soon?" She looked anxiously at Paul for confirmation.

"I guess so. Damn if I know where he went, though. Could be a job after all. Try calling Johnny Schultz."

Nobody home at the Schultzes'. She didn't know who else to call; she knew no other last names or phone numbers in the band. "But they could be together. That does make sense. Someone did call Mike last night, I remember now. They must have arranged to play somewhere tonight."

"Yes. . . . No, he couldn't. He didn't know then that he would have his horn back today. Unless he—" Paul considered, then shook his head. "No, he wasn't faking for sympathy—I don't think. . . ."

"Of course not. He wouldn't try to trick you."

"Wouldn't he? That kid has pulled some real shrewdies in his time. When he wants something bad enough, he goes all-out to get it. Me first and the hell with you, man."

"But he's changed," Kathy insisted angrily. "He's settled down, you know he has. He's an ROTC officer, he's taking a nice girl to the Ball, he's almost ready to graduate, his grades are— well, good enough. He's really just fine now."

"Oh, sure, he's just fine. He's a perfectly healthy normal well-adjusted high school senior, seventeen years old. So he misses his dinner one night and stays out alone after dark and you're climbing the walls ready to call the police. Why?"

"Because I don't know where he *is*," she almost sobbed. "I don't know what he's *doing*. Paul, what if he doesn't come back? What if he's left—for good?"

Paul looked startled. "Run away? *Now?* What makes you think he could have?"

"I don't know, I—I just have a feeling he might, but— He couldn't, could he? Not when everything is going so well for him. Just sneak away and go, without a word— He couldn't do that!"

"No," Paul said without conviction. "It wouldn't make sense now, not just before—" His voice trailed off as he contemplated the possibilities. Then he pulled himself together. "Well, that's something we can check."

Together they went into Mike's room. A fairly neat room, showing few marks of ownership—the small white radio beside

236

the bed, a portable record player, records, the mildly littered desk of any schoolboy, an almost life-sized poster of smiling Bill Rhodes, courtesy of Columbia Records, taped to the closet door. A fairly normal teen-age boy's room. . . . The ROTC uniform hung crisp and fresh in a cleaner's bag, ready for Friday. Kathy searched the closet quickly and blew out a breath of relief. "His tux is here!"

"Right, he would take that. Don't worry, he'll be back. The prodigal son will return. How many ration points for a fatted calf?"

"More than I have. He'll eat cold charred hamburger and like it. If he comes." She picked up a shirt that had slipped from its hanger, shook it out and hung it back where it belonged. Knowing that Mike had taken no spare clothes wasn't as reassuring as it might be. To run off unprepared was even worse, a crazy impulsive mistake that he would pay for bitterly. Hungry, shivering, alone in the night far from home, sorry but afraid to return for punishment or forgiveness— "Prodigals don't always come home, you know. I didn't." It slipped out before she thought; no way to jerk it back. "I never went home again. They told me I shouldn't go, but I didn't believe them, I thought they were full of banana oil. I thought I knew better than the whole town of Standish, Illinois, so off I went."

"To South America?" Paul said puzzled. He didn't know what she meant, of course, how could he guess? She could say yes, South America, and smooth it over, keep the awful story locked away where it belonged, where no one else would ever know what a fool she had been. Whose business was it except her own? Not Paul's surely. If he found out, he would leave in disgust at her youthful stupidity; he could never respect her again. Unless she could somehow make him understand that it wasn't her fault, not her fault at all. "I couldn't help it. They said I had talent; they called me a second Hayes, a second Cornell—a fat lot they knew about it, hometown drama critics of the high school play—but I believed them, of course. At seventeen you'll believe anything that sounds exciting. And Standish was such a boring little town full of boring people. I had to get away and see the world before I died of stagnation. My parents flatly forbade it, of course. They said Broadway was the shortest route to eternal hellfire. They said any girl who painted her face and paraded herself on a stage

237

before men for money was no better than, well, they said Jezebel. But I knew better. So I took my college money and packed my suitcase and went straight—to hell!"

Paul took the shocking news calmly and with a smile. "Non-stop?"

He still didn't understand. He equated "hell" with the silly old-fashioned standards of Standish. . . . But if Paul thought that, then she was still safe; she hadn't incriminated herself. Her Broadway career was only an amusing anecdote out of the past, a story to pass the time while they waited for Mike to come home. She *could* tell him, then, a little of it anyway.

"Not quite nonstop. For two months I lived at the Y and walked to all the producers' offices every day—and they're *all* upstairs—and I met producers' secretaries and producers' office boys. 'No Noo Yawk experience? Sor-ry, nothing at present, come back next week.' When I heard that Steinberg was casting a road company of *Saint Joan* I thought, ah, perfect, there's my role, if only I make him notice me out of all the mob. So I splurged a hundred dollars, half my bankroll, for a Saks dress and new shoes and a genuine fox scarf, 'used for posing only' the ad said, a fantastic forty-dollar bargain. I went up there armed for battle to the death. Battle! Can you imagine fifty supersophisticated ingenues in cloche hats and gloves and furs, crammed into one dinky waiting room for three hours on a boiling-hot September day, all of us cutting each other down with haughty killing glances, all of us determined to convince Mr. Steinberg that we were born for the role of a simple French peasant girl who heard voices?"

"And the producer's niece got the part," Paul said. "Well, that's show biz." He was smiling; to Kathy's surprise she found she was smiling too. Well, it was funny, wasn't it? The incredible naïveté of a sunbonnet hick from the country trying to make a splash in the tough world of Broadway. If she had only known when to shrug and give up and go home, while it was still funny, before it became deadly serious.

"Did your genuine furs impress anyone else?"

"Only Jerry—" She bit her lip and stopped. Dangerous ground. But still funny in an ironic sort of way. Sunbonnet Sue meets City Slicker. "Right after that fruitless interview I stopped at a Nedick's stand and Jerry was there and he started talking to the

238

fox. I mean literally conversing with it—'Hello there, Fido, hot day, isn't it?' and some cute crack about ladies putting on the dog. I should have cut him dead and walked away but—well, I didn't; I laughed because it was so true. Then he wanted to spike my orange juice with gin he had personally imported from Canada in a trombone case—typically Jerry, waving his flask right under the nose of the corner policeman, nonchalant as all hell. He seemed so close to the theater world. He claimed to know Steinberg's girlfriend and he offered to arrange a private interview for me."

"Oh-oh."

"Yes, well I believed him, that's how dumb I was, what a foolish little gullible idiot from Illi*noise*. Green as the cornfields. My money was running low, just enough left for trainfare home, but I didn't want to go home a failure, too humiliating after my high-handed flaming departure. Jerry kept saying stay a little longer, it'll work out, I promise—"

She broke off again. No, the rest could *not* be told. No one would ever hear about that dreadful first winter, the month she stayed in Jerry's room while he was on the road—cheap chow mein and the red sign across the street flashing Danger, Danger through the window until he came back and found her ready to die of loneliness, ready to die for love. . . . Companionate marriage was all the rage that year. Everybody tried it, except of course the old fogies of Standish, who knew it was even more lustful and wicked than jazz and show business. So of course she couldn't go home then, a fallen woman. . . . The bootleg booze made her sick, a hangover of guilt for a wild night among pink clouds and purple whirlpools, never again, never, she couldn't bear such incredible pleasure and pain. . . . Then Jerry said there's this stuff you can take to get rid of it; you've got to, Kathy, for your own good. It's better than a back-room butcher with a rusty knife, he said; I knew a girl who *died* from that, she bled to death on a kitchen table, do you want that should happen to you? He said will you go home then? How could she go home? They would kick her straight into the snow. She said she would sooner jump off the Brooklyn Bridge and in fact maybe she would do that, since he obviously didn't care and what else could she do? "Don't give it a second thought," she told him. "You want to get rid of the baby anyway, so forget it. When we're both dead, you won't have a care in the world!" Then Jerry got scared at last. He said, "Well, I guess we're stuck with each other." And they were. Stuck, trapped, glued face to face in a sticky web of lovemaking that stiffened into holy wedlock, wholly deadlock. . . .

"And so they were married and lived unhappily ever after," she said aloud, and slammed the door of Mike's room on the rest of the buried unforgotten past.

There. It was over. Kathy's hands shook as she lit a cigarette. They sat at opposite ends of the couch with the absent Mike between them, the link in their lives and the separation as well. Mike brought them together; Mike kept them apart. If Paul had three grains of sense in his head, he could understand why she never showed her face in Standish again. As a legally married woman she could have gone back to visit, perhaps, could have shown off her handsome New York husband and her not obviously premature baby. As a legal divorcée she surely could have let them know she was alive and well in Chicago, bravely rearing her child alone in the Depression world. But she didn't. The swine husks of Chicago were easier to swallow than the prodigal daughter's guilt and pride. If she must suffer for her sins, she would suffer alone and nobody else need know why. As long as she had Mike, she could bear it.

As long as she had Mike. But without him? Without Mike there was no point in going on this way. And when Paul left—as of course he would, now that he knew the truth about her—then there would be no one, no one at all.

Finally Paul broke the silence. "How did your parents save you from making your mistake?"

"Save me?" She stared at him. Dear God, didn't he understand *yet?* "They *didn't*, that's what I just told you. They raised such a fuss about sinful playacting and painted Jezebels that I had to go, just to prove that *I* wouldn't fall into the Pit. And then I did. I did exactly what they said I'd do, I fell in love with a no-good crumb and had to marry him. I thought marriage would solve everything, but it didn't, it only prolonged our troubles for five more years. I'd have done better to jump off the bridge in the first place." She was shuddering now, trying desperately to hold back the tears of shame.

Paul pretended not to notice as he went on talking in level tones. "Looking back now, do you think there's any way they could have stopped you?"

She gulped. "I don't know. I suppose not. They forbade me and

240

I went anyway. If they had said, 'Go ahead, but you'll be sorry,' I still would have gone because I was so sure I knew better. Kids only learn the hard way."

He nodded and sat silent again until the answer welled up in her.

"But I *can't*, Paul. I can't let Mike make that mistake too!"

"It might not be a mistake for him. You admit you had no talent, but he's got a lot of it. He'll never be a second Rhodes, but he could make a good living in a big band, even right now. If that's the only thing that will satisfy him, why not let him do it?"

"It's not the only thing at all. He thinks so now because he's stagestruck like I was, a head full of stardust. The glamor of it excites him, and showing off, making a big noise, making people listen. That's a cheap way to waste a life, following Father's crummy footsteps. Jerry wasn't worth anything better, but Mike is and I mean to see that he gets it. If he isn't drafted, he'll go to college and find a real career, a decent one that—"

"College? Are you kidding? Mike won't go to college."

"Oh, yes, he will. He'll do whatever I think is best for him, and I say he won't waste his life chasing show biz rainbows."

"All right," Paul said almost angrily. "Mama knows best. Okay. When he comes back tonight, what will you do? Lock up his horn again? Chain him to the bedpost until June and then four more years? And then what? Even if you win, even if by some miracle he turns out neat and square, even if he gets a college degree and marries a nice girl like Joyce and goes to work in a *bank*, for God's sake, sooner or later he's going to move out and live his own life. Then what about *your* life? What will you do from then to 1990? Type letters all day till your eyes get blurry, come home to an empty apartment and knit sweaters for your grandchildren, if any? It's a life, I guess, but it sounds pretty thin to me. What are you trying to do, anyway—punish yourself eternally for one mistake? I think you paid for that a long time ago. Maybe Mike being born was an accident, but he was born and he's living and his music talent is part of him. You can't deny him the chance to use it and it's no use making yourself eternally miserable over it. Mike is what he is. You've done your best for him, so quit smothering him. Let him alone. Give your love to someone who really needs it, someone who knows what to do with it."

"Paul, don't—"

"I know, I shouldn't say it. I wasn't going to. You've got problems enough without that. I told myself I'd never bring it up until you settled things with Mike once and for all. Next June, I thought, after he graduates, then you'd be able to let him go his way and start thinking for once about your own future. I waited this long, I said, I could wait a little longer. When she's ready, she'll let me know. And I think you did let me know, just now, talking about Broadway and Jerry and yourself, what *you* did, what *you* wanted. It's the first time I've heard you admit that you ever had a life of your own, apart from Mike. Sure, you had a crummy first marriage. You fell for a selfish man and he gave you a bad time. But it doesn't have to be that way and it won't be; I can guarantee you that it won't. I love you and Mike can take care of himself now. It's you I want to take care of."

He said it all and then he sat there, looking not at her but straight ahead across the room while the ash of his forgotten cigarette burned nearly to his fingers. She took it from him gently, at last, and stubbed it out beside her own. Still he didn't move or reach out to her. He had said it all, but the move was up to her. She had to do it herself, had to cross the gap between them.

But his arms were strong and his kiss was comforting, all the strength and comfort she could ever need. She laid her head against his chest and listened to the strong, slow heartbeat. Not red-hot selfish passion—gimme, *I* want, hurry up, *now*—but slow-paced compassion and understanding and strength enough to last a lifetime.

"What should I do, Paul?"

"Let him go," Paul said quietly. "Tomorrow, next June, next year, whenever he's ready to go, just let him go. He'll go anyway, you know, with your blessing or without it. There's no point in making him feel guilty, the way you felt, afraid ever to come back if things don't work out right. Do you understand what I mean?"

Her fingers touched the faint healed line of scar on his cheek. He never spoke about that, but it was there. The scar and the limp were reminders that Paul had lived through his own private hell of pain and loss, more recent than hers, more acute, more final. He had no one left to love. When Mike grew up and left her, as sooner or later he must, she would be alone too, with perhaps half a lonely lifetime ahead.

She lifted her eyes to meet Paul's steady gaze.

242

"Yes," she said, and kissed him again.

Mike stood literally at the feet of Bill Rhodes, jammed against the chest-high ledge of the auditorium bandstand while two hundred other jealous fans tried to shove him aside. He had fought hard to win his favored position, inch by inch through the crowd with sharpened elbows and opportune footwork. Once placed, nothing could budge him until the Last Trump. The general audience was thinning out now. By midnight those who came only to dance had begun to drift away. But the professional listeners stood staunch as ever, earning back every cent of their dollar-fifty admission fee, absorbing every move and note and gesture of the Gospel according to Rhodes.

They pelted questions at the brack boy who stood intermission guard over the famous trumpet. "What's he doing right now? Sleeping. . . . No autographs, it's too much hassle. Once he starts he can't get away. . . . Last night? Minneapolis. Tomorrow night Denver." Mike wondered where *he* would be tomorrow night. He felt like saying, "Hey, need another trumpet? Tell old Bill I'm available, man." He had parked the Bach in a pay locker at the Greyhound station, the handiest safe place. He wouldn't risk leaving it in Dean's car exposed to all the trumpet lovers of eastern Nebraska, and carrying it in his hand all night would look silly.

Johnny shoved through the crowd and tapped him on the arm. "Hate to tell you, old buddy, but we're cutting out. It's a working day tomorrow."

"That's okay, you go ahead. I'll catch a ride later."

"Are you sure you can?"

"Oh, sure," Mike said loosely. This was the moment to tell his plans, but he didn't want to, not even to his best buddy. Telling might jinx it up somehow. "But since you're such a flush workingman, I could use a couple of bucks insurance in case I have to take the bus."

Johnny grinned and pulled two from his pocket. "Just add it to the ten you already owe me."

"I don't owe you any ten."

"You do, but don't sweat it. I'll collect when they let you out of jail next June, maybe. See ya, Mike."

Just for a minute Mike was tempted to call him back. *Hey, wait up, I changed my mind.* But he swallowed it and stayed by the stand. A good guy, Johnny, a real good guy. He would miss him.

Rhodes' sidemen looked faintly tired as they began their final stint. Mike knew the feeling well. By midnight your wind is nearly shot and your lip starts to go. The crowd thins down and melts away. You coast through the slow easy ballads and curse the jump tunes. When some idiot requests a repeat of "Two o'Clock Jump," you wish him dead, but you play it again, stretching for the top octave chromatics, hoping you won't miss one and look like a fool. . . . Bill didn't miss any, though. Not one blessed note did he miss. He had played "Stardust" just once, early in the evening, clean, straight, beautiful—but looking, Mike had to admit, a little bit bored. Maybe he was. After the million times he must have played that tune he could be getting sick of it. On the best jump tunes he let himself go, ad-libbing like a wild man. He let his cheeks puff out in a way Mike wouldn't be caught dead at and wound up red-faced and breathless with his hair in his eyes and a satisfied beat look on his face—oh, man, what a blast. But in the final hour he played mostly ballads, sparing himself and his tired men. Mike suspected that he was occasionally hoking it up on purpose, thickening the vibrato a little, exaggerating the eyebrow lifts and shoulder shrugs, kidding the fans with a caricature of his own style—Rhodes imitating Rhodes and overdoing it. At one particularly blatant lip smear in "Velvet Moon" Mike started laughing; Bill looked right at him and gave him just a suspicion of a wink. But apart from that he stayed detached, almost unaware of his fans as they crowded around his feet calling requests and waving autograph books. Mike didn't blame him. It was a tough business leading a name band and playing a sensational horn—an arduous exhausting way to make a million dollars in a few big years. A man could burn out at thirty if he didn't keep cool and save his strength.

At one o'clock on the nose the band drove into the closing theme—that's all, folks, show's over. The hard-core fans didn't give up easily. "Don't quit yet, man, the night's still young! How about a little jam session? Give us fifteen choruses of 'Sing Sing Sing'!" Bill gave them nothing but a tired absentminded smile as he walked off the stand. The girls of his fan club dashed squealing for the exit, hoping to catch him outside in a final try for autographs and souvenirs. A gang of boys whom Mike had already pegged for nonunion semipros stayed by the stand, recognizable by their loud jackets and slicked-back long hair and attitude of cool professional criticism. They watched until all of Rhodes' sidemen had packed up and left, until a couple of muscular ushers came around to chase them out. "Okay, boys, break it up now. You had your money's worth."

It was over. Mike redeemed his horn from the bus station locker. On the vague guiding principle that California sat at the western end of the rainbow, he caught a streetcar to the west side of town and started walking out the highway with one eye behind him for a possible ride. Past the university, over a long hill and down to the last outpost of nowhere, a cluster of closed gas stations. Few cars passed at this hour; those that did weren't interested in hitchhikers. He had time to study the future from all angles and realize that he had already made one mistake. He should have stayed the night in the Greyhound station, warm with a bench to sleep on. Now he was stuck at Seventy-second and Plowed Ground, freezing his balls off and watching the trucks roll by.

Ah, a car coming down the hill. Hey, you nice people, give me a ride, I'm going we-e-est. . . . Shit. No milk of human kindness around here. No milk at all. The hamburger he ate with Johnny before the dance was long gone, only the onions lingered on. God only knows where he'd eat breakfast, or when. He counted his cash by starlight. How long can a man survive on two dollars and seventy-five cents? Not even to Denver, let alone Los Angeles. And nothing with him but his horn, no working clothes, not even a toothbrush. Stupid damn way to launch a career.

When a kindhearted truck driver finally picked him up, he had done some more heavy thinking. Now he knew the way to do it. He would head west with a small detour through Connor City. No, he wasn't giving up, certainly not, not by any means. But Connor was practically on the straight route west, only a few miles out of the way. It only made sense to stop off and pick up what he needed, his tux and a few more clothes, and say good-bye to Mom, and maybe tap somebody for a little traveling money. He'd look like a fool stranded dead broke in Denver. Let Mom have the satisfaction of a big hairy dramatic parting scene, crying and carrying on and pleading with him to reconsider ere it was too late. She couldn't stop him, so let her try. If he was a man, he could leave home like a man, fair and square, not sneaking off like a runaway kid in the night without dollars or sense.

The truck took him most of the way on Alt 30, but he did the last fifteen miles on his own, walking some of it, rattling the last few into Connor in a piggy-smelling pickup at seven o'clock. Five hours to cover eighty miles, Jesus, and only sixteen hundred more to go. He might reach L.A. by the Fourth of July—an excellent place to celebrate Independence Day if he survived to see it. Hitchhiking was for the birds, man. But he would do it somehow. She couldn't stop him.

Primed and ready for the farewell scene, he let himself into the apartment. And stopped cold in the doorway. Mom was there all right, but so was Paul. Paul—at 7 A.M.! They were eating breakfast together, a very cozy twosome. Mom was pouring Paul's coffee; when the door opened, she nearly dropped the coffeepot. Mike searched desperately around the room for reassurance that things were not the way they looked. They *couldn't* be. Not them, not Paul and his mother, not on the first and only night Mike stayed away from home— It was impossible and he knew it. He saw Paul's rumpled clothes and the blanket and pillow on the couch and started breathing again. Of course not. They were two quiet respectable adults, not a couple of crazy kids like him and Darleen. They could get married any time they wanted to, fair, square and legal. They didn't need to fool around first. But why should Paul be there now? Why should Mom let him stay at all under any circumstances? It sure did look funny.

"Well, I guess you weren't expecting me, huh?" Nobody reacted to that, so he tried again. "Don't let me disturb you or anything. I'm not staying. I just stopped to get some stuff." Still no reaction. "I'm moving out."

"Oh?" Mom said. "Where?"

He gave her the blast right between the eyes. "I'm going to California for a band job, and it's no good saying I can't, because I'm going. I've hung around this square town too damn long, and now I'm getting out."

"All right," she said quietly.

Braced to meet the opposition, he swayed and nearly fell on his face from lack of pressure. All *right?* Didn't she understand? "It's no joke. I really am leaving. So if you've got any last words of wisdom to offer, you better offer them quick."

"All right," she said again. "Your suitcase is in my closet. Do you want some breakfast before you go?"

"Breakfast! Are you trying to be funny or something? You don't believe I mean it, do you? You're humoring a little five-year-old kid running off to join the circus. 'Be careful crossing the street, dear, and don't forget to write when you learn how!' That stuff is so old it stinks. You can't kid me out of this. I'm going and you can't stop me."

"I'm not trying to stop you, Mike." She hesitated a moment and looked at Paul. Paul just sat there sipping his coffee, very comfortable, very much at home, shirtsleeves and needing a shave. Just as though he were already married, moved in and settled down.

"Oh, now I get it," Mike said. He could feel a wave of anger rising in him, anger and jealousy. The man of the house returned from a business trip and found his rival had beaten his time. "You *want* me to go, don't you? Two's company and I'm the crowd. I get it. You didn't waste any time after you finally made your minds up. I see you spent the night," he said to Paul. "How—how was it?"

Paul took the outrageous accusation with a smile. "The couch was very comfortable, thanks."

"Oh, yeah? I'll bet. I'll just bet it was. Listen, if she won't let you stay in her bed tonight, you can use mine. I won't need it."

Paul's face was getting red now, a tightness of anger along his jaw. He set down his cup and half rose from his chair. Mike tensed for action. Okay, man, I'll take you on, I'll take you on any time. But Paul thought better of it suddenly and sat down again. "You'd better go get that suitcase."

"I think I'll have some breakfast first," Mike said. He walked around the table and sat down, suddenly very tired. Mom got up and said, "Eggs?" and he said, "Yeah, anything." He looked at Paul, but Paul ignored him, sitting and smoking a cigarette in domestic bliss. Mom brought the eggs and sat down with her coffee again. After a minute Mike got up and poured himself a glass of milk. Pretty lousy service all of a sudden. Nobody seemed to know he was there. Didn't know and cared less. They only wanted him out of the way so they could get together. "Funeral baked meats," he said to himself. Mom said, "What?" and he said, "Nothing." Once in a while they taught a guy something

247

worthwhile at school, a real true fact in the midst of all the classical garbage. *Hamlet*. A dopey story, but some of it made sense. Well, that was all right with him. He didn't care what they did after he left. All the better if Paul was there to keep her company.

But they weren't really giving in so easily, were they? There had to be a catch somewhere. After all those years of fussing over him Mom wouldn't turn around and let him go just like that, without a fight and tearful hysterics. And if all she wanted was to marry Paul, Mike wouldn't stand in her way. He didn't need to leave just because of that. Three was no crowd; they could all get along fine together until June anyway.

"Rhodes really sounded great. That's where I went, you know, Omaha, to see him. Really great."

"Don't tell me, let me guess. He *hired* you." Paul said it so sarcastically that Mike started laughing and choked on his milk like a little kid.

"Sure, man, how'd you guess? I went up to the stand and said, 'Mr. Rhodes,' I says, 'I understand you need a second trumpet. Just let me show you what I can do.' He says, 'Why, certainly, son.' So I drew my trusty horn and I ripped him off a few choruses in my famous inimitable manner and he—what's the matter?"

"Nothing," Paul said, coughing a little. "Just your inimitable manner. Go on. So he signed you up for five hundred a week and you're off to California in his big red convertible, right?"

"More or less."

"Good going, Mike, that's really great news. The ROTC Band will sure be proud to hear you finally made good. Isn't that fine, Kathy? Your son is a real professional musician now."

Kathy pushed back her chair quickly and went into her room. After just a second of hesitation Paul followed her. Action at last, Mike thought. When they came back, he braced for the big scene, the lecture, the tears, the pleading, the ultimatum.

"Here's the suitcase," Mom said. "You'd better not keep them waiting for you."

Mike swallowed. "There's nobody waiting for me, Mom. That was just a gag about Rhodes, you know that. I don't have any job lined up."

"But you *are* going." She almost failed to make it a question.

He looked from one to the other, trying to read the truth

behind their expressions. Mom might be anxious, but she hid it well—so well, in fact, that he couldn't be sure. Paul's face was easier to read. Paul didn't give a damn where he went or what he did, as long as he went and did it elsewhere. *You can go to California or you can go to hell, sonny, I don't care. We're through fooling with you. You had your last chance and you blew it, so get out.*

"Yeah," Mike said. "I guess I am."

He took the suitcase into his bedroom. He looked at the bed and what he wanted to do, what he really wanted to do was crawl in and sleep for forty-seven hours straight. He felt as if he hadn't slept for a week. Come to think of it he almost hadn't. Sweating over Darleen had left him pretty sleepless. He wanted to go to bed and forget the whole darn thing. But he couldn't. They were throwing him out.

He packed his tuxedo and his good black shoes and a couple of white shirts. He tried not to see the uniform in the cleaner's bag. A tux was his only uniform now, all he needed, a sideman's working clothes. Have tux, will travel. Must travel. Fifteen minutes to hit the road before they called the cops. But they wouldn't call the cops to bring him back because they didn't want him back. They didn't want him messing up their lives anymore. Nobody here needed him. Joyce didn't, even Darleen didn't. Darleen was married to some slob of a sergeant who would probably knock her around good if she tried to cheat on him. She was too young to be married. She just wanted to have fun, but— Well, she didn't need Mike now. And Mom and Paul didn't need a big teen-aged son messing up their domestic bliss. Paul was a pretty soft guy, a real easy touch, easy to push around up to a point. But when he reached that point, look out. That's all, brother. Three strikes and out.

Socks and underwear, shaving tackle. The suitcase wouldn't hold much and he ought to travel light. Hitchhiking was risky business. People worried about getting robbed by hikers, but it worked the other way too. A guy who looked too prosperous could easily get mugged. But his trumpet case looked like an ordinary suitcase; no one would guess that it held a two-hundred-dollar baby. When he reached the Coast and had money, he'd buy new clothes. This schoolboy wardrobe wasn't worth carrying. He had all he needed.

He was checking the room one last time when Paul came in.

249

"Well, are you all set?" Mike nodded vaguely. He closed the suitcase lid and snapped the locks down.

"It's a long way to California this time of year," Paul said sort of uneasily.

"It's a long way any time of year, man." Was Paul going to try to talk him out of it after all?

"I mean the traveling. How do you figure on doing it?"

Mike jerked a thumb.

"That's what I thought. Got any money?"

"Some."

"Yeah, well, it's a pretty long trip. You'd better take this. Might help with busfare if you get stuck halfway."

Mike took the bill automatically. A twenty. Well, that was pretty damn decent of Paul, considering everything. Or was it? Twenty bucks wouldn't pay his fare to California. It would just get him far enough started that he couldn't change his mind and come back. Pretty shrewd parting gesture.

"Thanks," Mike said. "Uh, do something with my records, will you? Give them to somebody who wants them. I mean don't let Mom throw them in the garbage. She'd do that. She doesn't understand about stuff like that, what it's worth."

"Okay, I'll see about it."

Now there was nothing left for him to do, except go. He went as far as the kitchen doorway and stopped. Mom was washing dishes and didn't even turn around. She stood there with her hands in the suds and her back to him, so he couldn't see her face.

"Well, I'm leaving now."

"All right."

"Uh . . . good-bye," he said. I'm sorry, Mom, I'm sorry. I don't want to go, don't throw me out. Please don't just stand there and let me walk out of here. I'm *sorry*.

But he didn't say it and she didn't turn around.

"Good-bye, Michael," she said.

He put on his overcoat and picked up the suitcase in one hand and the trumpet case in the other, pretty slowly. Paul opened the door for him.

"Well, see you."

"Take it easy," Paul said.

"That's the only way I ever take it, man," Mike said, and walked out the door. Nobody stopped him. Nobody called him back. Paul shut the door behind him.

250

Mike took a breath and started down the stairs, whistling. California, here I come. Go west, young man. You're free as a big bird, so go ahead and fly. Keep flapping those wings because if you don't, you'll fall flat on your face. Go show the world what a talented SOB you really are. They're waiting to hear from you, so go blow your horn, Little Boy Blue. Blow it good and loud and strong and keep on blowing it, because it's all in the world you have got.

FIC Ric   Richoux, P
The stardust kid.
DAN AF

Athens Regional Library Syste

3 3207 00119 832(

Madison County Library
P O Box 38 1315 Hwy 98 West
Danielsville, GA 30633
(706)795-5597
Member Athens Regional Library System

DATE DUE

FEB 2 7 1974		
AUG 3 0 1974		
APR 2 2 1975		

GAYLORD		PRINTED IN U.S.A.